Critical Praise for
Burt Hirschfeld's *Flawless*

"Perfect."

—*Cosmopolitan*

"His research is solid, the settings stylish . . . his many readers will enjoy his polish and skill."

—*Publishers Weekly*

"The narrative is pure thriller. The action moves swiftly to many countries, and the intrigue becomes more and more devious. A voyage into an area rarely explored by purveyors of international thrillers."

—*John Barkham Reviews*

"Hirschfeld spins his story out with verve and style."

—*Chattanooga Times*

"Hirschfeld gives us a nice dollop of international intrigue, seasoned with a tantalizing view of the diamond industry."

—Cleveland *Plain Dealer*

BURT HIRSCHFELD

Family Secrets

CHARTER BOOKS, NEW YORK

FAMILY SECRETS

A Charter Book/published by arrangement with
The Simon Jesse Corporation

PRINTING HISTORY
Charter edition / August 1986

ISBN: 0-441-22729-5

Charter Books are published by The Berkley Publishing Group,
200 Madison Avenue, New York, New York 10016.
PRINTED IN THE UNITED STATES OF AMERICA

PART ONE
1958

1

"PLEASE," THE BOY said.

The girl, plainly pretty, and wearing a soft brown pageboy which gave off sparkling glints under the changing carnival lights, ducked her head. She wore a pleated skirt, a sleeveless blouse, and penny loafers. She was a sophomore at Old Brixton Regional High School. "My folks are going to ground me for life," she complained.

The boy held her hand, leading her forward. "Come on," he urged. "Nobody's going to tell."

"Not anybody?"

"You can trust me."

"Give me your word."

"On my honor."

She looked up into his face. Sweet thing, he was, nearly a year younger than she. Sweet sixteen and tall for his age, with dark curls tumbling over his ears. He had round, moist eyes with a mouth to match, a soft, luscious mouth. No other boy was more beautiful or more gentle. She loved him dearly, she was convinced of it. Never would she love another boy. Not ever.

"I *do* trust you."

"Then you'll go?"

Her eyes wandered past him to where the brass band of the Captain Ronald P. Simpson chapter of the Veterans of Foreign Wars was playing a Sousa march. Blaring horns drowned out the shriller sounds of the calliope and the carousel, all blending into the insistent buzz of the crowd on the midway. At the rear of the parking lot, an explosion of fireworks lit up the warm night sky, its distinctively muffled crump faint with echo. Her spirit soared; she was the center of the universe. The words she spoke might be the most important words of her life, her decision monumental, words and decision that would certainly alter the condition of the world, she felt. It wouldn't have occurred to her that no one was listening, that it mattered to no one else except herself and the boy.

"My mother says, she made me promise—'Don't ever go up to the Point in a car and let some boy have his fun with you.' She made me swear."

The boy laughed, a warm, liquid sound that left her disarmed. "I don't have a car," he reminded her.

She echoed his laugh, leaning against him. His arm went around her waist, leading the way. "We can walk. Get away from all this noise, all the people." He made an expansive gesture that included the great lawn behind the porticoed facade of the Old Brixton Women's Club building. "Where'd they all come from?"

The wide expanse of lawn was alive with rides, games of chance and skill, and stands that offered hot dogs and hamburgers for sale, as well as Polish sausage and Italian grinders, soft drinks and cold beer. No hard liquor was sold, but in the shadows men pulled at bottles of cheap whiskey or acrid, pungent red wine.

The Fourth of July Fair, fifty-third edition, attracted people from all over Owenoke County and beyond. A three-day affair, it was designed to raise funds for the various charities of the Women's Club. That afternoon, under the bunting festooning the crude wooden stands surrounding the Little League field, the Old Brixton girls' softball team had beaten the Kerrville girls by a score of 23 to 21. The boys had lost to Whitney 3 to 0, a heartbreaking defeat; the boys had not won a game from Whitney in seven years. There had been wrestling and three-legged races and apple bobbing and canoe races on the Owenoke River. People were already saying that this year's fair ranked with the best of them.

The girl made one last, feeble defense. "I sure was looking forward to the Elvis contest . . ."

Fourteen boys were entered. Each dressed for the part in baggy trousers of rust or lime green with open shirts of contrasting sateen framing hairless chests hung with fake gold chains and crosses. Their pompadours were greased back and falling loose. Each was anxious to demonstrate his ability to imitate the King. The prize: Elvis Presley's most recent album and two tickets to the King's next appearance on the Ed Sullivan television program in New York City.

"I'll get you back in time," the boy said. "In plenty of time." He meant it. He believed he meant it. He wanted her to believe him, too.

She knew better. Not that he would lie to her, not him. But boys saw things differently, from a special point of view, boys being so unlike girls. She felt a certain anxiety, as if she had a gut memory for every other boy she'd ever known.

"If I show up with my skirt all grass-stained and dirty . . . you don't know my mother."

"Don't worry—my raincoat." He displayed it like a prize taken in combat.

She wasn't comforted. "You sure are pretty sure of yourself."

"Aw, it's all that Boy Scout stuff. Be prepared and things like that."

This time she didn't laugh with him. "You had it all planned." It was a rebuke. Whatever happened was supposed to be spontaneous. But the edge in her voice was tempered by a secret admiration for his foresight. Not only was he the best-looking boy she'd ever known, but he had to be the smartest.

His fingers tightened at her waist. "You know how much I love you."

The words thrilled her. Falling in love, being in love, it had changed her life. She had never loved anyone before, not like this, anyway. "On one condition."

"Whatever you say."

She faced him, her open face solemn and earnest. "Promise?"

"Sure."

"Well, okay then. No touching below the waist."

"I told you," he answered, a little too quickly. "Whatever you say. Okay?"

"I mean it."

"I mean it, too."

"Give me your word."

"Honest. Scout's honor," he said, raising his hand half-jokingly.

Partway up the slope, she paused.

"What is it? What's wrong now?"

"What if I change my mind? I mean, if I say stop will you stop?"

"Sure I will."

"You promise?"

"I promise."

Satisfied, she allowed him to lead her forward, going faster, holding hands and careful not to look at each other, climbing steadily up to Overlook Point.

Deep in the far corner of the parking lot, four young men huddled together in the shadows, passing a silver flask.

"Here's to us," Nels Proctor said in a resonant voice that projected assurance and authority, "and everyone like us." He finished a long drink, coughing and laughing at the same time, pleased with himself. He brought one scruffy loafer to rest on the gleaming front bumper of the white Mercury Turnpike Cruiser. It was a graceful gesture, full of pride and possessiveness. As he came around to face his friends, he was a lean, vaguely malevolent figure in the night, turned at the waist as if ready to spring, without stress or strain. He attended to the crease in his starched and pressed khakis, smoothing away all wrinkles, and permitted himself a small smile.

The Turnpike Cruiser had been a gift from his father the Christmas before. "Campus wheels," Richard Crompton Proctor had declared in that sonorous manner that came so naturally to him, intending to take the edge off his wife's disapproval. Lately Nels's mother had insisted they had spoiled their only child, that they'd led the boy to believe that all things were his by birthright.

"After all," she had pointed out, "he is barely twenty years old and this is his third automobile."

Mr. Proctor conceded his culpability. But what good was money and power if not used in the service of one's sole heir? Nevertheless he vowed, as he always vowed, to curb his spend-thrift impulses when it came to Nelson—out of concern for the boy's long-term welfare, as he put it. Mrs. Proctor knew bet-ter. Richard would continue to lavish expensive gifts upon Nels to fulfill the boy's slightest desire as well as his own most outrageous impulses, molding the boy after his own image.

Nels let his hand drift across the polished surface of the automobile. A seductive caress, a gesture of profound con-cern. The painted metal was cool and reassuring under his touch. Crouched in the darkness like some great alien beast, it was all flash, vibrant with latent power and speed. A single crimson chevron marked its glittering white extension, com-plete with flaring chromed tail fins, Merc-O-Matic push-button transmission, and Seat-O-Matic (forty-nine different positions). Hallelujah! Nels reflected. A boy's favorite toy. The world's most efficient Pussy Wagon. *I don't care if it rains or freezes, long as I've got my plastic Jesus* . . . Peeling out. Laying rubber. That's what life was all about.

He examined his friends without urgency, seeing again what there was to see, confirming earlier perceptions. His was the slow, penetrating glance of a warrior-prince evaluating flaws in his followers, assessing their ability to do his bidding, weighing the loyalty of each man, measuring the lengths to which he might go in order to extract obedience from each. There was a cruel insolence in his pale eyes, the eyes of a man who found inferiors at every turn.

Early in his childhood Nels had realized that he was able to exert some intangible but very real force over his peers, caus-ing them to respond willingly to his commands. He learned that in return for a charming smile adults would gratify most, if not all, of his wishes. Women, especially, melted when he turned the full force of his personality their way. They touched him, stroked his soft brown hair, planted kisses on his cheeks. Good things were his merely for the asking and he came to believe that his was a bright and limitless future overflowing with rich rewards and abundant delights. He be-gan to believe he could do nothing wrong. Rules that restricted other men did not apply to him.

In that moment, on that warm summer night, his friends clustered tightly around him, exuding silent declarations of

admiration and affection, anxious to please him in any way
they could. There was about him the eternal beauty of the
mythical hero. He was tall and muscular, the cutting angle of
his jaw made softer by the night. In any company, his was the
dominant figure, the focus of attention, the man other men
aspired to emulate. He was the best of them all.

He spoke in a voice faintly ironic, with a hint of controlled
mockery, as if amused by a private joke. "Next victim?" He
extended the flask in one finely boned hand, the fingers
elegantly tapered. Like a trio of famished eaglets seeking
droplets of nourishment from a parent's beak, they reached
for the offering. He considered them one by one before passing the flask to Hollis Whitehead.

"A friend in need is a friend indeed," Nels recited without
expression. He watched Hollis drink, observed this act laced
with desperation and relief.

Hollis, like Nels, had completed his second year at Dart-
mouth, readying himself for a career as a lawyer. He was pale
and yellow-haired, handsome in a less angular way, his
features smoothed around the edges. A soft, pliable face, not
yet settled, finished. There was a fullness across his chest and
shoulders, giving him a ponderous, somewhat bloated look.
He was an outstanding athlete in high school, startling
because, a big man, he walked as if stuck tight at the joints,
slightly pigeon-toed and effeminate.

From the time they were toddlers, born within days of each
other to parents who were friends and neighbors, Hollis
followed Nels's lead. He went unquestioningly, obediently,
giving tacit approval to whatever Nels chose to do. A secret
envy of Nels Proctor had left Hollis uneasy, nourishing a sense
of guilt seasoned by more than a dollop of unacknowledged
dislike. Some amorphous element in Nels's character troubled
him. At the same time there was something equally repellent in
himself that alarmed him and made him afraid. He allowed
none of this to surface lest Nels take offense and leave him
behind.

As they grew up, Hollis conceded Nels his due. Never had
he met a finer young man. Or one more worthy of respect and
obedience. Nels was the smartest of them all. The most daring.
The most courageous. All of it carried off with style and flair,
a young prince to the manor born. Hollis raised the flask a second time.

"Don't use it all up," Gary Overton grumbled. "Leave some for the rest of us."

Stocky, with a thick neck and powerful shoulders, there was an aggressive tilt to Gary's round, close-cropped head. His small eyes peering out from under shaggy brows were slitted and seldom at rest, constantly on the lookout for danger. At the University of Vermont, Gary spent most of his time skiing, partying, and plotting ways to get grades good enough to gain a degree without studying. His father was an architect and a builder, with no particular flair for keeping the money he earned. Gary longed for the power of the Proctors and the easy wealth of the Whiteheads. He was uncomfortable and resentful to find himself on a lower rung of the economic and social order than his friends. He yearned to succeed where his father had failed, to transform himself into a rich man, the richest man in Old Brixton, the richest man in the state. One way or another, he intended to reach his goal.

"There's plenty more where that came from," Nels said, quietly authoritative. "Two fifths of Chivas still to be cracked in the Cruiser."

Mollified, Gary drank in short, swift gulps before passing the flask on to Jay Newell. Jay raised it above his head in salute. "Here's to you guys. Here's to our friendship and to a fantastic summer."

Gary whooped and hollered. Hollis said he'd drink to that. Nels displayed his flashing teeth in a slow, accepting smile. The flask went on its way until it was empty and Nels, good as his word, brought forth a bottle. Pouring with a steady hand, he refilled the flask.

"To us," he said. "To the four of us."

"The Four Horsemen," Jay Newell said. From under his shirt he brought out a heavy gold pendant of four horsemen in full gallop, hanging from a thick-linked gold chain. Each of them owned a duplicate, gifts from Nels Proctor on the day of their graduation from high school. They were solemn and precious reminders of their glory years together, gleaming proof of their friendship, their mystical and transcendent fellowship.

"The Four Horsemen," they intoned as one.

The flask went around again.

The Four Horsemen. A sportswriter down from Boston had coined the name after watching them play football in the state

championship at the end of their junior year. They had run
wild, winning easily. Doing what they wanted when they
wanted. Nels called the plays and passed. Hollis ran with
speed, if not abandon. Gary blocked viciously and made the
short, tough yards when called upon. And Jay, with a decep-
tive stride and big hands, snatched passes out of the air and
ran down the sidelines untouched. What an incredible game it
had been.

The Merry Men, The Victors, Golden Boys, they'd been
called, but it was as The Four Horsemen that they had become
known; the first time four players out of the same backfield
had been placed on the All-State team.

"We really were something," Gary recalled.

"The best," Hollis said, drinking long and fast. "The ab-
solute best."

"We still are," Nels reminded them. "When we're together, nobody can match us."

"Nobody!" Gary hollered.

"We had it all," Jay mused.

Nels made the correction in that mild, firm manner of his.
"We have it still," giving added emphasis to the last word.

Of course he was right. Athletes, students, popular with
both men and women, born into the right families. Each of
them had been raised on Bluewater Hill, that aristocratic
elevation looming over river and town alike. From the time
Old Brixton had been founded—then a tiny farming community—in the years prior to the American Revolution, the
hill had been a bastion of entrenched wealth and privilege, of
far-reaching power.

In the beginning the hill had been a natural fortress, the
strategic heights to which farmers out on the surrounding
flatlands could withdraw when under attack by marauding
bands of Indians. Later it became the exclusive preserve of a
growing merchant class, always above the daily fray. Here life
was lived with style and grace. On the flats, it was referred to
as Blue Blood Hill where, it was said, the only insects allowed
were silk worms.

It was, The Four Horsemen would have agreed, the only
place to live.

Jay tipped up the flask and allowed a few drops to trickle
onto his tongue. He had yet to acquire a taste for drinking,
even beer. Unlike some of the people he knew at school, he

took no pleasure in getting smashed. He preferred to keep his wits, to know what was going on around him. He would remove himself when the partying became too wild.

Jay was the only son of Harvey Newell, owner of the Old Brixton Savings Bank, the only bank in town. But banking held little appeal for Jay. He harbored a secret ambition to become an actor. It was his intention to pursue a theatrical career after college, to move to New York and make his dream come true.

Harvey Newell, never considering his son's wishes, undoubtedly expected Jay to join him in the bank. To that end, he had insisted Jay study finance at his alma mater, Syracuse University. After graduation, Harvey intended to take Jay's postgraduate education in his own two hands. He would teach Jay everything he had learned from his own father, as well as more contemporary banking methods. He would shape the boy's future as he would shape the future of the bank. Harvey envisioned a period of steady and unbroken growth for the Old Brixton Savings Bank.

Aware of all this, Jay feared the day he would be forced to announce his choice of a career. But he was determined to follow the path that would make him happy, no matter what opposition he encountered.

"Good," he said, returning the flask to Nels. "Don't want to overdo. The chicks don't go for that."

Nels smiled, the cool deep eyes showing nothing. "We are not going to have trouble in that department, not us. Drink up, men, and let's get back to the Fair. I am in the mood for some action."

Gary let out another whoop of delight. "Have gun, will travel!" he crowed, falling into step with his friends. Nels led the way back to the midway with the others close behind.

2

"GO FOR IT!"

Emily Fowler clutched a soiled baseball in her hand, making a mighty effort to concentrate on the three wooden bottles stacked in a pyramid on the shelf along the back of the carnival booth. The ball in her hand was insubstantial—too soft, too long in use, and therefore too difficult to throw accurately. Behind her, onlookers pressed in closer, urging her on.

THREE BALLS FOR A QUARTER! WIN A PRIZE! read the banner above the booth. And Emily had been trying for almost thirty minutes to win one of those cuddly brown Teddy bears, failing again and again. She had her eye on one bear in particular, a sweet, soft creature with shining glass eyes and a white splash over its nose.

At that moment, nothing else mattered; she had to possess that bear. How many balls had she thrown? How many quarters had been spent? She no longer remembered. Not that it mattered. This was the last chance, the last ball, her last quarter.

Her first two tries had been off the mark. One wide, one high. This time she meant to do better. She set her jaw, eyes focused on the stack of bottles. She drew back her arm and let fly. The ball went fast and true, striking one bottle, then another, and—incredibly—bringing the pyramid down. A rousing cheer went up and Emily basked in the warmth of approval and accomplishment.

"A winner!" the man in the booth hollered. He leaned her way, breath hot and smelling of stale tobacco. "Which one's it gonna be, girlie?"

She indicated her choice and a murmur of approval followed as the crowd fragmented into smaller groups. Emily examined the bear with pride and affection, then displayed him to her friend, Lauren Poole.

"He's sweet," Lauren said.

"I think he's magnificent!"

"Okay, magnificent," Lauren agreed.

Giggling, exchanging girlish intimacies, they picked their way down the midway past the wheel of fortune, past the shooting gallery, past the balloon-and-dart game. The going was slower as they moved deeper into the surging crowd and the sound level rose sharply. Neither girl comfortable among so many people, they withdrew to a soft-drink stand and contemplated the bear, trying out various names, none of which caught their fancy, and sipping Cokes. They huddled together, ignoring the suggestive remarks of some boys nearby, making a point of not noticing the raw inspections of older men with faces flushed by the beer they had consumed.

Emily felt increasingly uneasy. Being the center of attention always discomforted her, even when pitching for the girls' softball team at school. She had lived in a state of war with her perceived shortcomings for seventeen years and had yet to win a single battle.

Tall for her age and wide-shouldered, she slouched forward in a vain effort to reduce some of the unwanted height. She chose clothes that would mask the new, round heaviness of her breasts, embarrassed as she was by their sudden prominence and the attention they drew. As usual, she was dressed conservatively, wearing a loose-fitting pink blouse over a straight skirt. On her feet were brown-and-white saddle shoes. The sole piece of jewelry she allowed herself was a gold circle pin.

No longer plain, she had not yet become pretty. But the signs were there to be seen: the finely etched cheekbones, the full lips, and the wide brow. Her skin was smooth and clear and her hazel eyes were soft and direct. Her dark, burnished auburn hair fell in waves across her shoulders. She moved slowly, looking out at the world around her as if myopically searching for something precious lost. Her gestures were brief, incomplete, careful not to draw attention.

Emily vacuumed up sights, sounds, impressions, fearful she might miss something valuable. She struggled constantly to find order in the chaotic ebb and flow of life around her. She longed for control over her existence, trying desperately to map a safe route over which to travel. More than anything, she yearned for kindness and affection, for love, anxious to share her deepest feelings with another human being. Instead she felt imprisoned by her own inadequacies, unable to measure up to imposed standards. And on those infrequent occasions when she was able to set aside her subordinate position in the scheme of things there was always a harsh mirror to reflect the reality of her existence. That, and her mother's ceaseless criticisms and vitriolic tongue.

Emily had known very few triumphs in her life; winning an occasional game for the softball team was the single exception. She shouted and screamed and jumped up and down when the other girls did, but those victories provided very little real satisfaction. Nothing she did seemed to matter very much. At school her grades were mediocre, she had very few friends —no one but Lauren, really—and, because of her height and, until recently, her long, shapeless body, boys seldom showed much interest in her.

Her friendship with Lauren was central to her life. Lauren was everything Emily wanted to be. Pretty, smart, and popular with boys and girls alike. She was president of the junior class, had starred in the school play, was the highest strutter in the marching band. None of those accomplishments, however, made much of an impression on Emily's mother.

"The girl is inconsequential," Cornelia Fowler had said more than once. "What can you expect? From an inconsequential family, you get an inconsequential child."

Emily resented any criticism of her friend but dared not challenge her mother. Cornelia was an experienced and clever woman, beautiful and sophisticated, immensely wealthy, a woman of background and culture, to be admired and emulated. Emily tried. Eager for her mother's approval, Emily looked for reasons to support her mother's arguments. After all, if Lauren had been a truly superior person would she have befriended anyone as ordinary as Emily? The answer: a person got out of life exactly what she deserved. No more and no less. Which is what her mother had been telling Emily all along.

"Listen," Lauren said. "The brass band has stopped playing. The dancing's going to start. Want to go over to the pavilion?"

Emily pulled back. "Oh, let's not. I'm not in the mood."

Lauren knew better. She knew how much Emily loved to dance, how much she enjoyed the attention of boys. They had exchanged their most intimate secrets, revealing to each other what neither had ever admitted to any other human being. They had matched their experiences with boys: Lauren's many, Emily's few. Yet it was Emily, despite her shyness and fear, who was willing to experiment more freely when along with a boy, who took more risks.

Her few experiences had made little impression on Emily. She still felt unattractive and undesirable, convinced that most boys wanted nothing to do with her. And those who did probably acted out of the worst of all motives—pity.

"Let's face it," she said more than once, "no boy wants to be seen in public with a girl a head taller than he is. I'm a freak is all, a pituitary case."

"Come on," Lauren said, taking her by the hand. "We'll dance. We'll have some fun."

Emily went along, clutching the Teddy bear to her breast.

The raw, driving rhythms of the dance band drew the young people to the wooden floor, already groaning under the pounding of the dancers, laid down in front of the gazebo. Emily remained at the edge of the dance floor, watching, keeping time to the beat.

She was certain no one would ask her to dance. Already Lauren was on the floor, her pleated skirt flaring as she danced, her round hips swaying in time to the music, her blond ponytail bouncing across her shoulders. Her partner was Nelson Evan Proctor.

There was such pleasure in watching him dance. That fine athlete's body was responsible and always under control. The jerkiness of the other dancers, the wild contortions, the quick, unfinished leaps and twists—it wasn't Nels's way. Smooth and polished, his movements were dictated by an inner discipline the others lacked.

Emily envied her friend. To spend time with Nels Proctor, if only for a single dance, was a major social coup for a high school junior. Not only was he the handsomest, the most desirable boy in town, but he was a college man, and famous. His athletic feats at Old Brixton High were still discussed with awe, as were his amatory achievements. It was rumored that Nels had gone to bed with the entire cheerleading squad during his senior year, not to mention countless less exalted girls. All of this made him even more desirable and slightly dangerous. Of course, Nels was the kind of young man Emily's mother appreciated, too. He was from the right kind of family with all the correct economic and social credentials, with all those impressive ancestors: generals, diplomats, politicians, industrialists.

What, Emily wondered, would it be like to dance with him? To look up into that classic face of his, to gaze into those wild, pale eyes, to feel his strong hands guiding her. What would it be like to be kissed by him?

She shivered at the possibility. Nels Proctor was no pimply-faced high school kid to be teased and taunted. Spend an evening with him and it would be Nels who set the rules, she knew. He would determine the game to be played. To be with him a girl would have to act like a mature woman, to treat him like the man he was. Her eyes fluttered shut and she imagined herself naked, Nels hovering over her, his nearness blotting out the rest of the world as he persisted in taking what he wanted.

"Wanna dance?"

Her eyes shot open to see Hollis Whitehead, an empty grin plastered across his pale face, looming over her. Most girls found him attractive, too, second only to Nels. But Emily perceived him as cunning and sly, often a bully, and always subservient to Nels. Still, he was the only one asking her to dance and he was, she acknowledged, a head taller than she.

"If you don't mind a *ménage à trois*," she said, giving the words a suggestive undertone she didn't feel. She displayed the Teddy bear and pressed it to her cheek. "My newest friend."

Hollis, leading her onto the floor, leered. "Why not? I can handle that. As a matter of fact, I can handle anything you can dish out . . ."

In the river below Overlook Point, water foamed up over black rocks before falling into a gentle pool where it gained

strength to continue its meandering journey downstate until it
fed into the Connecticut River on its way to the Long Island
Sound. In the darkness, the roar of the rapids provided a constant reminder of the dormant power in the otherwise gentle
and slow-moving stream. On the Point, the river noise faded
into the background, lost in the brittle cacophony of carnival
sounds rising up from the fairgrounds.

A dirt track, carved into place by the hundreds of cars that
made the journey each year, twisted through piney woods to
the crest of the Point. A natural clearing opened onto the river
and the town beyond, offering a view that many Owenoke
natives had admired at some time during adolescence.

Along the track, a massive elm tree marked a turnaround
for any driver changing his mind. The leafy shadows provided
a secluded parking space safe from prying eyes. Across the
track, the trees grew closer together, crowded with thicket and
bramble, thick with leaves at this time of year. Behind the wall
of brush, no more than twenty feet from the old elm tree but
securely concealed, the boy and girl lay contentedly in each
other's arms. They kissed, at ease in the darkness, comforted
by the warm, still air.

"You taste good to me," he said.

"I shouldn't let you kiss me the way you do."

"Don't you like it?"

"If I didn't like it I wouldn't do it. It's just not right, you
know it isn't."

In answer, he fit his lips to hers. She sighed, her breath
warm in his mouth, and accepted his tongue. He slid his hand
onto her breast and when she made no objection he opened the
buttons of her blouse, fitting his hand under her brassiere. Her
breast was firm, the skin soft, the nipple erect. She gasped at
his touch.

"Did I hurt you?"

"It's not that. What if somebody found out?"

"There's nobody up here at this hour except us. Nobody's
going to find out."

"I mean, the way boys are, all the time bragging about how
far they get with a girl."

"I'm not like that."

"I didn't say you were, only—"

"I won't tell a soul. Not a solitary living soul. You can trust
me."

"I guess I trust you."

He manipulated her nipple and waves of sensation spread downward. Her muscles grew tense. "You promised," she whispered. "Not below the waist."

He shifted around and the hard bulge of him pressed into her belly. She longed to have him touch her everywhere, all at once. She wanted to touch him . . . how she wanted to touch him.

3

NELS, IN AN intimate, insinuating voice, said, "You wearing somebody's letter jacket?"

"Uh-uh."

Slow dancing, Lauren was acutely aware of his body against her own, his hand low on her back, fingers drifting across the rise of her hips. Being with him raised doubts and undefined fears in her—the temptation to surrender to a will greater than her own. The scent of him made her light-headed as she breathed in the unsettling mix of expensive cologne and body heat.

He held her more tightly and she pulled back. *I'm wise to the rise in your levi's*; all the kids said it and now she knew what they meant. She averted her eyes.

"A great-looking chick like you, you don't mean to say you haven't got somebody special?"

She glanced his way, taking in the crooked flash of those sparkling teeth, the almost white eyes vacant and disconcertingly steady. As beautiful as he was, Nels should have been a movie star. Nels Proctor wasn't, she told herself, a very nice boy.

"Why should that matter to a college man like you?" She

eased herself away from him. "I'm just a kid compared to you."

"I don't know. Used to be a little green, but you're pretty slick these days. Hot lips, bedroom eyes, all the right bumps and curves."

"Oh, you're the slick operator, I'd say."

He leaned her way, eyes boring into hers, sending her brain spinning, and the lights, the sounds, the heat of the summer night, suddenly were all too much. She wanted to be home in the safety of her room, listening to her Johnny Ray records or reading the poems of Marianne Moore.

"Know what I think?" he crooned.

"I bet you're going to tell me."

"You are ready to do the deed."

What would it be like? To give herself to a man. To know at last what all the fuss was about. To cross that mysterious barrier that separated a girl from womanhood. But not with Nels Proctor, she reminded herself. He was too pretty for her, too clever, and certainly too remote. She longed for a man who was gentle and loving, someone she could trust and love in return.

"You," she said in a bright, lively manner, "have got the wrong party."

"You wouldn't kid me, would you?"

"I mean it, all right."

He released her and they stood without moving in the middle of the floor, dancers circling around them. His expression never changed. "In that case, maybe I'll let your friend have a shot at the brass ring."

She wove through the other dancers, his mocking laughter trailing after her.

The Four Horsemen assembled behind the Bingo tent. From inside they could hear the numbers being called, the wooden clicking of markers, the cries of delight or defeat. They took turns pulling on the silver flask.

"I," Gary growled in mock ferocity, "am about to go up a wall. I got to get me a little cooze."

"No woman would put out for an ugly little runt like you when she could have me or Nels or Jay," Hollis said, goading his friend.

"True, true," Gary said, eyes scrunched up in contemplation. "But I am prepared to make concessions. I will overlook the cooties on some of these chicks. I will even forgive them their zits. Main thing is to dip the old stick." They laughed and slapped him on the back. Pleased by the response, he went on. "You check out the body on the one Nels was dancing with, that Lauren Poole? She is really put together."

"Made for action and comfort," Hollis said.

Gary made a wolfish face. "I'd crawl through a mile of broken glass just to kiss that girl's ass."

"Lay off, guys," Jay Newell said evenly. "She's a nice girl."

"That's what I'm after," Gary answered. "Some *nice* pussy."

Hollis put things in perspective. "Nels put his stamp on Lauren. Isn't that right, Nels?"

"Forget it," Nels declared, his tone imperious. "The kid is a loser. Not worth the effort."

Gary hooted and clapped his hands together. "The chick shot Nels down!"

A glance at Nels told him he had committed a monumental blunder. Nels fiddled with the Cartier watch on his wrist, the one that matched his father's. He cracked his knuckles one by one, looking off into the night.

"What Poole deserves," he said, "is to be taught a lesson. A good gang-bang is what she needs."

Gary laughed nervously. "I'll go that route."

Hollis upended the flask and took a long drink. "First in line," he announced, his speech thickening. His face was flushed, his eyes were moist, his mouth had gone slack. "Size places, everybody."

Jay laughed and accepted the flask. "No slippery seconds for me." He was beginning to feel out of place again. An insider by birth and by experience, he felt nevertheless that he never truly belonged, that he was a member of The Four Horsemen by sufferance. "I'll get my own, thanks," he concluded.

Nels held out his hand. "You'll take what you get." Jay surrendered the flask.

"Think she puts out?" Gary asked, watching Nels drink.

"You must be joking," Nels answered. "Both of them are hot to trot."

"Forget it," Jay said. "They're just nice girls, still kids."

"They're ready," Nels insisted loudly.

"If you say so, pal," Hollis seconded.

"Well, I say so."

"I'm with Nels," Gary said quickly, trying to regain lost ground. "What we have here is a matched pair, waiting to be had."

"They," Nels said, looking from one to the other, "are going to get an education."

"What do you mean?" Jay said, suddenly apprehensive.

"And how?" Hollis demanded. Resentment had begun building in him, resentment that he was once again being told what to do. When to do. How to do. All his life he had been taking orders. From his father, his older brother, Nels. To hell with this! Courage born of Chivas Regal caused him to speak out. "I've had my eye on Lauren for a long time. That one belongs to me."

Nels, surprised by the opposition, let nothing show on his face. "I intend to teach her a lesson."

Hollis knew he should stop, but he couldn't, and the words poured out nonstop. "How come you always get the pick of the litter? Back in high school. In college. Every damned time. This time you'll take Miss Ugly of 1958. Anything Poole has to learn, I'll teach her."

Nels drank from the flask and handed it back to Hollis. "Have another drink, it'll steady your nerves." Nels's brilliant smile came and went. "Okay, pal, what you want is what you get. At bottom, they're all alike. Look out Emily Fowler, tonight's your big night."

Relieved, a rising cackle broke out of Hollis. "What if she's still cherry?"

Gary applauded. "Right! Who'd want to get cut up on that skinny thing?"

"Time she lost it in that case."

"What if she won't?" Jay said worriedly, looking for support where there was none. "They're nice girls," he said again.

"Wise up," Nels said. "Once I go to work on her, she'll come across, cherry or not. And you can put money on it."

"For how much?" Gary said, enjoying the game.

"Twenty bucks a man?"

"Make it forty."

"Forty it is. All bets are covered."

Hollis, through an alcoholic mist, considered the situation. "Deadline," he mumbled. "Got to have a deadline."

"Let's drop it," Jay said. "Get back to the Fair." He himself had long harbored a secret yearning for Lauren Poole but had never summoned up nerve enough to ask her out, certain she would find him boring and unattractive.

Nels ignored the comment. "Tonight," he said to Hollis. "Give me one hour from the time I make contact."

"How we going to know," Gary protested, "that you got it on with Miss Ugly?"

"I figured that in, too. Now here's what we're going to do."

Lauren saw them coming first. Picking their way through the crowd, people giving way before them as if they were too special to mingle with common folk. A shiver of anticipation and apprehension rippled along her spine. She touched Emily on the arm.

"It's late. We better be getting on home."

Emily, too, saw The Four Horsemen. Swinging in their direction, handsome faces glistening under the harsh carnival lights.

"Here they come," Emily murmured. This was one of the better nights of her life. Winning a prize for the first time, dancing, having *fun*. Maybe it was the best night. Maybe this time one of the other boys would ask to dance with her. Maybe even Nels Proctor.

"Those boys are getting pretty rowdy," Lauren said.

"They don't mean any harm."

Lauren shook her head, ponytail swinging. "That Nels is a little too fast for me."

Emily hugged the Teddy bear to her cheek, smothering a giggle. "He's just the right speed for me." She broke off, surprised by the temerity of her remark; aware, too, of how little chance anything would take place. Lauren, with her golden hair and stunning figure, was the one boys went after. And no wonder—how beautiful and lively she was, so much fun to be with.

Unlike Emily, who lived with her mother and her mother's latest husband, Peter, up on Bluewater Hill, Lauren lived on the northern edge of town, daughter of C. Arthur Poole, principal of the grade school, and his wife Linda, a first grade teacher. As dictated by their station, they lived modestly. A genteel and cultured couple, they read books and listened to what they called "good" music. They were possessed of one overriding ambition, that their daughter would one day marry well enough to raise them up on the social and economic ladder. It was tacitly understood that in Old Brixton this could be accomplished by a strategic marriage with one of the princes of Bluewater Hill.

"Those boys worry me, Emily," Lauren insisted.

Still, Nels Proctor was every girl's dream of romantic glory and exitement. Hollis, equally handsome, with a future equally bright, was a little too aggressive and had a whiny undertone in everything he said. And she actively disliked Gary Overton. He was crude, hostile, and not to be trusted. Besides, he had a neck like a fireman. Which brought her to Jay Newell. Some of her friends thought he might not be interested in girls, but Lauren didn't agree. He was a shy boy, reserved, and not at all like his father. Mr. Newell looked like a banker—a big man, hearty, with a voice too deliberately friendly, a manner too effusive, as if he were always trying to get something for nothing. Jay was sensitive, delicate, and friendly.

"They're no different than any other boys," Emily insisted, tightening her grip on the bear.

But they were different, Lauren was certain. Flirting was an accepted practice, even as was judicious necking with the right boy, but you could only go far enough to encourage and excite a manageable interest. The Four Horsemen expected more from a girl than that, and without much preliminary, to judge by Nels Proctor's approach. A girl had to be careful to demand respect, make sure she received it, Lauren reminded herself. It was a big leap from the flats up onto Bluewater Hill, a journey only a very few girls had ever been able to manage. Her common sense and experience emphasized the need to walk up the aisle to that rich and easy life in a long, white gown, trailing train, and lace as affirmation of invincible virginity.

"They've been drinking," she pointed out.

"Just having some fun is all." All her life Emily had been around people who drank. Martinis in the late afternoon, wine with every meal, brandy after dinner, a nightcap before bed. All her mother's friends drank. Whenever they came to visit, that is, whenever Cornelia Fowler was at home. "Nothing wrong with that."

The Four Horsemen stopped a dozen yards away. What a superb group they were. They were dressed similarly in their starched khakis, loafers, and Oxford cloth button-down shirts in varying shades of blue from Chipp or J. Press, open at the throat, sleeves rolled back to the elbows, revealing strong sun-tanned arms. Except for Gary, they were all tall and narrow at the hips, with long legs. They stood straight, agleam with good health, easy living, and the joy of being alive and young. Emily shivered and smiled.

"That Nels," Lauren said in a small voice. "He's the worst of the bunch, and getting worse all the time."

Emily smothered another laugh behind the bear. "As cute as he is, who cares? I think he's divine." She glanced sidelong at the boys. "What are they up to, do you think?"

"We'll get them in the Cruiser," Nels said, with the brashness of someone who had never had to take no for an answer. "Take them for a ride."

"Then what?"

"Then up to the Point to give Emily the time of her life, courtesy of yours truly. Check it out, men, the girl will beg for it."

Jay frowned, eyes on the ground. "What about Lauren?" If only he could warn the girls, lead them to safety. He didn't know what he should do.

"Lauren is Hollis's assignment. Think you can handle it, ol' buddy?"

"That girl is in good hands."

"You keep the chick occupied while I go into my dance with Emily."

"Be my pleasure."

Gary, protecting his wager, broke in. "How we gonna know, Nels? I mean, if we don't watch you plow the broad, how're we gonna know?"

"Fair enough. Here's how we'll do it. We ride around for a little bit, Hollis and me, loosen the girls up a bit. Then up to the Point. Meanwhile, Gary, you and Jay get up there. I'll park under the big elm and give you guys a lesson in how to deliver the goods. Only make sure you stay out of sight."

"Done," Gary said. "Let's us be on our way, boy."

Jay hesitated briefly before trailing after the shorter man. Maybe the girls would refuse Nels's offer of a ride. They were smart and would see through the charm and the glittering appeal of the Cruiser. *Maybe they would turn Nels down.* But he doubted it. No girl ever had.

4

"Wait."

The boy, mind and body in conflict, paused. Gripped by a searing urgency, he still managed to attend the girl's wishes. Pleasing her mattered to him, making her understand that he was a decent, caring person. He rolled away and strained to see her face in the darkness.

"What is it?"

"Listen."

Her ears were sharp, picking up the rumble of the Turnpike Cruiser making the climb to Overlook Point. The headlights pierced the night as the car swung into view, and came to a stop under the big elm tree, only yards from where the couple lay.

He reached for her again.

"No," she whispered.

"They can't see us."

The girl put her hand across his mouth and was struck again by the softness of his lips; the sweet taste of him was still in her mouth.

"We can't, not now."

He started to argue, but soon recognized the futility of it. The magic moment was gone. He sighed his assent.

Moving deliberately, the girl began to adjust her clothing,
sitting up finally. "We better go now."

The headlights had been turned off and the boy's eyes had
adjusted to the dark. "Not yet. If we're quiet, they won't
know we're here. Soon they'll be too busy to notice us leave."

The girl smothered a giggle. He was right, of course. Besides, she was curious. She lowered herself back down and
peered through the undergrowth at the Cruiser, trying to identify its occupants. The boy curled up against her, his arms
circling her in a comforting embrace, his hardness pressed
tightly against her bottom, a reminder of how much he cared.

"That wasn't much of a ride," Lauren complained from
her place next to Hollis in the back seat. Hollis had maneu-
vered himself up against her, his arm across the back of the
seat, fingers at play on her shoulder.

Nels, not turning, dismissed her objections with a laugh.
"Never guaranteed the duration, only the ride. Besides, it's
quality that counts, not quantity. Isn't that a fact, sugar?" He
directed his question to Emily.

She nodded, looking straight ahead. If only they were
alone, she and Nels. If only she could believe he truly wanted
to be with her. Then, fingers light against her chin, he brought
her around so that she faced him. He kissed her, a long, slow,
skillfully delivered kiss. Emily made no objection.

Lauren squirmed. She felt annoyed that she had allowed
herself to get trapped in this situation. "I don't like this," she
said in a firm voice.

"We're going to have some fun's all," Hollis said, leaning
over her. He reeked of whiskey and his speech was slurred.

"I don't like this, Emily."

Hollis tried to silence her with a kiss, but she pulled away.

"Emily, I think we ought to go," Lauren persisted.

"Hey," Hollis said, nibbling at her ear. "Just sit back and
we'll watch the submarine races."

Emily heard her friend as if from a distance. Nels's mouth
on her own made her feel faint and warm and when his hand
moved over her breast, she experienced only a rush of good
feelings.

"We shouldn't have come," Lauren said.

Reluctantly Emily disengaged, shifting around. "Okay,

we'll stay for only a little while longer, please?"

"Why fight the inevitable?" Hollis said, embracing Lauren, pinning her in place. One hand moved rapidly along her side. "Try it, you'll like it." He tried to kiss her again and again she avoided him. "What's wrong?" he said, licking her neck.

"Don't."

His hand went between her knees, his effort more powerful when she resisted.

"Relax and enjoy it."

"Let go!" she hissed.

"This is good for you—clears the complexion."

She raked her nails across his cheeks and he pulled back, swearing. Lauren opened the car door and got out, slamming it behind her.

"I mean it, Emily," she said in an overly loud voice. "I'm going home. Are you coming or not?"

"To hell with her," Nels suggested quietly.

Emily sighed. "She's my best friend."

"She doesn't rule your life, does she?"

"We came together."

"She knows the way home."

"Let me talk to her."

Nels sat back. "Suit yourself."

Emily climbed out of the Cruiser to stand alongside her friend. "Just a little while longer. I—I think he likes me."

"Right now."

"What harm can it do? A few more minutes."

Lauren's mind was made up. She shook her head vigorously. "They're up to no good. I'm going right now. I mean it, Emily."

"Make up your mind, ladies," Nels called from inside the Cruiser. "Tempus is fugiting, the night is growing short."

They could hear Hollis laughing in appreciation of his friend's wit. Emily looked in at Nels behind the wheel. She longed for guidance, some pat solution to the complex emotions that gripped her. Nels's noble face, the essence of masculine beauty, offered little help.

"Your choice, lady."

If this had been a movie, he would have been Clark Gable, always in charge of the situation. Emily felt herself the helpless, shy ingenue trying so hard to keep up with this special man she had only just met, trying to unravel her confusion. She turned back to Lauren and confronted a stern expression of disapproval.

"Can't you manage a little while longer?"

"No, Emily. Now."

Emily, surprising herself even more than she surprised Lauren, said, "Go ahead without me, all right? I'll catch up with you tomorrow. Maybe we can do something, okay?"

Lauren jerked her head once and backed away. She paused, almost pleading, "You're making a big mistake, Emily, you really are. I think you should come with me right now."

"Tomorrow," Emily said in a small, hopeful voice. She waited until Lauren disappeared onto the curving path that led back to town, then took a deep breath. Once back in the Cruiser, she was assaulted by a volley of contradictory feelings: guilt and exultation, shame and satisfaction, and an overriding sense of loneliness. Lauren, she assured herself, would still be her best friend. Always.

Without a word, Nels began kissing her again, his hand back on her breast.

She pulled away. "Please," she said, locating the Teddy bear. "Try to understand. She's my best friend. I can't let her go by herself." She slid across the seat and out of the car again.

"You lose, buddy," Hollis mumbled, sprawling across the back seat.

"The hell I do." Nels moved swiftly, following her out of the car, holding her in place with a deceptively soft hand. "I appreciate how you feel." His voice and manner, so sweetly attentive, made her want to stay with him even more. His hands were on her shoulders now, fingers working with gentle insistence. "We haven't got much time. My folks are taking me on an African safari in a few days and . . ."

"When you get back—"

"It's off to Hanover again," he cut her off. "Let's not waste this time together." When she hesitated, he went on. "You're concerned about Lauren out there alone in the dark. Of course you are and I appreciate the way you feel about your friend. It was unconscionable of me, of us, to let her go off by herself. I can make up for it—Hollis will go after her. Hollis!" he summoned commandingly. "Catch up with

Lauren. See that she gets home safely."

"But Nels—"

"And after you do that, head on out to where Gary and Jay are waiting for us. I want just a few more minutes alone with Emily, then I'll join you."

It took a moment or two for Hollis to decipher the meaning of Nels's words. With a wise grin, he obliged, staggering down the river path as if in pursuit of Lauren. Once out of sight, he doubled back through the woods to where Gary and Jay were concealed behind the big elm tree, joining them crouching in clear view of the Turnpike Cruiser.

Emily and Nels were locked in a tight embrace, mouths fastened together, Emily backed up against the Cruiser. The Teddy bear fell to the ground and Hollis could see Nels's hand move under her skirt.

"Oh, no," she gasped. "Please don't."

"I can't remember when a girl excited me so much."

"You hardly know me."

"I'm getting to know you better in a hurry. There," he said, moving against her. "Mmm."

"Nels . . . do we have to . . . go so fast?"

"You like it, don't you?" As if in answer; she shuddered, then shuddered again, overcome by the manipulations of his fingers. "I knew you'd like this."

"I like *you*, Nels. I like you a lot."

He guided her hand down to the bulge in his trousers. "You like this?"

"I never—"

"Go on, say it."

"What?"

Lauren had been right, Emily shouldn't have remained behind. But he held her hand in place.

"You like it, don't you?"

The words lodged in her throat. What she felt was unsayable, a swirling mix of emotion. Confusion mingling with fear and desire, along with a spreading panic.

"Big enough for you?"

Suddenly, as if magically, his trousers were open and he brought her hand back down onto his throbbing penis. He closed her fingers around it. She was stunned by the thick hardness of it, the soft feel of its skin, the heat it gave off, unloosing in her an overwhelming fear.

"You approve?" he asked huskily into her ear.

She had necked with other boys, had even touched some of them, but always through their clothing, shielded from this stunning, shocking reality by layers of protective fabric. She tried to remove her hand but he held her in place.

"Rub it," he commanded.

"Please, can't we stop?"

Nels paid no attention, working open the pink blouse, exposing her breasts to the night air, exclaiming over the unexpected treasures he revealed.

"I had no idea you were so big." His mouth on her nipple was hard and insistent, his overeager teeth inflicting stabs of pain. He misunderstood her tiny cries.

"You love it. I knew'd you love it."

Her brain spun and her limbs grew weak. She began to tremble, her body out of control. He dragged her panties down, tearing the pink cotton fabric away. He lifted her skirt and insinuated himself between her thighs in one swift movement, forcing her backwards over the hood of the car.

As good as done, he assured himself triumphantly. Another notch on the old gun. A little more difficult than some, easier than most. Almost too easy. When was the last time a chick had said no to him and meant it, made it stick? He couldn't remember.

"Stop! Please stop!" Her voice was shrill with terror.

"You feel so good to me," he coaxed. The right words spoken at the right time opened the locks, lowered the barriers.

"I don't want to. Please . . ."

"You want to see me again, don't you?"

"Can't we wait?"

"Here. Put it in." There was a sharp eloquent roughness to his voice.

He was so used to compliance that her sudden resistance surprised him. Before he could react she had broken away and confronted him from across a patch of open ground, legs firmly planted, breathing hard, her face pale and determined.

"I don't want to!" she shot across at him.

Had they been alone, unobserved, would he have let her go? It was a question he never considered. They were not alone. Gary, Hollis, and Jay were out of sight but near enough to see every move, hear her every word. She was turning him down in front of his friends, subjecting him to ridicule and scorn, bruising his reputation as a man. No way, he thought. No way.

He advanced, oaths flying off his tongue, sparking a growing terror in her. A clench of violence ignited his nervous system, and he named her what he wanted to believe she was.

"Tease! Slut!"

"No! No!"

His words compounded her horror and shame.

"Cockteaser!"

Almost in shock, she backed away, trying to locate her underpants. Spotting the Teddy bear, she bent to retrieve it. Before she was able to straighten up, he flung her to the ground. She scrambled and he went after her, ripping at her clothes, slapping her.

Immobilized by the unexpected blows, she lay still, until some semblance of pride and appreciation of the degradation he had imposed on her broke through. The falsity of his words and his seductive actions. All a charade leading up to this, she finally admitted. Wordlessly she came up, scratching and punching, her blows connecting. Driven back by her surprising counterattack, he went wild, striking harder with clenched fists against her face and breasts. Crying out, she tried to fight back but he battered her down to the ground.

Positioned between her legs, looking on as if from a distance, knowing that he would not stop, could not turn away with his friends looking on, he slapped her again. Once, twice, as if to reinforce his supremacy. She lay, her body slack, weeping softly as he entered her roughly.

"Damn," he rasped close to her ear. "*Damn you for trying to make me look bad*."

Finally a succession of strangely unsatisfying spasms brought him some relief. His muscles went slack and he pitched forward on her dormant body, sucking air through his mouth, wishing he were somewhere else, wishing she were gone. Presently he raised himself and adjusted his clothes, glancing around.

"Bingo!" he made himself cry, pursuing the performance without joy to its conclusion. "What we have here is a winner!"

Emily lay unmoving, her legs spread awkwardly. From the

fairgrounds below, the throbbing echo of the dance band pounded in his sensitized ears.

"Pay off, you guys!" he shouted, making sure he was heard over the insistent music. "I win! I win!"

Gary was the first to appear, grinning lasciviously, clapping his hands, then pounding Nels on the back. Then Hollis appeared. Jay, as usual, was hanging a yard or two behind, not looking at the prostrate figure on the ground.

"The Four Horsemen score again!" Gary yelled, fist shooting into the air.

"Touchdown," Hollis said, handing over two twenty dollar bills. Nels accepted his winnings and the plaudits, though he was suddenly silent and sullen.

Emily sat up. She covered herself, searching for her panties, for the Teddy bear. "Bastard," she sputtered. "All of you are bastards . . ."

Nels glared at her. How dare she interrupt his moment of triumph! How dare she dilute his victory! "Easy," he said in that superior voice he assumed so readily, to silence her. "Just another pushover."

On her feet now, shaking, a thin line of crimson trickling down her leg, she sought some way to strike back, to hurt him. "Another dud in the saddle," she said evenly, the words rolling across her lips like poisoned barbs. "Not half the man you think you are."

Without hesitating, he drove his fist into the soft flesh below her ribs. A second blow and she went down, moaning, clutching her middle.

"Okay," he said brusquely. "Who's for seconds?"

No one answered.

"I said, who is next?" he repeated, staring hard at the boys used to doing his bidding. No one met his eyes, no one moved.

"What's the matter with you guys? Here's some tail for the taking. Hollis, you were hot to trot before. Well, there it is, prime meat ready to go. Do it, damn you. Do it now!"

Hollis took an uncertain step forward.

"Get your cock out, stupid. Get down there. I'll see that she cooperates." He reached for her ankles, trying to spread her legs, to hold her in place.

Without warning, Emily kicked out, her heel catching Nels on the jaw. He stumbled backwards and she scrambled to escape. No use. He brought her down with a low tackle, working her onto her back, reaching for a firm handhold. Through the thickening haze Nels's voice jerked her back to the present.

"Do it, Hollis! Put it in and fuck the bitch!"

A shadowy figure appeared over her and she kicked out again, but this time without much force. An angry oath and a fist flew at her face. She fought back blindly, legs and arms thrashing against the night.

"Grab a leg, Gary! Jay, you the other one."

Knees clamped each of her shoulders to the earth and her arms were yanked over her head; she couldn't move.

"Damnit, Hollis, you want to get laid or not?"

With a harsh cry, Hollis launched himself forward, driving his middle up against her.

"Please, oh, please, don't do this to me, please," she moaned.

No one responded. The pounding went on and she was hardly aware when Gary took Hollis's place, his face grim and determined. Warm flesh pressed against her mouth and without thinking she bit down.

Gary howled. For her trouble, her head received a shower of blows. She didn't move again.

After a while, Gary lurched away, fastening his fly with nonchalance.

"Jay, you finish it off."

"Let it go. I'll pass this time."

"What's wrong with you?" Gary objected. "You some kind of a fag, turning down good pussy?"

Hollis, caught in a flash of reality, hated Jay Newell for refusing to join in, for refusing to perform and so validate the act completely.

"Go on," he said in a flat voice. "Do it. I did it, you do it, too."

As always, it was Nels who laid down the most telling argument, speaking flatly but convincingly. "You still one of us?"

"Sure, only—"

"One of The Four Horsemen, Jay?"

"You know I am. Always."

"Prove it."

"Show us your balls," Gary taunted.

"Or," Nels added, "have you lost them?"

With unsteady fingers, Jay opened his pants, lowered himself on top of the prone, still girl. She gave no sign that she knew what was taking place. Jay moved against her, going faster, grunting, until in a few moments he collapsed on top of her with a tiny moan, a gradual exhalation, no longer moving.

One by one, they let go of Emily and stood in a small circle, shuffling around, not looking at each other.

"Okay," Nels said, digging deep for energy, for enthusiasm, forcing a high note of triumph into his voice. "We got what we came for. You guys owe me and that money'll buy us a hell of a good time tonight."

They rode the Turnpike Cruiser back down to the fair, leaving Emily Fowler alone in the darkness of Overlook Point.

PART TWO
1984

5

MOLLY FAIRFAX FELL in love with Old Brixton during her first
hour in town. It had the ordered look and feel of a New
England landscape frozen in time. Everywhere she turned, the
past was preserved amidst a manicured serenity. Things were
exactly what they appeared to be, antique fragments of a long-
ago America that had managed to survive the corrosive as-
saults of progress.

She strolled down wide streets on narrow walks passing
under tall oak trees and thickly leaved sugar maples that
would soon be turning crimson and gold and orange. A tall
woman, she moved in quick starts, with quirky gestures and
abrupt changes of direction, drawn to new sights, determined
to miss nothing.

Under a mass of bobbing curls, her features were delicate.
Her mouth was full, uncertain at the corners, on the verge of
an unexpected smile. Her eyes were sea green and curious, ex-
pectant, peering into the distance. There was a lively quality to
her that made her seem even younger than her twenty-five
years. Even in Old Brixton, her vivaciousness and easy
sensuality drew admiring glances. She seemed oblivious to her
own physical being, merely an observer, inquisitive but detached.

Past large, columned houses she went, white houses with black shutters, gabled and shingled with slate, set firmly behind black-painted iron fences, fronted by sweeping lawns and hedges shaped with traditional Yankee industry and attention to detail. Her meanderings led her to historical markers that gave the date and marching orders of a redcoat invasion force during the early days of the Revolution, a monument that celebrated a victory by the local farmers over the British in the weeks after the shot heard 'round the world. In a tiny graveyard, she examined the narrow headstones sagging into the soft earth over the remains of nearly forgotten citizens. She counted four Protestant churches complete with high peaked roofs and cupolas, with ministers whose names resonated wih their early English roots: Brookswood, Turner, Greene, Packer. And she located St. Luke's Roman Catholic, which was set in the west end adjacent to the "flats," the tract where the old factory workers used to live, but not as far west as the mobile home park.

By her observations Molly learned something of the history of Old Brixton. Nestled down between Worthy and Bannister, along the Black Rock River, Old Brixton had depended, like so many Yankee towns, on manufacturing for its economic health. When the factories and the mills began to close, moving south to milder climes and a work force not yet unionized, the vigor drained out of the town. Without jobs, people started moving away. Schools closed down and Owenoke County eased its way into a gray depression. Empty red brick factory buildings loomed up like three-story ghosts, doors boarded up and windows broken by generations of rock-throwing boys with nothing better to do.

The town remained stagnant until the men of Nelson Evan Proctor's generation began to take the reins of power into their hands in the 1960s. They recognized the changing face of America, how their own states and cities and towns had been affected, and they determined to do something about it. If not for the good of the citizenry, they did so surely for their own personal profit and satisfaction.

First, new businesses had to be attracted to Old Brixton and the county. Nels Proctor alone believed it could be done. In the beginning he was thought to be a dreamer, the rich son of a rich father looking for some way to make himself feel important. Gradually, however, people understood that Nels was a hard-headed pragmatist, a man who did nothing unless it stood a good chance of succeeding.

He sold the potential advantages of Owenoke County to businessmen everywhere. He pointed out that a labor force existed that was bound to a tradition of hard work, honesty, and fidelity to their jobs. He reminded chief executive officers that two interstate highways ran through the county, one going north and south, the other east and west. He stressed the willingness of the county—with state aid—to build new roads and improve existing ones. Further, he guaranteed new housing for all employees who might be forced to relocate. He said that old, closed school buildings could be refurbished and reopened and, when required, new schools could be built. He spoke of tax relief, of political and economic assistance. He emphasized his strategic position, his many friends in high places, his access to political power at the highest levels and to the available sources of considerable capital for investment. It took almost a year before he found anyone willing to accept his arguments and eighteen more months before Smith & Malkin, makers of fine optics for private industry and the military, opened their new headquarters building in Old Brixton.

Others followed. Property values began to rise and corporate structures went up around the county. New housing appeared and the population flow reversed itself: people began moving back.

Old Brixton itself underwent changes, although Main Street remained the same, presenting a traditional New England face to the newcomers. Side streets were lined with old-fashioned gas lamps and newly bricked walks fronted the chic shops and boutiques that sprang into being. Instead of traveling to Hartford or Boston or New York to do their shopping, people started coming to Old Brixton.

The Chamber of Commerce, the Zoning Board, the Licensing Commission together managed to keep out Dairy Queen and Burger King and the other junk food operators from the center of town. The old grist mill was transformed into an arcade complete with a gourmet shop and a health food store and two new restaurants. A fancy vegetable market, piled with artichokes and yellow peppers, sold fresh Mexican strawberries in the winter.

A large computer company made inquiries about opening

an office and a foreign car dealer showed interest in relocating. There was no longer sufficient space for either.

A number of other companies made inquiries only to
discover that suitable space was not available to them, either.
It was then that Nels Proctor began putting together the
necessary land to form the first office-industrial park. Once
that deal was behind him, he came up with the idea of building
a shopping center, strategically located in the county, only a
few miles from Old Brixton itself. Later came the notion of a
supermall, a mall designed to draw trade from all over the
country and beyond, the largest and most spectacular in the
state.

To this end, County Center Corporation was formed. The
proper site for the mall was chosen, with easy access to the in-
terstates as well as to local roads, and efforts to acquire the
land needed were begun. At the same time, a financial package
was put together. Architectural plans were drawn up. The
mall, it was generally agreed, was an idea whose time had
come, a project that would insure financial stability in the
county for the foreseeable future. No meaningful opposition
was expected. Certainly no opposition that couldn't be readily
dealt with and overcome. Work went ahead on all fronts, as
optimism spread among Nels Proctor and his friends.

Molly Fairfax, however, knew nothing about the County
Center plans when she arrived in Old Brixton. She recognized
no signs of the changes taking place. She saw only the preserved, the old, the proven, the established good. And the contrast with her life in New York was dramatic and intense. The
joke in Manhattan was, "New York would be a great place if
only they'd finish it." Everywhere the physical representations
of the past, the old beauty, were being torn down, to be replaced with garish towers of glass and steel that reflected only
the sameness of the present. She viewed life in Old Brixton as
positive, hopeful, productive by comparison.

The rolling green hills and gentle landscapes, the clear,
sweet air and cottony clouds framed what was to her a picture-
perfect New England memory brought to life. Everywhere she
saw the warmth of the past melding into the rich promise of
the future. It was a healing vision.

Healing. That was it, then? That was what had brought her
to a place she didn't know, had never heard of until a short

time ago: this place, connected in some amorphous way to her mother, and therefore to herself. The need to find answers, and in those answers to find peace, an emotional release after so many months of bankrupting her emotional reserves on Joel Hammaker.

And the rest? Was it only an excuse—the book, the letter, the ragged Teddy bear—a rationalization to flee, to escape the hurt and the bitterness, the never-fully-realized rage that boiled in her over Joel's betrayal? It had left her feeling empty and isolated, full of despair and depression.

Here, in Old Brixton, she would see out her ancestral connection to the town and its people. And perhaps in finding out more about her mother she would discover more about herself, about her father, and thus fill in the voids she had carried around for so long.

So it was that she saw, perhaps, only what she chose to see and her positive response was immediate and powerful. She began to entertain the idea of buying a house. It seemed so simple; she would keep the apartment in New York, spend four or five days a week working at her art gallery, with long weekends in Old Brixton. A perfect arrangement.

The Main Street she encountered was in many ways not much different than it had been a century before. A hardware store was squeezed in between Maloney's Grocery and the Berkshire Diner and Pie Bakery, directly opposite Bill Colbert's Electric Supplies. Since taking over from his father, Colbert had begun selling electronic equipment as well as tapes and records. At the south end of what the natives called "downtown" stood the Joy Cinema: two showings every evening, matinees on Saturdays. The house was dark on Sundays. Had been for thirty years. Farther along, near New Bridge (Old Bridge had been replaced over forty years earlier), was the town's only gas station and repair garage. A few steps away stood the public library, a gritty stone building.

Inside, the library was a muted expanse of polished wood and shining brass. Green-shaded reading lamps were situated on massive oak tables. Only a handful of readers were scattered about, heads bowed in concentration. A brass plate on the front desk identified the woman on duty as Carolann Burke. She was young and slender with wide eyes peering through designer glasses. At the sight of Molly materializing out of the bright September sunshine, Carolann sat up straighter, her curiosity immediately piqued. Strangers seldom came wandering in off the street, certainly not anyone like this one.

To Carolann, Molly Fairfax might have been a movie star or a New York model, so dramatically different was she from any of the women she was used to seeing. Molly owned a certain weightless flair, the stylized beauty of a woman who looked good in clothes, no matter what she wore, no matter the angle of perception. Light cottons in watery tones of blue and green flashed and faded as she advanced across the reception area, a headful of glimmering curls, a winsome smile of greeting. Just looking at this newcomer made Carolann feel good.

"Hi."

"I'm Molly Fairfax." She deposited an old book on the desk. Its library binding was discolored, frayed at the edges.

"*Madame Bovary*," Carolann said. "I loved reading it."

"So did I, every time."

Carolann drew the date card out of the pocket inside the back cover and a brief, bright laugh issued from her mouth. "According to this, the due date was back in July of nineteen fifty-eight. That can't be right."

"I think it is."

Again that bright laugh. "That is a late return. One thing's for sure, you weren't the one who borrowed it."

"It was with Mother's things. She died last winter—an auto accident."

"Oh, I'm sorry."

"It happened in Austin, where I was raised," Molly expained. "I live in New York now. Anyway, after things got squared away, there were a few things left over, this book among them."

"And you made a special trip up here to bring it back?"

"In a way. Tell you the truth, I was curious."

"What about?"

"About what Mother was doing with a book from the Old Brixton Public Library. Thing is, Mother never mentioned this town, not even once."

"Maybe she was visiting back then. Folks spend summers here. Hiking out in the hills or fishing or swimming in the river. Most summer people have drifted away lately, though. I guess it's getting too built up for that anymore. Maybe your mother was on holiday?''

"It's possible. I hoped I could find the answer here.''

"She must have passed through at least once, the book proves that, unless someone gave her the book.''

"Is there some problem?''

A pleasant-faced woman in her fifties, plump, proper and cheerful, joined them, coming up behind the desk. "This is Mrs. Abernathy,'' Carolann said. "She's chief librarian. Miss Fairfax is returning this copy of *Madame Bovary*.'' Mrs. Abernathy examined the volume while Molly repeated her story.

"Yes,'' Mrs. Abernathy said, "this is our book, of course. But after so many years goodness knows what fines would total if we were to get into that. Besides, it's been written off as a lost or stolen item for a very long time now. You may as well keep it as a souvenir.''

Molly drew a faded blue envelope from her purse. "This letter—I found it among my mother's belongings. It's addressed to Emily Fowler in Tulsa, Oklahoma. But our family name is Fairfax and Mother never mentioned living in Tulsa. It's got a local postmark and is signed by someone named Lauren. Does that mean anything to either of you?''

Mrs. Abernathy's eyes narrowed.

"Nothing,'' she said crisply.

Molly went on. "I'm trying to discover what Mother's connections were to Old Brixton. It's such a lovely town and—''

"None, I'd say,'' Mrs. Abernathy interrupted. "Back in fifty-eight the world was a much different place. So was Old Brixton. I was still a young woman and I can recall how it was. Mills were closing down, people coming and going, workers, summer people. There were always some folks who failed to return the books they borrowed, even back then. All libraries confront the problem. Doesn't say much for people, does it? A considerable lack of respect for public property. People assume library books are theirs to keep, never to return them. There is no way apparently to insure responsibility in human beings. Or honesty. I can't help you, Miss Fairfax. No one here can help you.'' She turned abruptly, disappearing down a long hallway into the research department.

Guilt left Molly uncertain and afraid. What had she done to turn Mrs. Abernathy against her? What had she said? She wanted to hurry after the librarian, beg her pardon, ask for a second chance. But she was confused, stunned.

Unless coming to Old Brixton had been a mistake. Fragmented thoughts of her mother floated to mind; for so long they had lived in close harmony, mother and daughter, and yet never even a single mention of this place was made. Evidently Old Brixton had meant a great deal to her; those mementos she kept over the years attested to that, reminders of a life she cared about, people and events that had lived on in her thoughts.

Yet as soon as she mentioned her mother's name—or the name on the envelope—a wall had been thrown up, blocking her quest. Had she wandered into some dangerous maze filled with traps, deceits, and dead-ends? Why not retreat at once and leave her mother's secrets undisturbed? Asking questions, investigating some out-of-date mystery, this was not the sort of thing she had intended, Molly reminded herself. She belonged back in her gallery in the center of Manhattan, an active link between painters and that part of the population with taste enough and money enough to buy works of art. That was her peculiar gift, to be a bridge that served both worlds, to the benefit of both. Old Brixton's vital charm was slipping away. But many unanswered questions remained, and she had never been one to give up easily.

"What," she said, directing her attention to Carolann, "did I say to set her off?"

Carolann shrugged. "Mostly she's friendly, but I suppose once in a while she's entitled to act snippy. Like the rest of us," she added with an artificial laugh. "I wish I could help you."

"All I'm trying to do is find out if Mother lived here once upon a time. If she had friends, a life I never knew about."

Carolann chewed her lip. She spoke softly. "Why not try the high school yearbooks?"

But no one named Fairfax was listed among the graduating seniors for 1958 or 1959; no Emily Fowler, either. And she had no clue of Lauren's last name.

"Sorry," Carolann said. "Probably one of those enigmas folks sometimes leave behind to puzzle and distress their families."

"Maybe," Molly said, then thanked the librarian and departed.

But the explanation left her unsatisfied. Even more, she was troubled by the sudden alteration in Mrs. Abernathy's attitude, as if she had something to hide, something to fear.

6

ANGER WAS CARL Becker's dominant emotion. Anger and regret that he had failed to spend more time with his father. Anger and sadness that a man's life could end in such an empty fashion, alone and surely afraid. He should have been with the old man to help him in those last, unhappy days.

Becker stood with bowed head at the foot of the grave, set so obtrusively apart from the other gravesites. That too added to his anger. He raised his eyes to the temporary marker.

SAMUEL ABRAHAM BECKER
1914–1984

Becker reached for understanding and compassion for the living and, as so often was the case, his reach exceeded his grasp. He felt as though he were being asked to deliver much more than he was capable of. More, perhaps, than he chose to. Confusion augmented the anger and the sadness and the pervasive guilt that he had been carrying around for so long. Tears welled up in his soft brown eyes and he tried to blink them away, saying aloud in a gritty, resonant voice the words of the Kaddish he had learned at his father's feet.

"*Yisgadal v'yiskadash shmai raba.* Magnified and sanctified by His great name."

"*Yisgadal v'yiskadash shmai raba*," came the echo from behind. The Kaddish completed, the voice said, "Amen."

Becker wiped his eyes before turning around. "I didn't hear you come up." There was a citified edge to the way he spoke, laid over tonal echoes of his Yankee roots.

The other man acknowledged the rebuke in a gilded baritone. "I am Rabbi Tannenbaum. I presided at your father's funeral."

"Yes," Becker said. He walked along the narrow path between the graves, the rabbi following.

"I'm sorry," the rabbi said, when they arrived at the paved parking area that separated the small cemetery from the synagogue. He was a large man with the ruddy complexion of a man who spent a great deal of his time out of doors.

Becker appeared even more insignificant by contrast. Of medium height, his body, slender and wiry, gave the impression of being concave. His hair was dark and unruly, and he constantly brushed it back off his high brow. His eyes were large and intelligent behind prominent cheekbones and his nose was long and bony, his mouth wide and mobile. At first glance he seemed ordinary, without distinction, but then the parts pulled together to reveal a man of high energy with a quick, attractive smile and a lively intelligence.

"Last winter," he said reflectively, "when my father was buried, it was so cold. I remember wondering how the men managed to break that hard ground for the grave."

The rabbi responded after a moment of pontifical consideration. "A ditch-digger, a special machine," he felt compelled to explain. "We are a small community, we Jews of Owenoke County. There is only this one synagogue between here and Hartford. When one of our members passes away in the winter, we rent the machine . . . from the Overton Construction Company."

Becker edged toward his car. "Am I wrong that at the funeral I heard an odd note in your voice? More than commiseration, Rabbi."

"Your father was a good man. I enjoyed his company very much. Not that we were friends, to say so would not be precisely true. Still, I admired and respected him. I appreciated his intellect and the pragmatic way he looked at the world. What you detected in my voice—well, I was so sorry—'' He broke off, gazing across the valley.

"Sorry?"

"About the gravesite."

"I remember Sam saying he had purchased a plot. He didn't want to become a burden to the living, was the way he put it. It seems in an odd location, off at the edge."

Under his black suit, the rabbi's shoulders rose and fell. "Jewish tradition informs us—'' Again he cut himself off, gazing on high as some do for divine guidance. Perhaps he found it, as he continued in a steady voice. "Tradition informs us that a suicide must be buried at least six feet from surrounding graves. Should that not be possible, the grave is located near the border of the cemetery, as in your father's case. When I said I was sorry, it was that that I meant."

Becker was guarded, almost cross, when he answered. "Sam did not kill himself."

The rabbi stopped, unsure of how to proceed. "I'm sorry, is it possible I misunderstood? The police report, it stated clearly—"

"The police are wrong. Sam could not have killed himself."

The rabbi went on, ticking off theological points on his fingers, concluding, "There are also criteria of religion to be applied in such affairs. Many questions must be asked."

"Questions?"

"Of course questions. To come to such a decision is no simple thing, be assured. It can be made only by someone well versed in the spirit and the letter of Jewish law. Believe me, if there had been another way . . .''

"Whatever questions you asked, Rabbi, you came up with the wrong answers."

"Show me my error and I will happily put matters right."

"Depend on it, I will."

The rabbi spoke rapidly, anxious that Becker not leave with any misapprehensions. "Under certain circumstances, rectification can be made. Reinterment is not a simple procedure, you understand. But it can be done. Under certain circumstances."

"My father was not a pious man, Rabbi, but he was a believer. He was a Jew. He would have wanted a proper burial in the family plot."

"I will be only too happy—"

"When I set things right," Becker concluded as he climbed into his car, a white Saab. "That's why I came back," he said. "You'll be seeing me again."

The rabbi addressed the rapidly moving car. "I'm sorry. So sorry."

Alistair Burgess was his name, and it fit him very well, looking as he did every inch a proper English gentleman. MEN'S TAILOR, read the neat sign in front of his establishment just off Curzon Street. BY APPOINTMENT ONLY.

Twice each year Mr. Burgess traveled aboard the Concorde to the United States—specifically to New York City—to take orders from a few dozen prime clients. These were men who shopped regularly with him, tailor's models of whom stood patiently in the back room of the shop, the exact measurements of each client taped meticulously to its dummy.

Once a year, Mr. Burgess renewed those measurements, incorporating the most subtle physical change that might have taken place. Between selling trips, Mr. Burgess dispatched his second assistant tailor to the United States to conduct the fittings necessary prior to finishing off the garment in question. When you shopped Alistair Burgess you bought not only the finest fabrics available but the most reliable and traditional English tailoring. Mr. Burgess took pride in his work and his clients. Both, he liked to say, were the best around.

Of all his American clients, Mr. Burgess had developed a particular fondness and admiration for Nelson Evan Proctor. Everything about Proctor revealed the man's breeding and good taste. The carefully controlled distance he placed between himself and Mr. Burgess, for example: friendly without allowing an embarrassing intimacy to intrude on what was essentially a business relationship. Proctor was aloof without being unpleasant. He was a cultivated gentleman, a natural and worthy member of the American aristocracy. And Mr. Burgess harbored a lingering affection for the upper classes, no matter on which side of the Atlantic they resided.

Nels Proctor looked the perfect gentleman. No matter what he wore, he appeared casually correct and comfortable. His strong square shoulders insured a perfect drape to every garment. Tall and muscular, he had a cultivated, insouciant slouch that identified his lofty position in society. According to Mr. Burgess, Proctor might easily have been mistaken for a member of the royal household, with his proud, lean figure strung so tightly, so correct. Proctor was an incredibly handsome man with a shapely head capped by thick dark hair worn long and suitably shaggy, only recently beginning to gray in splashes at the temples.

His features were distinct, each perfect in itself, yet the overall look managed to exceed the value of its parts. The mouth was sensual, drawn down at the corners as if in disapproval, or in a slight pout. His cheeks were slightly hollowed beneath chiseled cheekbones, his jaw cleanly sculpted, leading to an aggressive chin. The eyes were fixed and deep, pale to the point of emptiness, eyes that missed nothing and revealed nothing. Being a proper English tailor, Mr. Burgess never discussed casually any of his clients, not even with Mrs. Burgess, whom he admired and trusted implicitly. Had he talked about any client, however, it would have been Nels Proctor; Mr. Burgess would have confessed to being thoroughly intimidated by the man.

When Mr. Burgess left Proctor's suite on the ninth floor of the Plaza Hotel, he carried with him an order for six suits, two dinner jackets, and two sports coats, along with complementary trousers. As usual, price had not been mentioned. When the work was done, the fittings completed, and satisfaction expressed, only then would Mr. Burgess submit his invoice, correct to the last decimal. It was, Mr. Burgess insisted, the only way to conduct business between gentlemen.

On his way to the elevator, Mr. Burgess passed a rotund little man in a baggy wash-and-wear suit of no distinction whatsoever, a man who seemed jarringly out of place in a hotel of such quality. To his surprise, he saw Nels Proctor admit the little man to his suite with an enthusiastic handshake and a flashing white smile. American Democracy, Mr. Burgess reminded himself, was still a system bristling with improbabilities and imperfections.

Jack Bresnahan had, by his own reckoning, spent more than half his life in hotel corridors, ballrooms, suites, and toilets, consummating deals he was unwilling to expose to even semi-public scrutiny. He had learned early on that bargaining was the essence of party politics. He could haggle like a fish vendor—buying, selling, able to make the best deal he could get. He made threats when the power was in his hands; he surrendered when defeat was inevitable, careful to avoid leaving

behind irrevocable animosities. Whenever possible, he com-
promised, trying to make both sides comfortable if not happy
with his deals. Most important was to keep his eye on the
target, aiming to get the men he favored elected to public office.

Bresnahan understood both the benefits of power and its in-
herent dangers and was skilled in its practical application. So
at this stage of his life, with retirement looming, he had no intention of abandoning the field to those who might subvert
everything he had accomplished.

He had assessed Nels Proctor objectively. The man had ice
water in his veins. He was remote and definitely unlikable. But
Bresnahan admired his cool pragmatism, his ability to get
things done, his willingness to ride out the bad times without
complaint and his uncanny ability to exploit the good times.
He was someone you could talk to, deal with, a man you could
do business with.

"The gloss is off," Bresnahan said as soon as he was seated.
He kicked off his shoes and folded his legs up in the lotus position, looking like a red-faced Buddha, his big cigar rolling
around his thick lips.

Nels, pouring coffee from a silver urn, cocked his head. It
was an acquired gesture intended to buy time, to collect his
thoughts, to frame a suitable response whenever a difficult
situation presented itself. Bresnahan was a shrewd and capable adversary, a man with whom he managed a decent
working relationship, carefully balanced to their mutual
benefit. The slightest shift in either direction, he understood,
could be disastrous.

"The godlike look of you, my boy," Bresnahan continued,
contemplating his cigar, issuing his words one by one. Nothing
on that face told him a thing; that was not Proctor's way.
"Too damned good-looking, that was the only flaw you had,
Nels. Scared most of the men around."

"Scared?"

Bresnahan chuckled nostalgically. "Some of those emotionally constipated types. Saw you as a JFK or a Gary Hart
—albeit Republican."

"Nothing wrong with the way Reagan looks."

"Ah, but the man is definitely aging. Creases and wrinkles,
chin dimpling, jowls sagging, throat shot all to hell. The man
may be popular but his days as a leading man are long gone.

Too damned good-looking, which made you either a fag or a threat to hearth and home."

"You never believed that, Jack."

Bresnahan addressed the cigar, rolling it between his thumb and forefinger. "I never believed you were a fag, Nels. But the way things go these days, who in hell can vouch for anybody?"

"I take that as a compliment, I think."

An artificial chuckle broke out of Bresnahan, his fat face crinkling. Behind wrinkles and folds, his tiny eyes were observant, seeking a telltale sign. "Nice," he drawled. "The way you have of not giving anything away. Right out of some desert dryness in you. If a man could squeeze you like an orange, my boy, I doubt he'd get himself more than a drop or two."

"I don't think I take that as a compliment."

Another chuckle. The cigar had gone out and he made a lengthy production out of lighting it, blowing smoke. "Let a man think what he wants, that's your way. Say what he wants, you ride it all out straight into the wind, never flinching. That's why you never made it in elective politics, my friend—the mixed feelings most of our people had about you. Hate to admit it, but too many of our best Republicans are walking around with a steel rod up their ass. Unbending. Disapproving. Full of all that talk about America the Beautiful that never did exist, except in dime novels, Barry Goldwater's speeches, and a set of some of the most fertile fantasies this side of a Chinese opium den."

Proctor watched the other man as if from a great distance. At first glance, Bresnahan appeared to be a prototypical Democratic ward boss—rough, vulgar, concerned only with the obvious material perquisites of political power. Yet somehow he had managed to work his way up into the hierarchy of Republican party politics, a man who pulled most of the essential strings. The columnists wrote about the White House Staff, about the leading Senators and Congressmen, but always there were men like Jack Bresnahan who made things happen, won elections for the GOP. He was a man to be feared, a man to be catered to, a man to be watched at every minute. Nels forced a humorless smile onto his face.

"Still no compliment," he said lightly.

"The thing is," Bresnahan went on, not missing a beat,

"you have managed to keep yourself afloat all these years.
Piled up a list of favors around the country that you've never
called in. Oh, yes, I've been following your travels with
supreme interest. Organizer, fund raiser, manager, speech-
maker. You've done it all and done it well and it's made you
the number one party man in your state and even higher up.
People have come to look favorably upon you, especially since
you've put a few age lines onto that handsome face of yours.
It's time you were state chairman."

He placed the cigar aside and took his time tearing off a
piece of seeded roll, spreading butter, chewing with relish,
washing it down with a substantial mouthful of coffee. "Wife
is giving me hell," he muttered. "Telling me to lay off the
starches, butter, and the like. My weight, cholesterol, blood
pressure, that kind of thing. But I've always been a weak man
and there are few pleasures left in my life. Nice of you to make
time in your busy schedule for me, Nels." His smile was
puckish and vaguely malevolent.

"I'd've come down to Washington, Jack. We could have
had our little meeting there."

"I like New York, Nels. Only real city in the country, but
don't quote me on it. Sophisticated. Cosmopolitan. High level
of energy. A man can really indulge his nasty habits in a town
like this."

"Long time since we had a chance to talk, Jack."

Bresnahan went back to work on his cigar. Clouds of smoke
rose up around his head. "Doesn't bother you, does it? No,
not a piddling item like the stench of a cigar. Drives Mrs.
Bresnahan right up the wall. Insists I step outside to indulge
my only public vice, unless you count politics, food, booze,
and sex, that is. Makes the little lady queasy when I serve
myself at the feast of life. Enough about me, let's talk about
nineteen hundred and eighty-eight, and the election of the next
President of these United States. More to the point, let's kick
around the primaries and the convention, the choosing of a
candidate, that is. Given it much thought, have you?"

"Well," Nels said, understating his interest, saying only
enough to keep the conversation going, "I'm sure Reagan will
be re-elected this November."

Bresnahan snorted and rolled the cigar from one side of his
mouth to the other. "As they say in Clancy Donegan's Irish
Bar and Grill, a lead-pipe cinch. Jackson, Hart, the rest of

those empty pretenders will knock each other off, leaving Walter Mondale as the Democrat's man of the hour. Fritz hasn't got a chance. Not a chance. It's Ron in a walk. Which is why I bring up eighty-eight."

"When there's no more Reagan."

"Which could be good or bad, depending on your point of view. What is your point of view, my boy?"

"It should be an interesting year."

"That's not a point of view, it's a mealy-mouthed way of avoiding the subject. Interesting, what a piss-poor word. Hardly reeks of blood and action, eh? Maybe that's why I asked for this meeting, to kick it around. Let me make my little pitch.

"It goes like this. Reaganism is going to run on after Reagan is tucked safely away back on the ranch. It is my opinion that the party is on a roll, rushing headlong into a glory period during which our esteemed President overshadows everything and everyone for the next forty years or so. Carries us all on his back, so to speak. The way FDR did for the Democrats.

"Unless something unexpectedly horrible takes place, we will have a lock on eighty-eight for damned sure. Now that's no secret. Most of the boys hold the same opinion. You want confirmation, you say? Okay, count the number of would-be candidates getting on line.

"This is how it looks from my seat. Most, if not all of them, will kill each other off. Just the way the Democrats are doing right now. An old-fashioned political blood-letting. The contest is already under way.

"Consider this—twenty-two Republican Senators are up for re-election in eighty-six. A lot of these guys will exhaust their political and emotional capital just holding on to their seats. No way they will be able to stand for national office two years later. That's why Howard Baker resigned the Senate, to make a run for the White House."

"You favor Howard?"

"I favor the man who will win. Candidates to become The Candidate, I call them. Baker, Jack Kemp, Dole, Bush, and a handful of others soon to make themselves known. All good party men and true who will sure as shit stinks knock each other off, I kid you not.

"You take Bush. George has been riding shotgun for Ronnie, kissing ass on network TV every chance he gets. Won't help him at all. The man comes across insincere and phony, one minute an Ivy Leaguer and next, one of your good ol' boys. Now Dole, he's trying to clean up his act. Change himself over from killer to constructive statesman, a man of the people. I don't think anybody's going to buy. Baker, just a cut-off version of George Bush. The Republican version of Mondale.'' He waited for his laugh and, when he got it, went on. "Kemp might pull it off if the conservatives can hold on to their gains and not fuck up. Personally I am convinced all four of them will cancel each other out. Bang, bang, bang, bang.''

"You've got your own man?"

"Bet your ass I do."

"If nominated I will not run," Nels recited mischievously. "If elected I will not serve. Or words to that effect."

It was Bresnahan's turn to laugh. "Good deal. A man who knows his place, that's a rare bird. You and me, Nels, we operate behind the scenes, pulling strings, pushing and pulling, wheeling and dealing, jabbing the old elephant and keeping him in motion. No, it isn't you I've got in mind."

"I'm too independent to be a candidate for office. I'd choose to insult the wrong group, criticize some power broker, put down some sacred icon of the American scene."

Bresnahan chuckled and relit his cigar. "Nice, the way you handle yourself, my boy. Telling people right off what's wrong with you, the disarming confession. That way they never have to think about what's *really* wrong with you, never get to find out."

A slight shift of features brought a cold, blank expression onto Nels's face. Quickly he produced a thin, icy smile. "Can't put anything over on you, can I, Jack?"

Bresnahan continued, as if the question hadn't been asked. "What I am after, and what the party needs, is a face fresh on the national scene. Someone with a good political résumé but without coast-to-coast enemies, a man who looks, or can be made to look, like a statesman. Somebody clean, insofar as folks are going to look at it. Somebody 'presidential,' whatever the hell that means, a man not yet chewed up in that Washington shark tank. I am talking about your boy, Hollis Whitehead.''

"Hollis?" Nels kept himself in check. No mocking laughter. No caustic wisecrack. No barbed humor. The idea of

Hollis as President of the United States was startling; the image provoked and intrigued him. Hollis was a soft man and pliable, able and willing to take orders. Nels's own creature. What a marvelous idea! "Why Hollis?" he said with manufactured earnestness.

"The man was made for the part. He's got physical size, which is reassuring. He's good to look at, but running slightly to seed, also a plus. He knows how to handle himself in front of a microphone and on the boob tube. He photographs well and he impressed a lot of the right people at that fund raiser in Akron last year. Said the right things and made a lot of friends, the way he came out in defense of the President's action in Grenada. Strong and forthright, just the right touch of belligerence. People noticed him and liked what they saw."

"You liked it?"

"I liked it, Nels, for what it was. A well-researched, well-written statement with just the right note of patriotism. No Joe McCarthy, Hollis, but nobody's going to question his national loyalties."

"Yes, put the words in his mouth and he can carry the mail in front of an audience."

"Can you make sure he keeps saying the right words, Nels?"

"Hollis depends on me . . ." His voice trailed off.

"Something's troubling you."

"There will be problems."

"My boy, there are always problems. It's my job—and yours—to solve problems. Or bury them. To keep our candidates out front and squeaky clean, to get them nominated, to get them elected. Long after the President, governors, and Senators are forgot, people like you and me are still around. Sure, there are problems and this is how I see them: it's up to you to bring Whitehead into the national convention of eighty-eight without too many wounds showing and with a fair share of delegate votes. A good primary campaign will help and so will a good-sized war chest. Money still talks. If—I say again, if—nobody's swept in on the first ballot, and I can virtually guarantee that ain't going to happen, I can promise a massive shift of delegate votes over to Whitehead which should lock up the nomination on round number two. How's that grab you?"

"I like it."

"It depends on how you handle things, my boy."

"I'll get Hollis there unscathed."

"If anyone can, you're the man."

Nels let the possibilities roll around inside his head, swiftly raising questions, answering them, going on to the next envisioned obstacle. President Hollis Carleton Whitehead; that would make Nels Proctor the force behind the Oval Office, the ultimate source of power. He controlled Hollis now, had controlled him for years, would continue to control him in the White House. If—

—Hollis won the nomination.

And could be elected.

If—

"Hollis is President of the State General Assembly," Nels said. "I've promised him a shot at the U.S. Senate. His wife Bunny has the hots for the social life in Washington."

"Nix to the Senate. The governor's chair is a much more stable launching pad. Let him prove he's a capable administrator. He'll be able to comment on national issues and at the same time remain aloof from all that nasty federal infighting. Check out Mario Cuomo's strategy. Follow his lead. The state house is the place for Hollis and you have two years to put him in there, if it can be done."

Nels made up his mind. "I can do it, and I will. From this moment on, Hollis is your man."

Bresnahan unfolded his legs, brought his feet down to the floor. "No, Nels, he is *your* man. You, you are my boy. You belong to me, now and forever. Is that understood?"

"Understood."

"Never had a doubt in a carload." He pulled himself upright, heading toward the door. "Whitehead for governor and you for state chairman. I'll provide all the help I can muster. Next stop, the state capital. And after that, Pennsylvania Avenue. Pull this off and you'll be surprised at how many friends you will have."

"And if I fail?"

Bresnahan eyed him quizzically. "In that case, I'll have to find somebody who won't."

7

WHEN HE WAS a boy Jay Newell had often seen white-tailed deer in the woods behind his father's house on Bluewater Hill. Beavers used to build a dam on the stream that wound its way through the property forming a pond deep enough to swim in. Late every spring, when heavy rains fell, the pond overflowed into the surrounding lowlands, running off into the river.

Eight years ago Jay had sold off the lowlands to the Owenoke Development Corporation. The corporation consisted of himself, Nels Proctor, Hollis Whitehead, and Gary Overton. Overton Construction had been hired to divide the land into two-acre building lots and run in the necessary utilities. This done, Gary built eleven executive colonials— four bedrooms, two-and-a-half baths, a modern kitchen, playroom, and library—no different from the hundreds of other such houses being put up along the Eastern seaboard.

The beaver were gone and not one white-tail had showed up in the woods since construction had begun. Once in a while a brace of ducks appeared and occasionally someone spotted a raccoon. To see anything larger than a gray squirrel you had to go up into the adjoining northern or western counties, in the high feeder ranges that led to the Berkshires.

Jay had enjoyed tramping through those woods, never

knowing when he might spot some sign of animal life, a life
that seemed so much freer and more rewarding than his own.
Once, out walking with his father, a skunk had scurried across
their path.

"He's so beautiful," the boy had said.

Not so, the elder Newell declared in that firm, executive way
of his. "Ugly, dirty beasts."

Jay had dared to argue. "Not to another skunk. All God's
creatures are beautiful and perfect, the most beautiful and
perfect they can be."

His father had mocked him for being sentimental. "They're
dumb and useless and if I had my way, I'd drive them all off
the land. Foul critters, every one of them."

Jay had given up the argument, as he gave up other
arguments with his father. All discussion with the older man
disintegrated eventually into a clash of wills, a clash always
won by his father. It seemed to the boy that his father won at
everything he attempted, getting his own way all the time, a
powerful and resourceful man. The kind of man Jay knew he
would never grow into.

Some time later they were resting on a fallen log, seemingly
fastened to the ground by a large and intricate spider web,
when Mr. Newell gestured for silence. His eyes followed the
swift, unplanned movements of a huge black fly. With surprising speed, his hand flashed out, and he captured the fly in his
fist. Almost tenderly, he placed the insect deep into the pocket
web. At once the spider appeared, marching with a terrible
single-mindedness toward the still struggling fly, snatching
it up at last and carrying it back to the depths of its nest.

"People like us," Mr. Newell, speaking in his leaden, imperious voice, had said, "are the spiders of the world. Never
forget that. The rest are all flies."

The spider and the fly, and his father's portentous declaration, were etched forever in some dark area of Jay's memory.
For years he had nightmares about that fly being thrust into
the savage and voracious jaws of death, reduced by a mighty
hand into nourishment for another creature. He saw himself
as that fly and searched for the essential flaw in his character
that encouraged such morbid feelings. Until, by force of will,
he taught himself to identify with the spider, with his father,
with the predators, with the winners of the world. Only then
did he believe he had achieved his true place in the natural

order of things, on his way to becoming the man his father expected him to be.

"Banking," Mr. Newell used to say, "is at the core of our precious civilization. Money is the fuel that keeps capitalism on the right road. Money borrowed, money loaned, money spent and earned. Free enterprise depends on the free flow of cash to remain healthy and grow. Our duty as Christians and Americans is to insure the progress of the nation, under God. We are responsible for the welfare of all of mankind."

The last walk Jay took with his father was during the spring break of his junior year at college. Mr. Newell had spoken in that measured, solemn, businesslike way of his. "It's time to discuss the future seriously."

Jay's pulse began to race and a cold sweat erupted across his shoulders. For the first time he was able to make his feelings conscious, to put them into words: *I fear my father. I hate my father.* Aloud, all he said was, "I've been thinking about that myself."

"Excellent. I think an advanced degree in business at Harvard or the Wharton School might be in order. Summers you'll be with me in the bank, of course, and later—"

Jay had stopped listening. He struggled to find the courage to tell his father what he had decided. The words came from him in a sudden rush.

"I've decided to become an actor."

His father stopped walking. "What did you say?"

"An actor. I'm in the drama club at school and I'm good, Father. I really am."

"That's impossible."

"It's what I want to do with my life."

His father's face froze in a look of incredulity and disdain. His lips barely moved when he spoke. "Who are you to think you could become an actor?"

"I could be a good actor. I—"

"Newells do not become actors," his father said simply. He never raised his voice but there was no debating his authority. "A momentary aberration. It's time to put such childish drivel aside. Grow up. Become a man. Assume your responsibilities. I can see I've been too lax with you. Directly after school, then, you'll come into the bank. No graduate school. I'll see to your training myself. That's the way we'll handle things, understand?"

And so it had been. Ten years ago, at his father's death, Jay had taken over active leadership of the bank. Not since that last talk with his father had he set foot in those woods. Nor had he ever acted again, or even made the trip into New York to see a play. He occasionally watched something on television with his wife, but only for brief interludes, claiming boredom, insisting it was such a waste of time for a Newell.

The Newell house sat up near the crest of Bluewater Hill. It was a rambling affair of two stories with an enclosed porch at either end and a greenhouse that faced the south. It contained twenty-two rooms, all with high ceilings and fireplaces, hand-carved wainscoting, and spacious hallways lined with family portraits done in a formal, colonial style. Two libraries contained thousands of volumes including collections of works by Jane Austen, Thoreau, Kipling, Robert Louis Stevenson, and Charles Dickens. Poetry by the Brownings, by Keats and Shelley, by Whitman, and other American poets lined two walls, and included many first editions. A Duncan Phyfe table was the centerpiece in the elaborate dining room along with a collection of Waterford crystal displayed in twin American pine hutches along one wall. A large still life by Morandi hung over the chestnut mantel which framed the fireplace.

There were two other buildings on the estate: a massive barn long since transformed into a heated garage, and the gatehouse where the caretaker and his wife lived.

Now that the Newell children no longer lived at home —Charles was a stockbroker in Boston, with a family of his own; Lucille was with the Peace Corps in Ghana; Theodore was a Second Lieutenant in the U.S. Army, serving with a tank unit in West Germany—much of the main house was closed off. Jay and his wife lived only in the rooms on the south side of the main floor, little more than a large apartment but sufficient to their needs.

On this morning, the same morning Molly Fairfax was visiting the library, Jay Newell stood on the enclosed porch staring out at the woods. He wished, as he had so often wished over the years, that he didn't have to go to the bank. That he could stay at home and read all the books he had collected but failed to read, that he could listen to music—Mozart and Bach were his favorites—that he could take long solitary walks across the countryside, coming and going as he desired.

Why not resign his office? Sell off the bank? None of the

children intended to follow in his footsteps, that much was clear. And unlike his father, he would never try to convince them to do so. Such a posture of insistence was beyond his capabilities.

They might travel. Lauren loved Europe. They could spend a year—or more—wandering about, getting to know some of the great cities, visiting the museums. He shook his head as if to clear it of such absurd imaginings.

He would go to the bank this morning as he did every morning. Banking was what he did. A banker was what he was. It defined his existence. It was incredible that one's life was the sum of hundreds of unconnected incidents, many of them accidents, others deliberately developed and brought to a climax. More and more he had begun to accept the influence of chance in a man's existence. Accident, luck, some random happening; these were the primary elements, shaping and conditioning the tone and texture of every life. He felt saddened by that knowledge, that he was enclosed by invisible barriers, trapped in a world without horizons, in pursuit of more of the same, his tomorrows little different from his yesterdays, without excitement or meaningful rewards.

Still, he knew he oughtn't complain. Life had bestowed much on him. He had a wife whom he loved, although there were times when he wondered how she felt about him. He wondered, but had never dared to inquire. Had she ever truly loved him? Did she love him now? Or had all feeling drained away, leaving only the habits of a quietly desperate existence?

As for the children, they were handsome and clever and he admired each of them. Yet he felt a certain protective detachment had sprung up between himself and his offspring, that none of them cared to know him better. Or was it that they had come to know him too well? He preferred not to dwell on such questions; the answers were bound to be disappointing.

A maid announced breakfast and he joined his wife in the room set aside for that meal. "Juice and coffee," he told the maid, and took his place across from Lauren, smiling in her direction. He found considerable pleasure in the way she looked. She was still a beautiful woman, her straw-colored hair cut short now. If anything, she was more attractive, her features softened by time, all the hard edges removed.

She was, he acknowledged, a kind person. She would, for example, make no mention of the night before, of his unin-

vited entry into her bedroom. She would never be critical of
his behavior, no matter how boorish, no matter how lacking in
consideration. She would do nothing to embarrass him or give
him distress. A good woman, she was an outstanding mother
and everything he had ever wanted in a wife; why then the
emptiness in his life, the sense of being always alone?

"Breakfast," she admonished, "is the most important meal
of the day."

His father used to say that, in exactly the same dead verbal
rhythms. Had she learned it from him? Not likely. He returned her smile, recalling their wedding day. How proud he
had been, how anxious to revel in that blond flesh, how fearful that he would fail to please her in all the ways a man was
expected to please a woman. His fears were well grounded. He
had never been the man she needed or wanted or was entitled
to. But neither had he ever been the man he wanted to be. Nor,
he now knew, would he ever be.

"I have a busy morning ahead of me," he said, as usual.

The members of the girls' basketball team of Old Brixton
Regional High School ran up and down the outdoor court
with considerable energy and good will but without an abun-
dance of skill. In green shorts and yellow tee shirts, they ran
through shooting and passing drills. Too often they passed
wildly or double-dribbled and seldom were able to put the ball
in the basket. At last one of the girls made a lay-up and Carl
Becker, from his place in the grandstand at courtside, cheered
derisively.

"Way to go, team! Now let's try for *two in a row*!"

The players ignored him, but the coach, a strong-bodied
woman with short iron-gray hair and bright, inquiring eyes,
glared at him through tinted glasses. Her lips compressed in
disapproval.

"Coach harder," he yelled, waving at the woman. "You're
in for a long, hard season."

"Be quiet," a firm voice said from a few rows back, "and
let them play."

He turned around slowly, a cutting retort ready to go. He
swallowed it at once. The woman behind him was shapely and
stylish in black slacks and a white blouse, a cashmere sweater
tied casually across her shoulders. Her steady sea-green eyes
sent a hostile message.

"If you can't help, don't hurt," she drawled.

"I'm a fan," he protested.

She appraised him with deliberation, allowing nothing of what she thought to show on her face. He reminded her of Joel, yet they looked nothing alike. Joel was a big man, tall and wide-bodied, giving the impression of great untapped strength, and that strength had once provided her with comfort. In his presence, in the protective embrace of his arms, she had always felt removed and secure from the threats of city life.

How ironic. For Joel had proved to be unreliable, dangerous even, able to exploit her most vulnerable side. For nearly two years he made extravagant declarations of love and fidelity, creating an amorous pool that stripped away the shield of ordinary skepticism and good sense that protected her, causing her to ignore the nagging uneasiness under the surface.

The betrayal, when it came, had been complete. First the wife, never before mentioned to her; a wife and children, living in another city, left behind while Joel pursued a career as a painter, a career advanced so effectively by Molly and her gallery.

"I'm getting back together with Alice . . . my wife," he had announced callously.

A wife, children, a renewal of the marital life. Leaving her with what? Vows broken, promises shoved aside, expectations shattered.

"That doesn't mean," he had said, peering down at her with that so charming, crooked smile, "that we can't keep seeing each other."

The pain had been acute and lasting, the fury directed at her own naiveté. She had been too willing to believe in a goodness he had never displayed. Abandoned and alone, she grew gunshy, determined never to allow anyone to hurt her again.

Her eyes fixed on Carl Becker as she pushed the past out of her mind. "A fan," he had said.

"A clown, I think," she answered with no modifying gentleness in her voice, refusing to lower the barriers for even a moment.

He winced and brushed the hair off his forehead, as much a nervous reflex as a practical gesture. He clamped his mouth shut, determined to say no more than he had to. He owed her neither explanation nor apology.

He said, "Could be you're right."

"Of course she's right," the coach said, advancing up the risers of the grandstand. "Picking on my players the way you did." She took Becker's face between her square hands and planted a noisy kiss on his lips. "Forgive him," she said to Molly. "He's been spoiled by the indulgences of a father who loved him dearly and the absence of a good woman in his life for too many years."

"Anna, I only came to say hello and lend you the benefits of my expert opinion."

The coach grinned. She was squarely built with strong round legs and a face to match. Her manner was lacking in all artifice, her style simple and direct. She raised her eyes to the woman in the grandstand. "You're new around here?"

"Molly Fairfax is my name." She made her way down and offered her hand. "A visitor in town. I've only been here a couple of days."

"How lovely you are. Don't be too hard on my friend. He made a bit of a splash as a ballplayer during his high school years and he's never gotten over it. We have to talk, Carl."

"It's why I'm here."

"Friday. Drinks at five. You, too, Molly Fairfax. That is, if you can tolerate this ill-mannered fellow for more than a few minutes. Now, if you'll both excuse me, my girls need me. It is going to be a long season."

"Isn't she some piece of work?" Becker said to Molly, watching Anna back on the court.

In answer, Molly started down out of the grandstand. He hurried after her.

"I'll see you at Anna's on Friday. I'll pick you up at four-thirty. Where are you staying?"

"Mr. Becker—"

"Carl," he corrected.

"Mr. Becker," she repeated pointedly. "I have spent a considerable amount of time avoiding men like you."

With that she was gone, disappearing into the tunnel beneath the stands.

He watched her depart, resentment mingling with admiration, and said to the spot where she had been standing, "You have made a very big mistake."

But he couldn't be sure he was right.

Gary Overton was still a compressed package of physical power. He was thick-bodied and hard. He lifted weights and occasionally ran with his friend, Nels Proctor, though more and more he was unable to keep pace, seldom finishing the prescribed distance. He felt he was becoming shorter, his neck virtually lost between his great, humped shoulders. He wore his hair long in back in compensation for all that had been lost up front. He was beetle-browed and his eyes were small and squinty. There was a pugnacious set to his jaw.

He walked as if leaning into the wind, his short legs moving fast to keep up with the rest of him. Dressed in a work shirt, jeans, and a corduroy jacket, he looked like what he was—a man in a hurry to get things done: to build, to profit, to pile up a fortune. Sitting back on his spine in Nels's office, displaying his wiseguy's grin, he swung his booted feet onto Nels's desk.

"You and Barney have a good time?"

Nels had recently returned from a two-day outing up-country in advance of the hunting season. "Best spring scout ever. Trails clear, tracks and droppings wherever you looked. No doubt about it, we'll find some prime bucks come October. Barney and I'll be going out first day, if you want to come along—"

"I don't think so. It's been six years since I last went on a hunt. Seems like I've lost my taste for it."

"Whatever you say." Behind the big nineteenth-century mahogany partners' desk, Proctor perched like some predatory bird, sleek and sharp, the eyes pale and distant, vaguely accusatory.

Poised for flight—or attack—Gary thought in silent admiration. Unlike most human beings, life never got to Nels, never wore him down, never sapped the energy with which he confronted each day, every new project. He still seemed to want everything, his appetite for living apparently greater than ever, and he seemed capable of achieving anything.

A hint of a smile softened his expression. "How's that lovely new wife of yours?"

Gary was quick to smile back. "That woman is a sex machine. Using me up, day and night."

"Next time don't marry a woman half your age."

"No next times for me. Leila keeps my head spinning, as beautiful as she is. I tell you, Nels, I never felt about another woman the way I do her."

"Good. As long as you don't let her take your attention away from the job."

"Not to worry. First things first. We are proceeding on schedule. Should be finished pouring concrete this time tomorrow."

"I wish we could pick up the tempo. The sooner we get the mall built, the sooner we'll start collecting income, the sooner we'll show a profit on the books."

"I can't take a whip to my men."

"Have you considered putting on more men?"

Gary shook his head. "They'd only get in each other's way. Let's leave things the way they are."

"Have you thought about a second shift?"

"That'd double our costs."

"And double our production. Again, the sooner we start making money, the sooner we pay off the loans, get out from under those interest payments. Think about what I'm saying, that's all."

"Sure, Nels," Gary said dubiously. "I'll think about it. I can do that much."

Nels leaned, one long finger pointing. "Remember, in this affair, your business is my business." He smiled to indicate he meant no malice.

Before Gary could reply, the door swung open and Hollis Whitehead appeared. The years had added considerably to Hollis. The sandy hair had faded, whitening along the sides and at the back of his head, worn longer and combed full over his ears, framing his bland face. Time, and an excessive amount of expensive whiskey, had coarsened his features. There was slackness around his mouth and his eyes were watery, blinking repeatedly. If, in his youth, he had been only partially completed, the ensuing years had served to blur him further, all distinction smeared the way an artist might smear the lines of an unsatisfactory drawing made with a soft pencil. He wore a mask of anxiety, covering irrevocable disappointment with himself, his life.

He arranged his bulk tentatively in a chair, testing for support, before settling down with a relieved sigh. He refused Nels's offer of coffee or tea.

"Wouldn't mind a little eyeopener, ol' buddy. It's been a long, hard night."

Gary snorted disparagingly. "Fuckin' boozer."

"Which is considerably better than being a damned asshole."

Gary came halfway out of his chair until Nels waved him back. "Knock it off, both of you." There was a threatening current in his voice. His eyes, blue-white below the pale iris, held steady on the big man until Hollis turned away. "You've got to cut back on the drinking. Lose some weight. Get yourself back in shape, Hollis."

A flash of resentment brought the bloated features back into focus. "I don't need any advice on my private life."

Nels, elbows on the desk, fingers forming a steeple, teeth revealed in a humorless arc, said, "A great deal more is at stake here than you know."

"And I'm doing my share, more than my share. Hell's bells, who was it got the variances on the zoning out in the county?"

"You did, Hollis."

"And who was it pushed through every one of those licenses?"

"You did, Hollis."

"And who was it got that tax abatement bill through the General Assembly in the face of all that opposition?"

"You did, Hollis."

"You bet I did. All of it. And I got the Environmental Protection Department to rein in its opposition to taking over the wetlands. I did all that, Nels. Those downstate bastards would have buried the entire project, if not for me."

"You did very well, Hollis."

"Politics," Gary growled. "Every politician is the same, his hand in somebody else's pocket."

"Spare us the self-righteousness," Hollis said with unexpected fire. Only recently had he come to realize that he'd never really liked Gary Overton, never accepted the muscular man as an equal. "We all know how you run that construction company of yours. Padded payrolls. Bribes to building inspectors. Kickbacks to purchasing agents. Peddling dirt by the ton. Specifications ignored—"

"Fuck off!"

"Enough!" Nels snapped. "Each of us has his job. Gary, you get the building done. Hollis takes care of the politics.

Both of you have done well and I won't tolerate any in-
tramural squabbling. I called you here to discuss what lies
ahead, and a great deal does. Just remember who you are,
who we all are.''

"The Four Horsemen," Gary intoned in a self-mocking lilt.

"Yes, The Four Horsemen," Nels repeated. "We have been
through a great deal together, good and bad. Done a lot with
each other, for each other. There's still much more to be done.
Last week I was in New York with Bresnahan.''

"How is ol' Jack?" Hollis asked.

"We talked about you, Hollis.''

"Oh?" Hollis was being careful, not pushing too hard. If
only he could have that drink. But he dared not ask again,
unwilling to submit himself to Gary's scorn or Nels's disapproval.

Nels went on. "Jack will see to it that I'll be named State
Chairman during the party caucus next month.''

"Fantastic," Gary said. "Got to help us, having you running things statewide.''

"There's more," Nels said. "Todd Henderson has finally
agreed to step down.''

"About time," Hollis said. "The man is senile.''

"The man has Parkinson's disease, to be exact. In any case,
he's out. We are going to put a good man in the state house to
take his place.''

"You'd make a superb governor," Gary said to Nels.

Nels shook his head. "I'm not built for elected office. What
we need is someone whose work is known around the state,
someone with lots of friends and not many enemies. A man
who will get the nomination and can get enough voters to cross
party lines in the election in eighty-six.''

"Who do you have in mind?" Hollis asked.

"You, Hollis.''

Surprised and pleased, at the same time Hollis was frightened by what he'd just heard. As president of the General
Assembly, he exercised a certain amount of influence and
power. He was an important statewide political force. But his
responsibilities were limited and the public's awareness of him
was even more limited. He remained a cog in the party machine—one of many assemblymen—his position due to in-
terparty arrangements and conventions. Governors were
required to step out to the head of the parade, their actions

scrutinized and open to criticism.

"I'm flattered," he said automatically, in his platform voice. "But I'm not sure I'm equipped for the job."

Gary applauded, breaking into song: "Happy days are here again, The skies above are clear again—"

Nels cut him off with a gesture. "Consider how much you could do for the people of the state, Hollis, if you were in charge."

"Jesus," Gary muttered.

Hollis donned a solemn, statesmanlike expression. He visualized himself presiding at official functions. Reviewing the National Guard. Delivering the State of the State address. The governor rated his own bodyguard, his own staff of personal advisers: academics, experts in various branches of government, a full legal staff, writers, assistants, secretaries. The state bureaucracy was loaded with beautiful and compliant young women.

"I am sincerely flattered," he murmured with appropriate modesty.

"The party would look on your acceptance as a favor, Hollis."

"And you could sure help line the pockets of your friends, Hollis."

"Be quiet, Gary," Nels said, "and take your feet off my desk."

Gary obeyed without comment.

Hollis folded his arms defensively. He wanted to please Nels, to elicit his approval, to maintain their friendship. But this . . .

"Bunny hates it in the state capital, Nels. Everybody knows that. Hickville, she calls it. Most of her time is spent here or traveling. But as the wife of the governor she'd have to be there."

Nels leaned, hands flat on the big desk as if he were about to spring. "I wouldn't want anyone to stand in the way of your career, Hollis. I couldn't allow that to happen."

"Bunny would never move . . ."

"Convince her."

"What if she won't change her mind?"

"We'll combine strategies. Use ingenuity. Unmake Bunny's mind. Or do you lack the courage to try, Hollis?"

"I didn't say that."

"Good, it's settled then. Talk to Bunny. Meanwhile, I will begin assembling the necessary forces for the campaign. By the time the state convention rolls around, you'll have a lock on the nomination."

"Um . . . Nels?"

"Yes, Hollis, what now?"

"What if I lose the election?"

Nels lifted his finely arched brows. "What a ridiculous question. You won't lose. I won't let you lose. You know you can depend on me, don't you?"

"Yes, Nels, of course."

Nels delivered his most benevolent smile in return.

8

THE POLICE STATION was set in what used to be the town hall, a building made of faded yellow stone scored by high, narrow windows and doors to match. Located on a low rise two blocks west of Main Street, it was surrounded by a parking lot crowded with police vehicles and confiscated cars. Built just after the turn of the century, the building had the weary look and mustiness of age and overuse.

Holding cells had been constructed along one side of the basement. There was also a large chamber which had been fitted with lockers and showers for the policemen. On the second floor the detectives held forth and it was here that the interrogation rooms were located. The main floor—reception area and squad room—was for the uniforms. Past the sergeant's desk, three rooms had been set aside where lawyers could consult with their clients. Beyond that, running to the rear of the building, was a wide corridor lined with offices and a conference room. The chief's quarters were in the northwest corner; the outer room had desks for two secretaries—both uniforms, one male, one female—with exposures on two sides.

Perry Maxwell greeted Carl Becker in the reception area across from the sergeant's desk. They shook hands, embraced quickly, and looked each other over, seeking the changes that time might have wrought. Maxwell was a stylish figure in the blue-and-gray uniform cut to fit his muscular body, tight across his pectorals. A thick red mustache softened his otherwise craggy face and lent a note of authority. Taller than Becker, and wider, he felt physically awkward with the other man.

"We never had a chance to talk at the funeral," he said.

Becker made a gesture of dismissal. "You were there. I appreciate that."

"I liked Sam. Everybody liked Sam."

They had known each other since kindergarten. In high school they had played on the basketball team, Maxwell the scorer, steady and strong, Becker the playmaker, with a flashy dribble and a good sense of the court. Neither had been deemed good enough to win a college scholarship.

Becker had gone on to West Point, graduating from the Academy and later serving five years on active duty in the Corps of Engineers. He managed to get a law degree from Georgetown University while stationed at Fort Belvoir, Virginia. When he left the Army, an inevitable step had brought him into the U.S. Attorney General's office.

Maxwell had remained in Old Brixton. He had done odd jobs around town, until he decided to join the cops on his twenty-second birthday. He had always admired the direction Carl's life had taken, yet he was satisfied with his own accomplishments. Becoming a cop was the best thing that had ever happened to him and, on a rapidly expanding force, no one could say how far he might go.

"Back on holiday, Carl?"

Becker brushed the hair off his forehead. His hands were surprisingly large for a man his size, with long fingers and thick, corded wrists. He spoke in staccato bursts and it was not difficult to imagine him hammering at a witness, intense, insistent, and toughly effective.

"It's about Sam," he said.

Shifting his booted feet, Maxwell looked away. "It must have been hard for you," he said quietly.

"I still don't believe it."

"Believe what, young Mr. Becker? What is it you don't believe so emphatically?"

Becker and Maxwell both turned toward the voice. Coming up behind them on a hunter's silent feet, his big right hand extended, was Chief of Police Barney Grubb. He pumped Becker's hand in a powerful grip, clasping him at the same time by the shoulder. Well into his middle years, Grubb was a big man, broad across the chest and shoulders, thick and hard, with only a suggestion of slackness under his heavy jaw.

"By God," he said in a jovial rumble, lips hardly moving, "you are getting to look more like old Sam every year, Carl. Heard you was back in town asking about your dad, which comes as no surprise. Lawyers do that—ask questions, that is. Thing is I figured you'd be around here before this, once you got over the shock and all of what took place. It's a shame, old Sam going that way."

"How are you, Chief?"

"Fine and dandy, which is about as good as you can get, ain't that a fact? No need to ask how you've been—the sight of the man, right, Perry? Looking like a million dollars on the hoof. Silk suit and tie to match, all gussied up. No wonder taxes are so high—it must go to dress up you government people beyond our means." Grubb laughed roughly, longer and harder than need be, amused by what no one else found funny. He wore a battle jacket with a .357 Magnum holstered to a wide black belt. His cheeks were darkened by a closely shaven beard, his eyes were clear and bulging, as if about to pop out of their sockets. His teeth were large and yellowed and plentiful when he grinned. "Come on into my office, boy, and we'll kick around old times." It sounded more like an order than an invitation.

The office was spacious, the walls painted an institutional green, gray metal furnished with standard issue desk and chairs. Grubb settled himself behind the desk, feet up, showing custom-made cowboy boots of snakeskin. He inspected Becker with professional suspicion diluted by good will.

"You done real good for yourself, Carl, the way I hear it."

"I enjoy my work," Becker ventured cautiously. "I prefer the law."

"Prosecutor for the United States Attorney General. I am impressed with that, boy, I truly am. Your daddy must've been proud of you. That why you've come home, to close out Sam's affairs?"

"Not much left to close out."

Grubb agreed. "Life is sometimes a bitch, you can depend on that. Plan on being around for some time, do you?"

"Long as it takes. I'm on a leave of absence from the job."

Grubb massaged his chin with the back of his lumpy hand. "Long as what takes, Carl?"

"Long as it takes to prove Sam didn't kill himself."

Grubb thoughtfully laced his hands behind his head. He stared up at the high ceiling, at the paint peeling at the corners. "Don't think for a minute I'm not with you on this thing. Sam was a good man, solid as they come, good as you could ask for. I enjoyed his company and held him in high esteem. Man gave up teaching college and turned to farming when he was what—fifty or so?"

"Forty-five. When my mother died, he had to find a new way to live, he told me. Put the old ways behind him. He felt a strong kinship for the land. Said if he had it all to do over again he'd come back as an Indian living as one with the earth and the animals, back before the Europeans came to the New World and fouled it all up."

"A romantic man, old Sam."

"In the best sense of the word."

"I remember you were no more than six years old when you moved into the county."

"Barely two. Sam raised me on that farm. He rebuilt the broken-down house with his own hands, from the ground up. He loved the land, but I think he loved that house even more."

"Folks used to say Jews couldn't work the land. Of course that was back before Israel and those kibbutzes and all. Old Sam was to be admired, he certainly was."

"What happened, Barney?"

Grubb exhaled audibly, looking down at his boots, choosing his words carefully. "Same as happens to lots of folks, I'd say. Life turned sour and there was talk about him being sick—"

"He had some back trouble, nothing serious. Nothing that would make him shoot himself," Becker interjected.

"I also heard it said he was drinking more than was good for him."

Wine and beer, that was all Sam ever drank, and sparingly. Becker opened his mouth to answer, then thought better of it. Anything he said would sound commonplace. Yet he was profoundly disturbed by his father's death, bewildered and enraged, and he longed to protest and attack this injustice life imposed with such random cruelty.

Grieve privately, he reminded himself. Mourn behind locked doors, conceal the dark resentment from probing eyes. Only by distancing himself from the anguish and the pounding disappointment would he ever be able to separate himself from the loss. But for now, questions continued to tease at his insides: Why hadn't Sam come to him for help? Why no farewell message—a phone call, a scribbled note, the slightest expression of love or regret? Hadn't Sam understood that by killing himself he would wound his only child deeply and forever?

If answers were to be had, he would have to find them for himself, in his own way. Until then, it was vital that he keep the roiled emotion tucked away in the shadow of a cheerful—if not stoic—facade.

"I suppose the shrinks say it best," Grubb continued mildly. "Suicide's the ultimate rejection."

"No note. Not even a phone call to Anna."

"I know, not a word to anybody. He just didn't show up anywhere for a few days. When Henry Streeter went over to visit and found him on the floor of his kitchen, the gun was still in his hand. An old Luger."

"Sam never owned a pistol. Just an ancient shotgun he used for varmints, and I doubt he ever hit anything with it. Didn't approve of taking a life, any kind of a life."

"Your daddy was in the war against those Nazis, wasn't he?"

"He landed in Normandy on D day and fought his way across France into Germany," Carl said with a hint of pride in his voice.

"Something of a hero, wasn't he?"

"He hated the killing, but he said it was the only way to stop the Germans."

"Well, there you are. Most likely he brought that Luger back with him, a souvenir he took off some Nazi officer."

"Maybe."

"Sure. Listen, I'd like to help you out, Carl, make you feel better, only what's a man to do except deal straight on with the facts of the matter? There was no sign of a struggle. No forced entry, nothing missing. Nothing to suggest robbery and murder. You want, I'll get you the medical examiner's report. Says clear as day what I'm trying to tell you—self-inflicted wound. Suicide. No evidence to the contrary, soft or hard."

"You knew him, Barney."

"I knew him, okay."

"He wasn't the kind of man to shoot himself. If he had, he would have tidied up his affairs, gone out neat and clean so as not to trouble anybody. He was that kind of a man."

"I'm not going to argue with you, Carl. Except that facts is facts." Grubb rose, signaling that the interview was concluded. "Any single thing I can help you with while you're here, Carl, you let me know. How long you figure on staying?"

"As long as it takes me to find out the truth."

9

IN THE MIDDLE of the morning, the Berkshire Diner and Pie Bakery was almost deserted. They occupied a booth and waited for their coffee to cool down. For once Becker was at a loss for words, as if he had used up all his energy convincing her to come this far with him.

"How did you find me?" had been her greeting, delivered with substantial impatience, when he showed up at her door. She was not, he conceded, a woman to suffer unwanted intrusions or foolishness with good grace.

It had taken a considerable amount of determination to go on in the face of her obvious coolness. But he had persisted. "Owenoke Inn," he had said, convinced he sounded like the clown she thought him to be, yet unwilling to pull back. "Honey-colored plank floors, original hardware, four-poster beds complete with ruffled canopies, hooked rugs and Early American antiques. 'Washington slept here,' and all the rest. Very stylish, very rich, very nostalgic in this high-tech era of ours. Where else would a classy lady like you stay? Besides, it's the only decent place within miles, except for the occasional bed-and-breakfast room," he ended weakly.

He felt like such a fool. He entertained thoughts of a quick retreat, but put them aside, unable to come up with a way to make a graceful exit. His thoughts flashed back on Martha Rutala, the prettiest girl in his high school and how she had erupted into derisive laughter when he asked her for a date. Adlai Stevenson said it best: "It hurts too much to laugh and I'm too old to cry."

"Sorry," he had said at her door, backing off again as he had in high school. "I didn't mean to intrude."

There was that about him, she observed silently, allowing nothing to show on her face. Aggressive, yes. But perceptive and sensitive enough to recognize that he'd pushed his way in where he wasn't really wanted. How unlike Joel, who had crashed parties and privacy with a harsh brashness, displaying no concern about other people, their desires and feelings. How long it had taken her to recognize his cold selfishness, his thick-skinned disregard for the needs of others, including her own. Joel had been so charming, so boyishly seductive, innocent; meanwhile, he was always scheming to get his own way, to satisfy his own appetites, no matter who he hurt along the way.

Would she have entered into the relationship had she known in the beginning that he was married? She couldn't honestly say, knowing how hard she'd fallen for him. He had swept into her life on a whirlwind leaving her little time to do more than succumb to his powerful sensuality and his overwhelming cry for attention.

"Sorry," Becker had repeated.

Joel had never apologized for anything in his life. He bulled straight ahead, taking what he wanted, enjoying himself no matter the price others were forced to pay, acting always out of crass self-interest. All that sweet, youthful appeal masked a child's single-mindedness and Joel's ultimate cruelty.

"Why are you here?" she had said with a directness that put Becker on the defensive.

"I hoped we could have breakfast together . . . " He took a backward step. "Maybe another time."

"Give me a minute," she had replied on impulse. "I'll be right out."

Now, seated in the booth in the diner, she watched him through her sea-green eyes, keeping him at a distance. "You were raised in Old Brixton?"

He managed a nod, all glibness gone.

He might be able to help, she reflected. He certainly knew his way around better than she did. He would know people and friends that she would never ordinarily get to meet, and could open doors that would otherwise be closed to her. But that was as far as it could go. No dating, no romance, no sexual involvement. Since that last night with Joel, there had been a numbness in her, an abrupt cessation of any deep emotion.

When Becker still didn't answer, she made an effort to bridge the silence and soothe his bruised male ego.

"This is how I wish it had been for me. A place relatively unchanging, same neighbors, same friends . . ."

He gazed out at Main Street, watching the cars slowly roll past. A lazy street not too different than it had been a hundred years before.

"It's changing, right before your eyes and mine." He faced her again. "You haven't been able to notice it yet."

"Still, it must be wonderful to live here. To own a house, a piece of land."

"It could be. It once was."

An unfamiliar note had sidestepped into his voice and she grew uneasy. The glib city boy was gone, replaced by a man with whom she was losing ground.

"Once?" she said.

He held his cup between his hands. "You're a New Yorker?"

"I am now. I was raised in Texas."

"Ah, that accounts for the drawl. It's nice, as nice as the rest of you."

She recoiled at the compliment. It came too easily, and she knew to distrust men who used language too well, slickly persuasive men who were always looking out for themselves.

"What brings you to our picturesque little village?" he asked.

She told him how her mother had died and of her enigmatic legacy: a book, a Teddy bear, and a letter. She made no mention of the money she had inherited which had so dramatically altered her circumstances. "At the same time," she concluded, "I'm hoping to find out something about my father."

"What about your father?"

"There's not much to tell. He died when I was quite young."

"Sorry."

"His name was Michael Fairfax. He was a career Army man, a captain."

"I was an Army captain, too—in for five years."

"My father was killed at the Bay of Pigs."

He tasted his coffee. It was bitter and had gotten cold. He scowled at the cup. "My impression . . . was that only Cubans were involved in the actual operation."

"It was all hush-hush. There never was much publicity about the part our people played. The powers that be only admitted to a couple of American pilots flying missions, and that was revealed only when they were confronted with the truth years later. A lot of information simply never came out. Father was a hero. There was a medal, a Silver Star."

"You have that, too?"

"Mother left it to me. They were very much in love and they had a wonderful life together.

"Whenever he could, we did things together. I remember a picnic he took us on. There was a river. Well, not really —more of a stream or a creek. I went toddling into the water and was sucked under. I couldn't swim. I was helpless in the flow and was swept downstream. I remember how frightened I was.

"Until two strong hands grabbed hold and lifted me out of the water, holding me high in the air. He made me laugh and took me back into the creek so I wouldn't be afraid of the water. He was a marvelous man, strong and handsome—like a god to me—and I loved him very much. Maybe you knew him when you lived here?"

"I don't think so."

"Isn't it odd—no one around here seems to."

"Tell me about your mother."

She threw back her head and laughed, a graceful, enticing movement. "All I know about her life here is what she left: a borrowed copy of *Madame Bovary* and a letter from someone named Lauren. Oh, yes, and a sash on the Teddy bear that reads, 'Fourth of July Fair, Old Brixton.' I've been able to make no other connections so far. Do you know anyone named Lauren?"

"In a town like this, half the girls have fancy names like Candace or Merle or Lauren. Cute girls with turned up noses and yellow hair, girls who peak by the age of seventeen."

"I think there may be a decent man inside that street-smart skin of yours. Why not let him out, Carl?"

He nodded once. "With your help, I might be able to pull it off."

"I'm afraid I'm going to be too busy conducting my little search to get involved in any human reclamation projects," she said with a chuckle.

"Okay. But maybe I can help you."

"How?"

"About your father. I've got some friends in Washington, contacts in the Army. Why don't I have them run a check, see if we can fill in the gaps?"

The offer took her by surprise. "I don't want to put you to any trouble."

"And it won't be difficult to turn up some information on your mother. Why don't we begin by finding out if she was born in Old Brixton and if she actually lived here?"

"How?"

"Elementary, my dear girl," he said with an affected English accent; "We will examine the birth records."

"Why didn't I think of that?"

"Because *you* are not a hot-shot lawyer, lady. Or is it lady, lawyer? Or whatever it is Groucho would say."

"Fool," she said, smiling.

"Shall we go?"

In the Hall of Records, in the basement of the new Town Hall, they came up with a birth certificate for Emily Louise Fowler, born May 22, 1941. Parents: Cornelia and John Fowler. A further search revealed that John Fowler had died shortly after Emily was born, a victim of pneumonia. One more step and they learned that Cornelia Fowler married again two years later, to a man named Peter Matheson; no death certificate had been issued for Matheson, Peter or Cornelia.

"That means he's still in town and alive," Molly said.

"Not necessarily." His caution was infuriating to her but his exactness produced results; he knew how to conduct an investigation, she conceded. Logic and patience were qualities she had not expected of him.

"What kind of a lawyer are you?" she asked while they examined the records.

"Prosecutor, Attorney General's office."

"In these parts?"

"In Washington."

He was, she admitted to herself, full of surprises.

He read off a voter's registration card dated 1958. "Number Ten Bluewater Hill."

"What does that signify?"

"Your mother was raised on the Hill, according to these records. She lived there with Cornelia and, I suppose, with Peter Matheson. Bluewater Hill is where the money was—is —the money and power in Owenoke County. I'd say your mother was in very good shape, no financial problems at all. A book, a medal, a letter, and a teddy bear. What else did she leave you?"

Molly averted her eyes. "There was some money."

"Some?"

She decided to tell him the rest. "We lived modestly. Mother worked most of the time, in different shops around town. I never knew about the trust fund until her will was read to me. Money used to come from Parmalee, Whitson and Phelan, certified public accountants in Austin, where we lived. A check came every month, regular as clockwork. I was curious and asked some questions and found out the money was sent by a bank in Tulsa—"

"Tulsa, where Lauren's letter was addressed. Your mother must have lived there at one time."

"I suppose so. I phoned the bank and was told that they were just a conduit for funds out of a stock brokerage in New York City—Brown Investors, Incorporated. They handled the trust."

"Who was the trustee?"

"A law firm also in New York, headed by someone named Robert Henderson. Mr. Henderson readily confessed his role in all this but said he was prohibited by the rules of the trust from revealing anything more about Mother or her background."

"No connection to Old Brixton?"

"None anybody was willing to talk about."

"Obviously the trail was designed to come to a dead end, to cut off your mother and you from Old Brixton."

"All those twists and turns. Mr. Henderson would say only

that the trust was set up in order to keep the capital out of Mother's hands.''

"That same somebody believed that your mother was incapable of handling her own affairs. Who sits on top of that money now?''

"I do. Principal and income, mine to do with as I wish.''

"And what do you wish?''

She laughed briefly. "I did what I've wanted to do for a long time—I opened my own art gallery.''

"I'm impressed.''

"Don't be. It's just an itty-bitty place on a run-down street on the unfashionable West Side. You could say I'm breaking new ground. Only thing is I haven't been able to sign up any famous artists. Just a few young people who show a great deal of promise.''

And the best of those had left, she thought ruefully. That's what Joel had been with that sweeping, daring style of powerful brush strokes and his unique use of primary colors. A friend had brought him around to the gallery a month after it opened and she'd examined his slides, visited his studio, and was impressed as much with the man as with his work.

She had no doubt he possessed a special talent and was determined to make the entire art world see his paintings as she did. More than ten months passed before he produced enough new work to be hung alongside the older pictures he'd done. They met every few days and it took all her persuasiveness and constant encouragement to keep him painting, until he began to believe in her judgment and sincerity.

She committed her entire publicity budget for the year to that one show, determined to make the New York art scene sit up and take notice. And it did. Overnight, Joel Hammaker was recognized as a bright new talent, acclaimed by collectors and critics alike. His entire inventory was sold in the first eight days, putting Joel and the gallery on the map. *The New Yorker* magazine ran a piece about the opening in its "Talk of the Town'' section. The *Times* did a Sunday feature on the gallery and its young, beautiful owner. *New York* magazine's lead story was about Joel Hammaker. So it went in the weeks that followed.

The opening offered another cause for celebration; that night Joel and Molly became lovers. Truly a night to remember. She gave herself to him, personally and professionally, with an enthusiasm she had never before displayed. And it grew. She built a new life for herself in New York, the gallery continued to attract a great deal of attention and promised to keep doing so. And she was deeply in love with a man who exceeded by far her most romantic fantasies. Life was delicious in all aspects.

Until it came crashing down. Without warning, one afternoon, Joel entered her office at the back of the gallery and made his announcement, that sweet, charming smile spread across his mouth. He was switching to other management, one of those glamorous galleries on Fifty-seventh Street, the sort of place an artist of his stature deserved.

"And by the way," he let out as an afterthought, "I'm getting back together with Alice."

"Alice?"

"My wife."

When he left her office that day, it seemed to Molly that Joel was very proud of himself. She had sat there for a long time, too stunned to weep, too weak to move, too confused to know how to react.

"We," she said to Becker guardedly, "are just beginning to establish a reputation."

"We?" he said quickly.

"The artists and me, that's all."

"Sounds like you're doing okay. Your own gallery and the money to back it up. Way to go."

She ignored the hard edge back in his voice, beginning to accustom herself to his abrasive style. She was sure the brittle shell masked an otherwise compassionate and likable man.

"Why all the mystery, do you think? It's so strange."

"As Churchill said, 'a riddle wrapped in a mystery inside an enigma.' Maybe along the way we'll clear things up."

"Peter Matheson . . . if we could find him, we might learn a great deal."

"That shouldn't be difficult," he said, and turned back to the voting lists.

Molly deflected Becker's effort to accompany her to visit Peter Matheson. Mind working, planning ahead, she made the drive by herself.

The Owenoke Home for the Aged, situated at the eastern

rim of the county, consisted of a number of low buildings connected by covered concrete walks, all put down on a sloping meadow. She had phoned ahead to make arrangements, and when she arrived, a male nurse wheeled Peter Matheson into a reception room. The nurse glared at her as if she posed a threat to his patient.

"Mr. Matheson has agreed to this meeting," he announced protectively. "But he isn't very strong and you are not to place him under any strain of any kind. You'll find that he has moments of lucidity during which his memory is quite good. At other times, well—" He made a gesture of helplessness and stepped back out of hearing range, arms folded defensively.

Once a tall, well-built man, Peter Matheson had, at age ninety-three, sunk in on himself. He was wispy, his head much too large for his emaciated frame, his skin thin and translucent, his eyes unfocused.

Molly began in a small voice, trying to reach the old man, to fix his attention. She told him who she was, who her mother was. "Emily was Cornelia Fowler's daughter, Mr. Matheson, your stepdaughter."

After a while, the dull eyes brightened and his chin raised up. "Ah, Corky. What a beautiful woman she was, the brightest, smartest woman I've ever known. I loved Corky since the first time we met."

"Can you tell me about Corky?"

"We traveled a great deal, Corky and I. Corky was born a traveler. She loved to go aboard the *Queen Mary*—suites that looked out on the sea, the captain's table, dressing for dinner. all of it. Corky only went first class, wherever she went. The best hotels in Paris and London and . . . "

He grew melancholy. "Of course, I had nothing. No money, not much of a career. But Corky, she was well off, very well off. Money meant nothing when it came to traveling. Corky was enamored of France and England. I myself am particularly partial to the south of Spain, the Balearics . . . " His chin fell forward, coming to rest on his chest.

Molly persisted. "Cornelia was my grandmother, I think. Anything you could tell me about her?"

He made no response.

The nurse stepped forward. "That's all for now. Mr. Matheson needs his rest."

As the chair began to move, the old man stirred himself,

eyes locating Molly. "Pretty lady," he whispered. "Corky was the prettiest lady I ever saw, and you look just like her . . . "

"I'll come again," Molly said, "if that's all right with you?"

No answer came. His face was placid and vacant, the face of a man at peace with his long-dead past.

10

THE HOUSE LOOKED down at the river, clinging to the side of Bluewater Hill like some great angular creature reincarnated out of a prehistoric era. Long I beams reached into the earth as if seeking nourishment from the rocky soil to help support the layers and turrets of weathered cedar and unexpected angles of the terraces and decks. Off to one side was a swimming pool made of poured concrete, encased in native stone with wooden walks. Cut into the side of the hill was a tennis court, outfitted with lights for nighttime play. A heated driveway led to the road that snaked down the hill. The wide garage at the back of the house contained a green Porsche, a silver Jaguar XJK, a red and black Jeep Cherokee for everyday use, and a restored 1958 Mercury Turnpike Cruiser.

The house had been custom-designed to Nels's exact specifications, to fulfill his every need and whim. Hardwood floors were polished to a golden sheen under the lofty beamed ceiling in the living area. A study was lined with books and modern black leather and steel furniture, complete with an elaborate entertainment center including a giant television screen, a sophisticated stereo system with speakers strategically located throughout the house, along with professionally-installed audio and video recording equipment.

Nels's bedroom was without clutter. A firm custom-built mattress rested on a handmade walnut platform. There was a chest to match. Recessed lights in the ceiling could be lighted individually, or they could flood the room with illumination. An antique Navajo rug hanging on the wall behind the bed provided the only color in the room. A keyboard, situated on the nighttable, controlled the lighting and the stereo system. The adjoining bath, complete with sauna, hot tub, and jet-spray shower, was finished in black Italian marble.

The kitchen was large and fully equipped, although it owed more to elegance than practicality.

There was no guest room. No one was ever invited to remain overnight. Nels preferred to sleep alone in his house, alone in his bed, to wake alone. He loathed the sounds people made in their sleep. Loathed their toilet sounds, the smells and emissions of their bodies, their feeble attempts to conceal or improve on natural shortcomings. People were seen to their best advantage, he had long ago concluded, when entertained in brief, structured interludes, their visits judiciously spaced out at suitable intervals.

So it was with Leila Overton.

As usual, the garage door had been left open so that she could drive her cherry red Italian sportscar out of sight from nosy passersby. On her way into the house, she closed the automatic door, locking her car away from the world outside, thus preserving the anonymity of her relationship with Nels Proctor.

Leila had been only twenty-one years old when she became Gary Overton's third wife less than a year ago. She, too, had been married twice before. Her first husband, a used-car salesman, had gotten her pregnant when she was seventeen. Two weeks after they were married, Leila had an abortion; appalled by what she had done, he left her two days later. Her second husband was her best friend's brother; she married him when she was nineteen. Three weeks later he discovered her in bed with a disc jockey and attacked the man with a baseball bat. The disc jockey, a black belt in judo, disarmed him and delivered a swift and punishing beating. A second divorce ensued. Leila had yet to mention either marriage to Gary and had no intention of doing so.

He found her at Crazy Joe's, a lounge in Chicago. She was working as a cocktail waitress. In black shorts and a white

satin blouse open nearly to the waist, she presented a spectacular picture. Gary appreciated what he saw and offered her
a thousand dollars to join him for a weekend in Las Vegas.
Much to his surprise—and her own—she refused the offer.

Gary, convinced that money could buy anything and anyone, was startled. And dismayed. He was determined to get
her into bed no matter the cost; he doubled his offer.

"No, thanks," she said sweetly, wondering what was wrong
with her.

He tripled the offer.

Leila leaned over the table, the satin blouse falling open,
and smiled into his face. It occurred to her that Gary's swollen
wallet coupled with his obvious passion for her presented an
opportunity that she could not afford to overlook.

"I'm not that kind of girl," she told him, with just the right
amount of indignation.

As he watched her walk away, he was burning with desire
and wondering what it would take to get her on her back. During the next two months, Gary pursued her by telephone, by
mail, with gifts and flowers, and frequent visits to Chicago.
He worked every trick he knew but she anticipated every move
and turned him away, leaving him confused and desperate to
consummate his desire. No woman he had ever known had
held out against such an onslaught of gifts and promises of
more gifts. He bought her clothes and jewels and finally a
mink coat. She returned them all with shy expressions of grat-
itude.

He told her that he loved her.

"And I love you, Gary, more than any man I've ever
known."

How in hell, he demanded to know, could she love him so
much and still keep him out of her pants? His fervor increased
until one evening, sinking deeper into a miasma of desire, his
brain whirling at the nearness of her, he pushed the right but-
ton.

"Will you marry me, Leila?"

Would she!

Did she!

She quit her job at Crazy Joe's and off they flew to Las
Vegas to be duly wed by a justice of the peace in the Blissful
Marriage Chapel, one mile out on the Strip. They spent the
best part of the next seventy-two hours gambling and Gary

lost more than thirty thousand dollars without uttering a complaint or a curse. Leila decided that anyone who could lose
that much money with that much aplomb was certainly the
man for her and she told him how wonderful he was.

She also told him he was wonderful, each time they made
love, wondering how the hell she was going to be able to spend
the rest of her life with a man who climaxed in what had to be
world-record time, always with a squeak and a whimper. She
hoped time and a subtle effort on her part would bring Gary's
performance up to a more acceptable level. She would, of
course, have to move very slowly and carefully, lest her new
husband suspect of her being less than the pure and simple girl
she appeared to be.

By the time they returned to Old Brixton, she had learned
that Gary was worse than a poor lover. He was often no lover
at all, suffering frequent intervals of impotence. He made excuses, blamed his gambling losses, his fear of not being able to
satisfy a wife much younger than he, business problems, the
lateness of the hour, or an excess of booze. It became clear to
Leila that compensatory measures would be necessary.

That's when Nels Proctor entered the picture. Her husband's best friend, he reeked of sexuality. He was the most
beautiful creature Leila had ever met, with his chiseled, movie
star face and the meticulously honed body of an Olympic
athlete. At night in bed with Gary, she thought about Nels and
attacked her husband's flesh with an amatory relish that left
them both weak and trembling. Three weeks after moving into
Gary's seventeen-acre estate, Leila made up her mind: Nels
Proctor was the solution to all her problems. She couldn't
have found a worse solution.

Through the back door, unlocked in anticipation of her
arrival, she made her way down to the lowest level of the
cantilevered house. She found Nels working out in his fully-
equipped gym. One wall was lined with mirrors, and there
were weights and exercise machines everywhere. Clad in loose-
fitting athletic shorts, Nels pedaled a stationary bicycle,
watching himself in the mirror and speaking into a telephone
at the same time.

When he was finished, he handed Leila the phone and she
returned it to its cradle. He continued to pedal. He was a
visual feast, that lean body in action. Muscles flexed and
receded, the golden tan skin rippling smoothly, his stomach

falling away in a succession of hard ridges, all gleaming. His legs were long and powerful and the sight of them fired her already fevered imagination.

"How long," she said, in a high and thin voice, "are you going to make me stand here this way?"

He kept pedaling. "You're early."

"Only a few minutes. Stop that silly exercise and pay attention to me."

He checked his pulse rate, and dissatisfied, pedaled faster. When at last he was pleased with his performance, he slid off the bike and strode across the room to put himself on the padded weight bench.

"Some presses," he said, continuing his workout.

She stood over him, excited by his power, the way his shoulders and arms swelled as he lifted. A thin coat of perspiration made his skin shine under the ceiling lamps, reminding her of some sort of mythical creature, an unreal divinity.

"Suppose I don't choose to wait? Suppose I leave now?"

He lifted, brought the barbell back down to his chest, and pressed it up again. "You," he said, voice slightly strained, "shouldn't have any trouble finding the way out."

"You have no right to treat me like this."

"Then go."

"You are a—"

"Watch what you say." The words came out in a low, steady voice made more frightening by its lack of expression. Nels Proctor was not a man easily manipulated. Each time she had tried, it had ended in disaster. The trouble, she acknowledged, was that she wanted him more than he wanted her.

But it was more than that, she admitted; she *needed* him. He just tolerated her, as a source of occasional entertainment and relief. If she didn't call him, she doubted he would bother inquiring about her. One mistake and she would be eliminated from his life.

"What if I didn't phone?" she said.

"What if you didn't?"

"Would you call me, ever?"

He considered his reply. "So far we haven't had to find out, have we?" he said, still lifting.

"Be nice to me, Nels," she said, in a whiny voice she believed was both childish and cute.

Discomfited by the enduring silence, she said, "Gary lifts

weights. He snorts when he lifts and sweats like a pig. That's what he is, a pig, with a face like a pig and a body like one.''

"Speak kindly of your husband."

"The only good thing that's come out of my marriage is that you and I got together." After an unsettling pause, she went on flirtatiously, "Think what you'd've missed otherwise, sweetie."

He eased the barbell into its cradle at the head of the bench and lay still, allowing the blood to flow out of his inflated muscles, willing his breathing to return to normal, closing his eyes against her presence.

"Or maybe you don't think so?" she said, with characteristic petulance.

Eyes still closed, he answered, "Life goes on. It would have gone on for each of us alone. What's the saying? 'You play the cards you're dealt.' ''

A familiar irritation skittered under her skin. Always he treated her with disdain, as if she were a lesser creature, a diminished being. And she believed he was right, which made her want him even more. He was unlike any other man she'd ever encountered. She didn't deserve him. Which did not lessen the obsessive craving she felt. How much she wanted him! His hands on her flesh, his mouth on hers, his body pressed tightly to hers. Pride and resentment fled, leaving only that insatiable craving.

"Take off those shorts," she demanded, with more confidence than she felt. If only he would make the first move just once. Why must it always be she who asked for these meetings? Once, just once, let it be he who reached for her. But she knew it would never happen and his lack of regard inflamed her passion even more.

"Beg," he said, without a smile.

She went to her knees, not daring to put her hands on him. "Please, Nels. Please take them off."

"You do it."

He refused to make it easy for her, keeping his weight solidly planted on the padded bench. She tugged with all her strength until she worked the shorts over his bare feet. Now only a narrow-banded jockstrap concealed his nakedness from her.

He reminded her of a statue of a gladiator she had once seen in a museum. Aging, like Nels, but still powerful, its stone genitals had been swollen with virility. Standing before that gladiator, she had grown faint with desire. The gladiator, like Nels, had been indifferent.

She stood up and took her clothes off and he watched her through slitted eyes, giving no indication that her nakedness moved him in any way.

She bent over him. The jock was damp, rank with the smell of sweat. The aroma filled the cavities of her skull. A small wail of despair broke across her lips, a sense of her own insignificance. She removed the jock.

Cheek to his thigh, she gazed in wonder at his flaccid penis, thick and heavily at rest on his testicles. No other penis was as beautifully shaped, as graceful or as large, as powerful a source of pleasure. A prominent vein scored it from the head to where it disappeared into his dark pubic bush. For the first time, she noticed a smattering of gray hairs and the sight was jarring. Until now she had viewed him as aging but without the marks of his years, immortal, one of the chosen few. She shifted closer and the smell was more pronounced, overwhelming, a mix of scents, thickly sweet and sharp, from the struggling workout. But he was the cleanest man she'd ever known.

"How long?" she dared to ask.

He remained silent.

"It's been two weeks since you let me come over. A man like you, how long since you last got laid?"

"What a refined, delicate creature you are."

"You stink—from another woman?"

"Why don't you leave?"

"Who is she?"

He sat up, swinging away from her. "You are not to question me."

"She was here earlier, before I came?"

"It's not your business."

"You bastard!"

"Don't call me names. You don't have that privilege."

"That's it—always we play by your rules?"

"If you can't abide by the rules, don't play the game."

"Must it always be your game?"

"Always." At the wet bar along the far wall, he filled a

glass with orange juice, mixing in a spoonful of wheat germ oil and stirring thoroughly before drinking it.

"You make me so hot," she said.

"All men make you hot."

"No, just you, I swear. I adore your cock."

"You adore all cocks." He returned to the bench, lay down on his back, feet on the floor, knees falling carelessly apart.

"Nobody makes me feel the way you do. Nobody makes me come the way you do."

"A snake could make you come."

"Oh, Nels, be kind to me."

"You'd hate me if I were, the way you hate your husband."

"You're the first man who made me come."

"Don't lie."

"It's true. With other men, it's always close but beyond reach. Just missing all the time. You don't know what an awful sensation that is, never to find relief, always faking it."

"Is that how it is with Gary—you fake it?"

She giggled. "He can barely manage it, I told you. No matter what we try."

She reached out tentatively and when he made no effort to stop her she moved closer. He grew large and hard before her eyes, only inches away. "Please," she whimpered, "please . . ."

She mounted him and groaned as he penetrated deep inside her. Her hips began to gyrate frantically, her head thrown back, one arm across her eyes. A series of small inhalations, a choking sound back in her throat, until a loud scream broke out of her, rising in intensity. "Oh, no!" she protested, as if she were being punished. "Oh, no, no, no . . ." And then it began all over again, going on until she slumped over on him.

He ordered her to get up and she obeyed, knees weak, collapsing to the carpeted floor. She embraced his thigh.

"You didn't come. Look at you, you're still hard. I can make you come, in a way you like. I want you to come, to feel the way I feel."

He freed himself and said with a hint of superiority in his manner, "That's not necessary. I'm fine the way I am."

"That's not normal," she said, watching him disappear into the bathroom.

"No," his voice came back, "it isn't."

*   *   *

After showering, he came back into the gym wearing a dark blue silk dressing gown, his initials neatly embroidered on the pocket.

"Get dressed," he said, climbing the steps to his bedroom to put on his clothes.

She appeared in the doorway, still naked, studying his movements as if to engrave them in her memory. "I've been thinking."

"That can be dangerous."

She laughed, but he didn't. "About us, I mean."

He put on a crisp shirt, then knotted his tie. A simple series of movements common to all men yet possessing a certain style when done by Nels Proctor. She swallowed with difficulty, her fear mixing with admiration and longing.

"Why," she said in a small voice, "couldn't I move in here with you?"

"That's all?" He shrugged into his jacket and it fell perfectly from his squared shoulders. A perfect body for clothing, exquisite taste honed to perfection, and Alistair Burgess's superlative tailoring. No one looked quite as good in clothes—or out of them—as Nels Proctor did.

"Do you know how much I love you?" she implored.

He ignored the question. He slid a gold Baume & Mercier onto his wrist, checking the time. "I have an appointment in fifteen minutes."

"I could make you happy," she said plaintively.

"You may shower, if you like. But make sure to clean up after yourself before you go."

"It's because of Gary, isn't it? He's your friend and you don't want to hurt him. You're such a fine person, Nels. With such noble intentions. But is it fair that we have to sacrifice our lives because of Gary? The marriage was a mistake. I don't love him, I never have. I'll tell him about us tonight, that I'm leaving him."

He faced her, the pale eyes piercing the air between them. "No."

"I can't go on this way."

"You can and you will. Those shopping trips to New York and Boston, those charge cards, that sports car you drive around in, you don't want to lose all of that. So you'll go on just as you are."

"You're afraid of him," she challenged.

"There are times when you're actually amusing. Unintentionally, of course. Wit is not your strong point. Don't become burdensome, Leila. Don't create a problem. You wouldn't care for the solution I'd come up with."

"Don't you love me, Nels, not even a little bit?"

The question surprised him. "I don't even like you very much. But you do provide an outlet for certain of my, shall we say, less socially acceptable impulses."

"I don't understand."

"Of course you don't. Now be a good girl. Obey the rules. Break them and you're out of the game. Off the team. For good. Understood?"

She watched him leave the house and only when she saw the Jeep Cherokee back away did she allow her anger to surface. "Bastard!" she shrilled out in the empty house. "Dirty motherfucking bastard!"

And then she dressed herself and went home.

11

NUMBER TEN BLUEWATER Hill faced away from Old Brixton, shielding itself from a world in which human beings existed on a lesser scale. It gazed out on a wooded valley that stretched to the east toward another line of green hills, unbroken by signs of human habitation. The two-story colonnaded portico and wide brick steps spoke of wealth predating the Revolutionary War, a reminder of a nearly forgotten time.

Molly counted five chimneys through the branches of the stately evergreens which framed the long driveway. The house sprawled over the low rise on which it sat, wings and juts and ells spreading out from the main house as if to further strengthen its inhabitants' claim on the land, all with the same careful carving and detailing of the central structure.

Molly made her way up the front steps, savoring the sensation of floating back in time. She half expected the gleaming, oiled chestnut door—complete with brass knocker made centuries earlier by a master craftsman—would slowly open to reveal the lady of the house in billowing hoop skirt and powdered wig.

This, she reminded herself with something approaching awe, was her mother's home, where Emily had been born and raised. The impact of the eighteenth century mansion was dramatic, putting her emotionally in touch with a long line of ancestors she'd never known, people who lived and labored and died in Owenoke County long before she had been born. They—and this gracious house—were also part of her legacy.

What had it been like to live behind those walls, in close harmony with all that history? Her mind ranged ahead and she was able to see the stenciled floors, even as they had been in Colonial times, the wainscoting in the entry hall made of fruit wood. There would be a low-ceilinged living room with wide cherry planks on the floor, clearly hand-pegged and lovingly cared for, wing chairs covered in fading apricot damask which reflected the soft coloring of the pine-cone Senna rug. On the walls would be hung portraits of the men and women who were her true ancestors; and there, her own great-great-grandmother, looking so much like her mother, not too different from the face she saw in her mirror each morning.

She raised her hand to the brass knocker, changed her mind, and picked her way around the house, passing through a carefully tended garden. Behind the big house, the look changed: a kidney-shaped swimming pool, complete with twin cabanas behind a painted wooden wall and plastic chairs and tables covered by large fringed umbrellas. A young woman lay naked on a chaise sunning herself, oiled skin gleaming, arms akimbo so that even her armpits were exposed to the tanning rays.

"Oh," Molly exclaimed. "I'm so sorry."

The woman sat up, making no effort to cover her nakedness. She inspected Molly with a certain dull resentment, as if measuring this intruder against a privately held standard of youth and beauty. "Oh, that's okay," she drawled, reaching for a large beach towel, wrapping it around herself. "Do I know you?"

Molly introduced herself. "This house, my mother lived here, many years ago."

"How about that!" Leila Overton said. "You could say that's a coincidence, couldn't you. I mean, I live here now, me and my husband. I'm Leila Overton." She extended her hand. "Whaddya think? Some swell layout, huh? I made Gary put in the pool, just for me. I've been doing the place over. You should've seen it before, what an old-fashioned dump! You want to look around?"

"I guess I've seen enough."

"Come on, I'll give you the guided tour. You can see how I improved things inside."

Molly hesitated. Why not? It was why she had come to Old Brixton, to look into the past, to fill in the gaps in her mother's life—and her own. What better place to learn about her mother than in this old house?

"Why not?" she said aloud.

"Sure," Leila said, leading the way.

They crossed the wide rear veranda, passing through French doors into the huge living room. At once any resemblance to Molly's earlier imaginings seemed impossible. The walls had been stripped, finished off in an electric yellow that was harsh in the light of day. The furnishings were modern, sleek, with sharp lines—white leather, polished steel, smoked glass table tops. It reminded Molly of the display rooms at Bloomingdale's, all flash and glitz, but without any real style or warmth.

"Great, isn't it?" Leila crowed.

Molly allowed that she'd never seen anything quite like it.

Leila's enthusiasm increased. "Lemme show you the upstairs. Most of the rooms, we still have to get to. But the master bedroom is a real winner now."

The bedroom was almost as large as the living room below, walls of adjoining rooms having been torn down to complete this one chamber. The walls were completely mirrored, as was the ceiling. In one corner sat a hot tub made of pink plastic. In another was a six-foot television screen. "Great for watching certain kinds of flicks at night," Leila said with a slow, insinuating wink. A round water bed stood at the center of the room. Except for a white bear rug, complete with head and bared fangs, the room was without further furnishing or decoration.

"I believe in keeping to basics," Leila gushed. "I call it my playpen, if you get my meaning."

Molly glanced around. There was no evidence of where other rooms had once been located; the past had been wiped out. Had her mother slept in this very spot? Played on this old board floor, now bleached out and sleek with polyurethane? Was this where Emily had dreamed and read and entertained her friends? Was this the room where she, Molly, might have grown up, had things gone differently? None of her questions would be answered here, she realized.

She made her excuses and left. Back in the "Silver Bullet," the name she'd given her Datsun 280Z, before she drove off, she took one last, long glance at her mother's home, determined to fix in her memory all that remained of the house as it had been when her mother was a girl.

But time—and Leila Overton—had exorcised that past; history and tradition had been put aside, out of sight, lost forever. For the first time since arriving in Old Brixton, Molly wondered if coming had been a mistake. Had too much time gone by to discover anything of value? Would she be wise to allow Emily's world to remain untouched, her secrets undiscovered? Should she be content to live only with the memories she already possessed?

Emily had been a kind and loving mother, always there to talk to or comfort Molly. Her death had been a terrible shock and, though she viewed herself as a mature and independent woman, Molly was only just beginning to understand the full scope of the role Emily had played in her life. Still played. She turned the car around and headed back down Bluewater Hill, without so much as a single glance back.

"By God, I miss your father!"

Henry Streeter was by tradition and by choice a New Englander. His ancestors had settled in Rhode Island only a handful of years after Roger Williams had fled to that tiny English colony. Fifty years later two Streeter brothers moved to New Hampshire and the son of one of them later moved on to Massachusetts. In 1790, a male Streeter traveling around the countryside happened upon Old Brixton and decided to stay. He built a small house and established himself as a blacksmith. Streeters had been part of the community ever since: farmers, shopkeepers, a school teacher, even a minister of the Congregational Church. Henry looked like the old Yankee he was: gnarled and knotty, his skin the texture of worn leather, his eyes far-seeing, deep in their sockets, his hands veined and thorny from years of hard work.

"He looked upon you as a good friend," Becker said. "He used to regale me with stories of how you helped him when he first moved onto the farm."

Streeter nodded, thinking back. "That man didn't know a plow from a billy goat in those days. But when your father put his mind to a thing, by God, Sam Becker got it right. Reclaimed that rickety old house, he did, built a good half of it himself, from the ground on up.''

"The house is gone now. The foundation for the new mall sweeps right across the ground where it used to stand. Not a sign of it left.''

"Sam loved that house.'' Streeter let his eyes swing past Becker, lighting on something beyond the horizon. "Going to change the face of the county, they tell me. Make life better for everybody. Business, they call it. Progress.''

"The house is gone, the farm is gone, Sam is gone. It's as if Sam never existed.''

"Folks remember your father, Carl. I sure as hell do; think of him a lot. It's good to see you again, son. I hear you're doing real good down in Washington, D.C.''

"I don't believe Sam shot himself, Henry.''

"Maybe, if you'd been here, things might have been different. Oh, hell, most likely not. Life has a way of doing to some folks for better or worse and nothing can stop it.''

"You believe he did it, Henry?''

Streeter shifted around in his chair. They were seated across from each other on the shady side of the porch of Streeter's house, no more than half a mile from the center of town. Streeter sat hardly moving in an old rocker and Becker was erect in a straight-backed wooden chair that had been around for many years. The air was warm and still, except for the insistent buzz of insects outside the screen. The two men drank lemonade over ice in tall glasses and Streeter smoked one cigarette after another. His forefinger and middle finger were stained yellow and the flat broad nails were striated and broken, the hands of a man who still and always performed hard labor.

"Hard to say about people, ain't it?''

"Why would he do a thing like that?'' Becker asked, not expecting an answer.

A honeybee skimmed across the narrow flower bed that fronted the porch, coming to rest on a white rose. They watched the bee at work until it lifted off and darted into the distance.

"He'll be back,'' Streeter said. "Him or his friends. They know a good thing when they see it.'' He drank some lemonade. "No need to tell you how it's been for farmers the last few years. Prices falling, costs going up. Costs more these days to raise a hog than you can get for him on the open market. The small farmer doesn't have a chance anymore."

"Sam never mentioned money troubles to me."

"That figures. Sam said you had your own life to lead. Said young folks had a hard enough time making their own way without their people hanging onto their backs and making it worse."

"That sounds like Sam."

"The farm is what killed him."

"Damn, Henry, I just don't understand. He owned it out-right, the land and house both."

Streeter poured more lemonade from a pitcher, the ice clinking. "Three, four years back, when the price of farm products was way up and looked like they was going to stay up, Sam decided to take a flyer. Bought some extra acreage."

"He never told me."

Streeter nodded. "Feed corn, he went in heavy for feed corn. Couple of other crops. That meant big investments—a new tractor, some other equipment, seed, fertilizer, that kinda thing. Even took on a couple of hired hands to help with the work. Not cheap operating on that scale, and once he had the land Sam didn't want it just sitting there and producing nothing. I warned him it was touch and go, but he wasn't about to listen to me or anybody else. Caught up, he was, with the notion of bringing in a supercrop, making a killing of sorts. Went to the bank and took out a callable loan and later another loan."

"At his age, going into debt—"

"Sam had his own ideas on how to do things. Shame of it is, most farmers are poor managers, extending themselves too much from time to time. I got to say it, your father could be the stubbornest old man, once he bowed his neck."

"How big were the loans?"

"Never did say exactly. But I put the first one up in the neighborhood of a hundred and fifty thousand."

"Damn."

"And then the second loan built up the debt even more."

None of it made sense to Becker. His father had been a practical man, dealing logically and sensibly with the realities of life. He confronted problems as they came along, one step at a time. What had driven him, once the farm was paid off, to go so deeply into debt again?

"What went wrong?" he asked.

"Prices went down. Two straight bad harvests didn't help. Meant there was no cash coming in and lots of trouble meeting the bank payments. Oh, Sam was always talking like he'd be able to turn it around but it was plain to see he was worried. He was afraid of losing the place."

"He should've come to me."

"He came to me. When things got real sticky. Sat right there where you're sitting in that same chair and said he had these problems and was willing to let me help him out. 'Willing to let me help'—those were his exact words."

"That's Sam, all right."

"I did my best for him, used up most of my savings so he could meet his payments. Until things began to turn for me. No cash flow, as they say."

"Those things happen."

"I tried."

"What happened next?"

"Next? Well, the bank carried him for a while. Mr. Newell did his best for Sam, I'd say."

"And then?"

"I didn't see Sam for a good stretch after that. Figured he was out trying to raise capital, until all of a sudden it was over. Finished."

"You mean he was dead."

"I was the one who found him, you know. Anna called, said she hadn't heard from him for a few days, that he wasn't answering the telephone. So I went on out to the farm to see what was what. You get old, you get to feeling all alone, and sorry for yourself. Thought maybe your father had a touch of that eating at him. Anyway, there was poor Sam on the floor of the kitchen, that damnable gun in his hand."

Not so, Becker almost cried out. Sam had never owned a pistol. Sam Becker had cherished life in all its forms, avoiding damage to even the least of God's creatures. Yet in the end he had given so much anguish to Carl, a legacy of guilt and pain, the awful pain. It wasn't Sam's way, Carl told himself again. Sam was a man aware of and sensitive to the feelings of other people, especially those closest to him. Neither a word to his best friend or to the woman he loved, nor to his only child.

None of it made any sense. Becker shoved himself to his feet and shook hands with the other man. "Thanks for seeing me, Henry."

Streeter clung to his hand, tears forming in the corners of his eyes. "You don't now how sorry I am, Carl. By God, I miss your father, I do sorely miss him."

"You didn't bring that young woman," Anna noted in a slightly accusatory manner, admitting Becker to her home. The house was right for Anna. Built of native stone, square, and meant to last, it had a solid foundation. It was unadorned but possessed a clean, functional beauty. There was a large central room with comfortable furniture scattered around a kilim rug; a number of green plants in large pots grew near the windows. A staircase to one side led to a balcony and the bedrooms. In the back, adjoining the kitchen, was a long, windowed space where Anna did her pottery. It was complete with potter's wheel and kiln.

She wore no makeup, not even a hint of color on her fluid, voluptuous mouth. Like her pottery, strong and useful pieces in rich natural tones, Anna was without artifice.

"Molly decided not to come," Becker said.

"I like her—there's a good honest look in her eye. You two lovers yet?"

A warm flush rose in Becker's cheeks. "We barely know each other."

Anna snorted and brought a teapot and mugs to the round wooden table she used for eating, motioning for him to be seated. "People always talk about the sexual revolution. Seems to me hardly a shot's been fired.

"Have some tea," she commanded. "I baked the cookies myself. Unless you're intent on having something stronger."

"Tea is fine."

"It's called Mango Indica Flavored Tea. Sam likes it." She spoke about Sam Becker as if he were still alive, still within reach, a man she dearly loved. "Sam eats a half dozen of my raisin cookies as a warm-up for supper." She assessed Becker openly. "You're a tad on the bony side, seems to me. Something the matter with you?"

"I'm fine."

"I like my men with something to hold onto."

"You are one ferocious lady, Anna."

"I am a woman who misses your father more than I know how to say, Carl. I certainly do love that man. Sam," she said, the name lingering on her tongue, warm with remembered affection, "Sam and me, we fit each other pretty good from day one. Plug and socket, you might say. A man and woman fail to fit and you can forget all about it. Still, some shaping and smoothing is always in order, that was the case for us both. Times I guess I pushed too much and other times Sam got his back up, the way he could. Now and then he needed space, to be separate and not be bothered. I had to learn the signs, to know when those times were and give him that space. When he came back to me—and he always did—he was full of love and gentleness, reminding me of how strong and giving he could be."

She filled her lungs with air. "Sam looks on death as the final act of living. Normal and inevitable, not something to be concealed and shunned. 'I'd like to go out holding to the same principles I've lived by,' he says. That's my Sam and he is a man who does what he says he'll do. You know your father, Carl; you tell me: ever met a man more set in his ways, too damned stubborn to give in to trouble or enemies or the elements?

"Sam won't sell out. Two hundred years ago men like Sam put down their plows to make a revolution in this country and went back to farming only when the fighting was over. He loves that piece of land and isn't about to give it up, not Sam." It was said in a firm, even manner, without much display of emotion. But anger and resentment supported every word and Becker understood that Anna—as she described his father—was the stock out of which a nation had been built.

"Maybe the times passed him by."

Behind her glasses, bright eyes flared. "Hell you say! Sam's a man who belongs wherever he is and whenever he is. Whoever put that gun in his hand, whoever pulled the trigger, isn't good enough to wipe his backside. Whoever it was, knows that. That's why Sam had to be killed. He was too much for all of them."

Becker straightened up. "What are you saying?"

"That Sam never gave in to anyone. The day they say he shot himself, Sam phoned me—said he thought he'd worked out a way to save the place."

"Did he say how?"

"Just what I told you. He was to come over and see me the next day—or was it two days after? I can't be sure. But he never did show up."

A faint smile flickered across her full mouth. "My God, how I miss Sam. Past seventy, he was more man than most I've known. So damned loving, so loving . . . " She looked around the room as if expecting to find Sam Becker hiding in some shadowy corner.

"If Sam was killed," Becker said, choosing his words with care, "who did it?"

Her head swung around. "Don't have a name for you. Accusing without proof is a waste of good breath. If I had a name, if I believed, by God in Heaven, that man wouldn't be around for very long." She glared at Becker. "What are you going to do about it?"

"I'm on a leave of absence from my job. I'm asking questions."

"And getting answers, I hope."

"There's the bank, the foreclosure, the auction to the mall."

"That's Nels Proctor and his crowd, all rich and powerful. They hang out together."

"Barney thinks the pistol might have been a war souvenir."

"What are you going to do next?"

"Keep asking questions, I guess."

"You're a good boy, Carl. Your father always said that, that you turned out well. If you need my help, you'll let me know?"

"I will, Anna."

They embraced, clinging to each other for support. "Come and see me, don't you forget."

"I'll be back."

12

"Why have you come to me?"

There was more wonder in the question than hostility, more awe than annoyance at the unexpected interruption in a normal morning routine. There was even a suggestion of relief, had Molly been attuned to the voice.

"I should have called first," Molly said, examining Lauren Newell with frank interest. What she saw was a handsome woman in her middle forties, looking every inch the patrician grande dame in an expensive and stylish riding habit. Straw-colored hair peeked out from under the perky hard cap she wore and her creamy skin glowed with good health. Her eyes were bright and probing. It was her mouth, however, that gave her away, drawn down in disapproval, stiff with repressed tension.

"Saturday morning is one of the few times I can do as I wish," Lauren said, to explain away her reluctance to entertain her visitor. "Who did you say you were?"

Molly repeated her name. "Emily Fowler was my mother."

"Emily Fowler." A slight unsteadiness settled in Lauren's legs, the same she felt when she pushed her body beyond its limits.

Molly proffered the letter. "It's signed 'Lauren.' I went

back to the high school yearbooks and you were the only Lauren I could find. Lauren Poole. It wasn't difficult to locate you after that, Mrs. Newell. A few questions about Lauren Poole was all it took. You did know my mother?''

"Emily Fowler," she said deliberately, "was my best friend. And you are her daughter?" She peered closer, taking in each feature—the line of her jaw, the faint, startled look in her sea-green eyes. "Yes, I can see the resemblance. Please, come inside."

She led the way across an immense living room decorated with eighteenth-century sideboards and they stepped onto the enclosed porch with its windows ajar allowing a cool breeze to sweep in from the river below.

"If it's too brisk—?"

"Oh, no, I love this time of year."

"So do I. The days are so bright and clear and spiced by that first touch of autumn." A servant materialized in the entryway. "May I offer you some refreshment?" Lauren asked.

"Nothing for me, thank you."

A silent movement of Lauren's head and the servant withdrew.

"What a lovely room," Molly said.

"My favorite. That wall of greenery across the garden, the color of the flowers. It's all so restful. Please, won't you sit down?"

They sat in white wicker chairs on soft cushions covered in green with tiny yellow sunbursts. Molly's eyes were drawn to the out-of-doors beauty for a quiet interlude. Turning back to Lauren, Molly discovered that she was under observation; the older woman regarded her solemnly, as if attempting to fix her in her mind.

"I can see Emily in you—the green in your eyes is more vivid, but the tilt of your chin, the set of your mouth, the color of your hair is the same. This is what Emily must have looked like when she was your age. You are so beautiful, my dear."

"Oh, no. You're the one who is beautiful, Mrs. Newell."

"Please." One hand rose, fingertips brushing off the flattery. "Once, perhaps. The years leave their marks, I'm afraid. Oh, dear, I think I'm going to cry." She dabbed at her eyes with a linen handkerchief. "There, enough of that. When you reach a certain point in your life, old memories bring on a rush of emotion, of half-remembered friends and events. The adventures you shared." A brief, apologetic smile touched her mouth and she looked down at the pale blue envelope she still held. "This letter . . . "

"It was among mother's belongings, along with an old library copy of *Madame Bovary*."

Madame Bovary. Visions of Emily came rushing back to Lauren, transporting her to her youth. Emily and she, strolling along the riverside, discussing Emma Bovary—that most marvelous of women—as if Emma had been real and walking among them. How many times had she herself read the novel, how many hours had they talked endlessly, placing Emma in Old Brixton, making her a part of their lives, imagining how Emma might respond to the sights and sounds and events they were experiencing. Those exchanged fantasies had caused many a spring afternoon to pass swiftly and pleasurably, had helped draw the girls closer to each other.

"Your mother loved that book," Lauren said, careful not to give too much value to the words.

"There was also a Teddy bear, moth-eaten and much of its stuffing gone."

Lauren ducked her head, eyes moist. "We were together the night she won that Teddy bear. The Fourth of July Fair. Three balls for a quarter. Emily was the pitcher on the school softball team and was sure she could win that bear. It took all the quarters she had . . . " Her eyes came up, still moist but steady. "It meant a great deal to her."

"She kept it all these years. And the letter—it is from you, isn't it?"

"Oh, yes. A month after she left town, I received a card from her saying she was living in Tulsa, Oklahoma, giving her address and not much else. I wrote back at once—this letter—but she never answered. I wrote her a few more times but they all came back marked 'No Forwarding Address.' I never heard from her again. How is Emily?"

Molly lifted her chin. "She was killed in an automobile accident nearly a year ago. On her way back from a visit to Mexico, just outside of Laredo. A couple of boys drag racing on Interstate 35. They'd been drinking and there wasn't enough room for both of them to pass her at the same time. But they tried. Mother was forced off the road and the car turned over and that was the end of it."

Lauren blanched. "Oh, I am so sorry. I hoped that one day

we would meet again, that things could be the way they once were . . . when we were girls. What kind of a life did your mother have? Was she happy? Did she marry?'' She tried to recall the words even as she spoke them, castigating herself.

The question took Molly by surprise. Then she shrugged it aside, smiling. ''You see the evidence of that marriage before you. Did you know my father? His name was Michael Colin Fairfax.''

Lauren pored over Molly's face in search of hints of other faces, the way an explorer might closely examine a map of alien territory in a hunt for expected landmarks. Did she actually recognize a familiar turn of that lovely mouth? Of the angle of a single tooth? Was the tilt of her nose reminiscent? She couldn't be sure. She didn't want to be sure. ''Michael Fairfax,'' she mused. ''Was he from around here?''

''That's just it, I don't know. I can't recall Mother ever saying. I had hoped you might know, that coming back here I could learn more about Mother's life, about my father.''

Lauren clamped her lips together against the volley of questions she dared not put to Molly. Questions that were certain to conjure up unpleasant memories and emotions, questions which, along with their answers, could serve only to damage so many people, including her own family, including herself. Careful, she warned herself. Careful.

''What was he like, this Michael Fairfax?''

Molly hesitated. How easy it would be to boast about Michael Fairfax, to characterize him as a man wonderful and special in so many ways. But, she reminded herself, the father she carried around inside her head was a man described—and therefore created—by her mother, a father scarcely encountered except in vague recollections and in carefully contrived fantasies. She admitted ruefully to herself that she had indeed built her father into a personality greater than any human being could really be. She arranged a wistful smile on her lips.

''He was a career Army officer without much background. A self-made man. No money, no social connections, no formal education. Mother's mother disapproved of the marriage and they eloped.''

Once again Lauren suppressed an impulse to reveal what she knew to be the truth about Emily Fowler. But that truth was no longer relevant. It would do Emily no good and could do irreparable harm to the living. No good purpose would be served by unearthing that long-ago summer. She matched Molly's smile with one of her own.

"Your grandmother was a formidable woman. So forceful and terrifying to a young girl. I know that I was frightened of her. How impressive she was—tall, a classic beauty, haughty. When she entered a room she completely dominated it. In some ways you remind me more of Cornelia than of Emily. You're much softer, of course, more approachable and accepting. That accounts for it, then," Lauren continued, reaching for a convincing explanation, "why Emily left so abruptly and never returned for her last year in high school. The elopement, I mean."

Molly grew uneasy. Best friends, yet Lauren was so uninformed concerning Emily's activities, almost totally ignorant of the great love of her mother's life. An elopement; the socially proper girl from Bluewater Hill and a career soldier with few prospects. It was as if Lauren had never heard about it before. It made no sense. But before Molly could speak, Lauren was reminiscing again.

"I've thought so often about your mother. Emily and I, we were inseparable, closer than sisters . . . "

And yet, Molly thought silently. And yet?

"Seeing you is like seeing Emily come back into my life. What an eerie sensation. The family resemblance is uncanny, even to the rhythm of your speech, though you do have a bit of a drawl."

There was so much left unsaid. Molly evoked a profound awareness of Lauren's personal flaws and shortcomings, her failures, so much that she'd tried so hard to put out of sight. Shame rose around Lauren in a contaminated cloud and she shivered. She longed to embrace Molly, to express her true feelings of regret, to confess her sins. Instead, she remained silent, knowing the awful consequences this unexpected visit could bring down on her and hers.

"Mother trailed father around, from post to post. Being an Army wife is like that—"

Lauren broke in, "That must be why she was in Tulsa."

"I suppose so. The final posting was Fort Sam Houston, in San Antonio. From there Father was put onto some very hush-hush assignment which turned out to be the Bay of Pigs invasion. That's where he was killed, trying to save the lives of some of his men who had been wounded. They awarded him a Silver Star posthumously."

"Your father sounds like a splendid man."

Molly managed a soft smile. "We left San Antonio soon after that—San Antonio had too many sad memories for Mother. I was raised in Austin, mostly, and went to the university there."

Confronted by the anguish Emily must have endured, aware now of how desperately she had struggled to fabricate a new life for her and her daughter, to shield the child from an unhappy past, Lauren felt herself succumbing to dangerous emotion. Words of regret—and explanation—rose up in her throat, words she dared not utter lest they bring down everything she had built over the last quarter-century. Unable to confront her own past any longer, Lauren pleaded a busy schedule and ushered Molly out of the big house on the Hill, vowing to support Emily's version of the past, committed to extending the deception to the end of her days.

Lauren was one more in the lengthening roster of people who were reluctant to talk about Emily Fowler. Or, at best, seemed to be secretive, cautious, holding back. What exactly were they hiding?

More than ever it was vital that she learned more about her mother's life in Old Brixton. Coming here had seemed like a reasonable thing to do, a needed holiday from the routine of her life in New York. Even more, a way of leaving the sharp memories of her shattered romance with Joel Hammaker behind. All that had receded somewhat and now more than ever she craved solid answers to the growing list of questions forming in her mind.

Her mother had never mentioned Old Brixton, had never referred to her existence among these people. Why?

Why no mention of Cornelia, Emily's beautiful and ominous mother?

That house on Bluewater Hill. Another omission.

And Lauren—why keep her a secret, as Emily had done?

There was so much more: Peter Matheson, for example; Emily's substantial inheritance; friends, schoolmates, relatives. All kept tucked out of sight.

So much mystery, a mystery that continued still. Lauren and the others all erecting barriers meant to keep Molly from

unlocking the past. One thing she was certain of: she would
not leave this place until all of her questions were answered.

Molly strolled along the path edging the river, watching the
water pick up speed as it dashed toward the rapids, listening to
the steady roar that seemed both threatening and reassuring at
the same time. Her meeting with Lauren Poole Newell had
been a disappointment: she had hoped to learn more. Instead
of having her questions answered, she had merely informed
Lauren with news of her mother.

She formulated a set of new questions: What if an un-
suitable marriage had not caused her mother to leave Old Brixton? If not, what other reason could there have been? What
mistakes had Emily made? What crimes committed? Had she
been forced to go? What had gone wrong? On impulse, she
turned back and walked rapidly to the police station where
she spoke to a bored desk sergeant.

"Lady, nineteen fifty-eight, that's a long time ago. Anyway, what did this party do?"

Molly realized how foolish she must appear. Her questions
were vague, her search for information unstructured, without
a single target. "That's just it. I don't know if she did anything."

"Was a crime committed?"

"I don't think so. I don't know."

The sergeant's impatience showed through. "That makes
two of us, lady, who don't know anything."

Molly was about to retreat when an idea surfaced, taking
shape as it came. "Is there anyone around who was on the
force back then? Somebody who might remember?"

The sergeant stuck his tongue in his cheek. "Only Chief
Grubb. You want to talk to the chief?"

Barney Grubb rose when Molly Fairfax entered his office,
as much in admiration as out of politeness. Women as spectacular as this one seldom paid him a visit. He watched her approach with considerable pleasure, watching that long, easy
stride, her clothes undulating in counterpoint to the swing of
her shoulders, and the stretch and reach of her legs. At first he
figured her for one of those models out of a slick fashion
magazine, but she was too full in the body for that, with full
breasts that swayed when she moved and a fine curve to her
hips.

He delivered his best, most paternal smile, letting her get comfortable before settling himself back down behind his desk. He laced his fingers and smiled again, his massive and powerful essence of law and authority managing somehow to appear benign.

"You've made my day, miss."

"Why is that, Chief?"

"Not often I get such a beautiful girl coming to visit."

"Woman," she corrected gently, an elfin smile lifting all but the slightest criticism off the word.

"Right." How easy it was to misread the pretty ones, he thought. There was a core of steel in Molly Fairfax. "Hard for an old cop to learn an entire new vocabulary, miss. Now, how can I help you?"

Once more she repeated her story, telling him about the library book, the letter, the Teddy bear. He listened attentively and when she finished said her mother's name aloud, trying to get it right.

"Mother lived on Bluewater Hill twenty-six years ago."

"I was just starting out as a cop back then, only on the force for a short time. Naturally, I didn't know everybody in town. Bluewater Hill, you say?"

"I've established that for sure."

He shifted forward, elbows on the desk. "And how'd you manage to do that?"

She told him about her conversation with Lauren Newell. When she finished, he leaned back in his chair. "Good people, the Newells. Important people. Mr. Newell, he owns the Old Brixton Savings Bank." He chuckled softly. "Of course, it's the only bank in town, but there's talk of expansion. If Mrs. Newell says she knew your mother back then, then by all that's holy she knew your mother."

Molly uncrossed her legs and crossed them again. She saw Chief Grubb's eyes follow the movement and she made a quick, judicious adjustment of her skirt. She sensed that he, too, might be trying to dissuade her from continuing the search—he reminded her of the chief librarian, the abrupt change of mood, the icy wall of reserve thrown up at the mention of her mother's name.

Why?

No answer sprang to mind.

"My grandmother married a man named Peter Matheson,"

she said, almost as an afterthought.

His reaction was immediate. "Cornelia Matheson, you mean? Well, sure. I remember Mrs. Matheson. And I believe she did have a daughter. Seems to me the girl ran off a long time ago."

"That was my mother," Molly said with a surge of enthusiasm.

"Emily Fowler. Well, maybe that does ring a little bell after all."

"Can you remember anything about her, Chief? Anything that would have caused her to leave town?"

"Can't say that I do. Just up and disappeared, was the way I heard it."

"Would your records show anything?"

"Not unless there was a crime connected with it. Anyway, a lot of the old records got destroyed years back when we made the move to these quarters."

She stood up. "Thank you for your time."

"Looks like you came all this way for nothing, Miss Fairfax."

She turned her inquiring eyes his way, holding his gaze. "As lovely as Old Brixton is, I'm curious as to why a young girl would suddenly choose to leave—that is, unless she had to."

"Had to? I don't know what you mean."

"Neither do I, Chief. But I have the feeling that there's a lot I'm not being told."

"I wouldn't know about that, miss." He tugged at his blunt nose, thinking it over. A random thought surfaced, tickling his often bent sense of the ridiculous, a notion that served his need to accomplish a number of goals in a single sly move. "Tell you what, there is a man may be able to help. Man knows all there is to know about this town. Member of the Historical Society, Sons of the Revolution, and so on and so on. Family's been in these parts since the first Englishmen set foot ashore. He'll be pleased to give you some of his precious time, tell you whatever he's got to tell. Why don't I give him a call?"

"Who is this man?"

"Name's Nels Proctor. You're going to like him, miss. Everybody does. Leave your number with the desk sergeant and I'll let you know what Mr. Proctor says."

*   *   *

Alone in his office, Grubb settled down behind his desk. His mind ranged forward and backward, assembling bits and pieces of information as if putting together a puzzle, measuring one fragment against another until a picture that satisfied him came into focus. Pleased with himself, he made the call.

"Counselor," he began.

"What can I do for you, Barney?"

"Had a visitor a short time ago I thought you might be interested in. A girl by the name of Molly Fairfax."

Nels Proctor sifted through his memory. "The name means nothing to me," he said, making no attempt to soften his impatience. Barney Grubb was an itch he couldn't scratch, an irritation making its presence known in small but not-so-subtle ways, recalling favors done and demanding rewards that were never quite justified. Nels made the chief out to be a man who merely endured his lot in life, waiting, provoked by a dark drive for an as yet unreceived payoff.

In some unspoken way, Grubb made it clear that the slate had never been wiped clean; and if it threatened to be, he, Grubb, was always on the scene to perform a service—wanted or not—and thus raise the level of liability. Nels appreciated the way Disraeli had put it: "Debt is a prolific mother of folly and of crime." Putting people in his debt was Barney Grubb's primary talent, as he made it appear that his assistance was indispensable, his special abilities vital to everyone's welfare.

"All right, Barney," Nels said curtly. "Get on with it."

Grubb grinned into the phone. What a case Nelson Proctor was, one of nature's truly gifted specimens. All that energy, the animal magnetism, the effortless way he got things done—his way, of course. There was a mysterious, almost mystical aura about Proctor as if he belonged elsewhere; an alien from another time warp. And on top of it all, his arrogance, carried off with style, made it clear to everyone he came in contact with that all good things accrued to him by simple reason of his being.

Grubb understood how it worked. To Nels, no man was his peer. There were only subordinates, drones who did his bidding and were pleased to bask in the cool bright light of his approval, willing to profit from their connection to him, no matter how tenuous or brief that connection might be. Nels inspired fear in other men. Fear of his caustic wit, fear of the open scorn he sometimes displayed, the occasional outbreak of rage often undefined and uncategorized.

But an association with Nels Proctor provided benefits. As for Barney Grubb, if not equal to Nels, he viewed himself at least as a lesser noble living on a nearby land grant, a warrior bought and paid for, but not yet as rich or as powerful as he intended to be.

He wondered, was Molly Fairfax the opportunity he'd been waiting for? Or was it Carl Becker, back in town to wash away his guilt over a deceased parent too long neglected?

"Try another name, Counselor—Molly Fowler."

Nels entertained the name, made all the connections. "Is there a point to this call that escapes me, Barney?"

"I am talking about Emily Fowler's daughter."

"After all these years? A daughter?"

"Just the right age, the way I add it up, and a real beauty, besides."

"Meaning?"

"Meaning that knowledge is power. I thought you might want to know about her."

"I'm still listening, Barney."

"Seems like Molly has come around to discover what her mother's life here was like. The mother was in an automobile accident some time back and died. Now the daughter has returned to the nest to claim her birthright."

Nels felt his annoyance rising but he pushed it back, keeping his voice level and smooth. "What birthright is that?"

"Good question. The house on the Hill went to Matheson when Cornelia died and he sold it off before moving into the home. I'm sure Cornelia owned a great deal of property out in the county, but you'd know more about that than I would."

"The family never engaged the services of my office."

"Point is, the girl is going around asking questions, trying to find out why her mother left town. She tells me Emily found herself a soldier boy to marry, name of Fairfax."

"That causes me no difficulty, Barney."

"But it might. Fact is, when people start asking questions there is no way of telling what answers they are liable to come up with."

Nels spoke firmly. "I have no interest in this girl, Barney."

"Sure you don't. Only I let slip that you were the foremost authority on this town and its inhabitants, due to your own people going back so far, plus your widespread and abiding interest in local history. I suggested that of us all, Nels Proctor would surely be the one most able to help her out. Did I do wrong, Counselor?"

"One of these days, Barney, you will go too far and then—"

"And then?"

When Nels replied, his voice was tranquil and controlled. "Perhaps you're right. Seeing the girl might spruce up my day. Tell her to be at my office at five o'clock."

"If that's what you want, Counselor. And one more thing, I'd appreciate it if we two could have a meeting soon, Counselor. At your convenience, of course."

"To what end, Barney?"

"To discuss my future."

"I didn't know you had one," Nels said, putting a chuckle in his voice.

Grubb laughed, full-throated and joyful. "Indeed I do. A very bright future. And very rich. And getting richer all the time," he added, before he hung up.

13

◦◦❧◦◦

BUNNY WHITEHEAD WAS a majestic woman, always in command of the space around her. She plowed through life with
the inexorable assurance of a battleship plowing through the
sea, parting the waters before her. She was tall, with an imposing physique and a haughty demeanor. A halo of white hair
flared out from her head framing a face youthful by contrast,
a face notable for its smooth, ivory skin and sparkling blue
eyes. She sat proudly with her back straight in her favorite
chair, a ladderback rush-seated chair made out of local chestnut by one of her early forebears and handed down through
the generations. It was a chair that reminded Bunny Whitehead that she was a Middleton, a historic name in these parts,
a heritage of substance and status.

She sat with her back to the French doors that led to the
patio, the afternoon sun streaming in and causing Hollis to
squint and cock his head in self-defense. Her pale, unmarked
hands were folded in her lap and her impressive bosom in a
high-necked floor-length gown gave her the semi-grandeur of
an old English bronze.

When she spoke, disapproval laced her cultivated voice.
"Your speech is slurred, Hollis."

"I don't feel very well."

"You've been using Valium again." Disapproval and disgust were her reactions to so much of the life she saw around her. The world was shattering before her eyes. Standards were depressed, values lost in a contemporary rush for instant gratification, beauty reduced to an ever-changing fashion. Life had lost its grace and meaning, society had been reduced to an unintelligible jumble of crude and vulgar public personalities. She longed for a happier, more structured time when it was possible to remain outside the frenetic combat of ordinary people. She spoke to Hollis as if he were a recalcitrant child.

He answered with an immediate denial. "No. You've got it all wrong this time." He wanted her to accept the lie, wanted desperately to believe it himself.

"One phone call, Hollis, and it will be back to Golden Acres for you."

He shook his head vehemently. "No, I won't go. Not again. You can't make me."

"I am through coddling you. No more will I stand by and watch you become useless to yourself and to me because of drugs and whiskey."

"I promised—"

"Your promises are empty. No more drugs, I told you. No more drunken revels. No more of those revolting activities you so delight in from time to time. I have protected you and carried you for a very long time, Hollis, and I am sick of it. No more."

He summoned up his courage. "Don't scold me. I am a grown man and—"

"A grown man with an emotional age of ten. Self-indulgent and self-abusive and making the rest of us pay the price."

"I am responsible for my own actions."

She uttered a scornful sound. "If you were, life around here might be a great deal more tranquil."

He wilted under her unrelenting scorn. She was too strong for him, too demanding, too unwilling to accept his human foibles.

"We must talk, Bunny," he said, almost pleading.

"Very well, talk."

He filled his lungs with air, afraid of succumbing to oxygen deprivation, aware of his rising panic. The pulsing of his brain lessened and his heartbeat slowed. "Nels and I had a long talk the other day."

"A despicable man."

She had never approved of his friendship with Nels, nor accepted his need to continue it. "He's been very good to me over the years."

"He is without scruples, without morals. He snaps his fingers and you respond like a trained circus animal."

"He and I have known each other all our lives; he's my best friend."

"Nelson Proctor has no friends, only toadies and sycophants. There is in you, I'm sorry to say, a great deal of both. And what saddens me most is that you revel in the role."

"I'm not here to be insulted."

"Very well. Speak your mind, Hollis, and we'll end this encounter."

Panic clutched his throat and he became aware of a building pressure behind his eyes. "Forget it," he heard himself say. Another Valium would bring him back to where he wanted to be. In lieu of that, he made his way to the bar across the room and poured some Scotch into a glass.

"You are not to drink," she commanded.

He hesitated, then decided to risk her displeasure. "My first today."

"Another lie. Put down the glass."

With a swift, practiced motion, he swallowed the drink and at once felt better. Braver. Stronger. More capable of confronting a world in which he was never comfortable. He came around to stare at Bunny's face. A face pale and velvety to the touch. How long had it been since he had been allowed that touch? The texture of her skin used to remind him of a snake's cold white belly. And the scent of her—sweetish, cloying— made him think of spoiled flowers left around too long.

"You are weak, Hollis."

"I've told you," he said without much force. "You are not to speak to me that way."

She reminded him of his mother, an equally oppressive, distant woman, equally demanding and at all times critical. At her funeral, Hollis had not shed a tear. People had remarked about his courage, his strength; he had neither, just relief that she was finally dead and gone forever.

"You're a confirmed alcoholic," Bunny said.

"Don't talk to me that way."

"An alcoholic and an addict."

"I am managing my problems."

"Only with my help and the connivance of that best friend of yours. I'll give him that—he does try to help, for all the good it's done. Were it not for the two of us, you'd have gone under long ago. Now what do you have to say to me?"

He would have walked away, left her sitting there, had he not given Nels his word. A man kept his word to his friends.

"Nels," he said, not meeting his wife's eyes, "would like me to run for governor."

"Governor! You?" She began to laugh.

"Nels thinks I would make a very good governor. I'm a very competent administrator. I am."

"With you as its president, it's a wonder the General Assembly continues to function at all. With you as governor, the state would collapse in a year."

"It's nice to know you have such confidence in me."

"You fool," she hissed. "Don't you see what he's trying to do? Tuck you away in that ugly mansion in the godforsaken little city where you'll never be heard of again. Neither one of us. Well, it isn't going to work. I will not be buried alive among all those second-raters, those political hacks and their sleazy women."

"You make it sound worse than it is."

"Impossible. No, you are going to become a United States Senator if I have to buy you a seat myself. We are going to move to Washington where we can socialize with sophisticated and vibrant people, worldly people. You may go back to your dear friend Nels and tell him Bunny Whitehead isn't having any of it."

"I gave him my word."

"No, no, no. There is no chance Bunny Middleton Whitehead is going to settle in to that provincial backwater this state calls its capital. No, tell him I said no, Hollis. You tell him, or I certainly shall."

The office of the president of the Old Brixton Savings Bank had been cleverly designed by a young architect to summon up an impression of solidity, longevity, and dependability. The walls were paneled in dark oiled walnut, the rug was a thick and soft Persian, with muted colors, the design traditional and plainly expensive. The furniture was solid, comfortable to sit in, reassuring to look at.

The president's desk was oversized and without extraneous matter; neatness and cleanliness were Jay Newell's abiding passions. An uncluttered desk, he liked to say, reflected a mind clear of useless minutiae, geared up for clear thought. A clean office indicated a man who was meticulous and thorough, concerned not only with the way things looked but with the way they in fact were. Jay had raised his children on such maxims and made sure that he, too, lived by them.

He greeted Carl Becker with an effusive show of hospitality, an offer of refreshments from a full-stocked bar—or coffee or tea—to be served by a secretary standing at the ready. His handshake was a banker's handshake, reassuring and earnest.

"Nice to see you again, Carl."

A study in contradictions, Becker observed silently. Jay Newell was a big man running to fat, his athletic past a dim memory. He played golf, undoubtedly, a concession to his business, the greens a much more amiable environment in which to make a deal than his office. He reminded Becker of so many of the politicians he saw around Washington, well-fed men, almost arrogant in the certainty of their positions, their way of life. Clean, well-barbered men with empty, suspicious eyes and prim little mouths. Would such men look different had they chosen another way to live, another line of work? Or was it the political world that attracted such men? He was tempted to start off this meeting with a question—Isn't there something else you'd rather do with your life, Mr. Newell, than sit in this office and make money with your money?—but he said nothing.

"Shocking news about your father, Carl. Mrs. Newell and I were profoundly distressed."

Becker made no response.

Newell anticipated him. "The farm. You've come to inquire about the farm."

Bull's-eye! Becker waited.

Newell went on. "The bank was forced to call in your father's loans."

The bank. Not Jay Newell. Not any other human being.

Lives uprooted, families divided, careers ruined; all done at some remove—impersonal, without human interference. The bank did it.

"Forced?" Becker queried.

"Payments weren't being made and there were no indications that your father had access to sufficient funds. I spoke to him a number of times."

"Didn't he tell you he believed he could come up with the money?"

"Oh, yes, he vaguely mentioned some possible source. A friend—or perhaps friends—but he refused to supply us with any concrete information."

"So you called in the loans without giving him a chance?"

"Try to understand, Carl, farming in these times is a difficult way of life. Declining government supports, the steadily rising cost of equipment and feed, labor. Interest rates are up and the market is unreliable. Believe me when I say that the situation was not of the bank's making."

"Mr. Newell, you knew my father. He was dependable, a man who fulfilled his obligations. I happen to know that on two previous occasions the bank carried him until he was able to turn things around."

"In my father's time at the bank, yes."

"Why not now?"

"As I explained, no prospects. Besides, the timing was wrong. Every banking institution has a responsibility to its depositors. To its shareholders. There are outstanding obligations. There are federal rules and laws and guidelines that must be followed. A web of unfortunate circumstances. That's it exactly, a web of circumstances that your father was caught up in. Believe me when I say it is all very complicated, much too complicated for a layman."

"You should've have contacted me, given me a chance to help."

"That's asking too much."

"I don't see why."

"This institution is not in the farming business. We don't go skulking around looking for someone to pay off a bad loan—that's up to the borrower."

"It's not as if I am a stranger."

"You refuse to understand. These affairs cannot be put on hold. No way I can rationalize owning such a piece of property on a profit and loss statement. No matter how sentimental some of us may feel about the client, we do not keep properties we acquire any longer than is absolutely necessary.''

"You sold the farm as soon as you could after calling in the loan.''

"We are obliged—''

"You never tried to move it to one of the other farmers in the county.''

"It's not our job to—''

"All of them knew Sam. They would have sold the land back to him when he had the money.''

"Sealed bids,'' Jay Newell said, making it sound like a blood oath of allegiance. "The property went to the highest bidder.''

"Which just happened to be County Center Corporation.''

Jay's face hardened under the puffiness. "So, you have found some answers, I see. Why are you wasting my time, Carl?''

"This business, Mr. Newell—the farm, my father's death —I intend to find out what really happened. Why my father was killed and who did it. I want you to know: I won't be stopped.''

"You still don't understand!'' Jay called after Becker's retreating figure. "Let me help you to understand . . . '' But Becker was gone and Jay was all alone in his carefully planned and ordered office.

He was, Molly told himself, the most attractive man she'd ever met. There was a pared down look to him, no excesses anywhere. His face reminded her of Michelangelo's David, yet leaner, with character etched into those exquisite cheeks by time and experience. His pale eyes might have been a statue's marble orbs, revealing no hint of what lay behind them, all thought, all emotion locked securely away. She felt like a child, helpless and lost, out of her element, as he offered his hand in a greeting.

"Molly . . . '' He hesitated and the hesitation introduced a boyish quality to his personality, unbearably sweet and appealing, vulnerable. No, she corrected. Whatever else he might be, Nels Proctor allowed vulnerability no part in it. She saw at once that he was disciplined, every nuance of tone and manner under control. "Molly Fairfax.'' He tested each syllable as if

trying to make sense out of the name, to find in it the key to
her persona, her history.

"Mr. Proctor." She rescued her hand from his, reluctant
and relieved at the same time. How absurd to react so strongly
to a man she'd never before seen, a man old enough to be her
father, a man belonging to a world that could not possibly
coincide with her own.

She placed herself in a chair, adjusting her skirt over her
knees, uncomfortably aware of the calculating way his eyes
traveled up and down her body, settling finally on her face,
dissecting each feature.

He leaned back in his chair and smiled. "You are a
remarkably beautiful woman." He made it sound like a
caress, a caress delivered without affection, delivered by rote,
done for effect.

"Chief Grubb was kind enough to suggest you might be
able to help me."

"You're new to our little village." A smashing smile il-
luminated the lower half of his face, a smile incredibly white
against his tawny skin, marked by a single incisor tipped
slightly out of line and more interesting for that.

"I've been here only a few days."

"You're staying at the Inn, I imagine."

"It's a lovely place. From my room I can see the river, the
rapids, all those rocks."

"Sunday dinner at the Inn is a tradition for many of our
people." He neglected to mention that he held a majority
financial interest in the Owenoke Inn. "I hope you're comfortable."

"Oh, yes, the room is perfect." She felt as if she were being
interviewed or filling out one of those forms one found in
motel bedrooms asking for reactions to accommodations;
ambiance? service? "Antique furniture, a four-poster bed,
a hooked rug that must have been made two hundred years
ago . . . " She was unable to stop chattering, certainly telling
him more than he wanted to hear, babbling about inconsequential things, trivial matters that had nothing to do with
why she had come to see Nels Proctor.

He listened attentively, making her feel each word uttered
had a special meaning to him. He listened and compared the
soft turn of her cheek with what he remembered of her
mother. Her lips, full and quick to smile; was Emily's mouth

the same? The tilt of her jaw, the set of her head on a graceful neck. Emily's daughter, but lovelier than the mother. Or had Emily looked equally delicious at the same age? Had Emily possessed that same bold look, the same green eyes? He could not recall. Curiosity, and a suggestion of apprehension, sharpened his need to know everything about her, about her mother. Why, after so many years, had she turned up in Old Brixton? What was she after? Caution, he warned himself, caution and control were required.

"I don't usually chatter this way," she explained.

He glanced at his watch.

"I'm keeping you," she said, made shy in his presence, her confidence waning. "This is a bad time for you."

"Not at all. I am finished here for the day. Let's find a quiet place where we can talk, someplace comfortable. Everything is much better over a drink . . . "

"Why not?" she heard herself say, an uncertain reply.

He came around to where she sat, drawing her out of the chair. "Why not, indeed?"

14

⤷ꙮ⤶

ONLY TO LOOK, he assured himself.

Just to drink in the youthful beauty of the girl, nothing more. To fire his imagination, to make him remember what it had been like to be young, to touch female flesh unspoiled by time, to take in all that nubile sweetness. How many times had he seen her? Two or three? Only when he stopped in at the Blue Heron, the roadside restaurant adjoining the Yankee Clipper Motel. He'd make it four times, just to have some coffee to make him alert enough to make the drive back to Old Brixton, soberly.

She was eminently worth looking at. Hollis, positioned in a back booth over a second cup of coffee, studied her moves. Out of eyes swollen and streaked crimson, he watched her clean off a table, her buttocks outlined under the tight white uniform trousers she wore.

She sensed his attention and a quick glance over her shoulder confirmed it. She straightened up and came his way, chin down, eyes fixed, giving a contrived sultry set to her otherwise cherubic face. Emanations of sensuality signaled her approach. She seemed like someone out of a forties movie. Golden hair was piled high, glistening and sprayed into place. Her eyes were painted blue and lined, lips a slash of carmine

red—cheap and cheerful colors designed to make her look
older, more sophisticated than she was.

"More coffee?" she said.

"It might help."

She looked into his eyes, exhibiting a maturity he had never
had at her age.

"You make it sound like medicine."

What was her age? The sound of her soft voice playing
against that lush womanly body nature had provided, had him
unsettled by her nearness. She smelled of cheap perfume too
lavishly applied.

"I've been drinking," he said contritely.

There was no condemnation in her response—so unlike
Bunny. "Over at Marnie's Place?"

It was his favorite spot. Never too crowded, lights always
low, making it possible for him to drink steadily without being
bothered or recognized. "You go there?" he said, adding
quickly: "Certainly not, you're too young."

"Legal tender," she said, avoiding his eyes this time.
"Cream?"

"This is perfect." Was he reading something into her manner that wasn't there? Be careful; all signals were red. Stop
now. Young girls had tempted him before, caused him trouble
before. "I'll stay away from them," he had promised Nels the
last time. "Never again," he'd vowed to Bunny, on his knees
before her, begging her not to leave him. That had been three
years ago and the longing, that deep, dark craving, still
plagued him. The gnawing insistence that took hold of him in
his weakest moments refused to turn him loose. "Legal and
tender," he murmured.

She made a dismissive gesture that was without force.
"You've been in here before."

"I didn't think you'd noticed."

Her face closed up, pouty, a childish surliness. "I noticed
you noticing me."

"Well, now," he protested feebly.

"Is that why you came, to check me out?"

"Coffee, I told you."

"Oh, okay, if that's the way you want it." She started to
walk away.

"Hold on a minute." She turned and waited, hand on her

hip, an elaborately patient pose, as if she'd been through all this before. "Of course I noticed you. Who wouldn't?" That drew a pleased grin. "You're a remarkably pretty girl. And so young."

She took a step closer, voice more intimate. "Not so young," she said. "I'm eighteen."

Not even close, he thought. Off by at least two years. Not that it mattered. All this was nothing more than talk, a harmless flirtation. Just talk.

"It gives me a great deal of pleasure just to look at you."

"Ah, that's nice. I like you, too."

Cut it short, he told himself. Send her away. He said, "Why is that?"

"Well. Right away I was able to tell, you're somebody special."

Pay the check. That's what Nels—or anybody else with his head on straight—would do. Leave a nice tip and go, never to return. That would be the smart move. Anything else would bring him up to the edge of a precipice, to some horrible cataclysm that lay in wait. Her tongue was at the corner of her mouth, shining pink at its pointed tip. How tantalizing. How tender and enticing. So full of lush, wet promise. Images of her naked and writhing in passion were made vivid on the screen of his mind and his voice grew heavy and thick.

"What," he managed huskily, "makes you say a thing like that?"

"A man with your looks and style, we don't get your kind in here that much. Mostly construction guys and truck drivers, that's all."

A false smile formed on his mouth. "What if I told you I was a truck driver?" The notion pleased him—a rugged and solitary man, making his own way at the wheel of an eighteen-wheeler, speeding through the night, no one able to tell him what to do.

She looked him over. "No way. No truck driver ever wore a suit like you got on. Must've cost a couple of hundred dollars at least."

Made to order by a wop tailor off Newbury Street in Boston, Hollis thought. Cost? Nine hundred dollars.

"I know all about you," she said with sudden shyness.

He almost recoiled in fear; she knew who he was. Go, he

commanded. Leave now. Before it gets sticky and dangerous.
He drained the remaining coffee from the cup and started to
slide out of the booth. Her words kept him in place.

"Hollis Whitehead, president of the General Assembly.
Lots of people know you."

He couldn't help being pleased, flattered by what celebrity
he had to her. He reveled in the admiration in the eyes of
people he met, in the eyes of this sweet young girl. How lovely
she was, how desirable. He watched her fill his cup with more
hot coffee.

"I should be going," he said.

"Where?" she said with the directness of youth.

"Home." He swore at himself for extending this playful
moment beyond its due. But her nearness provided the kind
of excitement he craved, her attention shored up his sense
of worth, her obvious beauty provoked his manhood. A few
more minutes, that's all, he promised himself. "You have me
at a disadvantage."

"I do?"

"You know my name."

"Oh. I'm Nadine."

"A pretty name for a pretty girl."

"Talking to you like this is nice. Maybe we can do it again,
if you want."

"Maybe. The next time I drop in for coffee."

"What if I'm not here?"

"Where would you be?"

"I mean, if it's my day off or if I get fired or I quit, something like that."

"I'm sure you won't be fired, Nadine."

"Sounds swell, the way you say my name. I really do like
you, I really do." When he said nothing, she went on, standing closer now, the nearness of her leaving him light-headed.
"I finish up here at five. That's in half an hour."

Bunny would destroy him, he reminded himself. If she
found out. Cold bitch. How long since they had last made
love? A year? More like two. Dessert for the deserving, she'd
once taunted. Damned woman had cut off his balls a long time
ago and, worst of all, he'd allowed it. Spread his legs and invited her to perform her cruel surgery. This business with
becoming governor—why not? He'd be a good governor.
Anybody who knew him knew that; Nels knew it. But Bunny

with her snobbish ideas about where she wanted to live, about the kind of people she wanted to associate with, was going to screw it all up. She had no right, no right to keep him from advancing his career. No right to control him that way. No right at all.

"Marnie's Place in thirty minutes," he said to Nadine. "I'll buy you a drink."

She made a face, a wrinkle of distaste. "Oh, that place. I forgot my ID—they'll kick up a fuss. I wouldn't want you to be embarrassed."

How young was she? He dared not ask, preferred not to know. Certainly too young, as young as he liked them to be.

"I could buy a bottle and we could drive somewhere."

She leaned forward, blocking his line of sight, his senses spiraling out of control. "You could take a room at the Yankee Clipper."

"A room?"

"Unless you're afraid?" It was Nels's voice he heard: *Unless you lack the courage for it?*

"Sure," he said.

"Better not use your real name."

"No, of course not."

"Let's make up a name." It was a game for her, a child's game, without seriousness, with no sensible notion of possibilities or problems. "I'll go first . . . "

"Okay."

She giggled, hand over her mouth. "Reagan, in honor of our President. Since you're both politicians."

He agreed.

"I'll phone over there in ten minutes and ask for Mr. Reagan and you can give me the room number. That way I'll be able to come straight up to the room without asking at the front desk."

How many times before, he asked himself. How many times had she done this, exactly this way? Not that it mattered. To the contrary, she was making it all so easy, taking care of all the troublesome details. He tipped her lavishly before he left, much more than she could have hoped for.

She entered the room dressed in black parachute pants and a baggy white cotton blouse under a lightweight gray vest. She looked like a player in a hard rock video, slightly out of sync.

"You're late," he said, with considerable petulance. He had begun to think she had changed her mind, wasn't coming. "You were supposed to be here half an hour ago."

She blew him a kiss. "You didn't want me showing up in that icky uniform, right? I had to change into something pretty for you."

"You went home?"

She twirled, displaying herself. "That's where my things are. I wanted to shower and all. Do I please you?"

Home to whom? Mother? Father? Tall and violent older brothers? What in hell had he gotten himself into? He felt awkward and inept, unable to pull his eyes away from her.

"You live alone?"

"Of course not, silly. With my mother."

He felt his knees grow weak and he sat down on the edge of the bed. "You told her you were coming here, to see me?" He loosened his collar. He swallowed half a water tumbler of Scotch and stared at Nadine. What incredibly stupid blunder had he committed this time?

"She wasn't there," Nadine said. "Nobody knows where I am at, no-bod-y." She batted her eyes at him. "You going to offer me some of that good Scotch whiskey, honey?" She took the glass from his hand and drank, then gave him back the glass.

"Maybe I should ask to see your ID."

She laughed and undid his tie, slipping it from around his neck. "Big enough, old enough." She touched his cheek. "I like being here with you, Hollis, I truly do." She began to unbutton his shirt and exclaimed over the gold pendant hanging on its gold chain. "How beautiful! What is it?"

He explained that it had been a gift from his best friend a very long time ago, told her how much it meant to him, to each of The Four Horsemen.

"May I see it?" She lifted the chain over his head and examined it closely.

He grew nervous and drank some more Scotch, watching her warily. Aware of his eyes on her, she very deliberately undid the buttons of her blouse to the waist. She slipped the heavy gold chain over her head, adjusting the pendant so that it fell between her breasts.

"What do you think?" she purred. "How does it look?"

He reached for her with one trembling hand.

She spun away, mocking him with laughter. "Not too fast, Hollis."

"You are so beautiful."

"I know what you want."

"Yes, yes."

Out of reach, her chin lowered, eyes peering at him. "I want to play a game."

It was difficult for him to speak. Blood rushed through his veins, swelling his body, warmth spread along his nervous system. Most women failed to understand; he was not the middle-aged, cuddly creature they imagined. His passion, the obsessiveness of his needs, overwhelmed them; they were always startled by the raw, hard power of his body.

"What game?"

Posing against the low bureau, one hip outflung, she sucked tentatively on her thumb.

"You be daddy."

"Daddy?"

"And I'll be your innocent little daughter, staying out too late, much too late. I've been naughty and you are mightily upset with me."

It took all the willpower he could muster to keep his hands off himself, to keep from exposing himself, to tear the clothes off her. He watched, fascinated, as she slowly, very slowly, opened the remaining buttons of the white cotton blouse, one at a time, exposing the pale rise of her young breasts.

"You see how naughty I've been?"

He saw. He understood. He yearned to bury himself in that incredible young flesh. "Where the hell have you been until this hour?" he demanded, all harshness and condemnation, deep into the game.

Something in the voice, in his manner, was more ominous than she had anticipated. She straightened up, not convinced she should go on. A nervous little laugh escaped her, reminding herself that it was all play, and she was making the rules. Her tongue traced the circle of her wet lips.

"Out." A hint of defiance; out, old man, out having a good time. "Girls just want to have fun," she sang, expecting him to react.

He'd never heard the song before. "Look at you, your blouse half off. What have you been doing till now?" On his feet, shuffling, edging forward.

"Sitting in the car, talking."

"Talking? You expect me to believe that's all you were doing? Tell me the truth."

She shivered in delicious anticipation. "He kissed me, that's all."

"Kissed you and you let him."

"Yes."

"And what did you do?"

"I don't know what you mean."

"You know, damnit. Did he touch you? You let him touch you, didn't you?"

Her hand moved to her breast, sliding under the cotton shirt. "Yes," she said softly. "It was nice. He caressed me and made me feel good and he kissed me. Here, right here."

"You're just like your mother—a tramp. No damned good."

"Don't you dare talk about my mother that way! Shall I tell you what else he did?"

"I've heard enough."

"He touched me and I touched him."

"Bitch!"

"Here," she said and touched him, squeezing the swollen hardness. "Oh, you do like to hear about it. I touched him and it felt good to me and he took it out so I could feel it naked and make love to it with my hands—"

"Shut up!"

"—And with my mouth."

"Cunt!"

"And that's not all I did . . ."

He dragged her back to the bed, across his lap, and began spanking her.

She gasped and challenged him to hit her harder. She urged him on and he responded until the blows came with such force and frequency that she began to protest.

"Hey, take it easy!"

When he struck her again she tried to twist away. He was too strong, but she continued to struggle, striking back, sliding to the floor onto her knees.

It was then that he punched her for the first time and she went over backwards, too startled to cry out. He kept hitting her until, whimpering, she tried to shield her face from the blows. But they kept on coming.

15

JAY NEWELL WAS enjoying a solitary martini on the sun porch
facing the woods at the rear of his property. How long had it
been since he last went tramping through those woods? When
had he last fished for trout or gone boating on the river? All
that was behind him now. Aside from work, golf was his only
activity, and that was really another extension of his office. A
great deal of business was done while riding a cart along the
fairways of the country club. Deals were made. Loans were
agreed upon. Golf permitted him to bring together people with
mutual business interests, always for the profit of the bank.

"Golf," his father used to say, "is truly a gentleman's
game."

The delicate sound of the door chimes broke into his
ruminations. Not that he responded. That was the job of the
servants. Or Lauren, if she could manage to beat them to the
door. All these years his wife, and Lauren still hurried to
answer the door. Afraid the caller might depart. Or have his
feelings damaged. Unable to shake off entirely her early, less
privileged ways.

There was, he had long ago decided, much to be said for
being born into the correct circumstances. For being raised

with style and purpose. For learning early what your position
in society was and where it was you belonged. Not that Lauren
didn't belong up on Bluewater Hill. Now, that is. She was as
much a part of the tranquil scene as the isolated placement of
the house, attuned to the ways of their neighbors, even more
concerned with their attitudes and opinions than he was.

Lauren looked the part of a Bluewater Hill matron, in-
digenous as any of the other flora and fauna. Meticulously
dressed, her clothes selected at Bergdorf's or Neiman's or
Saks, she attracted no undue attention. Any hint of the perky
strutter from the flats had been squeezed out of her over the
years, leaving a lovely, well-groomed shell.

Morgan, a slight man in a starched white jacket, materialized in the doorway, silent, all-seeing, his stance crisp and
military. His full name was Arthur Morgan MacTavish and he
had begun his working life as a stable boy for Jay's father.
Later he had helped around the garage, washing cars and
doing minor engine repairs. Still later he became Mr. Newell's
personal chauffeur. By the time Jay's father died, Morgan, as
he was known, was major domo, in charge of the entire estate,
discharging his duties with a firm and gifted hand. Jay had
never been fond of Morgan and longed for some excuse to get
rid of him, an excuse Morgan had so far been too clever to
provide.

"Mr. Carl Becker to see you, sir."

Jay thought about refusing to see Becker. Especially in his
home. Another meeting could be only to Becker's benefit.
What, he wondered, would Nels do in the same situation? See
the young man, certainly; learn every iota of information your
enemy was willing to supply, that was Nels's theory. By all
means, see him.

"Show Mr. Becker in."

Enemy? How odd to classify Carl that way, even in the
seclusion of his thoughts. Why not be gracious and accommodating? Becker was no threat. After all, he was one of
them, a member of the Old Brixton community. A bright
young man on the way up; one never knew when a lawyer in
the U.S. Attorney's office might become helpful.

"Carl!" he said, coming to his feet and extending his hand.
"How nice of you to visit. What would you like to drink? I'm
working on a martini. Morgan makes them better than anyone
else in town."

"Nothing for me, thanks."

"Ah, you don't know what you're missing. A refill for me, Morgan. A touch drier this time, if you don't mind."

Morgan placed the empty glass on a small tray and carried it away. Jay got Becker seated and waved a hand toward the outside. "What a marvelous time of year. The air is clear and crisp, warm enough for only a jacket and with merely a suggestion of the cooler days that lie ahead. We're so fortunate to have such a spectacular view from up here. You've seen it many times before, I'm sure."

"Never from inside a house on the Hill, Mr. Newell. Growing up, Bluewater Hill was definitely not my stamping grounds."

"Too bad." The slight bite of privilege and pride put a serrated edge to Jay Newell's voice. He turned a slow, beneficent smile on the younger man. "If not for the scenery, Carl, why have you come?"

"Following our conversation, I had a second talk with Henry Streeter."

At that moment, Morgan returned. He placed the martini on the small table alongside Newell's chair and departed on silent feet. Jay sipped his drink. "There is an undeclared war going on between Morgan and I. I keep telling him to make my martinis drier and Morgan insists on adding an extra splash of vermouth every time. More vermouth and less crushed ice. A subtle adversarial situation, as you lawyers like to say."

"The beginnings of revolution."

Jay was delighted and said so. "But I find it impossible to envision Morgan as a latter-day Lenin. Still, one never knows. How would you deal with the problem?"

"I'd mix my own martinis."

That drew another laugh. "And spoil the game? I think not. You see, it is a game—most things are. Morgan pressing to find out how far he can go before I openly chastise him. He's testing us both, you might say, pushing each of us to the far edge. Trying to discover who will suffer a loss of nerve first."

"Who will it be, do you think?"

"Morgan, of course."

"What makes you so sure?"

"Morgan believes he knows the rules of the game and that I'll continue to abide by them."

"But you won't?"

"Of course not."

"So you change the game as you go along."

"Change the rules would be more precise."

"Is that fair?"

"Fair never enters into the equation. The important factor is to win, always, and to occasionally remind the servants who the master is. It's a question of character, you see."

"Wouldn't it be simpler to fire Morgan?"

"Too simple. Besides, I'd have to adapt to another player and that's not worth the effort. It's clear that you don't know how the game is played."

"I've never been a member of the team."

"Yet here you are, on Bluewater Hill."

"To talk about Henry Streeter."

"Oh, yes, Streeter."

Becker repeated the substance of his talk with Streeter, indicating what he had discovered about County Center Corporation, its officers and the limited partners. Once finished, he waited for Newell to respond.

The banker sipped his martini, head cocked and listening. "Hear that? A woodpecker. At this time of year, he's around every day. In the cool of the afternoon. Busy little fellow. Think of it, working that hard and having no apparent impact on the world in which he lives. Pecking constantly away, to no good affect. The tree doesn't give a damn, does it?"

"And you see me as a woodpecker, pecking away in some futile exercise against immovable objects?"

"My mind is not that subtle, Carl. Metaphor is not my style. I'm a banker, not a poet. Not a lawyer, either," he ended, with a sleek, professional turn of his soft mouth. This exchange, he told himself, was a great deal of fun.

Becker understood—still another game. Being played by rules that only Newell understood. He decided not to play.

"About Streeter," he said.

"Oh, yes. Let's see if I can anticipate you. You learned that County Center purchased your father's farm at auction. You discovered also that I personally handled neither the sale nor the purchase. Old Brixton Savings functions strictly according to law and accepted banking procedures.

"What else have you learned? Oh, yes, that Streeter owns a

few shares in County Center. Why not? It's a sound investment and many other people have likewise invested."

"You gave Henry his shares."

"Gave? Oh, my, no. I suggested he buy in, if he could afford it. Apparently he could. Give away stock—that would
not be sound business, would it, now? Besides, Henry has a
comparatively modest stake in all this. No more than ten
shares, if I remember correctly."

"Twenty shares at five thousand dollars a share."

"His purchase, his money, his risk."

"It looks that way on paper. But I'm convinced no money
ever exchanged hands. Or if any did, it was no more than a
quarter of that hundred thousand."

"Pure conjecture, Carl, and impossible to prove."

"Granted. But are you going to deny pressuring that old
man to stop lending money to my father?"

"Another empty accusation. It is an accusation, isn't it?
But without proof. Does Henry allege that? If so, we'll have to
ascribe it to his age. Fading health, the onset of senility."

"He's sharp enough."

"Pressure him how? Freely, of his own will, he sold his
farm to County Center so he could pay off his debts."

"I did a little nosing around and guess what I came up
with?"

"You're going to tell me, I'm sure."

Becker ignored the sarcasm. "At first I believed Henry's
land was the initial purchase made by County Center. I was
wrong. Prior to that, you bought Tod Blacker's farm, upland
from Henry. Water irrigating Henry's property came directly
off the Blacker place. Once the transfer of ownership was
complete, that flow was cut and Henry was without water, except for his well. He went to Nels Proctor for legal representa-
tion but the question never came before the courts. Henry sold
out to the corporation."

"You left out the matter of wetlands, the preservation of
the nesting grounds for the ducks and Canadian geese that
come through each fall. EPD was involved and it got to be a
mess, until things were sorted out."

"Thanks to Hollis Whitehead."

"Hollis? Well, the man does represent this assembly district
in the state capital. Hollis did his best to help us get through

the bureaucratic fog. A man in your line of work in Washington, you know how clumsy and obstructive the bureaucracy can be."

"Are you going to deny that you forced Henry to stop lending money to my father?"

"Is that what Henry did, lend money to Sam and subsequently cut him off? No mention of such loans were ever made during my talks with Streeter. I know how distressed you must be about your father, Carl, but please, please don't make something out of this that never was. Business, after all, is business."

"Is that all my father's death means to you—business?"

"My conscience is clear. In every aspect of this affair." He stood up, taller than Becker and broad, but with no hint of strength or agility to his big frame. It was as if he had left his athlete's body back on the high school football field, along with his courage, despite his attempt at genteel bravado.

"I performed my duties as Chief Executive Officer of the bank in a way that I am expected to, nothing more and nothing less. And now, if you'll excuse me, other business demands my attention."

Later, strolling through town, Becker grew impatient with himself for committing too many errors of judgment and strategy. What had impelled him to visit Jay Newell? Certainly he had no reason to expect the banker to own up to illegal complicity in the acquisition of Sam's farm. Or of forcing Streeter to withdraw support from his father. Or of having a hand in Sam's murder.

Murder.

The word ricocheted crazily around Becker's skull, echoing wildly, causing him to question every step he'd taken up to now, causing him to wonder what he hoped to accomplish with the flabby tactics he'd been following.

Bankers needn't commit murder in order to foreclose on small farms. Rising interest rates, increased debt loads, weakening Federal supports, a strengthened dollar making the export of farm goods more difficult; these were the weapons and tactics of the day.

Murder Sam Becker.

What an absurd idea.

No trained lawyer would accept the flimsy fragments of circumstantial evidence he had gathered. Certainly not a hardened prosecutor, cynical and skeptical, geared by experience to go straight for the jugular. Not even Sam's only son believed that. Why, then, couldn't he chase away the gut feeling that murder was precisely what had taken place?

16

HE BROUGHT HER to Maison François, a small French restaurant set behind low stone walls out in the country, on the edge of a small pond inhabited by a brace of swans. She told him it was a lovely place, in a beautiful, peaceful setting.

He apologized, a cool, cerebral declaration that he issued as if rehearsed. "Nothing in Owenoke County is first-rate. To get top of the line cuisine, you have to go to New York or Boston."

They sipped a chilled Chardonnay and exchanged pleasantries until, with disarming ease, he began to tell her about his life in Old Brixton. He was self-mocking at times, always modest, smiling benignly. His spectacular good looks, that easy manner and quick smile, his presentation of himself warts and all—she felt herself drawn into his personality as if it were a warm, seductive pool.

"When I was young, marriage was never important to me. I never perceived myself as a married man, never as a husband and a father. At the same time, I was expected to marry. Part of the Proctor heritage. To find a wife, raise a family, continue the name and advance the family history."

"What is your wife like?"

Disappointment flared. Married men, that was not her

style. Relationships could be stressful enough without the
added complication of becoming the second woman in a
man's life.

Too bad—Nels Proctor was a special case. Incredibly attractive with that aristocratic cast of his head, the lean, aggressive jaw, the tension in his stance, as if poised for flight.
He used his hands with balletic grace, fluid gestures with
tapered fingers and neatly pared and polished nails.

"I've been divorced for ten years," he said. "I live alone."

Relief replaced disappointment, tempered by a residual
wariness. Men like Joel Hammaker, like Nels Proctor, were
almost too attractive, too perfect in what they seemed to offer
a woman. She reminded herself of the promise she'd made to
herself when Joel had returned to his wife: to keep a safe
distance from any man, to stay clear of another emotional
commitment.

His fingers came to rest on her wrist. Concentric circles of
desire and fright made her feel skittish and jittery. He went on
without noticing. "And you, is there a special man in your
life?"

"No one."

"The men in New York must be very stupid, then, or
blind."

Without moving, she recoiled, almost as if he'd made a
threatening gesture. He was too good to be true, the embodiment of all her romantic dreams. But she saw him also as
elusive and enigmatic, with an explosive quality held carefully
in check, adding an element of danger. She suspected that he
was a man who was used to getting his own way and expected
to get it with her, too.

"Now," he continued, leaning her way, steering the conversation the way he wanted it to go. "Old Brixton doesn't attract
many women as lovely as you. Why are we so honored?" He
ended with a reassuring smile.

"It has to do with my mother." She told him about the car
accident, about the legacy of the book, the letter, the Teddy
bear, even the money left to her. She described her mother and
spoke of their life together in Austin. Later, over coffee, she
told him about her father, the kind of man he had been, and
how he had died.

"Michael Fairfax," she said, "was awarded a Silver Star
for bravery."

He sat back, not allowing the relief he felt to show. Molly Fairfax, daughter of Michael and Emily Fairfax, all legal and registered somewhere in Texas. Here only out of a transient curiosity about her mother's early life. Satisfy that curiosity and she would depart, leaving the past undisturbed. He brought his attention back to her.

"Mother used to take me to San Antonio, where I was born. We'd visit the zoo and go for walks along the Paso del Rio—the river walk—and have lunch in one of those chic little restaurants while watching the paddle boats in the water. We'd go out to Fort Sam Houston where my father used to be stationed to look at the deer and the geese that roam around the quadrangle. Coming here, it was like filling in some empty spaces in my history."

"Surely your mother told you about Old Brixton?"

"Never."

Out of the details of her finely boned face, Nels summoned up an image of Emily Fowler. The resemblance was clear, but certainly Emily had never been this dramatically beautiful, so casually seductive; those deep green eyes, the full lower lip, the firm set of her jaw. It had been a long time since he had come across a prize like Molly Fairfax. He silently thanked Barney Grubb.

"How can I possibly help you?" he said.

"I've been asking questions all over town. But as soon as I mention Mother people seem to pull back, as if afraid if they admit to knowing her they'll be involved in something awful."

He laughed and took her hand in his. "You must be imagining things."

"Becoming paranoid, you think?"

"Just overly sensitive. Even in a town as small as Old Brixton was when your mother lived here, not everyone would know her."

"Some did know her—"

"For example?"

"Well. Lauren Newell, for one. She wrote the letter I told you about. She and my mother were best friends. You'd think she could answer all my questions. You'd think she'd want to. But she wasn't very happy about talking to me."

"Maybe I can fill you in. Lauren Poole was her maiden name. She was a couple of years behind me in school."

"Then you knew Mother?"

He sipped some Courvoisier and considered his answer.
"No better than I knew Lauren. We were never friends. When
you're eighteen or so, a girl two or three years younger seems
like an infant. I doubt if we ever exchanged more than a dozen
words."

She was disappointed again. "And my father—did you
know him?"

Careful, he warned himself. For the first time the worm
of doubt that had been nagging at him surfaced and he was
forced to consider it openly. He searched her face for some
clue that might relieve the spreading sense of danger he felt
and found only that familial resemblance to the Emily Fowler
he had been with that one night twenty-six years before. Was it
possible that he, or one of the other Horsemen, had planted
the seed that had given life to Molly Fairfax? She might, he
conceded, be his own daughter. The possibility fascinated
him.

"The soldier?" he said, in answer to her question. A cold
chill surged through him. Was Molly more than she seemed,
clever and devious in ways he had not fathomed, working him
into a corner, trying to connect him to the events of that
Fourth of July night so long ago? Was she baiting a trap for
him? She could hurt him in a way he had never before been
hurt—damage his reputation, empty his purse, even send him
to prison. No; he could not permit that to happen.

Still, there was an internal logic to her story about Michael
Fairfax . . . a beginning, a middle, and an end. A despairing
young girl in need of affection and protection marries a tall,
handsome soldier who carries her off to exotic posts around
the world. He fathers her child and goes off to war, perform-
ing heroic deeds and getting killed in the process. Thank you,
Michael Fairfax, for coming along at the right time. For re-
lieving Nels Proctor of the fear of any delayed repercussions
of one short night of drunken revelry. Thank you, too, for
fathering this great-looking girl and placing her in Nels
Proctor's way. Thank you for another round and another
game.

"Michael Fairfax," he said. "Maybe I do recall the name,
the boy your mother married. Not that we ran in the same
group, and I wasn't invited to the wedding. But in a small
town very little goes unnoticed. Now that I think about it, I

must have read your father's obituary in *The Call*. I am sorry. I barely knew the man.''

The meal finished, he returned her to the Inn. They sat in the green Porsche before parting.

''It was a lovely evening,'' she said.

His manner mildly guarded, he said, ''I suppose you'll be going back to New York soon?''

''Not for a while. I've thought about settling in around here. I love Old Brixton. Maybe I could buy one of those great old houses. Wouldn't that be fantastic?''

''I doubt if any are for sale,'' he said quickly, then, ''Have you made up your mind—is it definite—about relocating in Old Brixton?''

She mistook his reply for an expression of personal interest and that pleased her, despite the caution she'd been exerting. ''I'll let you know what I decide,'' she answered playfully, sliding out of the Porsche, leaning back in to bid him goodnight. ''Thank you for a lovely evening.''

''We'll do it again,'' he said in a soft, insinuating voice as she closed the door and stepped up on the curb. She watched the Porsche disappear into the night until she could hear only the peepers and crickets along the riverbank.

17

DIRECTLY AFTER BREAKFAST, Molly visited Peter Matheson a second time. She located him, sunning himself in the garden, wrapped in a plaid blanket. To her surprise, he recalled their previous meeting and greeted her with a shy smile.

"Emily's girl," he started out, pleased with himself.

She told him how well he looked and he credited the weather. "This was always my favorite time of year. Autumn in New England . . . soon the leaves will begin to turn, all that color coming out. The last cry of summer, I used to call it."

"What a lovely way to put it."

He squinted at her. "You're not here to talk about the weather."

"You've got me there, Mr. Matheson."

Pleased with himself, he sat straighter in his chair, revived, a gleam in his eye. "What is it you're after, Emily's girl?"

The question caused her to reflect. "Coming here, at first I wanted to find out what connection my mother had to this place. But now, well, I'd like to discover more about my roots here, my father, about my grandmother—"

"Corky," he muttered, and she watched him withdraw into himself, eyes losing their brightness and focus, looking back into his past. "So pretty, my Corky was. More beautiful than any woman I ever met. Followed her around like a puppy, I did. Glad to be in her company. I could always make her laugh and Corky liked to laugh. That was my only talent, making Corky laugh. Traveling was her passion. We went everywhere together. The best hotels. The finest restaurants. Best seats at the opera and the ballet. Her dresses were made specially for her by . . . by . . . I can never remember his name, that Frenchman . . ."

"It doesn't matter."

He snarled as if stung. "Does so matter. Matters to me. I have to remember everything about Corky, *everything*." The snarl dissolved into a reminiscent silence. "Coming home was good, too. Comfortable around here. Nice people. Nice country. Only Corky hated it. Small towns, she said, smothered people like her. Kept her from growing, from becoming her best self. Maybe she was right, I don't know. Tell the truth, if it weren't for Corky I'd've never left Old Brixton . . ."

"About my mother, Mr. Matheson."

"Emily . . ." Out of empty eyes, he gazed past her. "Such a pretty girl, going off that way. Everything could've been fixed. The doctor would've done his part. Corky would've arranged it."

"The doctor?"

The question evoked a slightly animated response. "Only one doctor in town back then. But she was stubborn. Stubborn, your mother." He grew agitated, eyes rolling, spittle forming at the corners of his mouth. "Young people—don't know how life has to be lived, compromises, giving in now and then. Young people are so quick to blame. Corky and me, the doctor, we'd've helped. We'd've helped, you know . ." With that, the old man sank back into his silent reveries.

County Medical Center was a complex of low brick buildings connected by covered concrete walks spread across sloping lawns. Under shade trees, patients rested on wooden benches, attended by nurses. The administration building was sleek and shining, a mural depicting medical history covering one long wall. Floors and ceilings were soundproofed and an intrusive hush permeated the corridors.

Ralph Ortner's office was at the far corner of the building, a simple room designed more for efficiency than comfort. Ortner was a tall man with a face that might once have been handsome, the nose long and flat, the eyes soft. He had a long body, with a slight paunch around his middle, under an expensive sports coat that did little to disguise the weary slouch of his shoulders. He greeted Molly affably, saw her into a comfortable chair.

"My secretary indicated you're conducting a series of interviews, Miss Fairfax. Is this for a magazine or a newspaper?"

"There's been some miscommunication, doctor. What I said was that I've been inquiring about my mother."

"Your mother?" A look of disinterest came across the long face.

"She lived in Old Brixton about twenty-six years ago. I understand that you were the only doctor in town back then?" He acknowledged that with a slow nod. She repeated the story of her mother's death and of the peculiar legacy passed along to her. Ortner listened as if taking a medical history, speaking only when she finished.

"Your mother's name was Fairfax?"

Molly said, "That was her married name. When she lived here her name was Emily Fowler."

Ortner straightened his desk calendar. He arranged the six ballpoint pens on his desk in perfect marching order. He squared off the prescription pad and flicked a spot of lint from his jacket sleeve. When he finally spoke, there was no inflection in his voice.

"What is it you wish of me?"

"What can you tell me about my mother—anything at all? She left town so suddenly."

He straightened up in his chair. "How is it you come to me?"

She told him of that morning's meeting with Peter Matheson. "He talked about something being fixed. Said the doctor would have done his part. You were the only doctor in town at the time."

"Peter Matheson," Dr. Ortner said. "I look in on him from time to time. He's still one of my patients." A pitying smile curled across his mouth. "Hardly someone to depend on nowadays. Suffers from Alzheimer's, you see."

"Still—you did know my mother?"

Ortner sighed. "That was so long ago. Long before this
hospital was built. That would be Cornelia Fowler's daughter,
I suppose." He hesitated. "You remind me of Cornelia, most
beautiful woman I ever saw."

Molly inched forward on her chair.

"Cornelia was one of a kind. Unique, you might say. At
least here in Old Brixton. Lots of money and spoiled. Spent
most of her life traipsing around the world, what we called a
playgirl back then. A social butterfly. Hobnobbing with all
sorts of people. Her picture would show up on the society
pages and in the columns—Winchell, Ed Sullivan, Cholly
Knickerbocker, and the sort. There she'd be, dancing at the
Stork Club in New York City or at El Morocco with some
movie actor. Even managed to get herself engaged to a
member of the British royal family for a while. A prince or a
duke, or some such. Oh, our Cornelia was a busy one."

He frowned and pulled at his nose. "Can't honestly say I
approved of Cornelia as a mother, though. Left Emily to her
own devices mostly. Nannies and housekeepers, that sort of
thing. Not the way to raise a child, in my opinion. Not that
Cornelia ever asked for my opinion. As far as I can tell, she
never asked for anybody's opinion about anything."

"What happened to Emily?"

"Happened?" The question seemed to take him by surprise
and a few beats passed before he was able to frame the answer
he wanted to give. "Disappeared is all. Left town. Ran off and
that was that. Never seen around these parts again."

No mention of a marriage, she remarked to herself. Just
that she disappeared. No talk of eloping, as if it never happened. How odd.

"What could have caused her to run off without a word to
anybody?"

He frowned again. "Not exactly what I said. As far as I
know, she might have explained her reasons to a dozen people,
but not me. I was never privy to her motives for whatever it
was she was up to."

"Can you think of any reason—?"

He broke in. "I've given up trying to understand young
people and the things they do. It was coming up to the sixties
and young people were throwing off the reins of parental
guidance. Expressing themselves, they used to say. Rebelling.

Making it a better world. Can't say they did too well at it, things being what they are. I couldn't answer for Emily Fowler or anybody else.''

Molly phrased the question delicately. "Some people I've talked to refuse to discuss my mother. Sometimes I wonder what they're trying to hide.''

"There are no secrets in Owenoke County.'' He produced a small, bland smile.

"Specifically, what can you tell me, doctor?''

"Emily Fowler. Well, she was a patient, if that's what you want to know. Everybody was, I'd say. No other doctor within thirty miles or so of town. You probably don't remember what a G.P. was. General Practitioner. Internist, gynecologist, pediatrician, orthopedist, dermatologist. You name it, I did it—minor surgery, whatever came along. Patients would show up in my office without an appointment, waiting their turns. I kept the records, paid the bills, got paid when I could. Around here, lots of folks were out of work and nobody had much cash. My goodness, how long ago that was. Adults and children alike, I fixed whatever ailed them. Eventually other doctors moved into the county and the nature of medicine in these parts underwent a radical change.''

"Do you recall anything special about Mother?''

"Special?''

"A question of health, I mean. Was she ill, anything that might have given her trouble?''

"I really can't say. I wish I could help, my dear, but so much time has elapsed, so many patients.''

"Your records?''

He chuckled softly. "When the hospital was built, many of the old records never completed the transfer . . . no need to tell you how it is when things get moved around. Naturally you can't expect me to remember much about an individual patient after so long.''

It was not until hours later that Barney Grubb's words came burning back into her consciousness. "A lot of the old records got destroyed years back when we made the move to these quarters.''

The coincidence was troubling. Even more troubling, Ortner—so smooth and cautious—had revealed nothing that she didn't already know. Like Chief Grubb, he had managed to keep her at a distance; even as Lauren Newell had done.

Were they in league, part of a conspiratorial silence meant to exclude her from her mother's history, concealing the very information she so hungered to uncover? Or was her imagination simply running wild? It was likely there were no secrets. No minds set against talking about Emily Fowler. Nothing special to talk about. A girl had left town without announcing her departure, left a house where she was a stranger, her presence unwelcome, seeking a better life elsewhere. Why not? It happened all the time, she reminded herself. Didn't it?

Molly began househunting the next afternoon. The real estate agent was a small birdlike woman with a pronounced Yankee twang, impeccable manners, and an intimate knowledge of every house in town, down to the last squeaking floorboard. With each house she showed, came a detailed social and architectural history, including the names of each of the family members, their occupations and marital status, the causes of their deaths. She included structural changes made, as well as an authoritative assessment of the builder's talents. She knew which driveways froze in the winter and which basements flooded during the spring rains.

By four o'clock they had examined eight houses, none of which was exactly to Molly's taste. Anticipating her client, Helen Garnett said, "Shall we call it a day, my dear? Househunting is wearying work and we've reached the point of diminishing return."

"Sorry," Molly said. "I guess my mind's cluttered with other matters. Tell me, Mrs. Garnett, did you ever know my mother?"

"Your mother?"

"She was born and raised in Old Brixton. Emily Fowler was her name."

"Of course, I remember Emily. We were in school at the same time."

"Then you were friends?"

"Not exactly friends. She lived up on the Hill, The Four Horsemen and all that . . . a bit too fast for my crowd. My father was a foreman in the Brass and Wire works, a conservative blue-collar man. On school nights, I was expected to be in the house no later than nine o'clock, and that when I was a senior in high school. Weekends I was permitted to stay out until eleven. Once I didn't get home until eleven-forty-five and my folks grounded me for a month.''

''The Four Horsemen,'' Molly repeated. ''The name seems to ring a bell.''

Helen laughed, a small brittle sound. ''Word gets around about The Four Horsemen. You already know one of them—Nelson Proctor. Nels was the leader, star quarterback on the football team, most popular boy in his class, four years running. All the girls were crazy about him, including me, I'm ashamed to admit. Not that he even knew I was alive. Oh, once, there was an off-handed kind of a move in my direction, sort of a reflex action. It had to do with the fact that I was the only girl within reach at that moment. Blunt and to the point, our Nels, surprised when a girl said no to him. Lots said yes, I've been told. But not me. Not that it bothered him. Nels just went about his business and found himself another victim.''

The words grated in Molly's ears. She forced a question out of the back of her mind. ''Did he date my mother?''

''Nels and Emily? Not that I know of. And as nosy as I am, I'd've known. Still, one never really knows, does one? What people do in the dark, I mean.''

Back at the Inn, Molly said she'd contact Mrs. Garnett when she was ready to make another excursion into the real estate market. Halfway to her room, she changed her mind and went back outside to where her Datsun 280Z was parked. A thin layer of dust dulled the silver skin of the sleek sports car and she vowed to have it washed before too many days passed.

She drove across New Bridge and up the winding road to the crest of Bluewater Hill, passing no one along the way, a circular driveway bringing her to a stop in front of the Newell house. A servant led her to the greenhouse in back where Lauren was tending her orchids.

''I appreciate you seeing me without warning,'' Molly began.

Lauren brushed a strand of yellow hair off her brow. Devoid of makeup, her skin glowed with good health, but her mouth was drawn down and there was no friendliness in her eyes.

''And I'd appreciate it if next time you called ahead.''

''Would you have seen me if I had called? I was afraid you might refuse to talk to me.''

"I have no reason to avoid you, Molly. I have nothing to hide."

The words were jarring. *I have nothing to hide.* A gratuitous denial—why?

"I've been talking to a great many people."

Lauren removed the protective gloves she wore and led the way into an adjoining sitting room.

"The orchids can be tiring," Lauren said, tossing the gloves aside. "What can I offer you?" Morgan had appeared silently in the doorway, although no apparent signal had summoned him.

"Nothing for me."

A gesture of dismissal sent him away. "What have you discovered? About your mother, I mean?"

"Not very much. It's as if . . . people have something to hide."

If Lauren noticed the peculiar choice of words, she gave no sign. "You're an outsider, my dear, and to a dyed-in-the-wool Yankee that is anathema. You might as well have just come in from Outer Mongolia."

Molly wondered if it was that simple. Only, she told herself, if she didn't examine too closely the responses she was getting, the abrupt mood changes when she asked people about Emily, their sudden withdrawal.

She brought her eyes up to Lauren Newell, to that serene face. This was the face of her mother's best friend; how had the years altered it? Someone had written that people were responsible for their own faces, once past the age of forty. Had Lauren's life been so peaceful, so full of satisfaction, without any of the negative experiences and emotions most people seemed to suffer? Molly perceived no resentment in the older woman's expression, no lines of anger or bitterness, no suspicion or ill will. How nice to have lived so long and suffered little. Was it possible? No answer came.

She arranged a pleasant smile on her face, careful to take the sting out of her words. "I get the feeling there is more to it than my being an alien. Mention my mother's name and people turn away, refuse to talk as if about a dangerous memory."

"I doubt that." Had a swift frown passed over those placid features? Molly could not be sure.

"Tell me, Mrs. Newell, about my mother and her mother. What was their relationship like?"

Lauren considered her answer. "What is it you wish to know?"

"Did they get along well?"

"Cornelia and Emily?"

"Were they friends? Did Mother have a happy family life?"

"So often that's in the eye of the beholder. Children growing up—conflict between parent and child, that's inevitable but normal enough, wouldn't you say? Cornelia could be difficult at times, I suppose. She was a unique woman, almost out of another time, if you know what I mean."

"I don't think I do."

"Well. A stickler for obeying the rules. As far as Emily was concerned, that meant Cornelia's rules. A haughty woman, with a deep sense of family, her ancestors, a history that went way back. Her place in society had been handed down—nothing could change that—history, wealth, accomplishment, those were the building blocks of the family and Cornelia never let you forget it, one way or another. She felt superior, and I suppose she *was* superior, to the rest of us in a number of ways. If Cornelia wanted something, she got it. Every time, it seemed. She was spoiled by normal standards—by her parents, by servants, by her friends, and especially by men."

Lauren peered more closely at Molly. "Of course! It's Cornelia you remind me of. You may be even more beautiful than she was, but softer, more human, more like Emily in that respect. Oh, Cornelia never was satisfied living in Old Brixton, yet she was married to the town by tradition. What a wanderlust she had . . ." Lauren lapsed into a reflective mood.

Reluctantly, Molly broke the silence. "What did Cornelia feel about Mother's choice of a husband?"

Lauren's eyes flickered suspiciously. "I'm not sure I understand."

"It seems to me that all the ties that connected Cornelia to Old Brixton should have kept my mother here. Yet she eloped. Why?"

Lauren hesitated, then answered too quickly. "Love makes a woman do any number of strange things."

For some reason, the answer didn't ring true to Molly. "Did Mother elope because she chose to or because she had to?"

"Had to?" Now Lauren's expression underwent a subtle alteration, the slightest narrowing of her eyes, the barest tightening of her lips.

"It seems to me, Cornelia being what she was, she might very well have disapproved of Mother's choice of a husband. Did she order Mother not to marry Michael Fairfax and did Mother insist? Did Cornelia throw Mother out when she refused to obey?"

"Oh, no! I mean, that doesn't make any sense. You said it yourself, Emily eloped, and Emily must have told you. Or did I say that to you?" she trailed off.

"What can you tell me about my father?" There was a demanding tone in Molly's voice, an authoritative ring absent until now.

The lines at the corners of Lauren's mouth seemed to extend, to recede deeper into her pale skin, and for the first time Molly noticed dark circles beneath each of those blue eyes. At once Lauren looked older, weary, a woman carrying an immense burden that had finally worn her down, a burden that made her profoundly unhappy.

"I am tired," she said, looking away. "Michael, wasn't that his name? There's not much to tell about him—a nice young man, of no particular distinction."

A light flickered in some shadowed corner of Molly's memory, faintly illuminating what seemed to be an expanding web of deception. Speaking carefully, she made sure not to challenge the other woman. "What puzzles me most is why Mother ever left in the first place. It's such a perfect place to live."

"Yes," Lauren agreed hastily. "Whenever we travel, Jay and I, we're always ready to come back after a week or two."

"The quiet streets, the big old houses so full of history, all of them beautifully maintained."

Lauren pursed her lips. "Still, it's not for everybody. An acquired taste, I'd say."

"You mean like caviar or sushi? Well, I seem to have acquired the taste. Helen Garnett's been showing me houses."

Lauren clasped her hands in her lap. "Why would you want her to do that?"

"I'm thinking about buying, about making Old Brixton my home."

"Oh, but you can't!"

"Any special reason?" Molly kept her voice dry and quiet.

Lauren made a mighty effort to regain her composure. "A young woman as sophisticated as you are, without friends or family—you'd be bored in a month."

"I plan on keeping my apartment in the city, operating my gallery, and spending weekends up here. As for family, the closest I come is Peter Matheson. You could call him a step-grandfather, I suppose."

"You've seen Peter?"

"Twice."

"I'm told he's senile. He is quite old."

"Not entirely. There are times when he's remarkably lucid. It's interesting, the way his memory unlocks without warning. He's been helpful to me in a number of different ways."

Lauren started to speak, thought better of it, and clamped her mouth shut.

Molly said, "I want to ask about The Four Horsemen." A flicker of interest came into Lauren's eyes. "Specifically, about Nels Proctor."

"What about Nels?"

"I had dinner with him the other night."

"You and Nels?" Pale spots appeared at the corners of Lauren's mouth as she bit down on her lip.

"He's such an attractive man."

"Am I to understand that you and Nels are seeing one another?"

"Wouldn't it be odd—here I am dating Nels and it's possible he and mother went out together when they were in high school."

"Oh, no," Lauren said swiftly. "Your mother never had anything to do with Nels. Neither of us did. He was older, you see, off to college by the time we began to think about boys."

"Well, that's a relief. It did make me feel a little peculiar."

Lauren hesitated. "Nels is—he's been married, you know, and divorced."

"Most men are, I'm afraid. In New York, every man I meet is either married or gay or sexually impaired." She laughed gaily. "Divorced at least shows some promise."

Lauren squirmed in her chair. She started to speak, then stopped, interrupting her thoughts as they advanced in complete disorder. "You haven't . . . I mean, you and Nels are not—"

"Sleeping together? What a surprising question, Mrs. Newell. Or maybe it's not. He is so handsome, it's hard to see many women resisting him."

"He's old enough to be your father."

"There's something to be said for mature men," Molly said slowly. It was clear that the subject disturbed Lauren Newell; more to the point, what prompted her to ask such personal questions? Watching the other woman closely, Molly went on. "Older men have so much more to offer than those my own age. But my private life would only bore you. I guess I've taken up enough of your time, Mrs. Newell. Thank you for seeing me."

"If only there were some way I could help," Lauren said at the door.

"If you come up with something, I'll be around," Molly replied over her shoulder.

18

BARNEY GRUBB WOKE at dawn, immediately alert, full of
energy and a sense of well-being. By nature a man of action,
Grubb was willing and able to respond instinctively to
whatever life presented. Obstacles were to be overcome. Problems were to be solved. Act and react, that was his philosophy,
if he had one. That, and take care of number one. Survival
was man's primary responsibility, in Barney's view; establish
that first and only afterwards might a man prevail, molding
the environment to suit himself. Up to now, Barney was
satisfied with himself on both counts, but he expected to do
much better.

As Barney saw it, most people spent too much of their time
involved in useless cerebral exercises. They did too much
thinking. Concerned themselves with the nuances of every
sentence uttered. Fretted over the smallest notion that entered
their heads. Worried every idea to death. People tested and
weighed every situation, trying to anticipate every possible
result, as if life were a series of logical progressions that led to
logical conclusions. In novels, maybe. In university lecture
halls, perhaps. In theory, sure. But not in the real world.

Barney brought life down to basics—you were hungry, you
ate; you were horny, you humped; you were in danger, you

eliminated the threat. And when the main chance showed up, a man took it by the horns and wrestled it into the dirt. No doubt about it.

Once out of bed, he did a hundred push-ups and a hundred sit-ups. He skipped rope for a quarter of an hour, hardly breaking into a sweat. Most men who had lived fewer than his fifty years suffered by comparison. His amiable disposition and bulky torso faked people out; they saw him as a puppy dog of a man, soft, easy to know, always wearing a placating smile. Better to be underestimated, he figured, than to come up short.

Take Nels Proctor. Nobody smarter than Nels. Nobody with more fiber in his belly. Nobody better at picking over another man, spotting the weaknesses. But even Nels failed to read the police chief correctly. All muscle and balls was how he perceived Barney, a bull of a man short on brainpower, with minimal ability to plan ahead. Grubb had done nothing over the years to alter that opinion. Until recently, there had been no need. Now, however, the time for him to make known the scope of his ambition, the depth and intensity of his voracious appetite, had arrived. He was ready to make his move.

Nels Proctor, meet the real Barney Grubb.

He picked up the phone and dialed. Six rings before Nels came on the line. He was a heavy sleeper and enjoyed the privileges his position afforded him, often taking advantage—sleeping late, arriving at his office whenever he wanted, summoning subordinates and associates to meetings at odd hours. He resented being awakened and made that resentment known.

"It is six o'clock in the morning, Barney. What in hell are you up to?"

Grubb bared his teeth in soundless mirth. Nothing provided him with more pleasure than jarring his betters. No, not betters, superiors. Though born to wealth and power, men like Nels Proctor were no smarter than he was, certainly no more skilled in the ways of the world. And when confronted with certain rough kinds of work, they were helpless without a Barney Grubb to call on.

"Thought you might like to head out to Devil's Glen, get in some early morning casting while it's peaceful and quiet."

He could almost hear Nels struggling to control his temper.

Control, that's what Nels Proctor was all about, control of himself, control of the world around him.

"Fishing," he said in a voice flat and hard as stacked lumber. "Damn, Barney, why no warning? We could have set it up in advance."

"Thing is, Counselor, you and me have some serious talking to do without anyone else listening in."

Nels's attitude changed at once. "Trouble?"

Grubb visualized him swinging out of bed, bare feet hitting the lush wool carpet that covered the floor of his bedroom. That crop of perfectly styled hair, splashes of gray at the temples as if brushed in by a painter's steady hand, would be tousled. His silk pajama bottoms would be rumpled. But those nearly white eyes would be lively and penetrating, all sleep wiped away, his brain turning over rapidly.

"Could be serious," Grubb said. Proctor would be standing now, all the delicate sensors of command at work, all systems swinging into high gear, decisions being made.

"All right. Come and get me."

That's an order, was the way Grubb understood the words. "Fifteen minutes and I'll be carrying coffee for us both."

Devil's Glen was twenty-two miles downstream, where the Owenoke River divided north and south. North Branch descended into the Quinnipiac Gorge, bending to the west, continuing to fall until it emptied into the manmade lake behind the Howard Brody Memorial Dam.

South Branch continued twisting along, a minor artery of the Connecticut River, forming pools along the way. The largest of these was Devil's Glen, shielded on the north by a high rock wall and on the other side by a thick green curtain of spruce and pine with an occasional stand of birch. Every boy in the county had tried to conquer the rock wall, to demonstrate his courage and climbing skills on its almost sheer face. Few of them made it all the way to the top, their strength giving out and tumbling them back into the cool, still pool below.

During his sophomore year in high school, Nels had made the climb. It was not until he was a senior that Gary Overton dared attempt the wall; halfway up, he fell off. Hollis Whitehead never made it even that far. As for Jay Newell, he had never tried.

Leaving Barney Grubb's pickup back in the woods, the two

men, wearing waders, pushed thigh-deep into the gentle waters
and began casting. Both of them were using split bamboo rods
and Whirling Dun trout flies. They worked the flies over the
lairs where large and wise trout usually could be found,
avoiding the shallower water where small and less
sophisticated fish would strike at almost anything that moved.

Minutes later, Grubb made his first strike, netting a good-
sized fish. Ten minutes later, he brought in another. After half
an hour, Nels voiced his frustration.

"I could be back in bed, for all the good I'm doing here. I
haven't had a clean strike yet."

"Been a long time since we did this."

At least two years, Nels said to himself. He was giving
nothing to the other man. He waited, knowing Grubb would
get around to whatever was on his mind in his own good time.
That was Barney's way.

"You all geared up for the start of the hunting season,
Counselor?"

"That's why you brought me out here, to talk about white
tails?"

Grubb put on his best country-boy expression, complete
with sheepish smile. High above, through the canopy of
leaves, he spied a red-tailed hawk lazily working the currents
of air. Back in the woods, blue jays were squawking at each
other and, on the far side of the pool, some mallards swam
solemnly about, unimpressed by the presence of the two men.
The best days of the chief's life had been spent out of doors,
hunting, fishing, pitting himself against God's creatures, the
way life was meant to be lived.

"Less'n two weeks to go. Feel the tang in the air? Gonna be
nice and brisk when we go tracking them deer. Our usual bet
on who bags the biggest rack?" Season after hunting season,
Grubb always brought down the biggest buck.

"A case of beer," Nels said.

"Damn," Grubb said, pumping up his big chest with cool
morning air, "this is good for a man's soul."

"If you have one."

Grubb, pleased with himself, laughed aloud this time and as
if in answer there came a flutter back in the brush. Wild
turkey, maybe, or a nervous pheasant hen. Mist circled the
pool in a mystical shroud.

"By everything that's holy, I'd rather be out here than any place else in the world. You believe in God, Counselor?"

"Do you, Barney?" Grubb was full of surprises, but only tactical ones; the shallowness of the man was always in evidence.

"At times like these, I guess I do," the policeman answered. Then, with that amiable grin, attending to his line, "But mostly I believe in me, Counselor. And in you, of course."

"I'm relieved you included me, Barney. What else do you believe in?"

"In the special ability you and me have to get things done. When we work in harmony, that is."

"Nicely put, Barney. Which, I suppose, brings us to the real reason you brought me here. I was beginning to wonder if it had slipped your mind."

"Be a cold day in hell when I forget anything this important."

Nels said nothing, snapping his line, impatient with the fish he knew lingered beneath the surface of the pool, commanding the largest of them to end its life on his line to amplify his pleasure. No fish responded.

"Lady showed up yesterday at the station house to lodge a complaint. Just about the time shifts were changing. Desk sergeant was busy and I was around to listen to her. Nice looking woman, about thirty-five or maybe even forty, with a fine figure. Name of Betsy Wirth. Seems she works for Doc Ortner out there at the hospital answering the telephone and filing papers and the like."

"Get on with it, Barney."

"It goes like this. Betsy Wirth has a daughter who waits table at the Blue Heron. Out near Smithton along Franklin Road."

"I know the place." Nels felt a slight tug on his line before it went slack. "Damn!" he muttered, and reeled in to check his fly.

"Seems that the daughter, name of Nadine, who is a pretty thing developed beyond her years, I am told, let herself get talked into going to the Yankee Clipper Motel with one of our esteemed citizens." He glanced sidelong at his companion but there was no visible reaction. The tall man cast out his line once more in a smooth, practiced motion. Grubb went on with his story. "Thing is, nature being what it is, one thing led to another and Nadine got herself screwed and tattooed, as they used to say."

"What's the problem, Barney?"

"Problem is the esteemed citizen roughed her up more than a little bit. Abrasions and contusions, like they say."

"You ought to be able to handle that."

"Thing is, according to the birth certificate Betsy Wirth showed me, the daughter's only fifteen years old. What we have here is a clear case of statutory rape."

"Any evidence, other than the girl's word?"

"Seems like the esteemed citizen was wearing a very special pendant and Nadine walked away with it around her neck."

"Damned fool."

"My sentiments exactly."

"Charge him."

"Guess I'll have to."

Nels reeled in and cast again, good snap in the line this time. He watched the fly settle. "Why come to me with this?"

Another fish hit Grubb's hook and he fought it skillfully, netting it after a lengthy battle.

"Well?" Nels said.

"Well," Grubb replied, facing him. "The pendant is the same kind you're wearing around your neck, Counselor. The Four Horsemen. And the man in the case is the esteemed president of the General Assembly, the Honorable Hollis Carleton Whitehead—"

"Damn," Nels said in a small, tight voice.

"Exactly," Grubb answered with a slow, gloating smile.

19

⁓⁓

SHE STILL REGARDED herself as Lauren Poole. Newell, after so
many years, remained an alien label, one that never seemed to
apply to her. Three children and twenty-two years of marriage
and she continued to harbor a secret attachment to the girl she
had once been, never altogether grown up. There were occasions when she examined herself in the mirror, exploring the
time lines which transmuted her face into a stranger's mask.
The body that confronted her—faint stretch marks scoring her
belly, breasts sagging—was not the body she was familiar
with. It too belonged to someone else.

She was locked in to the tangled matrix of her own shadowed history. So much of the reality she had lived was buried
in memory, tucked out of sight of family and friends, impossible, even after so many years, for her to consider. An intrusive, fugitive thought was brushed aside, lest it illuminate
the dark past with the unforgiving light of hindsight. All her
life had been spent struggling on a slick and slippery slope, in
terror of sliding into the awful abyss that yawned at her back.

Of course you know Nels Proctor.

Everyone did. Throughout the county, throughout the

state; with friends and acquaintances, colleagues everywhere. Businessmen in California took him to lunch at the Polo Lounge. Women fussed over him at dinner parties in Sutton Place and in Boston's most prestigious salons. Politicians offered him deals in paneled club rooms in Washington.

To know Nels Proctor was to envy him. And to loathe him. To admire his ability to get things done and to deplore his cavalier attitude. People vied for his attention and competed for the privilege of catering to him. Nels Proctor—eternal youth—had transformed himself into what he had always longed to be: power broker, wheeler and dealer, a man devastatingly attractive in the light of day and insidiously corrupt in the dark.

Nels Proctor. *The most attractive boy I've ever known*, Molly Fairfax had said. Oh, no, not Molly. It was Emily, her mother, on that fateful night in the distant past, the best friend I have hever had. Lauren struggled to order the jumble of thoughts that flooded her brain, to separate muddled memory from current fact. Emily and Molly had blurred, coming together as one on the shifting screen of her mind.

Visions of that terrible night drifted into view. Nightmarish visions still vivid and nauseating after so many years. David Colfax, skin coated with sweat, supporting a battered and bleeding Emily on the lawn outside Lauren's bedroom window. She had rushed out to them, careful not to awaken her parents, alarmed at the sight of Emily—her mouth had been swollen, her cheek bruised, eyes rolling aimlessly in her head, blood everywhere.

"My God, what happened?"

David, sweet David, soft and compassionate, a friend to them all, had replied, painting a terrible picture of the events of that night. To this day, on those infrequent occasions when she and Jay made love, that shocking image would materialize and Lauren would see Emily being assaulted by each of The Four Horsemen, Jay being the last of them. Her husband, father of her children, violating her own flesh as he had violated Emily. Rapist, raping his own wife. The nightmare was always the same.

"Help me," Emily had whispered to her best friend. "Please help me."

Children is what they were, half formed, not equipped to

deal with the stunning cruelty of their own kind. Appalled by what had befallen one of their own. In awe of what could happen to any of them. Terrified of the disapproval of their parents. Society would condemn the part each had played in this awful drama. Blame for this abomination would accrue to each of them.

"Why?" Emily had sobbed repeatedly. "Why did they do this to me?"

Why? The word had lodged painfully in Lauren's throat, anger mixing with horror and guilt, ashamed that she had deserted her friend on Overlook Point. *Why hadn't Emily left when she did?*

"We have to do something," David had said. David, younger than either girl, consistently faithful to principles and standards he had yet to fully comprehend, was committed to act nobly in the face of man's ignoble actions.

I warned you! Lauren wanted to shout. Instead she said, "We better take you home."

Emily recoiled. "No. Please, no. My mother will blame me."

"How did this happen?" Lauren found it all too difficult to assimilate. Those boys were from good families, the *best* families, they were so . . . nice. Everybody thought so.

"It was a bet . . . a bet. And when he won the bet he made the others do it to me, one right after another, like animals."

Not Jay Newell. Please, not Jay Newell . . .

"All of them . . . how could such a thing happen to me?"

"Your mother's away," Lauren remembered. Away, the usual condition of Cornelia Matheson. In Paris or Venice or Buenos Aires or Istanbul. Places remote and expensive, glamorous. Partying in the world's most favored playgrounds, always on the run. Just back from a trip or about to embark on another one. Leaving behind her only daughter. Savaging the girl for not being more accommodating. For not being beautiful and graceful, the kind of child a mother could be proud of. Resenting the interest her new husband showed in the gangly creature, mocking his compassion and his kindness.

"We should take you to a doctor," David Colfax had said.

Emily refused, unwilling to submit her shame to another person's inspection. But with Lauren's support, David prevailed. They took her to Dr. Ortner and, afterward, brought her home, careful not to disturb the housekeeper.

All of that had been so long ago, yet it was still vivid and painful. Struggle as she might, the memories of that night remained alive in Lauren's dreams and in her consciousness, surfacing without warning to torment and haunt her.

The following winter, home from college on Christmas vacation, Jay Newell phoned to invite her to have dinner with him. Without explanation, she refused. He called twice more before returning to school and each time she turned him down.

"Why not go out with him?" Lauren's mother wanted to know, with her mild social logic. "He's a nice boy, from a good family, one of the best in the state."

Lauren translated her mother's words: The Newells had social prestige, political influence, and owned the only bank in town. Jay would be an extraordinary catch for the daughter of school teachers who lived on the Flats.

During spring break, Jay phoned again and asked her to go out with him. Emily had long since left Old Brixton and Lauren had pushed the horrors of that Fourth of July night into the darker recesses of her mind, keeping them out of sight and manageable, providing the emotional comfort she required to rationalize what she intended to do.

This time she accepted Jay Newell's invitation and he took her to the country club where they dined and danced. Jay was fun to be with, attractive and considerate, never pressuring her the way some boys did. She told herself that she should be flattered by his attention, aware that most of the girls in town would be happy to be in her place. Jay Newell was her big chance, perhaps her only chance; he was the fulfillment of her dream, of her parents' dream, that she marry well and live in a grand house on Bluewater Hill, a woman of means and stature.

She and Jay were married the summer after his graduation, on the lawn of the big house on Bluewater Hill. They spent the first night of their honeymoon in a suite at the Dorchester in London. Chilled champagne and flowers greeted them when they entered the suite. Alone in the bedroom, Jay had opened the spacious closet, dividing the fine wooden hangers into two separate groups, one at each end of the hanging bar.

"These are your hangers," he declared with solemn consideration, "and these are mine. That way there'll never be any conflict."

And in a similar fashion he compartmentalized the rest of their lives. His and hers. Yours and mine. Two people at opposite ends of the hanging bar.

Had she loved him then? She could no longer remember. Did she love him now? Another unanswerable question. Twenty-plus years of marriage had produced three children, each of whom put a great deal of energy into avoiding a visit home. The same barriers were erected between parents and children that existed between husband and wife.

A reasonable marriage. Seldom erupting into open conflict, contained and correct at most times, emotions that might disturb the balance of their unspoken arrangement kept under control. No anger, no declarations of regret or disappointment, no outward manifestations of passion. By the time they married, Lauren had managed to convince herself that what had taken place on Overlook Point no longer mattered much, might not have happened the way Emily said it had, believed that Emily might have exaggerated the occurrence. She told herself that Emily was emotionally unstable, unreliable, given to dramatizing the events of her life. But the nightmares kept recurring and memory gnawed at her like some malignant growth, working toward its inevitable and deadly end.

Of late, her life was teetering and for the first time she understood how flimsy a foundation she had built. Had Molly never appeared she might have gone on as before, able to cope. But Molly was a subversive charge about to go off, a charge that could destroy them all. Destroy everything she had clung to for so long. If Molly hadn't come along Lauren might have continued on her relatively smooth course, content with the arrangement that allowed her to survive the inner conflict. All that was changed now and her emotions were in turmoil. She needed help but there was no one she could turn to.

Surely not Jay. He had always succumbed easily to a commanding masculine figure. First his father and now Nels Proctor. And in controlling Jay, Nels controlled her, too, making decisions that shaped their lives.

She perceived Nels as an evil force dragging them all toward emotional and spiritual ruin. She loathed him, yet dared not give voice to her feelings for fear of damaging her relationship with her husband, who considered Nels an outstanding American, an outstanding man, the best of them all.

In time Lauren had come to loathe herself only slightly less than she loathed Nels, castigating herself as a weakling, a coward, a woman who had failed always in her responsibilities.

And still did.

20

BECKER AND MOLLY had breakfast in the dining room of the Inn at an old tavern table, eating off heavy blue and white crockery. Tea and toast for Molly, blueberry pancakes and sausage and coffee for Carl.

"I called you last night."

Guilt was her initial reaction. And yet she'd done nothing wrong, betrayed no one, harmed no one. Least of all Carl Becker, to whom she had no debt, emotional or otherwise.

"I had a dinner date." Her eyes challenged him to object, to criticize, to question. It startled her to realize he did none of those.

He cut a small triangle of pancake dripping with maple syrup and directed it with fastidious concern into his mouth, losing not a drop. He washed it down with some coffee.

"Nels Proctor," he said.

She lifted her chin defiantly.

He went on. "I saw you walking along the river with him a couple of days ago. A local legend, that's our Nels. The man always functions at the top of his game. The best of everything for Nels. Which is what he's got in you, the best."

"It isn't like that."

"Not yet," he said.

She took instant offense. "You have no right—"

He cut her off. "Right. I've got no right, no right at all." His manner softened and he spread his hands. "Can't blame a guy for trying."

She wanted to explain, to make him understand. "Nels," she said, her voice shifting speeds in a slight drawl, "took me to dinner once or twice. To lunch. We went walking in the woods and canoeing on the river. He took me fishing and I caught a trout my very first time. I've got a picture to prove it." She brought a snapshot out of her purse. "We took Polaroid pictures of each other. Corny, isn't it?"

"On the river," he said. "When I was a boy, we swam there all the time." He shrugged his shoulders and attended his pancakes. "Sounds like you had a good time. I wish it had been me."

"Oh, Carl, I am fond of you, only—"

"Only," he said, brushing the hair off his brow. "I spoke to my friend in Washington yesterday. That's why I called."

"About my father?"

"Yes, except he came up empty."

"What does that mean?"

"It means the computers failed to kick up any information about Michael Fairfax."

"How can that be?"

"Army, Navy, and Marines, nobody by that name fits the description."

"Army," she insisted. "Mother told me over and over again, Army. I can almost see him standing there in his uniform. He won the Silver Star—he was a hero."

"So you said, only we can't locate him."

"The bureaucracy," she said disparagingly.

"It can be deadly."

"Some kind of an administrative goof."

"Most likely. What we need is some additional information. Maybe he's tucked away somewhere, one of those specialized units that nobody remembers."

"You know everything I know."

"Do you have any official notification of his death—a letter, a telegram?"

"Nothing. My mother was a cheerful person—wouldn't keep something like that around, too morbid."

"Right. The point is, as far as Defense is concerned, nobody named Michael Fairfax ever existed."

She heard herself becoming shrill, felt a tightness across her chest, a thickening in her throat. "He was in Cuba. He was killed at the Bay of Pigs. Somebody's making a big mistake."

"Okay. But the machines are coming up empty. As far as my sources can tell, nobody by that name was in the Army at that time. Nobody by that name died in Cuba. Nobody."

An icy finger of doubt touched the base of her spine. "Maybe your sources are not as good as you seem to think they are."

"These are good people. Competent and thorough."

"This is crazy! This is—" She broke off and a knowing expression moved like a shadow across her face. "Of course, I understand now. It must have been CIA. Secret work for a secret organization. No wonder his name didn't show up on the regular rosters."

"No," Becker said.

"How can you be so sure?"

"We checked, down the line. CIA, DIA, National Security Agency. Nothing came of it. Besides, you said Army and according to military records Michael Fairfax never existed."

Never existed.

"The medal?"

"That, too. We checked the list—every Silver Star given out since the end of the Second World War. No medal winner named Michael Fairfax."

Madness, all of it. The possibilities suggested by what he was telling her caused her brain to reel. An insistent throbbing settled behind her eyes and on the other side of the table Becker faded in and out of focus.

"Sometimes," he said, offering her a way out, "people act in ways that are beyond understanding. For reasons that person alone knows. Your mother was by herself, with a young daughter to raise. Clearly a difficult time for her. She needed someone and maybe she created Michael Fairfax—"

"No! That's the craziest thing yet, all of this is crazy. I told you, he saved my life."

Carl sipped some coffee; it was bitter on his tongue and he pushed the cup away. "Something's certainly screwy here."

Her eyes were wide, staring, not registering anything in front of her. What if none of the stories her mother had told were true? What if Michael Fairfax had not died a hero's death that bloody day at the Bay of Pigs? What if he had not been an Army officer? What if it all was a lie? What had happened to her father?

"He was real," she said, almost reverently. "He was real."

"I'm sorry," Becker said.

Had there been a divorce? Or had Michael Fairfax run off with another woman, deserting mother and daughter? What terrible secrets had Emily chosen to keep to herself? Molly searched frantically for satisfactory answers.

"All right," she conceded, forcing herself to remain calm, the hard consonants sliding away. "Let's say it wasn't actually Cuba. The Bay of Pigs, it was a secret operation."

"That's true."

Encouraged, she hurried ahead. "Even today the military must still be keeping certain information secret. It mightn't have been the Bay of Pigs itself. He might have died during a training exercise in Guatemala or Florida, wherever it was they did those things. The Pentagon doesn't always tell the truth, everybody knows that. Those generals, they hide things to protect themselves. An accident might have taken place. A stray shot. A faulty hand grenade. Men drown during practice landings. I've read about such tragedies."

Becker could offer no comfort. The questions she asked were identical to those he had put to his friends in Washington, coming up empty every time. He spoke in a matter-of-fact voice, "I'm sorry."

"If he'd been doing secret work—"

"No."

"Records can be concealed."

"Not in this case."

"Official secrets, sensitive even this long after the event."

"No."

"Damn you!"

He watched her without speaking.

She grew pale, her lips trembling. "Are you saying my father never existed?" A shrill sound escaped her lips, almost a plea. "Don't tell me that! Don't say that Michael Fairfax never lived. I know better. He married Mother, I'm the proof of that, the living proof. I don't care about your sources, your bureaucratic friends, your computers. They're wrong. They've made a mistake, some ridiculous mistake. It's a bad joke, that's what it is. Isn't it?" she ended weakly. "Isn't it?"

He looked down at his hands. They were clenched into fists, the knuckles white.

After a while, she spoke again. "If it's the way you say it is—then everything was a lie. All the stories Mother told me were lies. All my memories, were they lies, too? Don't expect me to believe that."

He wanted to embrace her, make her believe everything was going to come out all right, but he couldn't. She'd listened to enough lies. She would hear no more from him.

"He's asleep," Bunny Whitehead said in her usual aloof manner. She admitted Nels Proctor to the marble-floored reception hall, an oval chamber that reminded visitors of a movie set of a Southern mansion. Dark blue silk lined the walls on which portraits of Bunny's parents, stern, handsome people, hung. Bunny carried a strong resemblance to each of them.

"How bad this time?"

"At a guess, he's been drinking for two days. Reeks of beer and cheap whiskey. Or is that a brothel he smells like?"

"Now, Bunny," Nels said, trailing her up the circular staircase leading to the second floor of the huge house. With any other woman he would have uttered an expression of solicitousness, embraced her, reassured her; but he knew that the Proctor charm would be counterproductive with Bunny. More than once she had made it clear that she had no use for him. "Don't be too hard on Hollis. We men have our weaknesses."

"Structural flaws," she bit off. "From the inside out, Hollis is damaged goods."

"You're not being fair."

"When we first were married there was some residual pride. A trace of manliness. Some element of ambition and courage. No more. All that alcohol's turned his brain to mush and his spine to jelly. The man is useless to everyone."

Not everyone, Nels reminded himself. Not yet.

They paused at the door to Hollis's room. "In there," she said.

"I'd like you to hear what I've got to say to him."

She backed away. "The smell of him is repugnant, the sight of him makes me sick." Nels reached for the antique crystal doorknob. "By the way," she continued, "Hollis and I had a little talk about your little talk with him. I made it plain to him as I am making it plain to you that there is no way I am going to bury myself in that backwater of a state capital."

"Ah." Nels gave her a long steady look from which she didn't flinch. "I had hoped for a more conciliatory attitude on your part, Bunny."

"Save the charm for those who appreciate it, Nels."

"I believe," he said, as if breaking down a complex thesis so that a child could understand, "that, despite his shortcomings, Hollis is on the verge of a remarkable career in politics."

"He's a hack."

"Professional is the word I prefer."

"With neither substance nor style."

"People change, they grow."

"Not Hollis."

"Ambition, duty, the love and encouragement of a good woman."

She began to laugh. "Spare me the Sunday sermonette."

"I'm serious, Bunny. Hollis is about to take on a new public persona. He is about to become a thoughtful political scientist. Hollis will soon be probing the problems that occupy men's minds."

"Save it for your faithful followers, Reverend Proctor."

"I intend to transform him into a solid thinker, a man who has dedicated his life and his fortune to the welfare of the people."

"Beautiful, Nels. Billy Graham in a snow-white suit couldn't have put it better. All you need is Kate Smith singing 'God Bless America' with a waving flag and a golden cross in the background."

"I mean what I say."

"Hollis as governor." She shook her head. "Hooray for our side, Nels. Shaft the people. Loot the state treasury. Let corruption run rampant. I no longer give a damn."

"You're much too cynical."

"Don't expect my help. I won't campaign with him. I won't be at his side when he's sworn in. I won't live in the governor's mansion."

One long stride brought him to her side, that devastating smile lighting his face, the icy eyes glinting with malice. "A great deal depends on you, Bunny."

"Not interested."

He shifted gears, his manner intimate, adopting a voice suitable to the occasion. "Consider the governor's chair as a first step."

"I don't know what you mean."

"The second step could be the White House, Bunny. You along with him. President and First Lady, how's that sound to you?"

She stared up at him in wonder, the ordinarily smooth brow furrowed. "You are the most outrageous man. Does nothing shame you? Is there nothing you hold sacred? Hollis as President—what an obscenity!"

"I can pull it off, Bunny."

"I believe you could. And you're the one who would run things, the reins of power in your corrupt hands. What a disaster that would be! A man without moral standards, without ethics. You believe only in your own predatory nature. I won't be a party to your insidious scheme."

"Not even if I can put you down right in the middle of Washington with all its rewards?"

"In the White House, no. There are limits even to my selfishness."

"How regrettable. Ah, well, that brings us around to Scene Two."

"Scene Two?"

With no change of expression, he said, "Scene Two concerns my hobby."

"You never struck me as the sort."

"Some men collect stamps, others coins, others tropical fish. I collect information . . . about people."

She took a single backward step. "You're going to make a point, I imagine."

"It's an expensive pastime requiring the services of private investigators. However, in the long run, it pays off. I keep files on just about everybody I've met—everybody that matters, that is. And you have always mattered to me, Bunny. A great deal—you and Hollis."

When she said nothing, he continued. "Your file is especially interesting, Bunny. Scraps of information, references to the many visits you made to Greenwich Village years ago and to Boston over the last five years. A number of names are mentioned but one keeps cropping up—a certain Mary Louise Gorman. I can cite every meeting you had with Miss Gorman,

Bunny, the nights you spent with her, the parties at which only women were present. There are photographs, too, Bunny, of you and Miss Gorman locked in what can only be called an intimate embrace. Shall I go on?''

"What a despicable man you are."

"I said there are photographs. I also have affidavits from people who were present at some of these parties. Evidence that might upset your social standing, shatter the Middleton legacy."

"You son of a bitch."

"We may not become friends, Bunny, but we can arrange a mutually advantageous truce. I don't hurt you, you don't hurt me. Neither do you stand in the way of Hollis's career. Together, we'll make sure Hollis is a good governor, responsive to the needs of the state.

"Then, in nineteen eighty-eight, amidst the political free-for-all that is inevitable among the front runners for the Presidency, Hollis will surface as a compromise candidate. Only he will be able to reunite the diverse and warring factions of the party. He will campaign as an extension of our present glorious leader, Ronald Reagan. Reaganism will be his theme and it should sweep him right on up Pennsylvania Avenue, and you along with him, Bunny."

"God save us all."

"He will," Nels said, smiling smugly. "He's on my side . . . ''

Hollis was asleep, snoring irregularly. Unshaven, unwashed, he seemed bloated and ungainly. Nels said his name but Hollis didn't stir. Nels filled a plastic tumbler with cold water and poured it in a slow stream onto Hollis's face.

He sprang into a sitting position, sputtering, confused. Gradually his vision came into focus.

"Nels. Full of jokes, you are. I guess it's time I got up."

Nels slapped him hard across the face. Gasping, Hollis fell back. Nels hit him again and Hollis started to sob.

"Stupid," Nels bit off. "Destructive. What a mess you are."

"I'm sorry, I'm so sorry. I shouldn't drink, I know. I must've been crazy . . . "

"Worse than that. Risking everything we've built so you can dip your wick into some cheap waitress."

A puzzled look passed over Hollis's face. "What?"

"You don't even remember. Nadine Wirth is her name, at the Yankee Clipper."

"Oh, my God!"

"She's fifteen years old and her mother intends to press charges—statutory rape."

"No!"

"You would not do well in prison, Hollis. Those cons would tear you apart within an hour."

"What am I going to do?"

"You are going to tie a very tight knot in that cock of yours, Hollis."

"I will, Nels. I will."

"No more young girls. None."

"That was a lapse, a temporary lapse."

"Go wrong again and I'm through with you. The party will be through with you. There's a great deal at stake here, Hollis, more than you know."

"You have my word."

"All right, here's the way it has to be. No more booze. No more girls. You go on a diet from now on—lose thirty pounds. Start exercising. Run every day. Get yourself in shape for the hard work that lies ahead."

Hollis clasped Nels's hand in both of his. "I'll never forget what you're doing for me, never." He kissed his hand. "You're the best friend I ever had." He lifted his eyes, asking, "What's going to happen now?"

Nels retrieved his hand. "I have to clean up the mess you made."

Molly felt herself drawn to Peter Matheson. Though the old man existed mostly in the mists of his private dreams, she felt a certain kinship, as if, through his marriage to her grandmother, he had become a blood relative. In his wheelchair, rocking slightly, staring vacantly into space, he was a living link to her past, to her mother's life in Old Brixton. Suddenly, for no particular reason, he straightened up. His eyes cleared, lit with recognition.

"Emily's girl," he said cheerfully. "You've come to see me again."

She leaned toward him. "Mr. Matheson, help me, please. Is there anything you can tell me about my father, Michael Fair-

fax? He was a soldier, he died fighting in Cuba. But now I'm
not sure. There's no record of a soldier by that name. Why
would my mother lie about him? Why?''

His eyes clouded over and he grew agitated, head bobbing,
squirming as if to screw himself tighter into the chair.

"No husband," he muttered finally. "Never had a husband, never. And such a pretty girl, too . . . ''

21

FOR THE OCCASION, Nels prepared himself with more than his usual sartorial concern. He chose a suit of dark blue flannel with a shadow stripe complete with vest, a soft blue shirt with a starched white collar, and a muted club tie. His black wingtips had been polished to a high gloss. He looked the part he chose to play: a man of power and wealth, a man who knew how to get things done.

He drove the Jaguar XJK, certain it would impress her most, with its sleek lines and expensive leather interior. In this situation, appearance played a large part in the game.

Betsy Wirth was already waiting outside the main entrance to Ortner's medical complex when Nels drove up. She was a pretty woman of no distinction, wearing a dress selected off the rack, Nels observed—a woman nervous and without style. Tension had thinned her mouth and no amount of makeup could disguise the unsteadiness in her eyes. She pulled at her fingers, watching him get out of the Jaguar, greeting her with his most charming smile, taking her hand.

"Mrs. Wirth?" She nodded and he looked deep into those tired, frightened eyes. "How kind of you to agree to see me." He opened the door of the Jaguar, helped her in, and got behind the wheel. "We'll have a leisurely lunch and get to know one another."

"I don't have a lot of time." Her eyes were never still, hands tightly clasped, face turned to the front. "Dr. Ortner doesn't like us away from the job for too long."

"Leave Dr. Ortner to me. Does Italian food suit you? I know of a pleasant place, northern cooking, of course, and the wine list is remarkably good, considering where we are."

"Whatever you say."

Not until they were seated in the restaurant, sipping a chilled Orvieto, did he address himself to the reason they were together.

"I know how difficult this must be for you," he started out.

Her jaw tightened. "He shouldn't've done it to her, that's all."

"Which is why I'm here, to put things right."

She snorted disparagingly. "How you gonna do it? You haven't seen my girl's face, her body, all black and blue on her boobs, her belly, all beat up the way she is. That man is a fiend."

"Let's begin with this: all medical costs, doctor's fees, everything will be paid for."

"That won't make the pain go away, the suffering . . . Nadine's just a baby and lookit the way he did her."

"To protect and shield your child, nothing is more basic to a woman. I understand that."

She nodded in agreement.

Seeing only despair and defeat in her posture, he decided it would be easy to solve the problem. "I'm here, Mrs. Wirth, to satisfy you and Nadine in every way possible."

Her head came up, face constricted, her eyes moist. He expected her to cry. Like so many men to whom a display of emotion is anathema, he failed to reckon with the tempered courage and strength at the core of Betsy Wirth. "I want that man punished. Hurt the way he hurt my little girl, taking advantage of her that way." When he didn't answer, she went on grimly, "But you can't do that, can you, Mr. Proctor? At least, you won't."

"Is it revenge you want or justice?" As soon as he spoke he realized he had made a tactical error.

Her eyes flashed. "Revenge *and* justice. I'd like to spread what he did all over the papers and on the TV. Let everybody know what kind of a pervert he is. I know who he is, Mr. Proctor. Nadine, she may not always do the smart thing, but she's got her share of brains. She knew who he was.''

There was no steam-rolling Mrs. Wirth, Nels decided. This called for a change in approach.

"With your help, we may be able to agree on a way out of this unsavory affair that will benefit both principals—" A flicker of scorn came into her eyes and he warned himself to be careful; Betsy Wirth had a nose for bullshit and would not be diverted. He sat back in his chair, opened his jacket, spoke quietly and with authority.

"Let's put it this way. I am a lawyer, an officer of the court, and no one knows better than I that without law man reverts to the jungle.''

"What are you saying to me, Mr. Proctor?''

"Suppose we send Hollis—Mr. Whitehead—to prison. Does he deserve that? Yes, by all means. Will that benefit Nadine in any way at all? Absolutely not.''

"Make her feel a lot better, and me, too.''

"Let's consider the harm it may do.''

"The harm's been done.''

"Worse could still come. Put a fifteen-year-old girl on the witness stand under a harsh cross examination by a skillful and hostile lawyer. Consider—she went to that motel room of her own free will. No one forced her.

" 'Question: How many times have you been in a motel with a man, Nadine?'

" 'Question: How much did you charge those men?'

" 'Question: What form of birth control device do you use, Nadine?'

" 'Question: Were you a virgin on the night in question, Nadine?'

" 'Question: If not a virgin, how many men have you had sex with? How old were you when you lost your virginity? Where did it take place?'

" 'Question: How many times have you had sex since that time with Mr. Whitehead at the Yankee Clipper?' ''

"That's rotten, Mr. Proctor, really low down.''

"Of course it is. I'm only trying to demonstrate the problem we face, should this case go to court. Then, of course, there is the matter of witnesses.''

"Witnesses?'' The ferocity dissolved, replaced by a quizzical expression, the look of someone confronting an enemy she hadn't counted on.

"We are going to have to place Nadine and Hollis in that room at the same time."

"The desk clerk . . . "

"I took the liberty of contacting the man. The register doesn't show Mr. Whitehead's name."

"He signed in as Mr. Reagan, kind've a joke."

His expression never faltered. "There was no Reagan on the register, no name remotely like it."

"His credit card?"

Nice try, he thought. "The room was paid for in cash, not unusual in such cases, I'm told."

"The clerk will be able to identify him."

"The desk clerk seems to have disappeared. Left without warning. Also not unusual. A lot of these fellows are essentially nomads, always on the move. Left no forwarding address."

She tried to clear her mind. "The people at the Blue Heron. They saw her talking to Whitehead. They're her friends, they'll testify—"

"To what? A waitress talking to a customer. Hardly unique. She could have been taking his order. Or, discussing the weather. Maybe he was questioning the check or just passing the time of day. Not much to go on."

She brought her gaze around, meeting his eyes, unblinking. "There is one thing," she said evenly.

"And that is?" He was ready to demolish whatever argument she offered.

She brought it out of her purse, spinning slowly the heavy chain sculpted in twenty-four-karat gold: The Four Horsemen. The pendant Nels had given Hollis so many years ago. "No way Nadine could've got her hands on this, unless he was in that room with her." In one swift move, she returned the pendant to her purse, clutching it in her lap, her point well made.

"I want that man put away," she said. "I told Chief Grubb everything and he's obliged to uphold the law."

"And he will," Nels said, proceeding more cautiously now. He cursed Hollis for being a drunken, lecherous fool. If there were less at stake, he'd let him go down the drain unaided. But . . . "Chief Grubb is a very thorough man. Experienced and at the core cautious, intent on protecting his own varied interests, if you understand my meaning.''

"I'm not sure I do.''

He pitched his answer at a casual level—a throwaway line—picking at the veal on his plate with no real interest. "Let's say that Grubb is one of those people who prefers to operate in the shadows, away from outside influence, you might say. Accomplishing much more in his quiet, diligent way than a more impulsive man might. If I know Barney—and I know him very well—he is determined to keep this situation from degenerating into a disastrous public circus. He's that kind of a man. Are you enjoying your spaghetti, Mrs. Wirth?''

"He's got to charge Whitehead. That's his job.''

"A cooling-off period is the way Chief Grubb explained it to me, giving both parties time to consider their options. Try some cheese on the spaghetti—it enhances the flavor.''

She stared as if seeing him for the first time. It was a mistake agreeing to this meeting; he was too smart for her, too worldly, and a lawyer to boot.

"Have you, Mrs. Wirth?'' he said.

"What?'' Keeping up with him was like trying to catch a fly, following his changes of direction. He was pouring more wine into her glass. Trying to get her drunk? Break her down, get her to drop charges against his pal? Not on your life, buster. No way. "What?'' she asked again.

"Have you weighed each of your options carefully?''

Options.

Defeat had always been the preeminent choice she faced. Should the good and the bad be offered, she inevitably chose the bad. Success or failure; she took to failure like to an old shoe. Bad times were all that were ordained for Betsy Wirth; nothing worked right, nothing went right. No matter how hard she tried, life consistently delivered one swift kick in the ass after another.

Oh, she knew. Had known for a long time. Nothing would ever change for the better. Two marriages, both ending in bitter brawls involving other women and, eventually, divorce. Divorce with no alimony. No child support. Just Goodbye Charlie, don't call me, I'll call you. Lovers; oh, how many lovers she'd had. Each one had cheated or beat her or disappeared with her spare cash. Two of them had tried to get it on with Nadine and one—that bastard, Ike—had actually succeeded.

A friend—her dearest friend, going all the way back before high school—had swindled her meager savings in one of those goddamn pyramid schemes, then run off with a blond surfer from Southern California. *Gonna make you rich, baby.* Gonna shaft you one more time, is what she'd meant.

All that, and a daughter with an itch that no one man could scratch. In more beds than Betsy had hairs on her head. Try and teach the girl, spare her pain and aggravation, try and save the child. Lot of good it did. Nothing ever went right. Nothing ever would.

"What options?"

"One always has choices." He used his soothing, paternal voice, giving her something to think about. "Have you ever considered relocating?"

"Relocating?" She dealt with the word as one might deal with a strange and exotic creature never before encountered.

"Go somewhere else to live. A gentler climate, for example. No harsh winters. No snow. An easier life. Let's say Florida. Let's say around Fort Lauderdale. I'm told it's lovely down there, a perfect place to live."

She sniffed. "Fat chance. I got no friends, no family, no job, no connections in Fort Lauderdale. Might as well be Timbuktu."

"Certainly a job could be provided. What do you make at the hospital? Thirteen thousand, five hundred. Barely enough to get by."

"Everything's always going up."

"Your savings account, under one thousand dollars."

"How'd you know that?"

"Nadine is destined to stay a waitress for the rest of her life. Picking up men, getting into trouble. Is that what you want for your daughter? Is that the kind of life you want for yourself?"

"Me move, huh. I can't afford even to think about moving."

"How does this sound to you? Fort Lauderdale. Sunshine all year 'round. A white sand beach. A condominium looking out at the water, bought and paid for. A job that will double your present income."

"Like a dream, that's how it sounds."

"Not far from Jacksonville, there's a private school that deals with girls like Nadine. Say the word and tuition will be paid, including room and board. Nadine will finish high school, learn a trade. Maybe even go on to college, if she's so inclined."

"Are you telling me—?"

He put his fork aside, touched his napkin to his lips, sipped a little wine. "I am telling you that in addition a bank account will be opened in your name containing twenty-five thousand dollars, yours to do with as you wish."

Her mouth curled in disdain. For him and for herself. "Guys like you, you always get your own way. No matter who gets stepped on. Father to son, you pass along the money and the power. Controlling people like me, buying and selling us like we were cattle. That's not what I am, Mr. Proctor, I am a human being."

He tasted the wine again. Not bad for Owenoke County. "The offer's on the table," he said. "I don't haggle."

"What about Whitehead?"

"With no witnesses, no hard evidence, it's only Nadine's word against Hollis's. Bring this to trial and my opinion is he'd walk away free."

"I still have the pendant . . ."

The cold, deep eyes seemed to withdraw deeper into his skull, all color gone from two seemingly sightless orbs. She shivered and wished she hadn't accepted his invitation.

"Consider this: by the end of this day, Dr. Ortner may be forced to fire you. The bad publicity that would come of this would certainly do his hospital no good. You'd be without a job and not likely to find another in these parts. Consider that resolution to this situation and compare it with the possibilities of Fort Lauderdale."

Fort Lauderdale. What bright and sunny images the name brought to mind. Water skiing, swimming, boating. Maybe, after a while, she might be able to buy a boat of her own. A Chris Craft, maybe, white and sleek; she visualized herself at the controls wearing a shiny black bikini. Of course, first she'd have to shed a few pounds, sign up for one of those aerobics classes. Who knows, she might even find herself another guy. She was still young enough, still good-looking enough, still able to show a man a good time.

"Oh, what the hell," she said, "what's done is done and can't be undone."

He waited.

"To hell with Whitehead."

Nels nodded slightly.

"To hell with you, too."

"I'll make all the arrangements. You can be on your way by the weekend."

"That soon?"

"I'll want that pendant returned."

"What? Oh, sure, once the deal is signed, sealed, and delivered. Maybe I'll hire a good lawyer."

"Maybe you should." He raised his glass. "To your new life, Mrs. Wirth, you and Nadine. Not everyone gets a second chance. I almost envy you."

"You," she said in a strong whisper, all energy drained away. "You are a devil, a true son of Satan . . ."

22

ON THE NEXT afternoon, Nels took Molly on a picnic at Devil's Glen. By the time they arrived, the fishermen had long departed and the glen was tranquil, the air still and warm under the leafy canopy, sun streaking the grassy shore.

"How lovely," Molly exclaimed.

"Isn't it," he replied, lifting a Louis Vuitton case about the size of an army footlocker out of the Jeep Cherokee. He carried it to within a dozen feet of the pond and set it on end, like an old steamer trunk. It opened outwards, each zinc-lined vertical divided into dozens of drawers and velvet-cushioned compartments. A small brass plate, engraved in Old English script, was affixed to the top left section: THE BREAKERS.

Molly admired the case.

"I found it in an antique shop in Newport one year during the America's Cup races," Nels explained, extracting a cloth of linen so finely woven that it folded into a drawer which couldn't have been more than an inch deep. "The Breakers was the Vanderbilts' summer cottage." Out came the napkins, of the same fine linen as the cloth and delicately embroidered with roses, white on white. Next an iced bottle of Chablis, grand cru, from its bucket, two Baccarat wine glasses along with a matching bud vase with a single white rose, lifted from its tin traveling case. "Cottages, to the Newport people, could have housed towns the size of Old Brixton. The wealth was enormous. Have you been there?"

Molly watched, entranced. He worked swiftly, as if he'd done it many times before, his movements stylized and confident. "Once," she answered, eyes enormous as Nels pulled out two pewter plates, matching utensils, and several serving pieces. "I was very impressed." He arranged a number of lined containers along one edge of the linen cloth. "Many of those old summer cottages are open to the general public, you know. Tourists." He removed the covers from each of the containers. "They line people up and pass them through these very grand rooms filled with the imitation antiques the Vanderbilts thought were so chic."

The two longest containers revealed two shelled cold lobsters, each on a bed of crisp romaine with a half-dozen halved lemons, some covered with cheesecloth and the others filled with mayonnaise. There was a spinach pasta salad with a pesto sauce that featured tiny slivers of prosciutto and minced olives and a platter of sliced tomatoes with fresh basil.

"This," Nels said, with a sweep of his hand, "is the sort of thing they did so inventively in the old days in Newport."

There were fresh raspberries in another container, whipped cream in a second, and chocolate-covered truffles in the last one.

"Voilà!" he said, returning the desserts to the cool, covered compartments of the case. "The best for last. And now, mademoiselle," he said with a flourish, "your chariot."

From the right side of the trunk he removed several mats woven from soft reed and flexible enough to fold to fit the narrow shelves. He opened and arranged them on the soft grass, each the size of a chaise.

"Shall we dine?" he said.

"Everything is perfect," she said, awed by the display and his performance.

He accepted the compliment with a graceful nod of his finely shaped head. "There is definitely no other way to go." He left no room for contradiction.

After dining—she could consider it nothing less than that; certainly this was like no picnic she'd ever experienced—they stretched out on the reed mats, shoulder to shoulder, thigh to thigh, hands entwined, listening to Mahler's *Kindertotenlieder* on the portable tape deck he had brought along. The music seemed to fill the glen, resounding off the rock wall in a faint echo.

"Songs on the Deaths of Children," Nels murmured.

"How sad."

"Mahler composed it shortly after the birth of his second child. But he meant it to be a requiem for his own dead brothers and sisters."

Parents and children. Her mind flowed backwards in time to her childhood in Texas. There had been so many happy moments, each crowded with the joy of discovery and the knowledge that she was loved and appreciated. Emily had spent every spare minute she had with Molly, lavishing affection on the child, taking trips together, visiting art museums in Dallas and Fort Worth, going as far afield as Atlanta and Sante Fe. They spent quiet interludes together, too, Emily often reading to the girl, exchanging ideas about what they had read. It was a rich, full period burdened only by the absence of her father.

Sometimes they spoke of him; that is, Emily spoke of him in loving, laudatory terms, describing Michael Fairfax in minute ways, recalling incidents from the years they had spent together. His absence left a sadness in Molly that she carried around with her still.

Later, when she was more mature, she sought hungrily after a male figure to take her father's place. No one had ever quite done so, however, not even Joel Hammaker who, with his stalwart build and classic good looks, his quick and agile wit, had come closest. Molly had invested more of herself in the relationship with Joel than with any other man she had known, and betrayal, when it came, cut deeply and painfully, lingering still.

Could it be that her father had never actually existed? Was he only a figment of her mother's active imagination, summoned up to fill the void in which each of them existed? If so, it had surely been an act of kindness, meant only to enlarge Molly's life; but it had also been an act of deception which might distort Molly's days and perceptions forever. Tears collected behind her eyes and she embraced herself protectively. The death of children was sad, the death of a parent equally sad; the death of a father who had never lived at all left her hollow and deprived, tinged with a lasting bitterness.

"What are you thinking?"

Nels's voice was lined with brass, summoning her back for his own reasons.

She brought her eyes back into focus and listened again to the music.

"Do you like it?" he persisted.

She listened intently. "There's a sinuous quality to it," she offered. "Almost oriental."

"That's very good." There was a tinge of surprise in his voice as if he had not expected her to respond so acutely to the music. He went on in a pedagogic tone. "With these songs, Mahler created a new kind of Romanticism. Not at all sentimental, but lyrical and extremely sophisticated."

His remarks intruded on her enjoyment of the music, shattering the mood. She wondered if he wasn't more concerned with displaying his knowledge of Mahler's life along with his critical assessment of the composition than with enjoying the music itself. Then, as if sensing her uneasiness, he leaped up, drawing her to her feet.

"Let's go for a swim."

She glanced at the pond, the water still and dark now, somehow ominous. She felt chilled suddenly. "The sun's going down."

"It's still warm and the water will be even warmer. Come on, you'll see. Unless you're afraid, of course . . ." The smile on his face was small, extended too long, holding an implicit challenge.

"Why should I be afraid?"

"I brought towels but no bathing suits."

She hesitated briefly before standing. "If you can handle it, sir, so can I." She stripped off her clothes and without a backward glance sprinted toward the pond, launching herself in a long, flat dive. The initial chill was soon gone, replaced by a sense of physical well-being as she moved across the bottom. A trout brushed her side and then another, as if she were accepted in their element.

Short of breath, she flashed upward, breaking the surface and falling back. Nels was nowhere in sight. She floated, gazing up at the cloudless sky through the leafy overhang. At peace with herself, by herself, she was comfortable in a way she hadn't been for a very long time.

Was it the frenetic tempo of life in New York that had left

her feeling vaguely dissatisfied, her desires undefined, her needs unfulfilled? The gallery took up so much of her time and its success had become vital to her. The work had meaning and rewarded her each day. Meeting with artists and sculptors was fun. They were an idiosyncratic bunch, artistically quirky, often in pain and lonely, with an obsessive need for recognition. She enjoyed helping them display their works, creating a market for that work, helping them grow.

Still, the pace was frantic, often taking over her social life until she could not separate one from the other. But the men she met seldom possessed much understanding of her needs, the emotional yearnings she experienced, her private obsessions. Here, in this idyllic setting, none of that mattered very much and she promised herself to contact Helen Garnett again and continue her search for a suitable house.

Without warning, Nels broke water alongside, reaching for her. Shrieking like a schoolgirl, she struck out for shore. Too late. He pulled her back into the shallows, arms circling her waist, mouth fastening onto hers.

Breathless, she broke away, nerves jangling, dashing to their picnic spot. She wrapped herself in one of the luxurious towels, covering her nakedness, rubbing hard against the rapidly cooling air. How convenient, she thought with pleasure and a just a twinge of resentment, to bring towels but not swimsuits. She cast herself down on the reed mat, head buried in her arms. A moment later he was beside her, making no effort to cover himself.

"You," he said in her ear, "have a delicious mouth."

She gave no sign she'd heard.

"Did you mind my kissing you?"

No man had kissed her since Joel and no man had been allowed to put his hands on her. How then had she arrived at this state? Lying naked alongside this comparative stranger—what had provoked her? Yes, he was attractive and sensual, provocative in so many ways. Still, she grew uneasy, unable to shake the niggling suspicions that bit into her consciousness, unable also to shed the shackles she had put on her emotions for so long.

Did you mind . . .

No, she thought. She hadn't minded the kiss; nor had it had any meaning for her. Merely contact, mouth to mouth, without deep sensation, without real excitement. Oh, the kiss was practiced and skillful, his tongue experienced at delivering promise; but she had felt nothing—neither passion nor revulsion—and whether or not he kissed her again didn't seem to matter. Would she ever feel that anticipatory tingling again, the desire to have a man caress her flesh, explore her body as she caressed and explored his? A tremulous uncertainty took over; was that once-vital part of her existence ended? She refused to think about that.

Nels was nibbling at her shoulder, manipulating her breast. Why was he inflicting these unwanted intimacies upon her? His arms circled her body and he shifted closer, trying to impose his erect desire on her flesh.

"When you ran to the water—what a magnificent body you have. There's so much I want to do . . . "

She eased back, working the towel between them, shielding herself.

"It might be better for us both if you told me more about Mahler."

She could feel him tense and she sensed his quickness to anger. He was not used to being refused. As quickly as it came, the tension went out of his body and he sat up and laughed, without amusement or mockery, a manufactured sound meant to bridge a momentary embarrassment. "Some more wine?"

"No, thanks."

He sat with his knees pulled up, sipping the Chablis and smoking a cigarette, gazing into space, the connection between them no longer in force.

She wanted to repair the breach. "All this makes me feel like a Hemingway heroine."

"Lady Brett, perhaps?"

"I've never been a Lady Brett, except in my most secret fantasies."

"Who then?"

"My literary heroines?" She weighed her reply. "Will you accept Lady Chatterley?"

"That's a surprising choice. You're too much the modern woman. Lady Chatterley was too subservient."

Subservient. Was that the nature of all of us, Molly wondered, all women? To demand and struggle for equality, freedom, opportunity, to become aggressive and assertive, and all the while remain secretly subordinate to some man?

"I guess Emma Bovary would be a better choice."

"The book that brought you to our fair village."

"You remembered. I'm flattered."

"It's easy to remember what you tell me, Molly." His fingers played across her bare shoulders, along her spine. She shivered, feeling terribly vulnerable in this situation. "Why Emma?" he asked with the familiarity of one who was intimately acquainted with *Madame Bovary*.

She answered without hesitation. "She was a rebel."

"Is that how you see yourself, as a rebel?"

"Maybe. Not really. I don't know. I read the book as an adolescent . . . to stand against society the way she did, what bravery, resisting all the pressures and strictures meant to suppress a woman of spirit. It was easy to admire her."

After a moment's silence, he surprised her. "You read your mother's copy of the book?"

"No. I never knew she had the book, she never showed it to me. I borrowed a copy from the library. Unlike Mother, I returned it. On time. I always return books on time. There you are—I'm not the rebel I might like to be. Later, I bought a paperback copy to keep."

He was at her shoulder again. Kissing lightly, tasting her warm skin, working her onto her back and finding her mouth. She turned slightly.

"It's late. We should go back."

Purple shadows had begun to reach across the pond and the air vibrated with the chirping of crickets. She could hear crows cawing at one another and a splash that signaled a fish leaping and falling back. It would be so nice, so easy and natural. He was the most attractive man she'd ever met.

He caressed her cheek and kissed her again. Without urgency or passion, sweet, lingering, lips soft and skillful against hers, his tongue beginning to probe.

She felt the response begin. Ripples of warmth deep in her belly. Odd spurts of tension along her limbs, up into her groin as his hands explored her flesh, spreading the towel, caressing her breasts, his hard nakedness pressed against her. She sensed his power, a power that exceeded the strength of his arms and his legs, a power unlike any she had ever encountered, and it made her afraid. She trembled when his mouth settled onto one breast, his hand spreading her thighs insistently, making her feel weak and insignificant. She spoke his name aloud.

He didn't respond.

"I am not . . ."

"What?" he murmured, hovering over her navel, tongue flitting.

". . . not sure." Was he laughing at her?

"I am," he said.

"Not so fast, please. I'm not ready."

Past and present came together in his mind, leavened by a growing rage, the ballooning need to have his way, muscling aside all the rules. Laws of God and man were for lesser beings. Nels Proctor created laws of his own and, when those laws became irritants, he amended them to suit his purposes. Mother and daughter, parent and child; convoluted images rushed into his head, accelerating the passion, sharpening his compulsions. For a frozen interval, he was unable to respond, up against the outer limits of control.

He sat up and lit another cigarette, sipped his wine, struggled to regain full authority over his emotions. He poured some wine into her glass and offered it, smiling reassuringly. Very tenderly, very neatly, he drew the towel across her body, protecting her from the evening chill. He delivered a sweet, gentle kiss to her brow.

"You are the loveliest woman I've met. It would be so easy to say that I love you and to mean it."

She shuddered and sat up, accepting the wine. "I'm not a child but—something, I felt so uneasy. I wish I could explain."

"No explanation is necessary."

"I'm not Lady Chatterley after all," she said softly.

"Nor Emma Bovary." A pleasant smile removed any possible sting from the words.

"No," she said, sipping some wine. "Not Emma, either."

On Saturday morning, Barney Grubb escorted Nadine and her mother to the bus stop for the ride to Boston where they would board the plane for Fort Lauderdale. All arrangements had been made. All details checked and guaranteed. A paper signed by both women absolved Hollis Whitehead of any wrongdoing, duly witnessed and notarized.

"The pendant," Grubb said before the women got on the bus. Betsy Wirth handed it over wordlessly, then she and Nadine climbed aboard.

That, Grubb said to himself, is that. The incident was closed.

He watched the bus disappear from view and only then did he turn away, strolling along Main Street as it began to fill up with early morning shoppers. Grubb was pleased. Pleased with his role in this affair. Pleased with his continuing ability to make the right moves. Things were going according to plan and that imbued him with a sense of his own growing importance, an importance that would soon be enhanced beyond his most secret dreams. Soon he would begin to collect his just reward. The biggest reward of his life.

23

THE FOUR HORSEMEN gathered around the long, coffin-shaped table in the conference room of Nels Proctor's office. Heavy drapes over the tall windows kept out the chill of the night air, blocked out the empty silence of Main Street. At this hour the shops were all closed, the Berkshire Diner and Pie Bakery empty. The only sign of life was at the Joy Cinema where patrons were captured by the adventures of the moving shadows on the big screen.

"You're looking good, Hollis," Nels said in preamble.

Hollis lowered his eyes. Still shaken by what had transpired, his body and nervous system had yet to return to normal. Occasional cramps and trembling fingers were reminders of his ongoing desire for a drink. But he knew how much was at stake and was determined to overcome his weaknesses. "I'm feeling much better, Nels. I've even lost a few pounds."

After nodding in approval, Nels let his gaze travel unhurriedly around the table. One corner of his mouth lifted in a canny, secret grin. "Before we get down to business, take a look at these," he said, withdrawing two Polaroid photographs from his pocket and passing them around. "Who does she remind you of?"

"Pretty girl," Jay said, handing the pictures to Hollis.

"Nice," Hollis said, being careful. "Reminds me of somebody."

"Check those knockers," Gary said. "Wouldn't mind getting some of that myself."

Nels had debated with himself over whether or not to tell his friends about Molly Fairfax—who she was, why she had come to Old Brixton. In the end, he had decided it was only fair. After all, they were part of this, too.

"Think back," he said. "Somebody you all knew a long time ago."

Nobody came up with a name.

Nels cheerfully retrieved the pictures. "Molly Fairfax is what she calls herself. Daughter of Emily Fowler."

For an extended moment nobody spoke. Until Gary broke the silence. "Jesus, yes! The resemblance is there. Where'd you find these?"

"I took them myself."

Jay put his hands flat on the table as if preparing to leap up, to flee from a clear and present danger. "You mean she's here? In town? Living in Old Brixton?"

"Visiting," Nels answered.

Hollis groaned and held his head in his hands. Now he really needed a drink.

"What's going on?" Gary, always the pragmatist, demanded.

"Trying to dig up some information about her mother," Nels replied in that deliberate style he so often assumed. "Molly wants to know what kind of life Emily led and why she left town."

"What the hell for?" Gary shot back. "That all happened a million years ago."

"She also wants to learn more about her father."

Gary studied the pictures again. "Her *father*?" he said with a leer.

"According to Molly, his name was Michael Fairfax, a soldier. Does the name mean anything to you guys?"

Gary tapped the pictures with one stubby finger. "From the look of the girl, I'd say Jay here is her daddy. Check out those eyes—lifted right out of your head, Jay." A derisive laugh seeped out of him; Gary was enjoying himself. "Last man in did the job."

Jay kept his face blank. "That's not likely."

Hollis decided to join the fun. "The way I see it, that crooked tooth matches Nels's bite exactly." Gary applauded.

"You boys are trying too hard," Nels said.

Hollis sobered quickly. "Is she going to make trouble, Nels? If she hangs around too long, finds out too much . . ."

Gary added, "Hollis has a point. Who can tell what she's liable to come up with? At a time like this, none of us can afford to be tarred with that old brush."

"Relax," Nels said. "I told you, her father's name was Michael Fairfax. He was killed during the Bay of Pigs invasion, an all-American hero. Molly's going to find out nothing. Who is going to tell her anything? Not anybody who knows anything. After a while, she'll get bored and take off."

"How can you be so sure?" Gary said.

"Because I have been investing a good deal of time escorting Molly around—pumping her, you might say."

Gary slapped the table top appreciatively. "Pumping her!" His laughter was lewd and raucous. "That's good, that is. First the mother, then the daughter. You got balls of solid brass, man."

Jay was on his feet, his face flushed. "Nels, you can't mean that. It's indecent, it's . . . you could be her father."

"A little incest," Gary snickered, "is good for the complexion."

"Her father," Nels said evenly, "was Michael Fairfax."

"Sure," Hollis said. "You don't think that Emily was some kind of an angel. I mean—"

"We all know what you mean, Hollis," Jay said, easing back into his chair.

"Come on, Nels," Gary urged. "Level with us. She as juicy a piece as her mother was?"

"Back off," Nels said, his voice soft and rich, meant to placate and calm. His mind reached back to the afternoon at Devil's Glen and the sleek, animal perfection of Molly's body as she went running for the pond. There had been nothing sexual about it, nothing intentionally provocative. She had moved with the swift, smooth articulation of an athlete, a perfect symmetry to her figure.

He recalled the taste of her mouth, the way she fit against him when they embraced, the sweet female scent of her that even now lingered in the corners of his mind. To his surprise, she had caused him to feel in ways he'd never before felt, unloosing emotions that startled and even frightened him. Was this what people meant when they spoke of love, he had asked himself for the first time.

What if Jay was right, what if he *was* Molly's father? Certainly it was possible. And that possibility perversely intensified his feelings, made him want her even more, quickening his desire to cross into forbidden zones, to do what others dare not do.

Hollis, meanwhile, slumped broodingly in on himself, remembering Nadine Wirth and the other young girls he had experienced intimately over the years. Each of them so young and lovely, untouched by time, so vulnerable and tremulous. Each of them had aroused him to new heights of passion, blocking out the rest of the world, the reality of his life. No matter the preliminary, no matter the games played, it came down to this: Hollis pounding at young flesh with his fists, imposing discipline, accentuating the weaknesses of the girls and his own strength and power, reducing each of them to a quivering, subservient mass.

And always, at the peak of his excitement, with all that nubile flesh under and around him, he was transported back to Overlook Point that Fourth of July night, to Emily Fowler lying under him, moaning, broken, her humanness battered away.

Next time, he told himself, eyes shifting in Nels's direction, he would be more discreet. He'd make no mistakes. Choose a girl who wouldn't go weeping and complaining to anyone. No way he was going to give up the one true pleasure in his life. Not for Nels, not for Bunny, not for anyone.

"Nobody can connect her to us," Gary was saying. "Can they?" he added with considerable concern.

"There's Ralph Ortner," Jay said.

"And Barney," Hollis offered. "There's always Barney."

Nels raised his hands in mock surrender. He displayed his teeth in friendship and compromise, eyes flat and penetrating. "Maybe you fellows are right. Maybe we'd be better off if Molly left town sooner rather than later."

"But how?" Jay felt the same way he'd felt that night long ago, weak and helpless, unable to flee and unable to resist the demands of his friends. Catastrophe loomed, and none of them could do anything to prevent it. "We can't force her to leave." Jay's eyes swung back to Nels, settling responsibility on the stronger man.

"All right, I'll take care of the girl," Nels assured them, and a palpable sense of relief went round the table. "Now, back to business. Gary, let's hear your report on the mall."

Gary climbed to his feet, clearing his throat, obviously pleased with himself. "I've got some good news and I've got some better news." He waited until the approving laughter died down. "First the good news. Construction is advancing at a rapid pace. As you all know, I put on a second shift. Well, two days ago I ordered work to proceed on a round-the-clock basis."

"The costs!" Jay objected.

"That's overdoing it," Hollis said. "A night shift means double-time and—"

Gary looked over at Nels as if for support, but Nels was slumped over a legal pad, doodling idly, remaining detached. Gary turned back to Jay. "Come on, you know how much interest we're paying on the loans. A hell of a lot's going out and not just to your bank, either. This way, we may pay increased construction costs but we'll finish ahead of schedule, which means earlier occupancy, and the sooner rentals will begin coming in."

Hollis grunted. "I suppose that makes sense. But I still think we all should have been consulted."

"It was my decision to make. Anything that affects construction—hell, I know what I'm doing. Besides, the night shift is temporary, only until the snows begin."

"It's a sound move," Nels concluded, not looking up. "Next topic."

"Any new renters?" Jay said.

Gary glanced at his notes. "My people are working hard and doing a first-class job. I have a letter of commitment from Sears—they want fifty thousand square feet and the contracts are being drawn up. There have been queries from Shearson/American Express for a branch brokerage, and Bloomingdale's is doing a feasibility study—I'm optimistic about them."

"That's great!" Jay enthused. "The quality names are of primary importance."

"That's right," Nels interjected. "I've been in touch with a

number of outfits about the corporate park. Perkin-Elmer is
one and Marketing Corporation of America is another. I'd say
both will go along, if modernization of Route 46 goes
through—''

"That asshole of a governor is still against it," Gary exclaimed.

"But no longer an issue. I pointed out that he's stepping
down in eighty-six and I'm certain that the new governor will
be more cooperative when it comes to allocating state funds.''

Gary shook his head. "That depends on who gets the job.''

Nels directed a slight knowing look at Hollis, silent rein-
forcement of what had earlier transpired between them. "The
man who takes over the statehouse will be sympathetic to our
needs here in Owenoke County. And what's more, our friends
in Washington inform me there's a good chance of running a
ramp between exits twenty-one and twenty-two off the interstate, so long as the county accepts responsibility for the
connecting arteries.''

"Will that be a problem?" Jay asked.

"Not at all," Hollis explained. "I've talked to the county
executive about this. Without making a public issue of it,
we're also asking for an additional ramp this side of Laugh-
ton, to make the mall easily accessible from north and south,
bringing in shoppers from the entire western half of the state.
Why go to Boston or New York when you can do all your
shopping at the County Center?''

"That ought to be our advertising line, huh?" Hollis continued, pleased with his contribution.

Nels straightened in his chair. "We are going to turn this
county into a magic kingdom. Which brings me around to
another project. I've been in touch with people from Disney
and Six Flags. The odds are no worse than fifty-fifty that one
of them will locate a theme park in the area. Think of the traffic that would bring in. Think of the development. Hotels,
restaurants, transportation; the future looks rosy indeed,
gentlemen, as I told you it would when we began our little
operation.''

There was a brief round of applause, The Four Horsemen
pleased with themselves.

"Finish your report," Nels said to Gary.

"Right. National General wants to operate the theater complex. That will mean five movie houses opening at six-thirty or

so and providing an increased flow in late afternoon and evening traffic, a great selling point to commercial renters.''

He checked his notes. ''I've had an inquiry from McDonald's. They want a fast food exclusive—''

''Absolutely not,'' Nels said at once. ''With thousands of hungry shoppers every hour, the mall will be able to accommodate half the food franchisers in this part of the state. Why close them out? No, McDonald's will have to take what we give them and like it. What's next?''

''We're covering the retail trade from soup to nuts. Clothing chains, shoe stores—Sam Goody is signed and sealed and so is Recordworld. Waldenbooks is coming in and so is B. Dalton. Oh, yes, a number of supermarkets have inquired.''

''Is that a good idea?'' Hollis said, anxious to contribute. ''Won't that make us seem a little ordinary?''

''Nothing chintzy,'' Nels agreed.

''I'm discussing terms with The Food Emporium,'' Gary said.

''I like their image,'' Nels said.

''On the subject of food,'' Gary said. ''You may have heard of Jean-Claude Farrand, the nouvelle cuisine chef. His agent has made a proposal. He wants to open a fancy French restaurant. The idea would be that we share in the expense of setting it up, something elegant and expensive, in return for a piece of the action.''

''We're not restaurateurs,'' Jay said.

''But Farrand is,'' Nels answered. ''It's about time we had a first-class food and watering hole in the county.''

''My thinking, too,'' Gary said. ''Sure, we want the peasants—we need them. But let's get the big spenders as well.''

''Run with it,'' Nels said.

Gary grinned with uncontrolled glee, turning to face Jay Newell. ''You're going to love this one, pal. Northeast Savings and Trust wants to open a drive-in branch.''

Jay took the bait, his voice loud and agitated. ''No, sir! Absolutely not! Our agreement was that I would get first crack at any banking done in the mall. I'm holding you to it.''

A round of laughter circled the table. Jay sank back in his chair.

''Careful, Jay,'' Hollis said in a slight mocking tone. ''You're getting all riled up.''

"Cut the bull, Gary. You've got an asinine sense of humor."

"Back off, everybody," Nels said, putting an end to the discussion.

Five minutes later, Gary completed his report, and a pleased expression settled on his face. They all murmured their approval, and the meeting broke up.

Alone in the conference room, Nels sat slumped in his chair, deep in thought. Finally he reached for the telephone and dialed. It rang three times before he heard Barney Grubb's rough voice.

"Barney," he began without preliminary, "there's a small favor you can do for me."

"Whatever you say, Counselor."

"It's a matter of talking to a few people, applying a little pressure, calling in a few chits."

"You know me, Counselor. What's the favor?"

That was the trouble, Nels reminded himself. He did know Grubb, knew how swiftly the police chief went from a standing start to the red line, too quick to embrace violence in order to get his way. Nels wanted to make sure nothing like that happened in this case.

"A little subtlety is what's required here, Barney. A case of harassment, you might say. No heavy work. None. Am I making myself clear?"

"Perfectly clear, Counselor. Whatever it is you want me to do, I'm your man."

Yes, Nels thought, that was the trouble. Barney Grubb was his man, always had been. If only there had been somebody else to call on. But there wasn't, so he told Barney what he wanted him to do.

24

AT NIGHT, IN the apartment over the garage behind the main house on what used to be the Janson Estate, less than a hundred yards from the Public Library, Carl Becker assembled dinner with the quick, practiced moves that come from cooking alone most of the time. A wedge of cheese cut into manageable chunks, bite-sized pieces of pepperoni, tomato slices arranged on a plate. Some two-day-old Italian bread warmed in the oven and margarine in a container with fluted sides, along with a bottle of cold Heineken. He had settled down to watch the finish of *Magnum P.I.* when someone knocked at the door. He put the food aside without regret, switched the television off with relief and opened the door. Perry Maxwell, in green corduroys and a khaki golf jacket, grinned in greeting.

"Saw your light," he said, "and decided you could use a little company, old friend."

Becker led the way inside. "Just about to have some supper. There's plenty for us both."

Maxwell surveyed the platter of food tolerantly. "The way you eat, no wonder you're pared to the bone. What you need is a wife. Or a cook. Certainly a nutritionist."

"Speak for yourself—why aren't you married?"

Maxwell ignored the question, eyeing the beer. "I am a touch dry in the throat, however."

Becker fetched a second bottle from the refrigerator. He began to eat, speaking around a mouth full of cheese and pepperoni. "What brought you into the neighborhood?"

"Just passing by."

"You might've phoned, made sure I was in."

"Just passing—"

"I know, just passing by." Maxwell had changed very little since high school. He still approached everything obliquely, feeling his way one step at a time. A cautious youth, he had grown into a cautious man. It was that caution that had prevented him from developing into a truly outstanding basketball player, always looking for the safe shot, never risking much, always striving not to lose instead of going all-out to win.

"I've been thinking," Maxwell said.

Becker knew his friend to be deliberate and thorough, and not to be rushed. "What about?"

"About old Sam."

Becker kept eating. In his own time, Perry would get to wherever he wanted to go.

"The way I see it, most suicides do two things."

Becker swallowed. "Which are?"

"First, they leave some kind of a message in writing. Or they call a friend or a relative, somebody. Some of the time it's because they want to be stopped before they actually perform the act. Others intend to go through with it but they feel honor-bound to tip their hats to the life they're leaving behind."

"Sort of a farewell gesture."

"You might say that. Am I making sense so far?"

"So far. Have some of this cheese. It goes great with the pepperoni."

"Just a taste, okay. Yeah, that's good. With a tomato slice and a small piece of that bread." Maxwell filled his mouth, chewing deliberately. "That's real tasty."

"Second?" Carl said.

"What? Oh, yeah, second. Second is when a man is about to blow his brains out he makes sure the gun is in hard contact with his head before he lets fly. No horsing around—bang.

That way the job gets done neat and quick, if you follow my reasoning.''

"I'm still listening."

"Here's my point: there are no accidents that way. No misses. No painful but unfatal mistakes. Boom, and it's all over. No time to reconsider and not much time to be afraid. How am I doing so far?"

Becker put his plate aside and wiped his mouth with a paper towel. "Are we discussing suicide in the abstract? Is this some philosophical beer-drinking sophomoric bullshit session? Or are we talking about Sam?"

Maxwell cleared his throat. "Well, sure. Seems I'm not making myself clear. Sam is who I am referring to. I'm here to tell you that the investigation didn't add up to even a small pile of gnat droppings, according to my way of seeing things. One look and it seemed like everybody was satisfied."

"Who headed up the investigation?"

"The man himself."

"Barney?"

"You got it, friend. The medical examiner's and forensic reports were issued about as quick as a blink."

Carl brushed the hair off his forehead. "Well, if nothing was out of line—"

"Did I say that? Did I say nothing was out of line? The thing is, the county people came down and did most of the work. Fingerprints, checking the weapon, taking photographs, stuff like that. The force isn't large enough here in town to keep all those technical people on staff."

"What are you getting at?"

Maxwell went on without pause, his manner calm, as if he was delivering an official report. "Nothing was missing, so robbery was ruled out as a motive for a possible murder. These days robbers do a lot of killing to eliminate witnesses to their work."

"I keep up with the news, Perry."

"No sign of forced entry," Maxwell said. "No indication of a struggle. Nothing out of place, nothing. The weapon was in Sam's hand, his fingerprints all over it. Nobody could quarrel with the conclusion."

"Suicide?"

"Suicide."

"Only you don't think so, Perry? Like me, you believe something is wrong. Out of line—something was out of line. What was it, Perry? What makes you think Sam was murdered?"

"Not so fast."

"That is what you think, isn't it?"

"That's always been your weak spot, diving in when there's no water in the old swimming hole. If you want to claim murder, you've got to show motive. No motive, no murder."

"What if I can provide a motive?"

"Go ahead."

Becker repeated his conversations with Henry Streeter and Anna Slocum. "The bank was after the farm and there was no way Sam was about to let it go."

"Banks don't keep hit men on the payroll, Carl; they have tellers to process deposits. Banks don't murder people, they foreclose."

"I'm tired of that song. The bank called in Sam's loans, we know that."

Maxwell flexed his arm, kneading the huge bicep. "Some people would consider that reason enough to support a suicide theory."

"Not where Sam's concerned. It wasn't his way. Which brings us around finally to why you're here, I imagine."

Maxwell cleared his throat and drank some beer, examining the neatly trimmed nails on his fingers. "There were flashburns on Sam's temple," he declared almost as an after-thought. "According to the m.e.'s report, from the amount of powder in place, I'd say the weapon was held no closer than ten or twelve inches from Sam's head."

Becker felt his pulse racing. "Then he didn't shoot himself?"

"From where I sit the odds are pretty good that someone other than your father pulled the trigger."

Becker, eyes closed, plumbing his own deep emotions, sucked in a deep breath. When he did speak it was in a somber voice.

"The gun? I have to know more about the gun."

"It was judged to be Sam's property."

"Damnit, how many times am I going to have to say it? Sam never owned a handgun."

"A Luger," Maxwell corrected him with professional specificity. "It's an automatic."

"Check it out for me, Perry."

Maxwell pushed his plate aside. "Why am I eating? I'm not hungry and I never did much care for pepperoni. Check what out?"

"Who owns the gun?"

"I told you—"

"And I told you, Sam didn't have a handgun. I heard him say it more than once—handguns were made for killing people, no other use. Check it out."

"We don't keep those kinds of records."

"Sometime, somewhere, somebody owned the godforsaken thing. There's got to be a name attached to it along the line."

"I could go back to the county boys one more time."

"And the state police."

"Okay, I can do that for you."

"And the FBI."

"Barney's going to have to know."

"No!" Becker saw the look of surprise in Maxwell's eyes. "Not Barney," he said more calmly, manufacturing a reassuring smile. "Not anybody. Do it on your own."

"I'm a cop, Carl."

"This is cop's work."

"Only you mean for me to do it outside of the department, if I read you right."

"Just this once."

"What if I come up empty?"

"What if you don't?"

"If Barney finds out, there'll be hell to pay."

"We can handle it," Becker said with a grin.

"We?" Maxwell said with mock complicity. "I'll remind you of that when I'm kicked off the force."

25

IT BEGAN THE next morning.

Molly had breakfast in the Inn's dining room at a small table alongside the windows that looked down on the river. A few dozen Canadian geese clustered along the far bank and some ducks swam about not far from shore. She lingered over a second cup of coffee before making her way into the spacious lobby with its huge walk-in fireplace made of domestic stone. The manager, a small man with a neatly trimmed mustache and a starched collar, hurried forward to greet her by name.

"I was wondering," he said formally, "what time you'll be checking out?"

A sudden chill seemed to sweep through the low-ceilinged chamber; she shivered slightly. "Checking out?"

"Yes. You understood, of course, that yours was a limited reservation."

"I don't know what you mean. No limit was put on my stay."

"Other guests," he said by way of explanation.

"I hadn't planned on leaving."

"I'm afraid you must. We require the room as of this afternoon. Check-out time is noon."

"There can't be a shortage of rooms," Molly persisted.

"Reservations have been made—"

"You have only a handful of guests."

"I don't wish to argue with you, Miss Fairfax."

"Why? Have I broken some house rule? Given offense in some way? If I have, please tell me."

"We need the room," he said firmly. "As of this afternoon."

She strengthened her voice. "Mr. Haas, I insist on some kind of explanation. Why am I being told to leave without warning?"

"A notice was put in your box."

"I received no notice."

"I'm sorry, but there you are."

"I will not leave."

"I'm afraid you must."

"And if I refuse?"

"Please, Miss Fairfax. Neither of us wants any unpleasantness, do we? By noon, please."

"Where am I supposed to go?"

He pursed his pale lips. "I'm sure I can't say. But I must insist—"

She walked quickly away, trembling with a combination of fear and anger, wondering how to deal with this sudden turn of events.

She spent the remainder of the morning trying to find another place to stay. At noon she returned to the Inn and surrendered the room, leaving her packed suitcases standing unattended in the lobby while she returned to the search. It was the middle of the afternoon before she located a room in a private home on a dead-end street within sight of the old brass works, its dark windows gaping at the world like unseeing eyes. She transferred her belongings and unpacked, leaving the 280Z parked in the street. When she came back outside, the car was gone.

The emptiness of the long street, rippling with streaks of sunlight filtered through the overhang of leaves, was jarring. She felt herself thrust into a Fellini landscape—stark, uninviting, forbidding—a stranger in a strange land. Startled by the absence, she questioned herself: had she parked the car elsewhere and forgotten its location? No. Her mind ranged over the possibilities until, at last, she decided someone must have stolen the Silver Bullet.

She suddenly perceived cause-and-effect at work. Here was the direct result of all the questions she was asking, questions that were bringing her closer to some long-held secret Old Brixton didn't want uncovered. The town was closing ranks against her, masking off its dark past, setting itself against any intrusion. What human swamp was her presence threatening to reveal? An icicle of fear ran to the base of her spine, causing her to shiver.

Violated. Her life intruded upon by person or persons unknown. Cold-hearted sons of bitches. Caught between the impulse to weep and to wound, she was unable to order her thoughts, incapable of acting. She looked around for help; there was no one in sight. She started back to the rooming house and stopped short; minutes after she had arrived, her landlady had departed. Molly stamped her foot in frustration and hurried back into town to the police station.

The desk officer listened to her complaint as if he'd heard it all before; drug dealers, rapists, murderers were at large out there—screw one missing set of Jap wheels, although the dame was a prize package, he had to admit.

"Does this sort of thing happen much around here?"

A fantastic mouth, he observed. Allowing for that one crooked tooth, she had a terrific smile. And how about those lips!

"Nah, not much. Last time was last month. A couple of kids went joy-riding in Tookie Golden's new Le Baron. Black and shiny as could be, a thing of beauty, that convertible. Red leather seats, too. We found it after a few hours out near the old Flagler place. With the boys still in the car. Passed out cold, they were, two empty bottles of rye whiskey in the car. Most likely it'll be the same with your car, miss. We're bound to find it for you."

"What am I supposed to do in the meantime?"

He continued admiring her face. "Can't say that I have an answer for you, miss. We'll get in touch when we have something for you."

"What happens now?"

"It goes into the computer and the other departments in the state pick up on it. Also the sheriff's department and the FBI.

Stolen cars is a big part of what they do, the FBI. Chances are okay we'll come up with it.''

"Meanwhile, I'm out a car."

"I guess so."

She went directly back to the rooming house, where her landlady was waiting for her. "I've been hoping you'd get back soon, miss," she began. The jangling of the telephone drew her attention and she answered. Finished, she addressed Molly. "That was Officer Ferrante over at the police station. Says to tell you they found your car."

Relief left Molly weak but grateful. "It was taken right off the street out front here. They certainly found it in a hurry."

"Good thing, too. You'll be needing it."

"Why is that?"

"To transport your things, miss."

"What do you mean?"

"There's been a mistake, you see. The room I put you in, it was rented to a previous party but I forgot all about it."

"Is this some kind of a bad joke?"

"Joke? Well, no, miss, it's no joke. I took it on myself to pack your bags for you. They're in the sitting room, waiting."

"I won't let you do this to me!"

Leila Overton's voice grew shrill and her girlish face turned white, tiny fists pounding against her thighs. "We were supposed to have this time together, Nels."

"You were out when I phoned."

"I had things to do. I planned for this afternoon."

"It will keep." His manner was direct, offhand, as if addressing an inferior. "It will have to keep."

They faced each other in the living room, each standing at opposite ends, faced off as if in battle. She raised one fist in warning.

"Maybe I won't keep," she said, knowing at once it was a mistake. He was not a man to threaten.

"Think pure thoughts, Leila." He was mocking her.

"I'm not being funny, Nels," she whined.

"You are many things, dear Leila. I agree, funny is not among them."

He was taunting her, toying with her as if she were some kind of a fool. "Don't you patronize me." Damn! Why had she said that? It was as if he controlled her, forced her to react according to his desires. "It's still early," she said, changing strategies. "There's still plenty of time."

"I'm afraid not. It's time for you to go. Now."

She closed the distance between them in a few strides, putting herself up against him, pelvis grinding, hands stroking his flanks, gazing up out of feverish eyes. Her voice thickened. "All week I've been waiting . . . for what we could do. What I want to do to you."

He disengaged and stepped back. "Save it, Leila. For next time."

"Who is it?" she cried, a shrewd glint in her eye. No man she wanted had ever resisted her, unless there were some other bitch. It could be no different this time.

"I'm expecting a visitor," was his cool, infuriating answer.

"I won't leave. I'll kill her."

"You're beginning to get tiresome, Leila."

"Please don't treat me this way."

"I'm treating you precisely the way I've always treated you, the way you enjoy being treated. Goodbye, Leila."

"Prick," she hissed, raising her claws. An attack would be warranted, but she thought better of it.

He walked past her leisurely and opened the front door. "It wouldn't do for you to be seen here, Leila. After all, you are a married lady." Common little bitch, he thought impatiently. Entertaining in bed but nowhere else. Even ordinary conversation with her was impossible. TV soap operas, the mechanics of sex, the price of gold—nothing else engaged her imagination, such as it was. A vulgar bore, not worthy of all this effort. His hand went to the small of her back, propelling her out the door.

"When am I going to see you again?"

"I'll phone when I can."

"That's no good. You never call. I'm the one who has to call, except when you want to break a date. I'm always making up little lies to tell your secretary so she won't know it's me. I bet she knows anyway. I bet you told her all about us. I bet you're fucking her, too."

"Goodbye, Leila."

"How long do you think I'll stand for being treated this way?"

"If you think it's time to stop seeing me—"

"Don't say that to me! Don't you dare. You know I don't

want to end it, Nels. Please don't send me away. Let me stay and show you how much I love you."

"Leave, Leila."

"Who is she?"

"Discussion is terminated."

"Somebody's wife, I'll bet. Wives are safe. Setups for you. Hungry for what they don't get at home. Desperate for a little romance, and willing to put up with your craziness to get it. That's what you are, Nels—crazy. You know that, don't you? Maybe not certifiable, but weird. Abnormal. A person without feelings is crazy. Do you treat all your women as badly as you treat me?"

"There are no other women."

"Hah."

"You can't recognize the truth."

"You lie all the time. Even when you tell the truth, I think you're lying."

That made him laugh, a velvety sound with a harsh undertone. "If I admit that you're right, you'll think I'm lying. And you might be right."

"You're making me crazy."

"Consider this, Leila. Perhaps you're the one who's insane. Certifiable. Ready to be put away. Isolated from normal society. Think about it while you drive home."

"Son of a bitch. Screwing your best friend's wife and treating her as if she's a whore. Gary says you're the best man he ever knew, the best friend. You're perfect, he says. If he only knew."

"Why don't you tell him?" Nels challenged.

"Maybe I will!" she shrieked as the door closed in her face. "Maybe I will!"

The telephone rang and he wasn't sure whether or not to answer it. After the fifth ring he lifted the instrument reluctantly.

"Yes?"

"Nels, it's Molly."

"You are supposed to be here." There was clear disapproval in his voice.

"I'm sorry." Her voice cracked, the emotional wave cresting. She offered him a catalogue of the recent events.

Carefully controlled, he made no reply.

She repeated, "Taken, I said. The police towed it away. I don't understand—the only car on the street. There are no signs prohibiting parking. No yellow lines. No reason to take it away. It's almost as if they had a tow truck standing by, waiting for the chance."

Still he didn't respond.

"They're trying to get rid of me!" she cried in despair.

He maintained his silence.

For Molly, it was an effort not to cry. "Oh, I don't know what to think. Keeping me from having a place to sleep, one place after another, taking my car."

Finally he spoke. "Nobody's doing anything to you. You're overreacting."

"Do you know where the car was while I was reporting it stolen? In the parking lot behind the police station. Nobody said a word. Then, as soon as I got home, the police phoned my rooming house. It's as if they were taunting me. They knew, Nels, where it was. They knew all along and never said a word. Why?"

"As far as your car is concerned, it was probably towed by the people who do that sort of thing. Maybe it shouldn't have been, but mistakes happen. Then to compound matters, it probably wasn't reported immediately to the officer on duty. Nothing sinister in that. A question of timing, a simple mix-up."

"And my room at the inn?"

"You moved, you said?"

"Forced to leave, is what I said. Evicted without notice. Some feeble excuse about the room being promised to somebody else. The place is half empty but they refused to give me another room."

"Would you like me to talk to the manager? I know Haas and he strikes me as a pretty straightforward sort of man."

"What's the point? I'm out of there now."

"You're right. Why make a fuss when it won't do any good? By now you've found another place?"

"Yes and no." She told him what had happened at the rooming house. "I thought she was going to throw me out bodily, she was so anxious to be rid of me. Packed my bags and had everything downstairs waiting when I got back."

"None of this makes much sense."

"Would I make it all up?"

"Of course not. It's just that people around here are friendly and cooperative, that's all. Let me look into this first thing tomorrow. But now, you need a place to spend the night . . ." She could almost hear his mind at work over the wire, crackling as he plotted and planned. "Here's what I want you to do. Drive up to my house—you'll stay here with me tonight."

"No!" she almost screamed. Calming down, she explained, "Nels, I feel as if I'm under attack."

"A couple of coincidental events, nothing more. You have no enemies in Old Brixton. Only friends. I am your friend."

She wanted to believe him, wanted to show she believed him, to please him. But there were restraints on her normally open reactions. She had lived most of her life without fear and now, for reasons she scarcely comprehended, she was afraid. Afraid of the town and the people who lived here. Afraid, she admitted thoughtfully, of Nels Proctor.

That day at Devil's Glen, there was no fear then. His arms had been reassuring and strong, his physical presence exciting. And yet she had resisted his advances. Certainly she was attracted to him. Why had she held back? What had prevented her from accepting his caresses, his kisses, of giving herself up to the passion she'd felt?

Fear? Other men had been in her life before Nels, and in each instance she had been able to give of herself physically and emotionally without reservation. But with Nels it was different. He was the most attractive man she'd ever encountered, the most personable, and she'd responded almost at once. At the same time, some camouflaged threat left her confused and frightened, even repelled. Why had she suddenly become so self-protective and defensive? What was she afraid of?

Nels had been so sweet to her. No, not sweet, she corrected herself. Distant and contrived, all hollow gestures, operating out of a vacuum, with a forced detachment from his own center. Or was Nels right, was she seeing hints of danger where there was only genuine concern and coincidental mix-ups? "I appreciate your patience, Nels. Your sensitivity. But if somebody touched me now I'd scream or cry or throw rocks."

He laughed. "Can't have rocks thrown at me. The important thing is to get you settled, find you a decent place to stay."

"I'm all right now. Somebody's taken pity on me and taken me in."

"Oh?"

"I'm calling from Carolann's house. She found me moping over a cup of coffee at the Berkshire Diner and took me home with her."

"Who is Carolann?"

"The assistant librarian."

He ran the name through the chambers of his mind, summoning up a face to go with the name. The young one, plainly pretty, of no interest to him. Until now. She'd just become a minor irritation that would have to be treated.

"As long as you're safe for the night—"

"I'm fine now." She laughed to make the point. "In the morning, I'll call you at your office."

"I wish you were with me now, Molly."

"Me, too," she said lightly, not at all sure she meant it. "Good night, Nels."

"Good night."

For a long time he sat without moving, considering the situation. Visions of Molly naked at Devil's Glen intruded and he could almost taste her mouth again and feel her fine, firm flesh under his hands. Her beauty was stunning but there were qualities about her he could not define that made her even more desirable. How much of what he felt was rooted in who she was and in what he'd done to Emily Fowler? He had no answer.

It was too bad, he decided. No matter what might transpire between them, she had to go. He could not afford to have her around much longer. None of them could. He would talk to Barney, get the police chief to step up his actions against her, drive her away. Only then would life return to normal and allow him to attend to those things that really mattered.

It was still dark when Molly woke and sat straight up in bed, feeling lost and afraid. Sweat broke out across her shoulders, trickling into the hollow of her spine. She made an effort to clear her mind, to put herself back to sleep—it didn't work. Each time she closed her eyes, the events of the past twenty-four hours flashed into view.

She dressed herself in slacks and a cotton sweater, a loose-fitting suede jacket, and a pair of old tennis shoes, and went

out, careful not to disturb Carolann. She walked swiftly
toward the river, following the narrow path that bordered the
stream as it bent and changed direction below town.

She reached back to that day on Bluewater Hill, when she'd
been taken through the house that had once belonged to her
mother. Correction: had belonged to Cornelia. Emily had
been only a barely tolerated stranger. How awful it must have
been for Emily—so often alone, yet controlled and diminished
by Cornelia. A child without love amid so much material
splendor, Emily had been deprived emotionally and psycho-
logically, causing her, Molly reflected, to grow into a woman
in retreat and hiding.

So much was clear now. Emily's secretiveness about her
past, the body of lies she had erected to shield herself and her
daughter from that unloved and unloving history. What
choice did Emily have, except to put considerable distance between herself and Old Brixton?

And now, for Molly, too, Old Brixton had become a hostile
place. The barricades had been raised, the truth distorted and
withheld, while some concealed puppeteer manipulated the
forces aligned against her. She felt alone, isolated in a world
hostile and ominous.

Once, pausing, she thought she heard footsteps, but when
she looked around she saw no one and so continued on her
way. Abreast of the rapids, she was startled to see a man
blocking her way. She paused, then began a slow retreat.

He came after her. She broke into a run but he anticipated
her move and overtook her after a few strides, yanking her
around by the shoulder.

"No!" she gasped, struggling to free herself. He avoided
her blows and spoke in a low, rough voice. "Give me trouble,
lady, and I'll have to hurt you."

All strength and resistance drained away, and she felt
helpless in his powerful hands. Nothing she said would
dissuade him from delivering his awful punishment. Nothing
she did could keep her at last from getting exactly what her
fears and anxieties had been warning her about . . .

26

THE CALL CAME only a few minutes after seven in the morning. By then, Becker had completed his daily run of three miles, showered, shaved, and was working on his second cup of coffee. From the sound of her voice, he knew immediately that something was wrong.

"What is it?"

"I need your help."

Anything, he almost said. Anything, anytime, anywhere. He couldn't remember experiencing so much feeling for a woman he had known for such a short time. It went beyond her dramatic appearance and her obvious intelligence, into a metaphysical realm where souls were irretrievably joined into infinity. Love, lust, companionship, respect—all were part of what he felt, a mix that intensified each time he saw her. Knowing her made him feel great, top of the line, king of the hill. He sounded, he had to admit, like a lovesick fool, living out a hackneyed song lyric.

"Where are you?" he said without hesitation.

"I've been arrested—I'm in jail."

Less than ten minutes later—the time it took to pull on a pair of faded jeans and an old L.L. Bean shirt and run all the way—he was at the police station. He identified himself to the desk officer as Molly's attorney and as a federal prosecutor; the man was not visibly impressed.

"What are the charges against my client?"

"Soliciting."

Startled, Becker stared in disbelief. "Again, please."

"Soliciting. You know—it means she was on the street trying to peddle her ass."

"I know what it means. I want to see Miss Fairfax. Now."

"You got it."

When Molly was brought into the interrogation room, she looked disheveled, her eyes were rimmed with dark circles, and her mouth was drawn down. Otherwise, she seemed unhurt.

Becker waited until they were alone. "What the hell is going on?" She mistook the anger in his voice for accusation, his distress for disapproval. She began to weep, more out of despair than shame.

"Please don't berate me. I've done nothing wrong, nothing. I won't be blamed. I won't be badgered. I called you for help, not to shout at me."

"I'm not shouting."

"You're doing it again."

He tried to control his emotions, then started over again. "Please, tell me what this is all about."

Each sat in a straight-backed wooden chair, a small table between them. She sat with her knees together, hands clasped in her lap, her chin lifted defiantly, struggling for control. A pulse beat loudly in her ears and she had to blink back the tears that threatened to flow. She swallowed hard and began to recount the things that had been happening to her since the previous day.

"It started when I was put out of my room at the Inn . . ." She spoke in a low voice, artificially calm, finally coming around to the events of the night in question.

"I went for a walk," she said. "A walk . . . because I couldn't sleep—my mind kept leap-frogging around. Along the river, it's so peaceful and still. I thought a walk might help. Until this man appeared out of the darkness and dragged me off."

"A cop?"

"Of course a cop." Then, remembering: "I don't know. He never said."

"He never identified himself as an officer?"

"I don't think so."

"Did he place you under arrest?"

"I don't remember."

"Did he read you your rights?"

Her indignation increased. "No! He brought me here. He manhandled me. He pushed me and he swore at me. When I stumbled, he jerked me up as if I were a rag doll. I was terrified."

"Of course you were. When you arrived at the police station, what then?"

"They insisted that I identify myself. But I wasn't carrying my purse or any identification."

"Then? What happened next?"

"They put me in a cell."

"Before or after you called me?"

"Before. Only later, when I calmed down some, did I remember that I was entitled to make a call."

"And you called me?"

She hesitated. "I called Nels Proctor, but there was no answer."

A jealous spasm made Becker's skin twitch and he accused himself of being an over-emotional child. He held no claim on Molly. After all, he reminded himself, Nels Proctor was also an attorney. "What happened next?" he continued evenly.

"They fingerprinted me, took pictures, asked me a lot of silly questions, and put me back in the cell. It was a foul place. That's when I thought about calling you."

Again he hurt—he'd been her last resort. He filled his lungs with air and exhaled audibly, forcing the tension out of his face. "What did you say to the arresting officer prior to being taken into custody?"

"Damn!" she shouted with surprising force. "You're treating me the way they did. Like you're a moving part in the bureaucratic machine. I'm a human being, so treat me like one, okay?"

He held back a heated response. "Okay. Tell it your own way."

"He said I was to go along with him. If I resisted I'd be sorry."

"Did you?"

"Did I what?"

"Resist."

"Are you mad? The man was a six hundred-pound gorilla. How could I resist? Maybe I tried to free myself from his grasp. He was hurting me."

"That can be construed as resisting arrest. Who spoke first?"

"Spoke first? Why are you asking me that? He did, of course."

"Are you sure?"

"I don't know. Maybe I said something. Hello. Good evening. Something along those lines. It's called friendliness. Does it matter? My God, Carl, you sound like you're on their side."

"Molly, I'm on your side, and yes, it matters. It could matter a great deal. I'm trying to determine exactly what took place, that's all."

"I don't go around picking up strange men at four o'clock in the morning."

"Of course you don't. Funny, isn't it?—him being there, almost as if he'd been waiting for you."

She thought about that. "There was . . . I thought I heard footsteps. Behind me, first, then later on off to my right, as if somebody was hurrying to get ahead of me. But I didn't see anybody, so I put it out of my mind."

"There was no way he could have known you were coming out when you did, right?"

"What are you saying?"

"You must have been under surveillance. Who knew you were staying there?" When she hesitated, he coached her. "Carolann knew, naturally. Who else?"

"Nels."

"Anybody else?"

She shook her head.

Becker spoke with a great deal of conviction, "The guy who made the collar must have been watching the librarian's house, trailed you down to the river before making the pinch."

"This is insane."

"Maybe not. Maybe it's just logical." He stood up and moved toward the door. "You're forced out of the Inn, you are evicted from the rooming house, you lose your car, then you're picked up for soliciting. All of this could be connected and we just don't understand the logic that hooks it all together."

"Meaning it's all part of some master plan?"

"Meaning," he said, opening the door, "I am going to get you out of here now."

At the front desk, he asked to see the duty officer. "That'd be Lieutenant Williams. He's out on patrol, making a last swing around town."

"Who do I talk to to get my client released?"

The officer frowned. "No bail, Counselor. Judge Harris doesn't set up shop until ten a.m. You see, we don't usually get much night business around here."

"I want my client out of jail. Miss Fairfax is a woman of substance and what you people have done opens you up to a lawsuit for false arrest, damages, harassment, and entrapment."

The officer ignored the threat. "I'd like to accommodate you, Counselor, but I don't have the authority."

"Then find someone who does."

"Will I do?" came the careful rasp of Barney Grubb, just entering the police station, his fresh uniform giving him the look of a man very much in charge. He greeted Becker and turned to the officer. "Okay, fill me in, Frank." The officer obliged and, when he finished, Grubb drew Becker to one side, speaking confidentially.

"The arresting officer, Hood, is a good man."

"He made a bad mistake this time."

"Maybe the lady had the shorts, Carl—a pressing need for funds—and hit the streets. More than one hooker got started in the life that way."

"Molly Fairfax owns an art gallery in New York, Barney. She also inherited a great deal of money after her mother's death. Millions, in fact. She doesn't need to hustle for a buck."

Grubb rolled his big shoulders. "There are some girls who do it just for kicks."

"Come on, Barney. You've seen the lady. She's not the type."

"Well," Grubb said reluctantly, "let's say my man made a mistake—"

"Let's say he damn well did."

"Still, Hood's a good cop. A little impulsive at times, but solid. Maybe the lady approached him."

"She couldn't sleep, so she went out for a walk."

"At four in the morning? That would make most cops suspicious, Carl; it comes with the job."

"A hooker would starve to death looking for johns in Old Brixton at that hour. This town rolls into bed with the evening news."

Grubb chuckled appreciatively. "You've got a point. Riverside Walk ain't exactly the Minnesota Strip. Tell you what I'd like to do, Carl. I'd like to clean this up as much as you would. But with nobody getting hurt. Not your client, not my man, either."

"How do you suggest we do that?"

"The girl gets turned loose, right now. End of story."

"With all records destroyed. No arrest on the books. No prints. No photographs. Nothing."

"Done," Grubb said. "None of this ever happened."

"There's one more thing," Becker said, plunging on.

"Oh?"

"I'm talking about my father."

Grubb allowed himself a small, agreeable nod. "What about him, Carl?"

"I'm convinced Sam was murdered." Grubb, head lowered, resting one hand on his gun butt, listened. "A man committing suicide by gun puts the weapon into his mouth or against his head—"

Grubb broke in, not meeting Carl's gaze. "Sam shot himself in the head. The right temple. Forensics, everything pointed to suicide. The weapon in his right hand, his finger still on the trigger—everything."

"Two things bother me," Carl said smoothly. "The amount of powder on Sam's temple indicates the weapon was held about a foot away when it was fired. Suicides don't do that."

Grubb's head snapped up, and he looked directly at Becker, challenging. "Is that a fact?" He puzzled over Becker's words, barely suppressing his anger. That information came from the m.e.'s office and could only have reached Becker through someone with access to the files, someone in the department. Who was snitching to Becker?

"A man intent on blowing his brains out permanently doesn't do it from a distance."

"Conjecture, Counselor. You want to get this case reopened, you'll need more than that, I'd say." A slow grin of victory spread across Grubb's wide, fleshy mouth. "You said two things were bothering you?"

Becker looked the police chief directly in the eye. "Sam would never have used his right hand to shoot himself, Barney. He was a southpaw, a lefty all the way," he said. Turning his back on Grubb, he headed for the interrogation room to release his client.

They went along slowly, their minds sifting through all that had happened, searching for answers. It was Molly who finally broke the silence.

"Doesn't the idea of it bother you, so much happening so quickly?"

"Ordinarily I don't believe in conspiracy theories, but this time—"

"I feel as if the town has turned on me, that it doesn't want me here anymore. Why? All I've done is ask some questions, tried to find out more about my family. Who am I hurting?"

"My guess is that you're coming close to something that someone doesn't want revealed. Someone, apparently, feels threatened."

"What is it, do you think?"

He shrugged. "Something damaging, obviously. Something to do with your parents."

"But Mother left here so long ago, the summer of nineteen fifty-eight."

"Whatever it is, it's still a problem for our guy."

"Is this the way it was with Mother? Was she treated the way I'm being treated? Was she forced to leave here? For what reason?"

All good questions, Becker had to admit. As sensible and logical as those he was asking about the circumstances surrounding his father's death. Like Molly, he had felt the resistance, as if push had finally come to shove and a powerful force, concealed in the shadows, was indeed pushing back. Henry Streeter had dissembled, had sought to mislead him; Barney Grubb, appearing strong and resolute in his chief's uniform, managed somehow always to be at hand, but at the same time offered no real help to either of them; Jay Newell, talking dollars and cents and the letter of banking procedures, never admitting that a human life might take precedence. Who else was involved? The opposition had erected a facade of tranquility and friendliness to camouflage a steel curtain to keep him and Molly on the outside. They were unwanted intruders, asking too many questions. And getting too few answers, Becker concluded.

Back at the librarian's house, they discovered that Carolann had left for work. A note on the coffee table in the living room was addressed to Molly: "Please call me at library. Important. *Very*."

Molly made the call. "I just got back," she said, "and found your note."

"Something's happened," Carolann said. "I'm sorry, but I must ask you to leave."

Molly set herself against the anger that lodged in her throat. "Why is that, Carolann?"

Over the phone, the librarian's voice grew defensive. "A man came to my door this morning. He identified himself as a policeman—"

"—and told you to throw me out," Molly finished for her.

"I'm sorry, really sorry."

"What reason did he give?"

"I asked him and he said it was none of my business. He showed me a plastic bag filled with white powder. He said it was high grade heroin. Oh, Molly, I was so afraid! I've never touched drugs, never in my whole life. He said he would claim he found it in my car and charge me with being a dealer. Unless you were out of my house by noon, he said, he'd come to the library and arrest me in front of everyone."

"Don't worry," Molly said, no longer angry with Carolann, but unable to anticipate the next blow. "I'll be gone before noon. By the way, did he give you his name, the policeman?"

"Hood. He said his name was Hood."

27

"I DON'T BELIEVE it!" Becker slammed the phone down, his face showing pure exasperation. "I've tried every motel, every hotel, and every rooming house in a thirty-mile radius and came up empty. The last three places—they didn't turn me down until I told them who the room was for. I called back, using my own name and, sure enough, they were prepared to rent me the whole shebang."

Molly smiled wryly. "Seems I've become a pariah."

"Not to me. Why don't you stay here?"

"I don't think that's a good idea."

"Nels Proctor?" he asked glumly.

"This has nothing to do with Nels," she said, not sure of her words. "But it would be better if I didn't sleep too close to where you sleep."

"Can't control yourself?" he joked, with a false grin and an exaggerated wink.

She couldn't match his mood.

"Why me?" she asked thoughtfully, aware she was under attack and not clear what she'd done to deserve it. Who had she antagonized? Specifically, what had gone wrong? She tried to answer the questions; she had offended no one, had harmed no one. And yet a very real hostility existed and was

growing stronger every day, as if some force was determined
to drive her away, to conceal from her the history of her own
family. "I've done nothing to these people," she said with
sudden intensity. "And I am beginning to get very angry."

"You're prying into somebody's secret, a secret he—or
they—mean to keep that way. Your mother and my father.
They never even knew each other, but I'm beginning to think
that they're tied together somehow."

" 'Curiouser and curiouser,' as Alice said."

"A looking-glass world. Nothing about this affair makes
much sense."

"One thing does: a substantial portion of the local populace
wants me out of the way." By now she had accepted the idea
that unknown enemies were acting against her. Her mind
began to sort out the information she had collected, working
to assemble a recognizable picture. "What," she asked, "are
your reactions to Barney Grubb?"

Carl sat up a little straighter, his interest sparked, reaching
back for a fleeting thought. It slipped away. "Barney means
to be helpful," he said without conviction.

"You're not sure, are you?"

"Barney's okay, I guess."

"Neither of us is too sure of him, it appears. The man is so
amiable, so full of homespun talk and cheerfulness and
whenever I turn around, he is on the spot. Getting me out of
trouble."

"Keep talking."

"Okay. His cops tow away my car and return it to me. One
of them arrests me, Barney turns me loose. Same cop gets me
thrown out of my room. What good deed will Barney come up
with next?"

"He does pop up now and then, doesn't he? For a while I
thought he might be instrumental in getting to the bottom of
my father's death. Now—well, I don't know. He is not exactly
putting obstacles in my way but he certainly isn't helping
any."

"Could he be the connection between my mother and your
father?"

"I'll think about that. Looks as if we've come full circle.
Now you see a link between your mother and my father and
I'm the one who's thinking it doesn't make sense."

"It might, if Barney's the link."

He started to answer, then cut himself short. He picked up the phone and dialed. "Sergeant Maxwell, please."

He waited, then: "Perry, Carl here. A couple of quick questions. In case anybody's within earshot, just say a yes or no. An officer on the town force by the name of Hood, do you know him? Oh? But you know who he is? I see. Do you know anybody by that name? Thanks, Perry, I'll explain another time." He hung up.

"Well?" Molly said.

"It seems," he said in a measured cadence, "that the peripatetic Officer Hood doesn't exist."

"Hell, yes, you were absolutely right to bring her to me."

Anna Slocum planted herself in the middle of her living room and inspected Molly with the same fierce concentration with which she might inspect a pot in the final stages of its creation. Full of aesthetic judgment, evaluating the work.

"Let me tell you," she declared fervently, as if Molly weren't present, "I certainly do like the look of this girl."

"You said that the last time," Becker reminded her.

Anna made a sound in the back of her throat, sensuous and approving. "You two lovers yet?"

A hot flush of embarrassment rose up Becker's neck and he brushed at his hair, looking away. "We are just—"

"Friends?" Anna supplied caustically. She grinned familiarly at Molly. "Just? Can you tell me why the hell people say dumb things like that? As if being friends was lower on the scale of human relationships than being lovers. As if you can't be one without the other. Thing is," she continued, sliding the words around in a conspiratorial, teasing tone, "I'd guess this one might be fair to tolerable in the hay. With proper training, that is. Even his father required a certain amount of pulling and tugging to get his act in order."

Becker backed away. "I don't need to hear any more of this."

She eyed him speculatively before turning back to Molly. "They say the acorn doesn't fall far from the tree. If that's the case, you've got a live one here—"

Becker spoke quickly. "Molly's got a friend."

"Is that a fact?"

"Nels Proctor."

Anna stepped back. "Nels Proctor." She dragged out the name.

"We've been out together a few times," Molly said defensively. "You don't approve?"

"Not a match I'd've made, that's all."

"You don't like Nels?"

"It's not the point—what I like—is it? What matters is what you like. All right, enough small talk. You and I are going to be housemates for a while. Now, give me one reason why anybody wants to squeeze a good lady like you out of town? Doesn't make sense to me."

"Nor to me," Molly said.

Becker said, "Something to do with her mother, maybe. Emily Fowler."

Anna lowered herself onto the frayed Victorian couch that stood against one wall, her back straight, square hands resting comfortably on her thighs.

"I used to teach a course in art appreciation at the high school until I went off and married Ben Trumpy, which was back in nineteen-sixty. Lasted eight months until poor Ben had himself a coronary and died on me. Forty years old and dead. What a waste!"

She managed a small, nostalgic smile. "Emily Fowler was one of my students. A gangly girl, just starting to get her looks. If you had any kind of an eye you could see it, the beauty she was going to become. Great round eyes and a spectacular head of hair. Same color as yours, thick and wavy, growing long across her shoulders. She was unsure of herself, shy, like one of those rabbits you come upon sometimes out in the woods. Hippity-hop for a bit and stop, not certain which way to go. That was Emily. She never finished her senior year."

"She left town the summer of fifty-eight," Becker said.

"Did you know her mother?" Molly said, hope rising in her like sap in a tree. "My grandmother was Cornelia Fowler. She was widowed and later married Peter Matheson."

"I knew Peter slightly. Nice enough fellow but without the belly to amount to very much on his own. As for Cornelia, she was a different can of beans. Treated everyone in town as if they were dirt. She saw us all as being lower on the social ladder, much lower. Nothing about Old Brixton pleased her, but she was rooted here as surely as any of us. No matter where she went, she always came back, sort of recharging her batteries, you might say.

"Cornelia was a case. Girls were 'coming out' back then. Debutante balls and all of that. Cornelia came out in New York City, at the Waldorf-Astoria Hotel. Must have cost her daddy a considerable sum of money, but then old Teddy Kilburn—that was the family name, you see—was that kind of a man. Lots of money and willing to spend it on his little princess. No more than a half-dozen families from town were invited—all from Bluewater Hill.

"Cornelia never looked back after that. She married an Arab prince when she was nineteen, and he was killed a year later in a racing car at Le Mans. Which didn't seem to slow Cornelia down one bit. The marriage had made her royalty and she played it for all it was worth. She ran around with an English duke, and after him one of the Rothschilds, and then she married John Fowler, whose family went straight back to the Mayflower. The marriage lasted a couple of years and produced one child—Emily. Fowler died of pneumonia. After him there was the Italian actor and then a Greek millionaire and so on and so on. Until she got together with Peter Matheson. Peter, well, he hung on for dear life. He sat a horse pretty good and could drive a fast car or a speedboat. He looked good in clothes and doted on his bride. Just about what Cornelia needed in a husband. Peter stayed with her until she died."

"What about Emily?" Molly said.

Anna flexed the fingers of her right hand. "Emily was a sweet child in need of more affection than she received at home. The sort of child who made friends with the children of folks who didn't live up on Bluewater Hill. Families without money or status."

"Underdogs," Molly offered. "Mother was always for the underdog."

"Victims," Anna asserted, thinking back. "Except for Lauren Poole. Lauren was pretty and perky and popular. The rest were a sad lot. Damaged goods, you might say."

"When her mother went traveling," Molly said, "did Emily go along?"

"Not even once, to my knowledge. She stayed in that big old house on the Hill. There were always servants to feed her and see she had clean clothes. But a child needs more than that. Poor Emily. Cornelia was never one for looking after anyone's needs but her own." She lifted her eyes to Molly's. "When were you born, girl?"

"March, nineteen fifty-nine."

Anna nodded her head. "Fits like a glove."

"What does?"

"Well, the reason your mother left town—you know why?"

"Nobody's given me a good reason yet."

Anna frowned, eyes going from Molly to Becker and back again. "You might not like what I've got to say."

"I'd like to hear it anyway."

"Emily got herself pregnant that summer. Pregnant with you, I'd guess . . ."

Long after Becker had gone home, late into the night, they talked over hot chocolate and homemade banana bread, Molly and Anna Slocum. Molly told the older woman all about herself, about her childhood in Texas, about her father.

"Michael Fairfax, you say?"

"You knew him?"

Anna's expression firmed up. "Never heard the name before."

Peter Matheson's frail image moved slowly across the screen of Molly's mind, his reedy voice saying, "No husband, no husband."

Molly shuddered. "You must have known him. He was one of the most popular boys in town, Mother told me."

"In Old Brixton, no. As long as I taught at the high school, there was no Michael Fairfax. As far as I know, nobody by that name ever existed. Never."

Anna was wrong. She had to be. When Molly woke the following morning she was convinced of it. She had mentioned her father to Lauren Newell and Lauren had not denied his existence. Nor had Nels; what was it he had said? Something about not attending the wedding. Proof positive that he knew of Emily's marriage to Michael, that he had heard of her father. Anna's memory was playing tricks, that's all. Older

people had memory lapses. That's what it had to be. Molly
did remember her father. Vivid and alive as if it had all happened yesterday.

To let Nels know where she could be reached, she told
herself, was her only reason for calling him. But she could not
conceal from herself the continuing perverse desire she had to
see him again.

Why perverse? Was it the fact that he was nearly twice her
age? Hardly; she'd been out with older men any number of
times and enjoyed their company. Older men were often confident and patient, willing to court a woman and deal with her
as more than an object of their own sexual cravings.

With Nels, the attraction went beyond age. She could not
deny how she responded to him. More than that, he was attentive and concerned, but somehow always detached, strangely
untouched by her presence. That afternoon at Devil's Glen—
her emotions had been contradictory, flowing erratically, as if
switched on and off by an invisible hand.

What if he had persisted? Would she have capitulated? Certainly her feelings for him were strong enough, powerful and
pervasive, and still she had not been able to give herself completely to him.

Why had he stopped so abruptly? At first she'd been grateful and relieved. But later, when she thought about it, she was
made uneasy by the willingness with which he'd acquiesced.
She surprised herself by not knowing her own mind.

"I've been trying to run you down for two days," he said
over the phone. *Run you down* . . . the words struck a discor-
dant note. A warning flag went up in her brain, elusive,
unidentifiable, and fading rapidly.

"One hour," he was saying, laughter easing the threat. "If
you're not here in one hour I'm coming after you." She received the invitation with pleasure and relief, hopeful that
under his protective wing she'd be safe at last.

"Your house," she agreed, "in one hour."

She prepared herself. A hot bath in Anna's oversized tub
relaxed and revived her. A strategically placed drop of her
favorite perfume, Opium, here and there before dressing. She
chose her chiffon wrap dress with padded shoulders and a
clinging sarong skirt. Black teardrop earrings and a brilliant

Bulgari ring which she had given herself as a present to cele-
brate the first consequential sale out of her gallery. One final
glance in the mirror assured her that the look was glitzy, fem-
inine, arranged in a casual, expensive style, a placid mask over
her clashing emotions.

In the house on the side of Bluewater Hill, they drank Dom
Perignon and nibbled Ossetra caviar on tiny squares of toast,
the Brandenburg Concertos playing in the background, while
she recited her adventures of the last few days.

"When you didn't call, I was concerned," he murmured,
taking her hand in his, "that I'd offended you out at the glen
the other afternoon." He brought her hand to his lips. He
kissed each of her fingers. He touched the tip of his tongue to
her palm with all the delicacy of a butterfly lighting on a
blossom. "You've been constantly on my mind. When I didn't
hear from you, when I was unable to locate you, I became
afraid for you. I see now, I was right to be."

"Carl Becker helped me."

His fingers tightened on her wrist. "I should have been with
you."

"I did phone you."

The deep, flat eyes revealed nothing. "You did?"

"From the police station, at about five in the morning.
There was no answer."

"That explains it," he said, releasing her hand. "I often
shut off the phone when I'm particularly tired. Pull the plug."
He poured more champagne into her glass and fed her some
caviar. She was still chewing when he kissed her lightly on the
lips. His icy eyes looked straight at her. "You and Becker,
you've become close?"

"He's . . ." She searched for the right word and came up
short. "Nice," she ended lamely.

"He's more than that," he corrected her, crisp and businesslike, delivering his professional assessment. "Becker is
smart and aggressive, a young man on the move, in my opinion. Agreeable enough but not part of the accepted social
circles in Old Brixton. He'll continue to do well in Washington—all that ambition, all that hunger, for success—making career points at those slick cocktail parties. I suppose he'll
be going back soon, his job . . ." A benign smile lingered on
his face. "More caviar?"

She accepted the toasted square. "Carl is convinced his father was murdered."

"Suicide is difficult to accept. In time he'll reconcile himself to what happened."

"Unless he's right and it wasn't suicide."

"Barney Grubb has built a very efficient police force. This is a fairly peaceful community, but when a crime is committed Barney generally gets to the bottom of it. And Barney says it was suicide."

"You trust him?"

"Trust Barney? Of course. He worked his way from ordinary patrolman to chief. He's smart, tough when he has to be, and understanding—a good man. I've known him since I was a boy."

She put her glass aside and adjusted the sarong skirt over her exposed thigh. "There's something about all that's happened that's out of alignment. One of Grubb's men—by the name of Hood—forced Carolann to put me out of her house."

"That doesn't sound like Barney. He's a cop, not a bully."

"Hood threatened to plant heroin in her car and charge her with dealing."

"Over the years, I've come to know Barney very well. He would never tolerate such behavior."

"Maybe not. But Hood is the same man who arrested me for soliciting. He dragged me into the station house."

"Why don't I have a talk with Barney?"

"There's more. When Carl checked with a friend of his on the force, he found out that Hood is not even a member of the department."

"I don't understand that."

"Carl is convinced that Hood is not a cop."

"But he arrested you."

"Carl believes Hood is a thug that Barney Grubb brings in whenever he needs some goon work done."

"I simply can't buy that line of reasoning," he said in a matter-of-fact tone. "Barney has no cause to harass you. Nor that librarian friend of yours. I'd better talk to Barney myself, ask a few questions."

"And if his answers are unsatisfactory?"

"I know Barney too well. He'll level with me. We'll get to

the bottom of this, don't you worry." He kissed the palm of
her hand, a fleeting, skillful touch. "There, satisfied now?"

"Not really."

"What else is troubling you?"

"I feel—I no longer feel comfortable here."

"In my house?"

"In Old Brixton. In Owenoke County. When I arrived I fell
in love with the place and the people. Everything seemed perfect, a picture-postcard town in a perfect setting. The hills, the
river, the green countryside. The people were so friendly."

He smiled paternally, indulgently, or was it patronizingly,
she thought with a start. "Molly, you've discovered our
secret. We are not perfect. Not the town, not the people.
We're human, with human frailties. But still, Old Brixton is a
pretty good place to live."

She shook her head. "It's more than that. Now, beneath the
surface, there's something smoldering, corrupting everything
and everyone, spoiling the way life should be."

"Should be?"

"Yes, should be. Could be. There's an evil side to everything that's happening, Nels, and it's almost as though my
coming here has set the decline in motion."

He sat back, careful not to touch her. "I wish you didn't
feel the way you do, but I understand. Not everyone belongs
in a town like Old Brixton, not everyone fits in. I hoped you
would remain, reclaim your heritage on Bluewater Hill. I
wanted us to grow close, closer."

In the flicker of the candles his eyes were glassy marbles, impenetrable, reflecting brightly but revealing nothing.

"You're suggesting that I leave?"

"If you're not comfortable."

"Do you want me to go?"

His arms went around her, drawing her to him. "I want you
to be happy—in New York, in your gallery, surrounded by
people you know and understand. We'll still see each other
—I'd like that very much. Exchange visits, and more . . ." His
mouth touched hers.

For a long moment, she submitted, passive and unrespon-
sive, until Nels pulled back with a rueful smile.

"You're still not ready," he said, mechanically, raising her
hand to his lips, eyes holding steady on hers. "I understand

that. As you will see, I am a man of infinite patience."

She offered no reply; there was nothing to say. More than ever before, she had a sense that Nels was a man who would hurt her in some unknown way. Hurt her deeply. And that, she had vowed, was something she would never allow to happen again.

28

"LOOKING GOOD," Grubb said approvingly.

At his side, Nels remained silent, conscious that the big policeman was unpredictable and therefore dangerous, a man who might go off in any direction for reasons known only to himself.

They were at the building site, standing alongside an idle yellow ditchdigger, watching workmen erect cinder block walls which later would be masked off with shiny green tile. The County Center Mall was beginning to rise out of what had recently been farmland.

"What you see before you," Nels remarked as if delivering a prerecorded message, "will change the nature of shopping in the county."

"And put a great deal of money in a great many pockets."

"Including yours, my friend."

"But mainly your pockets, Nels. You and those three pals of yours. I'm in for peanuts."

Nels chose to ignore that comment. From time to time over the years he had made sure to cut Barney in on one project or another, to enhance the policeman's financial position. Just enough to keep him satisfied, not so much as to make him independent and thus impossible to control. To Nels, Barney was another employee—often helpful, in some ways his services unique, but still an employee—one of many that Nels commanded.

"I asked you along because there are a few items that must be discussed."

"Fire away, Counselor."

"The subject is Molly Fairfax."

"I'm listening." Grubb appeared to drape an invisible, defensive cloak about himself, assuming a still, combative posture. There was that about him, the alarming swiftness with which he went from the amiable caretaker of the public good to a man of rage and violence, a man to be reckoned with. "You said I was to give her a hard time."

"I said you were to make it uncomfortable for her to stay in town."

"Which is what I've done, Counselor."

"Arresting her for soliciting—that's a bad move. The girl's no hooker."

"Maybe so. Either way, I rectified the error."

"Don't be too sure. That goon of yours, Hood—"

The big face closed down, armored against possible assault. The small eyes grew smaller and the muscles in his jaw flexed. "Who said anything about Hood?"

"Molly did. She found out he's not a policeman."

"How?"

"Sam Becker's boy and she are friends. Evidently, Carl is tight with one of your cops."

Grubb swore under his breath. "That'd be Perry Maxwell. That really tears it."

"You've got to get Hood out of town."

"I'll take care of him."

"Be sure that you do. Now back to square one. I want you to back off the girl, leave her alone."

"Getting to you, is she? She is surely one superior piece of work. I credit you, Counselor, I certainly do—mother and daughter, you diddle them both?"

"Watch your mouth, Barney."

Grubb's response was both sly and to the point. "The girl doesn't mean squat to me. So her mother got herself banged way back when—no skin off my nose. Nobody cares anymore, least of all me. What's done is done. All I've been doing is lending a helping hand, like you asked me to. Trouble is, it ain't the girl that's the primary problem."

"Meaning?"

"Meaning Carl Becker, that's who I mean. That fella is becoming a burr under my hide."

"Slow down, Barney."

"Don't you tell me to slow down." Grubb growled, his face turning red, the tiny eyes glaring sharply. He waved one thick arm, encompassing the construction site. "You wanted—you *needed*—Sam Becker's place. Jay Newell said it flat out, 'We got to have it to complete the parcel.' Hollis said more than once that without Becker's farm there wouldn't be a mall. You said yourself the deal would be blown without Sam's land."

"Nobody said he was to be killed."

Grubb snarled. "Nobody said otherwise. I remember your exact words: 'We've got to get rid of him, *one way or another*. What can you do to help, Barney?' is what you said to me."

"You were never ordered to kill Sam Becker."

"The hell you say! By meaning, by expression, by emphasis, that's exactly what happened. 'Kill the bastard!' was what you were telling me. What you begged me to do for you. Every single one of you knew there was no other way. Sam wasn't about to give up that farm. You knew it, we all did. That man had his back up and he was plenty smart. Somehow, someplace, he was going to raise the money he needed."

"Killing is not an acceptable solution to a business problem."

"You tried everything else, buddy—buying him out, scaring him out, driving him off the land. Nothing worked, which is why you dumped it in my lap. 'Do it for us, Barney.' You said it in a hundred different ways. You wanted him dead. You needed him dead. And no one else around had the balls for the job. 'I'd appreciate your help in this matter.' Remember saying that, Counselor? You knew what you were asking for and so did I. Well, you got what you asked for—and now it's my turn. Exactly like Newell's bank, I am calling in this debt."

"Oh?"

"What goes around comes around."

"You're going to explain that, I'm sure?"

"My time's come, Counselor, my time for moving to the head of the line, for putting myself on top of the hill. No more living down below, Counselor. I want a fancy wife in a fancy house with a fancy car in the garage. For a long time I've been doing dirty jobs for you and your family, for all of you. Twice I yanked your burning chestnuts out of the fire. Two separate times I saved your ass. I don't forget.''

"We could have bought David off, convinced him and his family to leave town."

"Like the Wirth woman? Not a chance. That boy was a straight arrow. The fool kid believed in Santa Claus and the tooth fairy. He kept talking about justice and the law, can you imagine that? Poor silly kid. He was the only eyewitness to what took place on Overlook Point that night and he would have pinned every last one of you to the wall."

"You didn't have to shoot him."

"You were standing right there, Counselor, when your father said it—'Get rid of the boy, Barney. Do this for me and I'll be in your debt forever.' That's what your father said and you were right there with a shit-eating grin on your face because you knew, him and me, we were going to take care of everything for you. Saved your ass, I did."

Nels, masking his unease with a soft, placating manner, said, "You did what seemed best at the time. And rose to become chief of police as a result. I brought you in on the first office park we built and that presented you with a tidy profit. Since then there have been other deals—equally good, equally profitable. You own stock in the mall. I'd say you have no cause for complaint. Be satisfied—"

"Satisfied!" Grubb almost choked on the word. "Is that what you and your friends are—satisfied? Not so's anybody can notice. Well, neither am I. I want more, a lot more, and this time around I'm going to get what I want. That supermall of yours gonna make millions for you. I heard Newell, 'The first of many,' he said. 'An entire chain of malls, I can see it coming.' ''

"That's a pipe dream."

"I want in on it."

"You are in on it."

"The stock? That's small change. I am talking about my rightful share."

An icy calm settled over Nels. He let the words out one at a time. "What do you perceive as your rightful share?"

"First, I mean to become security chief for the mall, for all the malls. I'll quit the cops, take my pension, start up my own company."

"That can be arranged."

"And I'll have to have a stronger stock position."

The corners of Nels's mouth lifted and Grubb took it for a smile of assent, convinced he had read the other man accurately. Like the others, Proctor was no different under pressure, backing down, unwilling to risk the consequences of hand-to-hand combat. Grubb matched the smile.

"My time is here, Counselor."

"So it seems, Barney."

"Then you agree to my demands?"

"You'll get what's coming to you."

"Make book on it. Nobody is about to do me out of a penny. Not you, not your friends, not that piss-ant Becker. No way am I about to let some smart ass Jewboy lawyer come in here and fuck me around. If he keeps going, he might get lucky and tag me for taking out his old man. And I am not about to let that happen."

"Stay loose, Barney," Nels said softly.

Grubb, certain he had won everything he was after, answered expansively. "Not to worry, it's all gonna work out. Great day, ain't it? Another couple of weeks and the hunting season kicks off. You and me, Nels, we are going to get us a couple of first class bucks this time. First class."

"I have to see you."

The message was waiting when Nels returned to his office. A bothersome note: *Call Leila*.

He swore under his breath. She was not permitted to leave her name, yet she had, thereby linking them up in a way he wished to avoid. Stupid woman. Alone in his office, he considered the best way to deal with her. She had become predictable, demanding, and boring. It would have been preferable if she had fallen away—as all the others had, without complaint or fuss—simply disappearing into the void. But she persisted, claiming more of his time, more attention than he chose to provide. Now she was a problem that had to be solved.

He made the call. "This is Nels."

"I must see you right away." Over the phone her voice was demanding, laced with a breathless sexuality. Her beauty, combined with that blatant sexuality, had drawn him to her in the beginning. Few other women he had known were as intense and passionate, so desperate to please and so insistent on being pleased. For someone as dull and uninteresting as she was usually, she knew an infinite number of ways to provide pleasure in bed.

And always there was Gary. Nels delighted in knowing that she loathed her husband and mocked him whenever she had the chance, reveling in Gary's sexual inadequacy.

"Not today," he insisted.

At other times, when he refused her, she had pleaded for a meeting. This time there was a rising demand in her voice he'd never noticed before and it troubled him. "I'll be at your house in fifteen minutes," she said. "If you're not there, I'll come directly to your office."

He considered testing her resolve but gave it up as too risky. What if she did show up at the office, make some sort of a scene? What if she made their affair public with an hysterical outpouring? He couldn't chance it. "Fifteen minutes," he said and put down the phone.

She was waiting when he arrived, trim and chic in a red wool jumpsuit with a standup collar and brass buttons. A soft leather belt was cinched tightly around her slender waist. She had arranged herself artfully next to the matching red Italian sports car, one pale hand resting lightly on the hood, as if posing for a fashion photographer.

He went inside without acknowledging her presence. She hurried after him and he swung around to confront her.

"What do you want?"

She perched on the high-armed corner section of the gray suede modular couch which had been custom made for him in Paris. "Bastard," she hissed.

He settled himself in the Eames lounge chair, adjusted the seams on his twill trousers, then raised his eyes to meet her. "I don't have a great deal of time, Leila . . ."

"You filthy son of a bitch," she said in a voice quavering with emotion. "You lied to me. I won't let you treat me this way."

He placed his hands flat on his thighs and pushed himself erect. "Get out," he said in an ordinary voice, made more fearful for being so.

She sank down onto the couch. "Do you know how long it's been?" she wailed, the pretty face screwed up in anguish.

He regulated his breathing. She was a minor annoyance, he reminded himself, easily disposed of. Of course, there were complications. Gary—her husband, his friend—could become a problem.

"Be nice," he said, "or leave now."

"You are so cruel. It's been two weeks, nearly two whole weeks. Who do you think you are to ignore a person for weeks yet when you snap your fingers I'm supposed to jump? Why do you treat me this way?"

"Is that it? What you came to say?"

She was on her feet now, her face distorted by anger. "You think you can put something over on me? Well, you can't. I know all about that girl, what you're up to. The whole town knows. Do you know how much I love you?"

"Leila, I want you to go. Another time, when you're calmer, we'll talk."

"I'm not imagining it. I saw her. I was here." An explosion of sound erupted out of her constricted throat, frustration and disbelief at the situation in which she found herself. In the past, men had always pursued her, sniffing at her skirts, pleading for her attention. But not Nels Proctor.

"The other night," she continued, "I parked up the hill out of sight. I saw her go inside and I know when she came out. Bastard, you never let me stay that long."

Vaguely pleased by this display of jealousy, yet apprehensive about where this might lead, he said noncommittally, "You are a married woman."

"Nels, Nels," she pleaded, coming forward. "She can't do anything for you that I can't. Whatever you want, tell me and I'll do it. You used to tell me I was the best, that I gave you the best sex you ever had. I'll still be the best, just give me the chance."

She went to her knees on the oriental rug in front of him, fumbling with his fly. He watched her with mild curiosity. Her mouth closed around his slack penis, sucking hungrily.

"What's the matter?" she said at last.

"There is nothing here for you."

"That never happened before."

"It's over, Leila."

"No" she said. Then, screeching, "No!"

"It would be better for everybody if we parted as friends."

"Friends? You're nobody's friend. You don't feel anything for anybody—there must be something wrong with you. That's it!" she cried, her voice undulating crazily. "You're queer, aren't you? A flaming faggot! Wait till people find out that the great Nels Proctor can't even get it up. Wait till Gary finds out that his precious pal, his all-American hero, his best friend, is a fairy—''

His hand shot out, grasping her by the upper arm, propelling her forward. She protested, struggled, struck out at him. He opened the front door and shoved her out, sending her tumbling along the rough brick path.

"Oh, please," she cried, on her hands and knees. "Please, Nels, I'll be good. I promise I'll be good. Don't throw me away . . ."

He stepped back into the house and closed the door behind him. Later, having showered and donned fresh clothing, he went out to his car. She was gone. It was over, he assured himself, and about time. He was rid of the bitch once and for all.

29

MOLLY KEPT HOPING for some kind of magic break-
through—all questions answered, all problems solved. She
was on her way to see Peter Matheson again, driving without
haste along a winding road, the sky blotted out by a tunnel of
greenery. Soon the leaves would begin to change colors, and
then the clouds of autumn would give way to the long New
England winter. Part of her was ready to give up her quest, to
leave Old Brixton behind, to put her mother's past out of
sight. But a deep stubbornness kept her going, along with the
certainty that, if she continued to ask the right questions,
sooner or later she would hit upon answers that made sense.
And Peter Matheson, she was convinced, was the key to the
puzzle.

Once again the old man mistook Molly for her grandmother, his wife Cornelia, and the tears began to flow. Whatever else Cornelia had been, she had played a profound role in
Peter's life. He drifted in and out of nostalgic reveries, mean-
ingless to Molly until he zeroed in on a night long ago, speaking of it as if it as still going on.

Late in the summer of 1958, Peter and Cornelia returned
from a three-month tour of the Mediterranean aboard a
friend's yacht, after spending the last weeks of their holiday

on the Greek island of Skiathos. They were tanned and sleek and planned to remain in Old Brixton until the beginning of winter, when they would head for Palm Beach.

For three days mother and daughter exchanged very few words, certainly none that were intimate or revealing. Their encounters were mostly by chance, their meetings strained, crackling with barely concealed hostility. Cornelia had never really wanted a daughter, had never wanted a child of either gender. She held Emily to be a burden that offered no pleasure. She considered the girl ungainly and plain, an embarrassment whenever Cornelia's friends were around. Thus it was more out of curiosity than concern that Cornelia inquired one morning when she heard Emily retching in the bathroom.

"What seems to be wrong?"

"I'll be all right."

"Shall I summon Dr. Ortner?"

"I'll be all right, I said."

"You look awful to me. Pale and gaunt. Get out into the sun, why don't you? Put some color in your face. People will think I mistreat you."

In answer, Emily began to weep. Cornelia, watching silently, wished as she had before that there was some simple way to unburden herself of this bothersome child. She was grateful that Peter, perhaps recognizing the limits of her maternal devotion, had never expressed a desire to have a child of his own. Should that have been the case, of course, the marriage would have been dissolved. To spend nine months of her life discomforted and shapeless, plus the indignity and pain of childbirth, plus the years of a wailing infant, an intrusive toddler, was more than she could ever bear again.

"Stop blubbering," she commanded Emily. "You never see me cry; tears indicate a flawed character. Get hold of yourself, young lady."

"I . . . I . . . I want to die."

Cornelia glared at the girl, her offspring, huddled on the edge of the bathtub, rocking back and forth—a miserable child with not a single redeeming feature. How could she have given life to this ugly duckling? What confluence of genetic deficiencies—all of which she ascribed to her late husband, Emily's father—had left her with this pitiful creature.

"Stop sniveling!"

Uncontrollable spasms jerked Emily's body until Cornelia grew alarmed. "Stop it!" she cried. "Have you become spastic?"

Emily marshaled her resources. "What am I going to . . . do?"

"Do? You are going to get control of yourself. Wash your face, make yourself presentable and start acting like a member of the human race."

Unaccountably, Emily began to laugh, an extended choking sound that carried on too long. Staring at her mother all the while, clapping her hands, slowly coming to her feet.

Cornelia was convinced, as never before, that the child had lost her senses. "What is wrong with you?" she demanded, clearly offended by this unplanned turn of events. "What are you doing?"

"I," Emily spat out in a thin, venomous burst, "am going to have a baby."

Cornelia absorbed the impact of those words in the blink of an eye, their current meaning and future impact. Color drained from her angelic face and she emitted a piercing cry of desperation. "Peter! I need you!"

He came running. "Is something the matter, sweetheart?"

"She," Cornelia declared, finger pointed with regal contempt, trembling with the enormity of her offspring's betrayal, "has allowed herself to become pregnant."

"I see," Peter said, thinking it over.

"Is that all you can say?" Cornelia said.

"When," Peter asked, out of concern, "is the baby due?"

Cornelia turned back to Emily. She could see this was something she'd have to take care of herself. "How stupid, to allow yourself to get caught. Have you no sense of right and wrong? How could you do this to me?" The words came rushing out.

The question—more an accusation—was so grotesque that Emily could not respond at first. Then, in a sudden outpouring, she recited the events of the Fourth of July night.

Cornelia raged on. "What possessed you to participate in such a revolting pastime? Have you no pride at all? Four of them, one after another."

"No, no! You don't understand."

"I understand precisely exactly what you've done."

The words reverberated with increasing effect in Emily's

mind. All her life had been leading up to this moment, to a new, meaner level of confrontation with her mother, a place from which there was no turning back. Guilt and terror seared her mind: she the victim, was being transformed into the criminal. *By her own mother*. A low wail escaped her lips.

"They forced me. Beat me and held me and forced me." She named her assailants.

"No more lies," Cornelia broke in. "You've always had an overly-dramatic imagination. Those boys—from the best families in town. Oh, I know what happened—you accommodated the filthy lust of some boy who saw you as an easy mark. Now you have to pay for your indulgence."

"They raped me!" Emily shrieked. "Four of them raped me . . ." Her voice trailed off.

"Very well," Cornelia said, in control once more. Her manner was crisp. "Very well. You've made a mess, Emily, and once again it's up to me to clean it up. Very well. But this time you are going to learn from your error." She glanced at Peter. "It shouldn't be difficult to arrange."

"Arrange?" Emily whimpered.

"Corky," Peter said, "Couldn't we discuss this later?"

"There is nothing to discuss. My mind is made up. We'll get rid of the brat, which is what I should have done years ago."

"No!" Emily screamed.

Her mother went on without pause. "Ralph Ortner will be able to put us in touch with a suitable person, if he's too squeamish to perform the procedure himself."

"I won't—"

"The arrangements must be made as soon as possible. Once this is out of the way, it's off to boarding school with you, young lady. It's clear that you cannot be trusted to look out for yourself."

"No!"

"You will do as I say."

"No, I said. I won't let you do this to me. I won't help you kill my baby. I want my baby."

"You're being hysterical and impractical. In years to come you'll thank me for helping you."

"No," Emily said again, backing away. "No."

Cornelia's temper escaped her control. "All right. If I can't force you to save yourself, I can certainly save this family

from disgrace and shame. I want you out of here today. At
once. Before nightfall.''

"Corky," Peter remonstrated mildly, "she's your daughter.''

"If you can't be helpful, Peter, don't get in the way."

"She's only a child herself."

"Old enough to get herself into this trouble."

"How will she live?"

"Oh, don't worry, I'll see to that." She swung back to
Emily. "You'll be provided with funds sufficient to your
needs. I'll establish a trust fund that will allow you to live in a
decent fashion, but you will not be permitted access to the
principal amount. You are not now and are never likely to be
responsible enough to conduct your own affairs. The necessary arrangements will be made with the lawyers, the banks,
whatever is required.

"But this is the end of it, Emily. You have inconvenienced
me for the last time, embarrassed me once too often. You are
not to look to me for additional assistance, no matter what
trouble you get into, after the lack of consideration you've
displayed. You are never to contact me again. Should you do
so, I shall not respond or acknowledge you in the slightest
way. You have, after all, brought all this on yourself, by
yourself.''

Molly wept for her mother, and Peter, palsied with age,
wept with her. "They oughtn't to have done it," he muttered
presently. "Not the right thing to do. That boy, he was a good
boy. He wanted to do the right thing. Poor, poor David . . .''

It was not until she was back in the 280Z, on her way back to
town, that she thought to ask, who was David?

Molly woke in the middle of the night, clutching the worn
Teddy bear, and in the darkness imagining her mother. The
Emily she perceived was only seventeen, rejected by her
mother, cast out and forced to live her life alone in a strange
place without family or friends. How frightened she must have
been. How filled with anguish and despair, sacrificing
everything for her unborn daughter. Waves of emotion broke
over her and she spoke aloud, saying, "I love you, Momma. I
love you.''

In the morning, as she drank her coffee, she heard the phone ring. Its harsh jangle startled her. She snatched it up.

"Yes?"

"Is this Molly?" a muffled voice said.

"Who is this?"

"I won't call again . . . The man you are seeing, he may be your father, your real father. Please, stop before it's too late." There was a click followed by a dial tone, and nothing more.

30

"YOU'RE SCREWING MY WIFE!"

The words echoed from the high walls of the abandoned rock quarry, bringing Nels around in the direction from which he had come. Emerging from behind some boulders that guarded the path up the quarry wall was Gary Overton, a Colt .45 clutched in one big hand. The weapon was pointed at Nels's belt buckle.

"Gary," he said in a carefully modulated voice, hands outspread, a winning smile on his finely shaped lips, "what is this all about?" He knew at once what had happened; Gary had found out about him and Leila. Had someone seen them together? Not likely; he had been careful not to be seen with her in public. Someone might have spotted her leaving his house; possible, but again not likely. He had taken every precaution.

That left only Leila. She had created this situation, seeking revenge. Obviously she had told Gary about their assignations. Damnable double-dealing slut, doing this to him. What could she have been thinking? He widened his pale eyes in simulated innocence, producing an even wider smile.

"Hey, Gary, pal. This is Nels, remember?"

Gary shoved the .45 forward, advancing behind it, his face constricted in unassuageable anguish, his mind concentrated on punishment deserved. The hand holding the automatic was trembling.

Nels weighed his options. Gary, closing the gap between them, blocked the only way out of the quarry. To Nels's back lay the dark water that had transformed the old quarry into a small lake. Off-limits to the youth of Owenoke County, it had nonetheless served all of them at one time or another as a swimming hole.

"You're screwing my wife," Gary said again, wondering how this had happened to him. This nightmare was an intrusion into the plans he had made for his life. To build, to sell, to make himself rich many times over. To fight when he had to, yes, but never to shoot his best friend. Never to be the wronged husband, betrayed and crazed. What had brought him to this moment, about to kill Nels Proctor?

Nels, his manner cool, giving no emphasis to the statement, said, "You've got it all wrong."

Gary shook his head, blinked; he couldn't think clearly. "I have to kill you, what else can I do?"

"You can put down that gun."

"But first I intend to shoot your balls off. An eye for an eye, as I see it."

Nels manufactured a confident, pleasant laugh. "Okay, let me guess. You've discovered coke, is that it? Let me tell you, pal, better change your crutch; the stuff you're using is destroying your gray cells."

"A few drinks is all I had. Who wouldn't after what Leila told me?"

That *bitch*. "What's to tell?"

"Bad enough she was fucking around behind my back, that didn't surprise me. I knew what she was when I met her, but I figured she'd get straight when we got married. But you are supposed to be my best friend."

"I'm still your friend, and it's ridiculous for us to be in this situation." He took a forward step, testing the water.

The automatic came up in a white-knuckled, shaking fist. "Don't you lie to me!" Gary growled.

Nels froze in place. He calculated the distance that separated them; he was not nearly close enough.

"What put this notion in your head, Gary?" He needed time to think, time to figure a way out of this dilemma, time to get the gun away from Gary.

"Stand still!" Gary pumped his lungs up with a succession of short, noisy inhalations. Do it, he commanded himself; shoot now. "I can't believe it," he said in final resignation. "She sat me down, put a drink in my hand and served me crackers and cheese. You should've seen the way she looked, all decked out in one of those long gauzy skirts I bought her down in the islands last winter. You can see right through it and she wasn't wearing a thing underneath, nothing. I told myself she was feeling horny and trying to work me up. She gave me that sweet, girlish look of hers and told me how much she liked to suck your cock."

"No," Nels said, his anxiety spreading. "This is some kind of a mistake."

"No, no mistake. Maybe I'm not the smartest guy in the world, but I can read Leila. She's not smart enough to make up a story like that and carry it off. Not Leila. Besides, I could smell her."

Nels inched ahead. "Smell her?"

"She was wearing this perfume that I paid a couple of hundred bucks for in France—she must've bought a gallon of the stuff. Some faggoty frog gets rich so that my wife can send out signals when she's got a hard-on for somebody."

"Not me, Gary, believe me."

"My ass. She told me straight out. 'I have been having an affair with Nels Proctor,' is the way she said it. My pal, Nels, my asshole buddy."

"It's some kind of a joke."

"That's another thing Leila's too dumb to do—joke. Never jokes, not about anything. Especially not about sex. When it comes to her nookie my Leila is grim and serious. It's her special talent, her only talent, the one thing she does well. Man, I hope you enjoyed her because that's the last piece of ass you'll ever get."

"Gary, listen to me."

"Right in the balls, Nels."

"Let me explain."

"Here you go—"

Nels charged. One quick step to the side, and he launched himself in a high dive at the other man. The automatic went off, echoing up and around the quarry. Down they went together, Gary struggling to bring the weapon to bear. Nels worked his knee onto Gary's gun arm, desperate to immobilize the .45. Once that was done, he swung his fists against Gary's face. Blood began to flow from Gary's nose but he continued to fight back, almost heaving Nels aside. Nels located a stone the size of a baseball and brought it down on Gary's gun hand. The automatic came loose and bounced down the rocks toward the water.

The weapon gone, Gary sagged. Nels wrestled him up into a sitting position, his back against a boulder, holding him in place, while both of them struggled to catch their breath. Every impulse directed Nels to destroy Gary, to eliminate this problem once and for all; more pragmatic considerations intervened. He needed Gary too much and would continue to need him in the foreseeable future.

"You very nearly made a bad mistake," he said.

"How could you do this to me?"

"Have you forgotten that night on Overlook Point?"

"You made us do it."

"I mean the second time, remember? The most important night of my life. It bound us forever in friendship; the four of us became brothers, blood brothers."

"You screwed my wife—"

"We took an oath that night."

Nels recalled it as if it had taken place only minutes ago. The events that concerned them—that concerned him so very much—had proved as nothing before how capable he was of imposing his will on other people, of getting them to act in his behalf. That night with Emily, without planning, without forethought, he had led them farther than ever before, breaking new ground, placing them in deep thrall to him. And he had intended to insure their subservience, their obedience, and his own safety, from that night forward.

He had composed the oath himself, committing it to memory, and three nights after they had done Emily Fowler, during a hard summer rain, he had recited it to them . . .

". . . and believe each other above all others. We swear allegiance and fidelity to each other, to support and defend each other, this to supersede all other oaths and promises, all other relationships, all other commitments, from this moment forward in time, no matter the provocation, no matter the forces arrayed against us. We are together. The enemy of one shall be the enemy of all. And this oath shall take precedence and force above the laws of man and the nation and of God.

Let the one who breaks this oath be damned forever."

They clustered in the rain under the big elm tree, on the ground where they had taken Emily Fowler, and as water dripped off their chins, their hands clasped as they did before a big game, they vowed never to be separated. No one, they swore, would ever come between them, until death claimed them.

"And beyond," Nels said.

"And beyond," they echoed.

"So do I swear," each of them said.

Later, they got drunk and ended up in Daisy Palumbo's whorehouse on the Old Post Road. It was, each of them agreed later, one hell of a night.

"How could you do that to me?" Gary, head rolling loosely on his round shoulders, complained weakly.

"You are my friend," Nels replied earnestly. "You are my brother. I swear to you now as I swore that night, it is not true."

"She told me everything. Details. The way she used her hands on you, her mouth, everything. Do you know how that made me feel?"

"It isn't true."

"Why would she lie about a thing like that?"

"You and me, Gary, along with Jay and Hollis, we belong in Owenoke County, we are part of it. Like the river and the hills, no different from the trees or the animals, a part of the earth itself. Leila—she will always be an outsider."

"That doesn't give you the right to screw a man's wife behind his back."

"I am not going to say a single critical word of your wife, Gary. You've never heard me speak ill of Bunny or of Lauren. It's not my way. You are my friend, so she is my friend."

"How could you do it?" Gary persisted.

"You want the truth?"

"Yes."

"You won't like it."

"Things can't get any worse."

"I wanted to protect you, prevent you from being hurt, that's why I never said anything. Leila came to me, Gary."

It hung in the still air between them. "Are you going to tell me she forced you to get into bed with her?"

"She phoned me. She wrote me love notes."

"I want to see them. Show them to me."

Nels shook his head ruefully. "Do you think I'd take a chance on somebody discovering them accidentally? Of course not. So I destroyed them. Twice I found her hiding in the bushes outside the house, waiting for me to come home."

"I don't believe you."

"I have no reason to lie. What do I gain by lying to you?"

"She seduced you?"

"I refused to do it, Gary. I couldn't. Not to my best friend's wife. When I refused, she began nagging me. Phone calls at odd hours. Threatening to tell you about us, to make up stories. I didn't believe she'd do it. As you can see, I was wrong."

Tears welled up in Gary's eyes. His body began to quiver. Nels went over to where his friend sat slumped on the ground and helped him up to his feet. He wrapped his arm around the other man's shoulders.

"It's time to go home, pal."

At the top of the quarry, Gary stopped. "What am I going to do?"

"She's your wife."

"You're my best friend. I need help."

"Can you continue to live with a woman who deceives you, who tries to create a rift between you and your best friend?"

The rage flickered. "I'll kill her."

"Send her away instead."

"If I see her—"

"Would you like me to handle it for you?"

"Oh, Nels, after what I tried to do—could you, would you, do that for me?"

"A phone call to Barney is all it should take."

"Oh, Jesus!" Gary sobbed.

"Leave it all to me. I'll take care of everything."

31

MOLLY, BEHIND THE wheel of the 280Z, drove swiftly along the Old Post Road, heading north. On either side of them, trees zoomed past, a succession of subtle greens and crimsons and oranges, early fall changes.

"I'm convinced I know who called me this morning," Molly said to Becker, both staring ahead as the road gently climbed away from the river into the low surrounding hills.

"You said you didn't recognize the voice."

"I said it was vaguely familiar. I kept hearing it in my head and now I'm sure."

"Hardly the kind of evidence I'd like to take before a judge."

"We are not in a courtroom, Counselor," she answered, with considerable churlishness.

Becker glanced at the speedometer. "Take it easy, I'm not ready to die."

She removed her foot from the gas pedal and the sports car began to slow itself. A glance in the rear view mirror revealed a car catching up. She slowed even more to let it pass.

She said, "The caller said Nels Proctor might be my father—"

"She didn't mention his name."

"Who else could it be? The man I'm *seeing* . . ."

"Does that mean we're dropping Michael Fairfax out of the deck?"

Molly gripped the wheel tightly. All this was so painful—to accept the fact that any one of four men might have fathered her in brutality and blood rather than love and affection. And her father—no, she corrected; the man she had thought was her father—where did he fit in this ever-changing equation?

So much deceit, so much that Emily had withheld or distorted or simply lied about—why not Michael Fairfax, as well? Which of her memories were real, she wondered, and which counterfeit, contrived to aid in the deception, to rig a false history in order to achieve some kind of public acceptance for a woman alone with an infant daughter?

Becker's voice broke into her ruminations. "We've been unable to track down Fairfax. Not even a trace of him remains. Doesn't that tell you something? The man who never was."

Molly checked the mirror again; behind them, the car was closing fast.

"As for Proctor," Becker continued, "I find that hard to accept, even of him."

"That he's my father, you mean?"

"That if he is, he'd commit incest."

Her voice was sharp. "From what I've read, incest crosses all social lines, all economic barriers. Maybe it's become the new national pastime." A shudder traveled down her spine. "My God, with my own father . . ."

"You can't be sure. An anonymous call doesn't mean it's true."

"Always the lawyer." The words were laced with irony and anger, a broad, unfocused rage directed at whoever happened to come into range.

Behind them, the car was barely a length away. A late model Cadillac, powder blue, with windows tinted almost black. The driver's face was completely obliterated, giving the Cadillac the high-tech, otherworldly look of a vehicle out of a science fiction movie. The Cadillac swung out, preparatory to making his pass. Molly cut her speed; she was in no rush.

"The plot thickens," she said with contrived cheerfulness.

The Cadillac pulled abreast and Molly glanced sidelong. The almost-black window on the passenger side lowered a few inches and from the corner of her eye she caught the glint of sunlight on metal.

For a fraction of a second she looked without seeing, until everything came rushing at her like some awful nightmare. "Look out!" she cried and stepped down hard on the brake. The Cadillac shot past, leaving an explosion of sound in its wake and sped around a bend in the road. Molly fought to control the wheel, finally bringing the car onto the grassy shoulder, drawing to a stop.

Shaken, Molly made herself get out of the car. An ugly scar was imposed on the hood, no more than twelve inches from the windshield. A quick, hollow queasiness settled in her stomach; it spread, leaving her weak and uncertain. Her knees began to quake and conflicting emotions scurried along her nerves. Sweat broke across her back and trickled like an icy finger into the hollow of her spine.

Becker circled behind her, wary, watchful, his voice turned thin and aggressive. "What in hell was that all about!"

She made a helpless gesture. "The man in the car . . . there was a gun . . . he shot at us." The weakness took over and she swayed, setting herself against impulsive tears, resolved to stay on top of her feelings. Her mouth opened and closed soundlessly.

Becker inspected the hood. "You're sure it was a gun?"

Suddenly, it was all too much, too much emotional wear and tear, too much fear. All that had happened, was happening—the barrel of the weapon peeking out of the dark window of the Cadillac, Becker's skepticism. Her voice climbed precipitously. "Damn you, Becker, I saw it!"

He shrugged in acceptance. "Whatever you say."

Her hand jerked up as if to strike out, then, dizzy with emotion, with resentment and fright, she stumbled and almost went down. He moved swiftly, arms going around her, holding her upright, supporting her with his body, silently strong and reassuring. The hard warmth he gave off seemed to penetrate her very skin; she sobbed into his chest and clung tightly. Then she was brought rushing back to the present, to where they were and the fact of their closeness, captured by the dark desires she had for so long buried. His lips sought out her mouth, in a kiss of vast hunger and delicacy that was charged with feverish promise.

Instinctively she responded, accepting his tongue, the warm penetration reassuring, and she was aching to be filled and fulfilled, her belly pressing forward as if to claim his power and his heat, unable to separate desire from terror or terror from confusion. His hands rode along her sides onto the roundness of her buttocks and she trembled at the touch. Until sanity floated to the surface through her passion, through her anxiety, through the surprise and wonderment. She pulled back, hands keeping him at bay. "No, no," she murmured. "No . . ."

"Since the first day in the grandstand, I've wanted to kiss you."

The thickness in his voice washed over her like a warm bath, and made her think of Nels, that afternoon at Devil's Glen. How excited she had become at his kiss, at his touch. The kiss muddied her emotions, and a vision of Nels filled her mind. How uncommonly attractive he had been that day under the fading sunlight, his naked body so sexual, exuding the promise of immense pleasures, his kisses skillful, provocative, triggering long-dormant responses in her. Still, she had resisted, pulled away even as she now pulled away from Becker. She blamed herself, her own fears, her own inadequacies; what was the matter with her?

"No," she said again, trying to get past the confusion, trying to deal with things as they were, not as she wished them to be. Unable to face Becker's inquiring gaze, she hurried back behind the wheel.

After a moment, Becker followed, taking his place beside her. "No point in saying I'm sorry—I'm not. For a moment there, I believed . . ."

"No!" she said with unexpected vehemence. "I was upset, that's all. Being shot at—that's a hell of a note."

"Nobody would like it. But the way you kissed me . . ."

"It was a mistake. Let it go, please. Let's not talk about it anymore."

He looked ahead. The road was empty, but filled with ghosts. "It's Proctor, isn't it?"

She refused to think about Nels, would certainly not discuss their relationship with Becker. Not at this instant of high stress and uncertainty. Not ever.

She shook her head. "What we should be talking about . . . somebody's trying to kill us."

He examined her in profile, and saw how each feature blended so smoothly into the next, how her reserve was intact despite what had transpired. She was a remarkable woman with an inexhaustible fund of resources, a woman of strength and courage to be admired and respected. He wiped his hands on his trousers, suddenly aware of his own fears.

"Maybe," he offered, "only one of us."

Her confidence came rushing back, and she was pleased. "Let's say you're right about Sam being murdered. Maybe you know more than you realize. The man behind the gun obviously feels threatened and wants you out of the way."

"Assuming he was after me."

She turned the 280Z back toward town, driving cautiously, unwilling to let Becker see the depth of her concern. "Or me," she replied, keeping it light, aware of the lingering taste of his lips.

He frowned. "Neither possibility exactly thrills me." And after a short interval. "We should report this to the police."

She shook her head. "What's the point? The gunman is long gone. At a guess, the car was stolen for the occasion. And I certainly have lost any faith in Barney Grubb's willingness to enforce the law."

Her own words heightened her apprehension. She wished she had never come to Old Brixton, never heard of the place. She'd arrived with only a few simple questions and a reasonable complement of expectations. In return she'd been given very few simple answers; in the course of her stay she had discovered more about her mother than she wanted to know, more about her father, and much more about herself than she needed to know. Along the way she'd encountered hostility and secretiveness, Old Brixton unwilling to confront its past truthfully. Where, she asked herself, not expecting an answer, and how, would it all end?

"Peter said my mother was raped by four men. Four."

The Four Horsemen, Lauren had said.

A silent groan filled the cavities of her skull, the hollow echo of despair and anguish. A rapist's seed. Nels Proctor or any one of the others. Someone had to know what took place that night, someone had to be willing to reveal the truth. She checked the rear view mirror, looking for answers in the deep reflection of an empty country road, swiftly fading in the distance.

"Where are we going?"

"Lauren Newell," she said.

"Why would she talk now?"

"Somehow, I'll make her talk to me. Being shot at—damn, Carl, that makes me nervous, makes me think it's time that I got some straight answers."

Twenty minutes later they drew up in front of the Newell house. Becker opened the door on his side but Molly called him back.

"Wait for me here."

He protested. "I'm good at this sort of thing. Asking questions, investigation—it's my business."

"I have to do it myself. I want to."

He sighed and sat back. "Okay. But if you need me, I'll be right here."

Lauren, wearing gray flannel slacks, a black cashmere sweater, and a delicate gold chain hanging around her neck, greeted Molly without enthusiasm.

"I'm rather busy," she began. "I'm president of the Historical Society and—"

"This won't take up much of your time." Molly went past her into the reception hall.

Lauren allowed that she could spare a few minutes and led the way onto the enclosed porch. Morgan appeared with tea and scones and butter, withdrawing on silent feet. Outside the afternoon sun was warm, the garden stippled with the vivid shades of mauve, red, and blue of poppies, salvia, and delphinium, and irises of several shades of purple. Between the garden and the green wall of the woods, water fell in transparent sheets over the lip of a stone fountain which was topped by a plump cherub.

"That was you this morning, Mrs. Newell, phoning me?" Molly began.

Lauren remained impassive and immobile in the white wicker chair. Molly admired her self-discipline; she would make an exemplary witness.

"I made no call to you, my dear, not this morning, not at any other time."

"You suggested that Nels Proctor might be my natural father."

A condescending smile drifted across Lauren's handsome

face and she replied with calm certainty. "If I'm not mistaken, you mentioned your father to me, Molly. Michael Fairfax was the name, I believe."

"You said you knew him," Molly said.

Lauren smiled again. "No, I asked if Emily had ever married. You told me about Michael Fairfax, asked if I knew him. You said they eloped and I remarked that the elopement might account for the dramatic and abrupt way your mother left town. Certainly you remember now?"

"What about Nels Proctor?"

Brows slightly elevated, Lauren said, "What about him?"

Molly decided to improvise, take the chance that Lauren would not recognize the bluff she was calling. "We know that Proctor and Emily were never lovers. That is, they never dated—"

"In which case, Nels could not have fathered Emily's child. Isn't that so?" she ended sweetly.

"If they had been lovers, you would have known, as close as you and Emily were?"

"Lovers." The word rolled off Lauren's tongue. "When I was a girl, very few of us took lovers. Not the way you young women seem to do today. We dated. Occasionally we necked. But nice girls never went all the way. Virginity was still in vogue."

"If Nels and Emily had been lovers, you would have known?"

"You're repeating yourself."

"You were her best friend."

"Young women were more discreet during my adolescence."

"Emily would have told you, I think. Why hide it? Nels Proctor—what a prize he would've been. Best-looking boy in town. Richest, from a socially prominent family. Outstanding athlete. Best catch around. And they were from a similar background."

She waited but Lauren offered no response. "If there was an outsider in the equation, Mrs. Newell, it was you. Your parents were teachers, always on the edge of financial disaster. You lived in the Flats and I've discovered what that means in this town. Marrying Jay Newell was a big step up for you, right on up to Bluewater Hill."

Lauren, emotions churning, stood up slowly. "I've heard

enough. You will leave now, at once." Panic rippled under her skin and it took all the control she could muster to keep from blurting out everything she knew. Guilt festered, bubbling toward the surface.

"Friends," Molly said quietly, "share intimacies."

"Your mother and I—it was different then. Attitudes, what people did, what they said."

Molly altered her mode of attack, the edge blunted. "Emily was pregnant when she left town."

Lauren sucked air between her teeth. "Ridiculous!"

"I know that she was, Mrs. Newell. You had to know it, too."

"Who told you that?"

"What matters is that she was pregnant with me. Cornelia sent her away, thereby allowing a number of people in the county to breathe easier." She opted for another gamble. "Up on Overlook Point, on the Fourth of July, I know what happened."

Lauren's eyes darted from side to side. "That's impossible."

"There's a witness," Molly said.

"No! There were no witnesses. There was nothing for anybody to witness." She staggered and almost fell, pointing unsteadily at the door. "You must go. Now. At once. Please, leave."

Molly placed herself squarely in front of the other woman. "Tell me about David," she insisted. "Or would you rather I tell you?" Molly waited, afraid she'd gone too far. Until she saw Lauren's mask begin to dissolve, pain reflected in her eyes. She began to speak in a soft, reflective voice . . .

David brought Emily, clinging fiercely to the Teddy bear, to Lauren's house. Startled at the sight of her battered friend, Lauren embraced Emily, cooing over her.

"Who did this to you?" she finally said.

It was David who answered, describing what he had witnessed. Fear had kept him from interfering, he said.

"When they left," David said, "I came down along the river path so no one would see me."

"Help me bring her inside," Lauren said. "I'll wake my parents, they'll know what to do."

Emily protested. "Nobody must find out."

"You need help," David said.

"We'll take you home," Lauren said. "Your mother . . ."

"She's in the Mediterranean. Oh, God, why did they do this to me? Home—oh, no! The servants, everybody will know by tomorrow. My mother will murder me when she finds out."

Lauren didn't know how to respond. She recognized how brutally her friend had been assaulted. At the same time, Lauren wanted to protect herself from the events of the evening; her entire future depended on her doing so. Shamed by the thought, she nonetheless was unable to shake it. Should she become involved publicly in this affair it would only reflect badly on her. Unlike Emily, she did not have a powerful family name to fall back on. And more than anything else, Lauren yearned to move up in the world, move into the rarefied atmosphere of Bluewater Hill. She warned herself to do nothing that might jeopardize that ambition.

Sensing her indecision, David took charge. "We have to get you to a doctor, Emily."

"No, I'm all right. I'll be all right."

"You're bleeding, you're hurt."

"I don't want anybody to know," Emily moaned.

"Doctors can't talk about their patients. They take an oath, the Hippocratic oath. It's a question of ethics. We'll both go with you."

Lauren drew back. "Oh, no." Her head grew airy, floating, her shame pervasive. "I mean, I can't go. My parents would have to know."

David settled it for her, for all of them. "Okay, Emily. I'll take you."

"And did he?" Molly asked Lauren.

"What? Oh, yes, to the doctor."

"At the hospital?"

"No. It wasn't built until much later."

"In fact, construction began that spring, which meant plans were drawn up during the fall and winter."

Lauren dismissed the remark casually. "You could be right."

"So Dr. Ortner treated Emily?"

"I told you that he did," Lauren said with some annoyance.

"But made no mention of it when I talked to him."

"I wouldn't know about that."

"Why would he hold back, Mrs. Newell?"

"I have no idea."

"Let me submit my version: keeping quiet about what happened to Emily that night was Ortner's part in this conspiracy."

"Conspiracy?" She wet her lips, eyes cast down. "What a peculiar choice of words."

"Is it? Wasn't the medical center Ortner's payoff for keeping his mouth shut?"

Lauren looked out at her garden. She loved working in the earth, preparing the soil, planting, nursing the fledgling plants to bloom. "I have told you all I can."

Molly spoke insistently. "Who were the rapists?"

Lauren was startled. "How would I know that?"

"Because my mother told you, she *must* have told you, that night outside your house. You managed to avoid mentioning their names."

"No," Lauren said.

"David knew who they were," Molly said. "He saw them all. Mother knew. And you knew, Lauren."

Lauren busied herself with pouring more tea. "It was night, pitch black on the Point, woods all around. It was impossible to recognize anybody, despite what you think."

"Mother had to know who they were and I can't believe she didn't tell you."

"No! Some boys from out in the county. Or maybe even out of state. Drinking too much, they went crazy. Boys right off the farm, in town for the fair. Drinking too much . . . it had to be like that."

Molly leaned forward, conciliatory, intimate. "You objected to my use of the word conspiracy. What else are we to think? A conspiracy of silence exists about Emily Fowler. No one is willing to admit what happened that night, and when some fragment of information does come out, a smothering blanket is immediately thrown over it. In my opinion, Mrs. Newell, half of this town is protecting somebody, a number of people, people important and powerful. Let's face it, somebody is exceedingly anxious to bury the past, no matter who else gets hurt in the process."

"Nobody's going to get hurt," Lauren said, not believing her own words.

"Somebody tried to kill me today," Molly said. "Or kill Carl."

Lauren stiffened. "What are you saying?"

"A man in a car shot at us," Molly said.

"That can't be."

"I'm afraid it is. Now do you understand how serious this is?" When Lauren made no reply, Molly went on. "There is someone who knows all the answers, who will tell us what we want to know."

Lauren gave no sign she'd heard.

"I'm talking about David, Mrs. Newell."

Lauren stared sightlessly.

"Where is he?"

Lauren brought her eyes back into focus, speaking in a monotone. "David? He died, a very long time ago."

Back in Anna Slocum's stone house, they drank dark beer out of oversized mugs and nibbled roasted peanuts.

"It isn't right," Molly said, "that anybody should have to endure the pain my mother was subjected to."

Anna, solidly settled on a tall stool in front of a drafting table across the living room, answered. "Your mother was a brave woman, and she survived a great deal. And she must have loved you very much, to birth you by herself, without family or friends, in some strange place, to stand against her mother the way she did. Cornelia Fowler was a formidable force to be reckoned with."

"I suppose you're right. Mother had to battle so many hostile forces." They drank beer, chewed nuts, and worked silently through their own emotions until Molly said, "I haven't been ready to face this, I guess, but if four of them raped Mother, any one of them might be my father." Her eyelashes fluttered, fighting back tears. Then a bitter laugh trickled from her lips. "It's so hard to accept. My memory of father is so vivid. All these years, I loved him dearly. And all just a myth."

"Emily gave you the father you deserved," Anna said evenly, "the father she wanted you to have."

"I feel as if I'm being torn apart, as if I'm being forced to kill my own father, the only father I ever knew. He saved my life—"

Becker broke in. "He never existed, you've got to accept that."

She looked from Anna to Becker and back to Anna, seeking answers; neither of them had any to give. All answers, all decisions, had to come from within herself. It never happened, the drowning, the rescue, the memory of Michael Fairfax snatching her to safety. Or if it had, someone unknown had saved her, not Michael Fairfax. That was simply one more story concocted by Emily, another false thread in the fantasy woven to deceive and protect Molly from a world Emily had perceived as hostile and dangerous. How many times had she listened to that story? How many times had she repeated it to herself, boasted of her father's strength and courage to her friends? Until it became real in her mind, part of her history. A shiver ran through her and her eyes met Becker's.

"The military records don't lie," he offered gently. "He served nowhere. There was no Michael Fairfax."

Anna, eyes fixed on Molly, nodded. "I certainly would have known the name."

Becker continued. "When Peter said, 'No husband,' he was telling us in his own way that Emily was pregnant, but never married. And that phone call you received—the caller was talking about Nels Proctor."

Molly made a small, guttural sound. "I don't want to think about that. Nothing seems real anymore. Are all my memories false? What is real?"

"Real is this," Becker said, summing up. "Four men raped your mother. There is reason to believe they were The Four Horsemen. Proctor—"

"That unholy bastard," Anna blurted out. She made it sound like a fact, one that had stood the test of time.

"Proctor," Becker repeated, "may or may not be your father, if four of them were involved. That has to be considered."

"What am I going to do?" Molly moaned, pitching herself at Anna, clinging to the woman potter. "How am I going to live with what I've done?"

"You've done nothing wrong," Anna said firmly.

Molly responded between clenched teeth. "You don't understand, neither of you. From the start, I wanted him—the desire was so strong . . ."

"You didn't know," Anna said. "You couldn't have known."

"I wish I were as certain as you are." Molly reached back to that day at Devil's Glen. "It would have been so easy and I was tempted, more than tempted. But something made me hold back—"

"There you are," Anna said, as if that settled the entire affair.

Through a closing fog that seemed to enshroud her brain, a thought pierced through. "I have to talk to Nels, to confront him."

Becker frowned. "What good will that do?"

"He must confess what he's done."

"Nels will admit nothing," Anna said. "I know the man. Give him the chance and he'll make you feel as if you're the guilty party."

"I'll go to the police, bring charges—"

"On a rape that took place twenty-six years ago?" Becker said gloomily. "Without an eyewitness, without a victim? No way."

"If only David were still alive," Molly said.

"David," Becker said, "is the hero of the piece. Brings a battered Emily to her friend and later to the good Dr. Ortner. And conveniently expires—too conveniently."

"Is that David Colfax you're talking about?" Anna said. "You knew him?"

"I remember him. He died—why, I believe it was that same year that Emily left, that same summer."

"Do you know what happened?" Molly asked, excitement rising in her. "How did he die?"

"In a town this size, not that many murders take place—"

"Murdered! You're sure of that?"

"I confess to my age, Molly, but I'll match my memory with anybody." She shifted around, her womanly breasts rising and falling under the thick fisherman's sweater she wore. "He was killed by someone passing through, it was generally believed. Robbed of whatever items of value he had and shot in the head."

"They never found the killer?"

"Never."

"Dead end," Becker muttered.

"Maybe not" Molly said. "There's something peculiar about this."

"Peculiar?" Anna said.

"Overlook Point—what is it known for?"

"As a lover's lane. Kids mostly go up there to 'watch the submarine races'—that's what they used to call it. Necking out of sight of disapproving adults."

"What was David doing up there?"

"Of course!" Becker cried.

"David brings Mother down to Lauren, by himself. He carries her to the doctor, by himself. Was he up on the Point by himself? A young, healthy boy in the throes of adolescence? Does that make any sense?" Molly demanded. "My best guess," she continued, "is that David was on the Point with somebody. A girl, a girlfriend."

"Making out," Becker said.

"Necking," Anna corrected. "Remember—we are talking about nineteen fifty-eight."

"Why hasn't she ever come forward?" Becker wondered aloud.

Anna shrugged her shoulders. "Listen—I have been trying to shed light on you ignorant youths. You don't listen any more than Sam did. Sex was not as openly dealt with then. This is a small town—working-class traditions, conservative, with traditional ways of doing things. People took a dim view of any girl who went too far. They still do, for the most part. If this alleged girl and David were having sex—"

Molly broke in excitedly. "She'd have more than one reason for not making her presence known."

"So she split," Becker concluded, "When David went to Emily's aid."

"Exactly," Molly said. "She allowed David to do his good deed without getting involved herself."

"And," Anna pointed out, "in the normal course of things in those days, existing by an adolescent's code of honor, David never mentioned his friend by name to anyone."

"Fantastic!" Molly said, clapping her hands.

Anna swung around. "What?"

"Don't you see? This means there is a witness, after all, an eyewitness who can testify to what took place, someone who can identify the men involved."

"If we can find her," Becker added, without optimism.

"We must find her. We will."

Becker brushed at the hair over his forehead. "Okay but where do we look?"

Molly smiled sweetly. "In the telephone directory, of course."

32

SHE WAITED FOR nearly thirty minutes before being admitted to Ralph Ortner's office. He greeted Molly as if they were old friends and saw her into a chair before settling behind his desk, gazing serenely at her from behind his rimless glasses.

"I confess, my dear, I am surprised to see you again."

"Why is that, doctor?" She had formulated a list of questions designed to bring her closer to the truth, and she didn't intend to allow Ortner to divert her.

He produced a self-conscious chuckle, a professional tool for reassuring a concerned patient. "To be perfectly honest, our little town offers so little in the way of excitement or entertainment that I was sure you'd be gone by now, back to the diversions of the Big Apple."

She tried to remember. "I don't recall telling you that I lived in New York."

A brief flash of annoyance showed in those clear eyes. He made a gesture of dismissal. "It must have been you—I've talked to no one about you." A smile came and went on his thin lips. "No matter. What can I do for you today?"

"No one?" she said, hoping to catch him in even an inconsequential lie. "Not Nels Proctor?"

The tactic failed. "Proctor? Why, no, absolutely not."

"Barney Grubb, then?"

"I don't see the point . . ." He leaned back in his chair, long face drawn down in a frown. "With all due respect, Miss Fairfax, you are not central to my existence. I'm a busy man, so—why are you here?"

Aware that she had lost ground, Molly drew back to her rehearsed position. "Last time we spoke you said you didn't remember anything in particular about my mother."

"That's true."

"No accidents, broken bones, any out-of-the-ordinary diseases?"

"She was, as I recall, perfectly normal in every way. Healthy, active, not unusual medically. Why do you ask?"

"If anything special had occurred, you'd remember?"

"I suppose I would. You appear to have something specific in mind. What is it?"

"Rape," she said tonelessly.

The blood emptied out of the long face and his hands came down flat on the desk. He blinked but said nothing.

She went on. "Rape is out of the ordinary, wouldn't you agree, doctor? How many rape victims have you treated in your career, doctor? How many have there been since nineteen fifty-eight?"

He rose slowly and walked to the door, opening it. "I find your manner offensive, Miss Fairfax. You will leave at once, please."

She remained in her seat. "The Fourth of July, nineteen fifty-eight. That was the night Mother came to your old office, doctor. You examined her. You treated her. About midnight, it was. Maybe a little later."

He closed the door silently. "What put such an idea into your head?"

"David Colfax brought her to you."

He went back to his chair and sat down, his movements tentative.

"Well," he said, licking his lips. "You never mentioned David Colfax up till now. He'd slipped my mind entirely, yes. But it's beginning to come back. Perhaps I do remember after all . . ."

In 1958, he said, the office was located in an extension built on to the back of his house at the end of Evergreen Lane. He accepted patients as they came, day or night, without appointments, making house calls when necessary. Seldom a case of major proportions: flu victims, measles, chicken pox, the full gamut of childhood diseases, minor cuts and bruises, occasionally a broken limb to be set. Nothing that prepared him for Emily Fowler that night.

Unmistakably the victim of a vicious beating, she was bleeding, with bruises on her face, across her shoulders, on her breasts. Between sobs, she told him what had happened, breaking down before she completed her story. David Colfax finished for her, starting to identify her assailants.

Ortner cut him off. "No, no more, you've told me enough. If you want to press charges, go to the police. I don't want to hear any more."

David fell silent, intimidated by the tall and dour physician.

As for Emily, her rage had dissolved into shame and self-accusation, to an inflamed sense of guilt that would cling to her for a very long time.

"No," she managed to say, "no police, please. I don't want anybody to know."

Ortner, relieved, had returned to his work.

"I advised her," Ortner recalled with fervor, "that I could not testify to her claims of sexual assault."

"She'd been beaten. She was bleeding. There must have been evidence of semen. If not rape, what would you call it?"

"I could find no reason to believe she'd been forced to do anything. She indicated she'd gone into the woods of her own free will with some boy. Maybe it was this same David, I couldn't be sure. Maybe she had tripped, fallen in the dark, injured herself."

"She was raped!"

"Raped?" Once more he donned the cloak of infinite authority. "Oh, how easily you women make that accusation. Cry rape and you evoke sympathy for the supposed victim. But more than one female has led a man on only to change her mind in the midst of the act itself. Well, I am not so easily deceived."

"There were indications that—"

"Indications that what? That your mother had intercourse? Oh, yes, that was plain to see. Perhaps more than once. Perhaps even with more than a single partner. Does that con-

stitute rape? It certainly does not. It may, however, define a
girl without morals. A girl with unnatural cravings. A girl who
will do anything with anyone. When I was a young man we
had names for girls like that.''

"Don't you dare!" Molly was on her feet, striding toward
the door. "My mother was attacked and brutalized, raped. I
will not allow you to blame her. There's been a conspiracy in
this town to hide what happened to her and you were part of
it. You failed in your professional and personal responsibilities then and you are still failing." She left, leaving the
door ajar.

He called after her. "Don't expect me to rewrite history so
you can rescue your mother's reputation!"

Her thinking was muddled, her emotions unsettled. She
yearned to wipe away the dirty pictures Ralph Ortner had
planted in her mind. She was overwhelmed by swiftly flashing
images of a guilt-ridden, sexually compliant girl succumbing
to the advances of four amorous boys on a warm summer
night, the night in which she, Molly, had been conceived.
Trapped by the apparently insurmountable walls of her dilemma, she sought a satisfactory answer, some element of relief. In that disturbed condition she hunted for a way to dispel
her doubts, which inevitably brought her attention back to
Nels Proctor.

She arrived at his house in an agitated state and he sought
to calm her, embracing her, uttering placating platitudes. She
freed herself from his arms and went into the spacious living
room that looked down on the river. The water moved lazily
along, the same as it had when her mother was a girl, yet so
very different.

"Can I get you something—a drink?" he said.

"Nothing." She came around to confront him. Never had
he looked more handsome, more stalwart, the stuff of which
adolescent dreams are made. Yet she felt only revulsion,
disgusted by what she knew, shamed by her role in their relationship.

"Somebody called me this morning," she said.

"That should come as no surprise. A girl as beautiful as you
are—men must phone often."

Girl. That was part of it. He managed repeatedly to subvert
her sense of self, to diminish her adulthood, reducing her to a

shaky adolescent. At that moment she despised him for steal-ing so much that was essential to her, for refusing to allow her to be herself. And she despised herself even more for permit-ting it to happen.

She stepped back, keeping a cushion of safe space between them, forcing herself to meet his gaze. "According to the caller, the man I have been going out with could be my father. You, Nels, that's you. Are you my father, Nels?"

For the first time they'd met, he appeared shaken, unsure of himself and out of control. But he recovered almost at once, dismissive, amused by what he had heard. He started toward her, arms outstretched in invitation.

"No." She retreated a step or two. "I don't want you to touch me."

He was laughing. "Every small town has its cranks and gossips, people with nothing to do but concoct strange and ab-surd stories. You make me sound like a character in a bad novel. Certainly you don't give credence to such a grotesque notion. It's nonsense."

She maintained her distance, fearful lest his slightest touch corrupt her even more, put her beyond the reach of decency again. She spoke, her voice hard and biting. "I'm not here to make small talk or invite you to flirt with me. I came about my mother."

No change of expression on that handsome face, nothing to show that he felt anything. Not fear, not remorse, not the slightest concern. He nodded once. "Go ahead, I'm listen-ing."

"Twenty-six years ago you took Emily Fowler up to Overlook Point."

"I'm still listening," he said, making it sound like a challenge.

"You—you made love to her. No, not love, not even lust drove you. It was something much less than that, something mean and venal, the need to make less of her and less of your friends, to exercise your power over them."

His pale eyes glittered like shining steel bearings. "You have a vivid imagination."

"It was a game for you. How proud of yourself you must have been. You raped my mother and forced your friends to do the same."

Still no visible reaction. Just that perfect composure, his

face all sculpted planes and shadowed hollows. It was, she told
herself, like the face of an aging Roman warrior, cruel and
ungiving.

"Ridiculous."

"There were witnesses . . ."

He touched the knot of his silk club tie, fingers curled at his
own throat like a spider poised to strike. "Are you saying
someone placed me up on the Point with your mother? That's
absurd—I barely knew the girl. As for rape, it's never been
necessary for me to rape in order to get a woman's attention."

Her face grew flushed but she persisted. "The Four Horsemen," she offered doggedly. "Heroes, every one of you."

He seemed pleased by the reference. "I didn't know you
were aware of the name. We grew up together, played football
together, hung out. We're still the best of friends."

"You raped Emily Fowler, all of you."

The small muscles in his cheek twitched. "Nothing of the
sort ever happened. I never dated your mother. I barely knew
her. Certainly I never raped her . . . or anybody else."

She wanted to believe him. "You remembered her wedding?"

"Hardly a crime."

"And you told me you read about my father's death in the
newspaper?"

"What bearing does that have on anything?"

"You lied."

Imperceptibly, the calm masking his features fragmented.
He blinked as if struck and he cleared his throat as if to speak,
but said nothing. One corner of his mouth lifted involuntarily
and fell back again.

"No one has ever dared to call me a liar."

He seemed to swell with self-importance, dominant, terrifying, giving off an aura of danger. But she set herself against
him, refusing to give in, determined to make him admit his
crime.

"There was no marriage. Her soldier-boy all a made-up
story so I'd have a father of my own I could be proud of. All
the love I felt was for a piece of blue sky, shaped by my
mother's imagination." She paused but he said nothing, and
she plunged on, unwilling to hold back anything. "There was
no obituary in *The Call*, no record of a marriage at Town

Hall. Nobody knew Michael Fairfax. Not the Army. Not Mother. Not me. Nobody.''

A spasm wrenched his tall frame and the tension left his limbs. That cool, detached expression faded back into view and a thin, awful smile revealed flashing teeth. "Apparently I made a mistake. To be honest, your mother played a role of no importance in my life.''

"What kind of a man are you?''

"What would you like me to say? That I raped your mother that night? That I fathered her child—you? I did nothing to hurt your mother. I've done nothing to hurt you.''

"You had me thrown out of the Inn, out of every other place I stayed. That business with my car and having me locked up for soliciting. And when none of that frightened me out of town, you had someone try to kill me.''

He frowned. "Nobody tried to kill you.''

She described the incident on the Old Post Road.

"No,'' he muttered, struggling to conceal the scorching rage that lodged in his gut. Grubb again. Damn the man! He was a loose cannon, out of control, and no longer to be tolerated.

"I,'' he told her with all the sincerity he could muster, "don't know anything about that. You must believe me," he ended, surprised that in some indeterminate way what had happened to her mattered to him. "Believe me," he repeated to her retreating back, as she walked out of his house. "Believe me . . .''

33

"BARNEY AND I have been planning this hunt since the close of last season."

Seated in a back booth in The Tin Whistle, Gary kept his attention focused on the mug of beer in front of him. For years he'd been an avid hunter—deer, duck, wild turkey. But all that was behind him now; hunting had lost its appeal. He was an expert shot; perhaps it had become too easy. All the fun was gone, the challenge dissipated. No more hunting for him.

"I'll pass this time, Nels."

Nels went on as if he hadn't heard. "We spotted some good deer trails. A lot of sign was put down during the rut. Those big bucks will be coming through again."

Gary washed his mouth out with beer before swallowing. "My hunting days are over."

"Is that what it is?" Nels held Gary's wrist in his right hand, staring into his eyes. "Or is it still that business with Leila?"

Gary freed his hand. "Oh, no, Nels." There was an undertone of melancholy in his voice, an absence of his usual fire and force. "I was a fool to believe her for even a minute. The bitch was not to be trusted, I know that now. You're my best friend, like always. What happened is over and done with. She's gone and I'm glad.''

"Glad?''

Gary emptied the mug of beer, examined the bottom as if searching for traces of meaning. "Ah, well. If I said I didn't think about her once in a while I'd be lying. I keep remembering how beautiful she was. Wasn't she beautiful, Nels? The most beautiful woman I've ever seen. Sometimes at night when she came to bed looking like an innocent young girl in one of the short nightgowns she wore, I'd get all soft and weak inside. Thing was, it was hard to believe she belonged to me. Thing was, she never did. Not for real.''

"You're lucky. You have some good memories.''

"Maybe so. But when I think about her I feel sad. I miss her, Nels. Maybe sending her away was a mistake. Maybe she just needed some time to grow up.''

"But she's gone and you've got to put that part of your life behind you. Go on to bigger and better things.''

"You're right. I know you're right. Anyway, Leila's going to file for divorce. Bound to cost me an arm and a leg, I bet.''

"Which is why this hunt will be good for you. Take your mind off your troubles.'' He reached over to Gary's shoulder, squeezing hard. "I need you with me.''

"You always get your antlers. What's so special this time?''

Nels fixed Gary, drawing him in with his pale eyes, holding him in place. "I am not going after deer this time.''

Gary was puzzled. "Nothing else around here worth the effort.''

"Bigger game.'' Nels tightened his grip and his eyes grew impenetrable, transmitting nothing, opaque. "Much bigger, and much more dangerous.''

Gary tried to disengage but Nels held on firmly. A chilling apprehension settled in Gary's middle and he knew he should flee, should get away from the other man.

"It's Barney.''

Gary squirmed, still in Nels's grasp. "What about Barney?'' He didn't want to know more, wanted this exchange to end, to evaporate.

"The man is out of control. He refuses to obey orders . . . He'll take us all down.''

"Maybe if we talked to him, if we explained—''

"There's nothing to explain. It's long past that stage. He tried to kill Molly Fairfax."

Gary shuddered. "Why would he do such a thing?"

"She was driving with Carl Becker, a car came up alongside, and the man inside took a shot at them."

Gary paled. "What are you going to do?"

"There's only one choice left to us."

They sat without moving, staring at each other, until Gary blinked. "My God, Nels, you're talking about murder."

"We have to get rid of him."

Gary swallowed hard. "Barney's shrewd. He knows all about killing. To go up against him by yourself—"

Nels tightened his grip. "Not by myself. The two of us, Gary, as a team."

Gary twisted in place. Bile rose in his throat and he was afraid he was going to throw up. He fought down the impulse, finally raising his eyes.

"Trust me. You do trust me, Gary?"

Gary hesitated before answering. "I always have."

"Imagine how it will be. We're going out with bows and arrows, Barney and me. That means we have to get a lot closer to a buck in order to make a kill. I've mapped it out, every trail, every step we'll take. You'll be in place, out of sight, safe, waiting for exactly the right moment." Nels released his grip on Gary and sat back, easy and tranquil, an approving smile on his face.

"You expect me to make the shot?"

"I'll set it up for you, maneuver him into range, provide a clear shot, easy shot."

"You expect me to zap Barney from a hiding place?"

"You're the best shot I know, Gary. I've never known you to miss a standing target—you won't miss this time. One bullet is all it's going to take. I'll see that you have plenty of time to get set, to zero in on the target, to get off the shot."

"And then?"

"You take off. When I see what has happened to my hunting partner, I'll go for help, report an accident. It will be clear to everyone that some inexperienced hunter made a terrible mistake, panicked, and ran. Hunting accidents happen every season."

"What about the rifle?"

"You will drive past Fredricks Lake, across the old dam. Make sure you're not seen, then toss the rifle into the water. It's about forty feet deep at that point and nobody will ever find it."

"Nels, this scares me."

"It has to be done." He touched Gary again, this time on the wrist, trying to reassure the other man. "If I could make the shot myself, I would. But Barney expects me to hunt with him, so he can show off his prowess with a bow. If I change plans on him, knowing Barney, he'll become suspicious. The setup is perfect, Gary. We may never get another chance like this."

"There must be some other way."

"Don't you think I've considered all the options? We can't scare Barney and we can't chase him. No, this is the only way."

Gary's lips were dry. "What about the others?"

Nels stared straight into his eyes, speaking in a low, intense voice. "You are my man. The others—as much as Hollis drinks, he's useless. And Jay's soft, self-indulgent, weak."

He leaned toward Gary, his voice strong and steady. "What happened at the quarry—"

Gary turned away. "I'm sorry about that. I had it all wrong. I was a fool."

"No, that is the kind of man you are. Strong and courageous. If the others had thought what you thought, do you think they would have taken a gun to me? No, only you have the backbone for it. Only you are man enough."

"I appreciate your confidence, Nels."

Nels continued intensely. "In three days, Barney and I are going out. That gives you plenty of time to back out, if that's what you decide to do. Time enough to warn Barney, if that's what you choose to do."

"I would never betray you—"

"Of course you wouldn't. We're brothers."

"What if I fail?"

"You won't."

"Or lose my nerve."

"Not you, my friend. But I want you to be sure."

Gary said he was sure.

"What we're going to do, you and I, will bring us even

closer together. Barney Grubb, no longer a threat, out of our lives once and for all. What do you say, Gary, are you with me?''

Gary, trying to make his voice sound strong, insisted he was.

34

JOHN AND REBECCA Colfax lived in a modest house on Owenoke Turnpike, which was not a turnpike at all, but merely a country lane little more than a mile in length. The house was set behind a row of tall spruce trees with a neatly tended lawn and a flagstone walk from driveway to front door that looked recently swept.

They were elderly and feeble, clinging to each other as if drawing nourishment from the contact. In the tiny living room, with its frayed and worn furniture—one corner of the sofa, leg broken off, was supported by a stack of books—they watched Molly seat herself, wary in the presence of the young and vigorous stranger.

She explained why she had come. "Your son's name came up in the course of my search. David Colfax was your son?"

"He died a long time ago," Mrs. Colfax said, hanging on to her husband's hand.

"Shot down like a dog in cold blood," Mr. Colfax said, his anger still fresh.

"What happened?"

"Never had a chance. Shot in the head and left to die alone in a ditch on a back road. Only a yellow-bellied coward would do a thing like that."

Tears came into his wife's eyes. "Such a sweet boy."

"Always willing to lend a hand. A Boy Scout from the time he was old enough to join. Got to be an Eagle Scout, with a ton of merit badges. A fine boy, a fine son."

"What is it you want to know, Miss Fairfax?"

Molly repeated the story of Emily Fowler's experience on Overlook Point. "David brought Emily down from the Point, took her to a doctor."

"That's our David, always trying to do the right thing."

"He never mentioned the incident?"

"No, never," the father said. "Never one to brag, that boy. Helping out, that was in his nature."

"I remember Emily," Mrs. Colfax said eagerly, as if fearful some detail might not be correctly recalled. "A friendly child, not like some of the folks up on Bluewater Hill. Used to greet you with a smile and once, when I was shopping for groceries, she gave me a hand loading bags into the car. That was when we had the Pontiac, John, remember?"

"I liked that car."

"Raped, you say? Poor child. Can't say I ever heard any mention of it."

"Most folks didn't. Almost as if it were being kept a secret."

"David never said a word."

"When did all this happen?" Mr. Colfax asked.

"Fourth of July, nineteen fifty-eight."

Mrs. Colfax drew her breath in sharply. "Three days," she said to her husband.

"Is that significant?" Molly said.

"David was shot on the seventh of July, that same summer," Mr. Colfax answered. "Robbed and killed and only sixteen years old. Boy never even got a start on life, did he?"

"I'm sorry, I know this must be hard for you," Molly began again.

Mrs. Colfax leaned her way, a knowing look on her crinkled face. "You haven't asked it yet, have you?"

"Asked what?"

"The question you came here to ask," Mr. Colfax and his wife said simultaneously. "Go ahead, ask."

"Okay. Did David have a special friend back then?"

"He had a lot of friends. He was popular."

"I mean a special girlfriend, someone he might have taken to the fair that night?"

Again, the Colfaxes answered as one. "That would be B.J. for BettyJane. A pretty thing B.J. was, sweet and lively. I do believe they cared for each other. B.J. Miller."

"How did you find me?"

Under the striped awning attached to her paint-poor trailer, she sat in a canvas chair in the autumn sun, wearing a heavy wool cardigan over a shabby dress of no distinction, rough, red knees exposed. She drank beer from a can and a cigarette dangled from one corner of her mouth.

"You are B.J. Miller?" Molly asked.

The woman inspected Molly and Becker out of eyes rubbed red. "B.J. is what they call me. Who sent you?"

"Mr. and Mrs. Colfax—David's parents," Becker told her.

B.J. squinted into the distance, peering into her own past, amused by what she saw, then said to Molly, "Wouldn't believe it, seeing me right now, I guess, but once I was pretty good to look at. Pretty as you are almost, miss. Never owned expensive clothes like those but the boys didn't seem to mind. They sure enough didn't."

She frowned, pulled on her beer and dragged on the cigarette.

"Hillerman," Molly said. "That's your married name?"

"Used to be Miller. B.J. for BettyJane."

"You knew David Colfax?"

B.J. struggled into a more dignified position, straightening up, tugging at her dress, making a pass at her hair. "Who was it told you about me? No reason for folks to talk about me, I ain't harmin' any of them. How'd you find me?"

"Once I learned your name," Molly said, "it wasn't hard. One person led to another until I got to the trailer court."

B.J. took another swig of beer. "What do you want, anyway?"

"Just to ask a few questions."

"What kind of questions?"

Molly said, "Can you tell me anything about David Colfax?"

B.J., a sullen set to her soft, dissolute face, muttered, the words coming out in a stream. "Bad luck is worst of all, I tell you. Thing is, once life turns on a person how are you gonna get out from under. Makes you wonder, has somebody out there got it in for you, so that nothing can turn out right, if you know what I mean.''

She tilted the can; no more beer. She placed the can under the chair, still mulling over her thoughts. ''Nothing worked the way it should. Not the jobs I had. Not the men. Lovers and husbands. Been married three separate times and not one of them was worth spit. Men really came after me in droves. I truly was something special in those days. You don't believe me, the way I look now? Can't say I blame you. But just you wait . . .'' Heaving, she made it up to her feet, plunged into the trailer, returning shortly. ''Just you look at this!''

She handed Molly a photograph. In it she saw a trim, perky girl with a bright smile and lively eyes, her tight, strong body displaying a short sequined skirt and a sleeveless blouse.

''That's me. Yes, it is. Me in high school. Best baton twirler the school ever had and that's a fact, ask anybody. Boys coming after me in swarms, like bees to honey.'' That made her laugh, a pleased, shy laugh, eyes turning flirtatiously toward Becker. ''Don't look much like honey now, but then —could've had about any of them I wanted. Any of them.'' She retrieved the photograph, pressing it to her breast. ''Admit it. Was I good-looking or was I good-looking?''

''You were lovely.''

''Damnit all to hell, I was. I was,'' she said, tears coming. ''What bothers me, what I never can understand, you see, is how it all went from being such a good thing to being such a bad thing. So empty and full of pain. Scratching at top speed every waking minute so's to keep things going, just to keep going.''

Back on her feet, eyes rolling again in Becker's direction, an awkward smile gave her face animation. ''I'd show you how I used to do it if I had a baton, but I don't.'' She tapped out a time step and began to do high kicks, exposing flabby thighs, dimpled and marked by a splash of broken blue veins. She whirled and leaped, stumbled, and went to her knees. The feisty cheerleader betrayed by the shapeless body of a weary, middle-aged woman. Molly helped her back into the chair. Breathing with difficulty, B.J. asked for another beer. ''Inside,'' she said. ''In the fridge.''

Molly went after it; she watched her drink, saw the color return to her cheeks.

"Tell me about David, please."

"That was a long time ago."

"You went up to Overlook Point with David just before he died—you were friends."

"Friends?" B.J. roused herself in defense of her memories. "We loved each other. We were going together. I'd've done about anything for that boy, anything at all." A suspicious look crossed her face. "What is it you're after?"

"Tell me about that night," Molly asked. "About you and David . . ."

Moist eyes rolling, snuffling, B.J. swallowed a long gulp of beer. When she spoke, it was hurriedly, as if she was impatient to get it over with, intent on ridding herself of a burden too long sustained.

"We went up to the Point, David and me, and got down on his raincoat. Not that we were doing anything we shouldn't've been doing. Most kids who went up there had autos but our families couldn't afford an extra car for any kid. Oh, maybe we kissed a few times—I was a good girl, and my mother raised me right. But I loved David and I loved it when he put his hands on me."

A warm, dreamy look came into her eyes as she recollected. "Well, after a while, there were some sounds. We peeked through the bushes and it was a Turnpike Cruiser carrying two couples parked nearby. One of the girls got out, saying she was going to leave, saying her friend should come along. But the friend stayed on. Next, one of the boys left, too. With all that commotion, David and me kept laughing to ourselves and whispering and having a good time about all the fussing. Only he, the boy who left, that is, he never went very far. He just tippy-toed around in a big circle and hid, back out of sight behind the old elm tree. That's when we spied the other two, also hiding out, keeping watch the way we were."

"What happened next?" Molly said, not wanting to know.

"Well, the second couple got out of the car and did it."

"Had sex?" Molly forced herself to say.

"You bet. Hot and heavy, lots of moaning and groaning."

"The boy forced her," Molly said, willing it to be so.

B.J. was surprised by the question. "Not at first. I mean,

who'd've blamed her, him being who he was and as good to look at as he was. But it was like she changed her mind and he got put out, started calling her names. She was about to take off but he wasn't having any of that. He jerked her around, began hitting her . . .''

"Go on.''

She turned away briefly and when she looked back, a shrewd, calculating expression had settled on her face.

Recognizing the look for what it was, Molly offered her something for her troubles, handing her a twenty-dollar bill. She eyed it with open disdain and Molly doubled the offer.

She snatched at the bills, tucking them inside her dress. "A lady's got to live. After all, these are hard times.''

"What happened next?''

"Four in all,'' she said, summoning it up as if it were taking place again in front of her. "One right after another. It was a bet, you see. The first one won his bet and so he insisted that the others get in on the deal. The girl didn't much care for that. They had to hold her down. She fought something fierce, kicking and scratching, even tried to scream. Only they knocked her around until she couldn't put up a fight anymore.''

"You watched them assault and rape her?''

B.J. nodded solemnly.

"And you did nothing to help?'' Molly, trying to control her anger, said.

B.J. shook her head pityingly. "Four of them and only David and me, what do you expect? They'd've beat up David and done the same to me, most likely. There was nothing anybody could do, you can see that, can't you?'' She described what happened next.

Flat on the ground behind the bushes, David had made a move as if to go to the aid of the beleaguered Emily. B.J. dragged him back down, holding tightly to his belt.

"Let's get out of here,'' she implored against his cheek.

"They're hurting her.''

"Those boys, she's the same as all of them, one of their own kind. If they don't care, why should we? David, I'm scared.''

He agreed silently, unable to watch any longer, the

malevolent rhythm of the unholy act pounding in his ears. Until at last it came to an end. Now a more searing hurt shot through him as he listened to the echo of his own failure.

"Please," B.J. urged, "let's get out of here." The four boys had gone, driving off in the gleaming Turnpike Cruiser, leaving the girl on the ground.

"Let's help her, she's hurt."

"She'll be fine, her kind always is. Money fixes everything."

B.J., on her feet, kept pulling at David's arm. He rose, looking back to where the girl was. "I can't walk away like this, I can't do it."

"I don't want to get involved. It's going to mean trouble for us both, you'll see. I'm not having any part of it."

He considered the situation, the choices open to him. "Head back to the fair. A couple of hundred feet back and you'll spot the lights. After that, it's easy. Go on straight home. I'll talk to you tomorrow."

"What are you going to do?"

"I'll be all right."

She watched him pick his way through the thicket, saw him make his way to Emily and then crouch at her side. The battered girl moaned at the sight of him and rolled away, clutching at her Teddy bear.

"No more, please. No more. Why did they do this to me?"

"I'm going to help you," David said softly. He wasn't sure what to do next. "I'll take you home."

She recoiled from his touch. "Oh, no, not home. Not home. If my mother finds out—she can't. Please . . ."

"You can't stay here."

She allowed him to assist her to her feet. "Lauren," she managed to say. "Lauren will know what to do. Lauren will take care of me."

"What happened then?" Molly prompted B.J.

She blinked. "Happened? Why, David was killed is what happened. Shot in the head. Dead at sixteen."

"Murdered to protect those boys?" Molly said.

"Nobody could do anything to those boys. Nothing touched them. Nothing harmed them. Like they owned the world and everything was arranged to suit them. Every last thing."

"What were their names? Please, tell me who they are?"

B.J. sniffed and turned away.

"I know who they are. But I need to hear it from you. A witness."

"Witness?" B.J. said. "Me, a witness? You must be crazy!"

"If not for me, then for David's sake."

B.J. sat up, looking directly at Molly. "David was killed because he put his nose in where it wasn't wanted. What those boys did was wrong, it was dead wrong. Only that didn't do David any good and it won't me. Can't no good come of any of this."

"If you're afraid—?"

"Sure I'm afraid. I was then, I still am, and with plenty of reason to be, I'd say."

"We'll go to the police," Molly said, aware of the emptiness of her words. "Make sure you are protected."

The look in her eyes told Molly what she thought of that idea. "What I got, this life of mine, it's not much. Still, it's all I got and I mean to hang on until the last breath in me. These days, that's enough."

35

"NOTHING," PERRY MAXWELL said, when he came out of the computer room. "The machine tells me zero about Emily Fowler. No rape complaint brought by her or anybody else during the time period we've been looking at."

Molly, disappointed, shook her head. "I kept hoping somebody might have spoken out. Have I been clutching at straws?"

"It's all in the computer."

"Unless certain records were never entered into the machines," Becker said.

"Very good, Carl," came the rumbling rasp of Barney Grubb, all amiability gone. "You have an instinctive grasp of how things are done."

Molly jumped in. "You're saying the records are incomplete?"

Grubb spread his lips in a mirthless grin. "I'm saying that not everything was entered into the computer. We went to the computer in nineteen seventy-two with a cutoff date of nineteen sixty-eight. Anything happened before that would be in the regular files. They're kept over in the warehouse, behind the fire station. Anytime you want, you're welcome to scrounge through 'em." Grubb shifted his attention from

Molly to Perry Maxwell, his manner stern and commanding. "Maybe you'd like to tell me what it is we are discussing here, Sergeant?"

"Rape," Molly said before Perry could answer.

Without looking at her, Grubb said, "I don't know about any rapes."

Maxwell, cool and correct, said, "Miss Fairfax is convinced her mother was raped back in fifty-eight. Raped and beaten by four locals."

"Whatever gave you an idea like that, miss?"

"It happened."

"If it did, I'd know about it, wouldn't I?"

"There were witnesses," she blurted out, then wished she hadn't spoken.

Grubb went on as if he hadn't heard. "I was on the force back then, and I'm the only old-timer still around. My opinion is that you are misinformed, wasting your time on what may be the product of some poor soul's imagination. No such crime ever took place."

"How can you be so sure?"

Grubb allowed himself a flat, truncated laugh, as if he'd had second thoughts in the middle of it. "Memory is a prime ingredient of police work. Memory for faces. Memory for gestures. Memory concerning methods of operations. Who did what to whom and when and how it was done. A good cop fills his head up the way a kid fills his head up with baseball averages. And in a small town like this one, it ain't so hard to keep track of things. Go ahead, ask Perry here. Bet he remembers every case he ever dealt with since he joined up. Ain't that so, Sergeant?"

"I try, Chief."

"There you are," Grubb said. "He tries. We all try, only some of us get better results than others."

"This happened twenty-six years ago," Becker pointed out. "There were other officers on the force handling other crimes . . ."

Grubb glowed with triumph and Becker realized he'd made a tactical blunder. Nodding sagely, Grubb seemed to agree.

"Back then only three of us were on the force. Whatever went down, each man knew about it. That takes care of that, I'd say."

"The other two officers," Molly said. "Where can we find them?"

Grubb's satisfaction was plain to see. "Well, now, Bob Meader, he ran his car off the river road in sixty-one, I think it was. Went right into the water and goodbye Bobby. By the time we got to hoist that car back onto dry land, it was rusted over, not even good for parts.

"Hillary Gault, he used to be chief. You can find old Hillary in the graveyard back of the Congregational Church, dead of a massive coronary. At least poor Hillary had a few peaceful years. Retired in fifty-nine and didn't pass on until seventy-two. Which leaves only me to remember the good old days, and I am guaranteeing you no event such as you describe ever took place. This ain't New York City or Chicago, or some such as that. We get speeders and fist fighters, some serious drinkers, kids doing mischief. But not much in the way of heavy stuff, not in a peaceful town like Old Brixton."

His eyes raked over them, settling finally on Molly. "We have learned that lots of rape victims don't come forward, okay. They reason that no matter the outcome, the hard time the system causes ain't worth the effort. So be it. Mostly, it's women like you, Miss Fairfax, who get raped, you know. Unmarried, white, your age or thereabouts. Statistics say rape amounts to about three percent of all violent crime in the good old U.S. of A. Shame, ain't it? But there you are. Maybe this rape you folks got on your mind was like that—nobody reported it. On the other hand," he ended, in a manner pointedly casual, "you did mention something about a witness."

"There were two witnesses," Molly said, determined to shake him loose of his arrogance. He reeked of abusive power and entrenched authority and she now believed he was capable of using his position for his personal good.

He responded in a voice soft and curious. "Mind telling me who they are, miss? I'd sure like to have a few words with them."

Molly glanced at Becker who nodded slightly. She said, "One witness is not ready to step forward."

"Is that a fact, a living witness to a crime that happened more'n a quarter century ago? Not that it matters. You see, we got a six-year statute of limitations on rape in this state, so it don't matter much, does it? Besides, a witness not willing to testify is about as useful as no witness at all." He experienced no relief, only frustration and a growing fury. "Who might that witness be?"

Molly answered, "When the time is right, we can produce the witness."

Grubb squared away, warning himself to rein in his anger. "And the second witness?"

"That," Molly said, "was David Colfax."

Grubb relaxed. Feeble, that's what they were. One witness who wouldn't talk and another long dead. But the threat still remained and would have to be dealt with.

"That's the boy got himself shot through the back of the head, I recollect. No need for them to do him thataway, was my thinking at the time."

"Them?" Molly said, probing gently.

Misses nothing, Grubb noted. Smartass female, not to be taken lightly. He arranged a pleasant expression on his big face. "Those people, whoever it was shot David, took his watch, a ring, and whatever cash he had on his person. A boy that age, most likely didn't amount to very much. Left the empty wallet alongside the body. Way I figured it, the killer was a stranger, just passing through. Had a need for a quick score and happened on the boy and took him out. Shame of it was that young Colfax was such a nice kid. That's the last killing we've had since."

"Except for Sam," Becker reminded him.

Grubb answered in a slow, meticulous way. "I wasn't referring to self-inflicted wounds."

Molly couldn't contain herself. "Do you count near misses, Chief?"

"Near misses?"

"Somebody tried to kill Carl and me."

Grubb raised his brows. "First I've heard about it."

"A man in a light blue Cadillac," Becker said. "Put a shot across the bow of Molly's car. You can see the scar."

"Why wasn't a report made?"

"Would it have done any good?"

"With sharp-thinking types like Sergeant Maxwell on the force, can't say what we might come up with. Get the license plate number, did you?"

"We missed that."

"Too bad. Well, we'll notify all our people. A Cadillac, you said. Maybe you got the year and model, Counselor?"

"When somebody shoots at me, I tend to overlook the details."

"Shame. Still, we'll do what we can. We might get lucky. Trouble is, we are not the FBI. Just a small-town force directing traffic and keeping the peace on Saturday nights. Ain't that a fact, Sergeant?"

Maxwell nodded once.

"Tell the truth," Grubb said, "I am putting all that behind me soon enough. Going to throw in my retirement papers by-'n'-by, go into business for myself. Set up my own security company. More pay for less work, and no risk to speak of. Private enterprise, the coast-to-coast all-American dream of wealth and glory, a man's own honest-to-God business. Ain't that the way!"

Later, when Becker and Molly had departed, Grubb summoned Maxwell into his office. "This here is a police station, Sergeant. Police business is conducted on these premises, not doing errands for your nosy friends. Oblige me by keeping that in mind from here on out. You hear me, Sergeant?"

"Loud and clear, Chief."

Back in his car and driving well within local speed limits, Becker said, "It's all connected in some mysterious way."

"What is?"

"My father's murder—"

"You're convinced it was murder?"

"I am. And what happened to your mother. And the shooting of David Colfax."

"That's stretching things awfully far."

"Maybe it's the way I want things to be, tied up in a tidy little bundle. One thing I am sure of, there are two people who have all the answers: Barney Grubb is one and Nelson Evan Proctor is the other."

36

THE SAUGATUCK RANGE extended due north before beginning its westerly run. At its loftiest elevations, the terrain undulated from grassy bowls to raw, rough ridges, intermittently masked off by strands of hardwood. Grubb, head down, set a killing pace as he led the way up a slope covered with pine scored by an occasional cluster of birch. His movements were surprisingly quiet for such a big man, each footfall carefully placed, covering ground swiftly.

Five yards behind, Nels Proctor offered no complaint. He had conditioned himself for this or any other test Grubb cared to put him to. The daily workouts in his home gym, the five-mile runs, had left him lean and wiry, his lungs sound. Admittedly, Grubb was in better shape than expected. After a while his tempo quickened as he bulled his way through thickets of oakbrush, overcoming obstacles that would have forced a lesser man to seek an easier way around.

Where the climb was steepest, where brute strength served best, Grubb gained ground; Nels closed the gap on the long, open areas. A thrill of recognition went through Nels and he called out. Grubb never paused, answering over his shoulder.

"Need a break, Counselor?"

Once again the police chief had transformed a cooperative

venture into a competition. To complain would be a sign of
weakness, to stop was to surrender. Grubb functioned in a
straight cerebral line, calculating all twists and turns in solitary
silence, factoring in all possible diversions, operating by rules
he alone knew. The game was familiar to Nels; only one man
could come out the other side feeling good about himself.

Rich man, poor man. Nels understood why Barney had to
win whenever possible. Hunting, fishing, shooting a game of
snooker, arm wrestling; pastimes at which Grubb inevitably
excelled. Grubb never gave an inch, never let up, determined
to prove himself the better man.

The hell he was, Nels thought grimly. "We're off the trail,"
he said, coming abreast of Grubb, who kept plowing ahead.

"Good. One of these days you'll turn into a real hunter."

A thin compliment reluctantly given, swiftly diluted. That
was Grubb's way. The policeman did not lead a noticeably
civil existence.

"We scouted farther east in the spring," Nels pointed out.
By now Gary would be closing in on the stand they had
chosen, putting himself in the proper frame of mind for his
new role as an assassin. Nothing could be permitted to in-
terfere, no way Grubb could be allowed to go off on one of his
tangents. "And made some fine sightings."

"On the nose. But the landscape is different now. The trees
thicker and the brush overgrown. No way to set a straight
course into the high country. Soon enough, we'll begin to circle."

"I'm right behind you, Chief."

Out here, Grubb fell naturally into his role as leader and
teacher, at home in the wild, comfortable in the huge spaces,
sensitive to every shift in the wind, to every movement in the
forest. "Bucks tend to conceal themselves when possible," he
lectured. "They'll keep to the swales, work behind the low
rises. One of those bucks can be as smart as a man. He'll drift
through cover instead of clinging to a previously established
trail. Staying alive is a full-time job for a buck and the ones
that make it from season to season are damned good at what
they do."

"Survival of the fittest," Nels said, playing to Grubb's ego,
not really listening to his words.

"You got it. Remember your best spot?" Grubb planted
one big booted foot as if on a marked point and pushed off,

heading due east, going still higher.

Grubb's instructions were succinct. "What looks like open terrain to you has plenty of cover for a buck. Hunting with a bow is short-range work and there's no room for error. A buck gets on to you, brother, and he is gone. One good leap and he's out of shooting range, one more and he's out of sight. In this business, almost don't count."

Grubb sat on a rock, bow resting across his knees.

"Getting tired, Barney?" Nels said, expressing mild concern.

Grubb didn't answer at once, squinting into the distance, plotting the moves of some unknown super-buck, adjusting his own game plan accordingly. "Had a small talk with your lady friend the other day," he said, gazing up the mountainside.

"Molly?"

Grubb made a small sound that gave nothing away. "Lady says she and Becker have come up with a witness to that business with her mother back when."

"I know, she told me. But there is no witness—there can't be."

"Since nobody ever came forward, we always assumed there was nobody else. Were we wrong? Suppose there is a witness lurking out there in the brush?"

"Statute of limitations," Nels said.

"Yeah. Still, wouldn't help your reputation or mine, would it? Might even tie somebody into the David Colfax case, and we can't have that."

"This shouldn't be happening."

"Exactly my way of thinking. Too bad whoever took a shot at those people missed. Would have settled everything."

"One witness," Nels said presently. "To an event that took place so long ago. It can't do any real harm."

"It can't do any real good." Grubb pushed himself erect. "Maybe whoever took a shot at those people will try again and this time not miss. That'd help, wouldn't it, Counselor?" He started up the side of the range once more. Nels, coming up behind, was thinking hard.

Gary's legs were giving him trouble. Legs that for so many years had been the main source of his power. Thick, muscular thighs had provided that extra drive needed to churn out the tough yardage down at the goal line, bumping heads with those huge linemen, never quitting. But the same strong muscles had been his weakness, too. Knotting up from time to time, tearing under excessive strain, until finally his football career had ended. Everything begins with the legs, Coach used to say, sending them out to run laps.

With deliberate caution he bellied down to the ground, stretching out, face cradled in his arm. That was better. In the shadows of the stand, the earth still held on to the morning dampness and he grew chilled and anxious. Using the binoculars Nels had supplied, Gary scanned the landscape north to south and back again.

Where in hell were they?

He checked his Rolex. What if the watch was running slow and he had missed them? At thirty-five hundred bucks a pop, the damned thing ought to keep proper time. He listened to it tick and warned himself to remain calm. What was it Nels had said? Hunting is not an exact science. Stay out of sight and wait. He glassed the high ground but saw no movement. He glanced to his rear; nothing. Very few hunters were likely to make the arduous climb to this high altitude, preferring to work the lower fields. The air was thin and crisp and breathing was difficult. He felt very much alone, isolated in his pact with Nels.

But at least there *was* Nels. If not for Nels, he'd still be locked into that lousy marriage with Leila, and her banging every stud in the county. Nels had caused him to see the error of his ways and he knew he was better off for it. Though there were still too many moments when Leila was on his mind.

Another look at the Rolex. Five minutes had elapsed. Nels and Grubb were due. Soon. And then he would demonstrate his ability to uphold his end of the bargain, any bargain. He held out his hand, his fingers trembling. No matter. When the crucial moment came he would be all right. Steady and ready. Prove himself to himself. And to Nels.

Proceeding along the western edge of the ridge, they picked their way through a low pass which opened on to a soft green basin that brought them steadily higher.

Nels brought one arm high overhead before lowering his hand to the top of his head. Certain they were under Gary's glass at last, the signal was intended to alert him to their identity. By now Gary ought to be in place set for the instant when Grubb would offer himself as the target. To make it appear like a hunting accident, however, it was up to Nels to maneuver Grubb into a patch of woods where his movements could reasonably be mistaken for those of a feeding buck.

Abruptly, Grubb went down to one knee. Ahead of him, a doe appeared, picking her way delicately toward higher ground. Soon a second doe passed from shadow into the shifting light, then was lost to sight in the thicket.

Grubb spoke in a hoarse whisper. "A dollar'll get you ten a buck'll be sniffing after them any minute now."

He started out again. Where the forest thinned out, he increased his pace, boots barely rustling the leaves underfoot, a man at home in his environment. He stopped again and Nels froze, not five yards to his rear; now, he silently urged. Shoot now. They were under the gun, lined up in Gary's sights.

Grubb gestured. "Up there, bedded in the pine."

Nels peered through his glasses, gradually bringing into focus the velvety tips of a buck's antlers. A magnificent beast.

Grubb voiced his admiration. "Must be six or seven years old. That's a twenty-eight-inch rack, maybe more."

Shoot, damnit. Shoot.

What was he waiting for? Perhaps Gary was looking for a closer shot, at a range from which he couldn't miss. If so, it was up to Nels to supply it.

Nels tapped Grubb on the shoulder. "From here it's an impossible stalk."

"Yeah, but I don't want him to get upwind of us before I get a shot off."

Nels jerked his head in the direction of the high ground. "Let's try it up there, let's let him come to us."

"Good thinking. Let's do it."

They set off in a great circle around the buck. They climbed without haste, silent and careful to make no sound that would startle their prey. The trees were smaller here and set farther apart, offering less cover. Keeping to the shadows, they went slowly. Step and pause. Look and listen. Time was held frozen, the existence of the buck the only unchanging element in the interminable interval.

At an elevation he considered safe, Grubb went down to one knee, looking back. Nels followed his lead but was unable to

spot the deer, until Grubb pointed discreetly. The buck again
was on the move, feeding as he went, the great antlers proudly
held as he raised his head to sniff the wind.

"Want to go higher?" Nels suggested.

"This is as far as I go. I'll take him from here. Once he
comes out of the brush, I'll have a clean shot."

Nels felt the tension drain away. At this distance, Gary
would have no trouble locating Grubb in his buffalo plaid
hunting shirt. A perfect target, that wide, powerful back.
Impossible to miss. A clean shot, Grubb had said. A clean
shot through the back was what Gary had now. Take aim,
Nels silently urged, taking up a position down and away from
his companion. Take a deep breath, exhale, squeeze the
trigger . . .

Gary's mouth was dry. Lips parched, tongue thick, too big
for his mouth. Spread out in the stand, he sighted down on
the two men below. He put the front sight in the middle of
Grubb's big back, right between the shoulder blades. His
finger reached for the trigger and at the same time Grubb
seemed to fade away into the haze of the forest, taking up a
more strategic position.

Gary blinked and waited, eyes scanning the wooded terrain
below. He changed his position, pushing the brush to one side,
assuring himself an unobstructed view. Once again he took a
firing position. Grubb was nowhere to be seen. But Nels, Nels
was in place behind a plane tree. On one knee, peering at the
buck coming his way.

Gary brought the rifle to bear. How easy it was; Nels had
been right about that. No way to miss. He laid his cheek along
the stock, sighting, lined up on Nels's back. Why not, he
asked himself. Why not take both of them out? No one would
ever suspect him. No one knew he was here. All he had to do
was dispose of the Springfield according to Nels's instructions
and he would be home free.

Nels was his best friend, he reminded himself, a blurred vision of Leila dancing before his eyes. Her eyes were bright,
and her taunting silent laugh mocked him. Oh, the bitch, that
duplicitous bitch. And with his best friend.

He flipped off the safety and steadied the Springfield.

No shot came. Nels, crouched behind the plane tree, began

to question his decision. Suppose Grubb was right? Getting rid of Becker and Molly once and for all might solve all their problems. Those two did present a growing danger. With Grubb gone, who would tend to such matters? This ambush—it might turn out to be an irrevocable mistake. From time to time, the Barney Grubbs of the world were necessary. He glanced back; there was no sign of Grubb.

Had he changed his mind, begun stalking the buck, too impatient to continue playing a waiting game? That wasn't Barney's style. To do so would have brought the police chief out into the open and he was too experienced to make that kind of blunder. Where was he, then? Changing his position, seeking to improve his chances for a killing shot? Yes, of course, that was it.

And Gary, he should have fired before this. The open shot had been there. Was something wrong? Had Gary lost his nerve?

The shot, when it did come, startled him. A cry of alarm went up, pain, fear, and a thrashing from above, back in the thicket. Nels charged up the mountainside.

He found Gary stretched out on the ground, unconscious, blood trickling from a small wound above one ear. Nels spoke his name, tried to rouse him without success. Only gradually did he realize that the rifle was missing. Commanding himself to remain calm, he stood up and drew an arrow from his quiver, placed it precisely onto the string of his bow. He took one hunter's step out of the stand and then another.

Clunk.

There was no mistaking the ominous sound of the Springfield's bolt being thrust into place, a live round jamming into the chamber. Nels spun around.

"Go ahead," came the words, Grubb's voice edged with malice and joy. "Try me on for size."

Nels allowed the bow and arrow to fall to the ground. A few counts went by before Grubb showed himself, the rifle pointed at Nels's stomach.

"Dumbness," the big man snarled. "You and your asshole buddy both. What were you thinking? To take me down like I was some dumb deer? From the start I was onto you. Acting so damn friendly, so agreeable, all that natural superiority of yours gone. Why, I asked myself. What is going on? And this fool—" He indicated Gary, who was beginning to stir.

"Whether you mean to kill an animal or a man, you stay still. No moving around. No leaves going the wrong way under the wind. No breathing too loud. No careless, noisy releasing of the safety. Dumb bastard never knew I was on to him until I bashed his head."

With every word, Grubb got angrier. His normally small eyes became slits and his cheeks grew mottled, his lips drawn back in a display of professional scorn and loathing for an amateur opponent. "For you it's a game" he shouted, the rifle trembling in his big hands. "A damned ball game with winners and losers. Well, lemme tell you, if it's a game, it's a game you ain't familiar with."

The shout faded into a thick rumble and, as if disappointed in himself, Grubb exploded into action. He drove the butt of the rifle into Nels's middle, sending him to his knees retching and gasping for air. Grubb kicked out, and Nels went rolling. Poised for another kick, Grubb decided against it. He hunkered down, the rifle across his thighs, watching. He lit a cigarette and considered the situation.

"See what you've done, making me mad this way. I don't like losing my temper like that. Dumbness—what you tried to do was dumbness. You disappoint me, Nels, a smart guy like you, trying to bring me down in such a simple-minded way."

He smoked and thought. "Doesn't make sense, does it? No reason for me to be pissed off at you people or you at me. You need me. I want a bigger slice of the pie—so what? Who is going to take care of certain items if I ain't around? Certainly neither of you guys. Not Whitehead or Newell. None of you is up to it. Oh, yes, I am sorely disappointed in you, Counselor."

Gary sat up, moaning, holding his head. "What happened?"

"Dumbness is what happened," Grubb replied evenly.

Nels managed to get his back up against a tree. His ribs ached and his hip throbbed where Grubb's booted foot had landed.

"You going to arrest us?" Gary said, with a supplicant's smile.

Under the weight of the question, Grubb's demeanor collapsed. He held himself and laughed raucously. "Jesus, but you are sincerely the dumbest of men. Arrest you? Let's just say I am out of my official jurisdiction."

Gary couldn't restrain himself. "What are you going to do?"

Grubb lifted the Springfield and leveled it at Gary's belt buckle. "Maybe do you the way you were going to do me. In my place, Counselor, what would you do?"

"You're not going to kill us, Barney," Nels said confidently.

The rifle swung his way. "Don't be so sure."

Nels felt his strength returning. Barney was right; what they'd done had been stupid. Inept and clumsy. He should've done the job himself. It was not too late; his chance would come. "What do you want, Barney?"

Grubb lowered the weapon, grinning that awful, toothy grin of his. "Balls of pure brass, I give you that, Nels." He sobered quickly. "What we have is an inequitable situation, which saddens me and leaves me a great deal poorer. It is time for us to reorder our relationship, as the saying goes."

Gary whimpered. "What's he talking about, Nels?"

"Getting rich."

"That's what I like about you," Grubb said. "Right to the point. Eliminates all the bull that way. Getting rich from this day forward, for now and forever."

"I'm willing to listen," Nels said, the old arrogance back.

"How rich?" Gary dared to ask.

"An equal partner."

"That's crazy!" Gary cried.

"In everything," Barney continued. "The mall. The corporate parks. Whatever comes along. Equal partner with an equal share and an equal voice."

"We can't do that!" Gary said.

Grubb swung the rifle back to him. "Sure you can."

"Sure we can," Nels said with a slight, imperceptible modulation in tone.

Grubb was magnanimous in victory. "There. That's smart. Common ground for our partnership. Listen closely, gentlemen, and I'll tell you exactly what our arrangement is going to be . . ."

37

IN THE DAYS that followed, winter signaled its imminence. The sky was glowering, the wind whipping out of the north, cold and penetrating. Throughout the county, householders split logs and opened chimney flues. Down parkas appeared on the racks in sporting goods stores and the sale of insulated boots increased steeply. Snow tires were examined with a frugal eye toward squeezing out another season's use and antifreeze began to appear in pyramids in auto supply shops. Stolid New Englanders reflected on the popularity of heading south when the snows set in, but few of them would do so; it wouldn't have looked right.

Anna Slocum spent much of the afternoon stacking firewood under the shed roof at the rear of the stone house. The pile grew rapidly, thanks to Molly's help, and when it was done the two women retreated to the cozy kitchen and huddled over mugs steaming with aromatic Chinese tea.

"The days are getting shorter."

"When I first arrived in Old Brixton," Molly said, assembling her thoughts without haste, "I felt at home—as if I belonged—and wanted to stay forever."

"And now?"

"I'm a stranger. I don't belong."

"You belong in my house," Anna replied with unexpected intensity. "For as long as you like. Having you around is good for me. Provides me with a taste of what it would have been like if I had a daughter of my own. My link with immortality, as it were, some distance removed." A wry smile spread across her face and her eyes crinkled at the corners. "Getting sentimental lately. Must be age creeping up on me."

"You'll never be old."

"Sixty." She tasted the word, its implications. "That's a big number. When your time comes, you'll understand. Sixty is close to retirement. The age when people start complaining, spending time in hospitals, and dying. Young people call you 'ma'am' and treat you with elaborate concern, as if you're liable to shatter before their eyes. Senior citizens, that's what we sixties are."

"Not you, Anna."

"This is when I feel it most. The wind whistling and the temperature falling. It's the lonely time, locked in by the cold and the snow. Since Sam died—ah, being alone is the worst part." She cupped the mug and breathed in the scented fumes of the tea. "Stay and become a part of my life, I want to say to you sometimes. Stay and make me believe that I'm not alone, won't be alone for the rest of my life."

"I would like that."

"A romantic notion. Young and old, making it easier for each other when the going gets rough. Wouldn't work, though. At your age, there are things for you to do. Adventures to have, victories, defeats. That gallery of yours, for example. Great artists are waiting for you to discover them, show their work, make them rich and famous, shove them down the throat of an uncaring public." She laughed. "Become a powerhouse lady."

"Actually, the gallery's been on my mind lately. Why do I limit myself solely to painting?"

"There are a great many fine young sculptors."

"And other media. Weaving, jewelry, ceramics."

"Namely my ceramics, you mean?" Anna threw back her head and roared with pleasure. "By God, girl, you are a decent piece of work. I am no artist. Just a craftsman, doing good honest work. Functional and meant to last, my pots and bowls."

"You could make other things."

"Wind chimes and wall tiles and coasters? No, thank you. I'll stay with what I do best. Sam used to say that, 'Stay with what you do best, a person can't go wrong.' Sam would have made a hell of a pioneer. Breaking sod, plowing behind a mule, fashioning furniture by hand. Doing the thousand little jobs that need doing. He was that kind of man."

She drained her mug. "And I'd've made a fine pioneer's wife. Rearing a handful of kids. Cooking. Cleaning. Making clothes for them all. Loving the hell out of Sam at night."

"You never had children?"

"Didn't want them when I was young—too much to do was what I told myself—and when I finally did want them I had become too old. You get caught up in things. Experiencing everything, going and doing, tasting of every pot. It's fun while it lasts, but it doesn't give you much to hang on to."

"I've never given much thought to raising a family."

"Well, it's about time you started thinking about it. Maybe doing something about it."

Molly allowed her eyes to close. "When I think about a man now . . ." A shudder shook her body. Her eyes opened. "I feel soiled, spoiled, ashamed of myself."

"Because of your reaction to Proctor?"

"Because of what I did."

"What you almost did, keep that in mind."

"I should've known."

"Nonsense."

"In a way I think I did know. There was an intensity, an acute, gnawing sense of danger and wrongdoing, as if I were crossing a line I'd never before crossed."

"Nor did you cross it."

"I wanted to. *I really wanted to.*"

"But you didn't. Whatever you felt—and none of us is responsible for our feelings—you didn't cross the line. There's nothing to blame yourself for: you did nothing wrong. And there's no point in laying what Nels Proctor did on all the males of the species. Just put it out of your head."

"I wish I could." She paused, then continued deliberately. "Anna, I've made up my mind. I'm going to leave, go back to New York."

"Maybe that's your best move after all."

Molly pulled on her tennis shoes and a heavy Irish knit turtleneck sweater. "A little air might clear my mind, help me to think straight."

"It's cold outside and night's coming on."

"I won't be long." At the door, Molly paused. "All this time and I've never set foot on Overlook Point. It's about time I visited the scene of the crime, don't you think?"

Perry Maxwell, looking every inch the prototypical police officer in perfectly tailored uniform, joined Becker at the counter in the Berkshire Diner and Pie Bakery. Becker drank coffee, Maxwell ordered a glass of cold milk and a wedge of strawberry-rhubarb pie.

"You got the word on the Luger finally?" Becker said.

"I went to the warehouse for those old files. You can thank Barney for reminding me about that. What a mess—nobody's looked at that stuff since they tucked them away. I found something."

"I'm waiting."

"You're not going to believe this."

"Try me."

"Turns out it once belonged to Barney Grubb."

"That son of a bitch!"

"It's not that simple."

"The hell you say! This is the crusher. Barney shot my father, made it look like a suicide."

"Take it easy."

"This pins his ass to the wall."

"It'll take more than the gun."

"Why more? This puts the murder weapon in his hand."

"You're not going to like this. Barney reported the Luger stolen."

Becker swore. "When? The day before Sam was shot? A good way to get himself off the hook."

"I said you wouldn't like it. It was reported stolen in July of nineteen fifty-eight."

Becker stared at his friend, trying to sort out what he'd just heard, make it fit into the puzzle he was trying so hard to piece together.

Maxwell said, "July sixth to be exact."

Becker's brain pulsed with excitement as the date registered. "That's one day before David Colfax was killed. By a drifter or drifters unknown and unapprehended. Twenty-six years later it shows up again in my father's hand."

"Coincidence?" Maxwell asked.

"Too much so."

"My thinking exactly."

"What's your explanation?"

"Careless is what it is," Maxwell said. "I checked ballistics and—"

Becker broke in. "The slug that killed Colfax matches the one that killed Sam."

"You should've been a cop, Carl."

"All this time and no one ever made the match before this. Why?"

"No reason to connect the two deaths. Nobody put the gun in two places before this. Nobody had cause to."

Becker, consumed by the desire to solve his father's murder, struggled to hold himself in check. This was no time to go off half-cocked. Logic was in order, logic and a tempered response.

"Barney's gun," he said quietly, "used in two killings. Nobody in his right mind would suggest Sam stole the Luger and murdered David Colfax."

"No," Maxwell said thoughtfully, "nobody would suggest that."

"Then only one conclusion remains."

"Don't be too sure."

"Perry, you're thinking what I'm thinking, I can tell."

"I'm a cop. I collect information. I build a case and, if it looks solid, I turn it over to the County Attorney for prosecution. What I don't do is draw wild conclusions."

"Not so wild."

"Be careful, Carl. You could turn a silk purse into a sow's ear."

"Somebody's got to say it, Perry. That Luger was Barney's backup gun, maybe one of many he owned years ago."

Maxwell pushed the milk away, toying with the pie. "Barney collects guns. All kinds. He's shown them to me. Must own a couple of hundred weapons, new and old, foreign and domestic, some functional, others useless."

"Makes the cheese more binding, to my way of thinking. He reports the Luger stolen, along with a few other weapons to make it look kosher—how am I doing so far?"

Maxwell recited in a lifeless voice. "A Hawes-Saurer Western Marshal single shot, a Bo-Mar winged-rib with a six-inch barrel, a Colt .45 automatic, a .22 target pistol—"

"And the Luger?"

"And the Luger."

"None of them particularly rare. None of them truly valuable."

"The Hawes-Saurer was a reproduction."

"None of them worth more than the retail price, I'll bet."

"You're doing okay so far."

"Once they're reported stolen Barney would be in the clear, if any of them were to be used in a crime."

"You said that, I didn't."

"And forty-eight hours later, goodbye David Colfax."

"Which proves nothing."

"Unless the guns were never stolen."

"They might have been stolen," Maxwell said doggedly. He felt uneasy in this situation, his loyalties divided. He was a cop and wanted to believe that his fellow cops were good people, straight and honest. But he knew better. Still . . . "There is no way to put Barney on the trigger."

"It had to be Grubb both times."

"You want it that way, Carl. But there are unanswered questions. What motive did Grubb have to take Colfax out? Without a motive, you've got nothing."

Becker worked it out as if it were all unfolding before him. He layed it out for Maxwell, step by step. "Colfax watched The Four Horsemen rape Emily Fowler. He recognized each one of them. Had it not been for B.J. Miller holding him back, he would have tried to help her. That was his nature, Perry. Instead, he waited until they left and brought Emily down off the Point. First to Lauren Poole and then to Doctor Ortner. Nobody—not Ortner, not Lauren, not Emily herself—was willing to make a police case out of the rape, each for his or her own reasons.

"David was different. He couldn't deal with that. The boy had been brought up to believe in truth and justice. This boy was a straight arrow, Perry, and he knew it was his duty to report the crime."

"There's no record."

"David reported the rape, all right, and it was his bad luck that Barney Grubb was on duty. David told Barney about the rape, named the four rapists and agreed to testify."

"Are you saying Barney destroyed the record?"

"Maybe there was no record. Maybe he never put anything down on paper. Maybe nothing had to be destroyed."

"And then Barney took out David?"

"After reporting the Luger stolen."

"Why?"

"To protect the rapists."

"You haven't convinced me."

"All right, try this. The Four Horsemen were not much more than kids themselves. They sober up and realize the gravity of what they've done. They are scared, some of them more than the others. If one of them talks, they all pay the price and the chances are excellent that one of them will crack, so they look for a way out."

"They go to Barney."

"Sure, why not?"

Maxwell shook his head. "I can pick holes in your case, Counselor. One: Nobody knew there were witnesses. The rapists couldn't have known what happened after they left the Point. They wouldn't know about David's visit to Barney, if there actually was a visit. Two: Why would they go to Barney? Like I said, he was a young cop, new to the force. If they approached anybody, it'd be the chief, the top man. No, Carl, it didn't happen that way."

"Unless," Becker pounced, "we've got it backwards. But you said the magic words—Barney was young, ambitious, but without much in the way of prospects. The town is small, the force is small, and he lacked seniority. He had no future. Until he saw his main chance and seized it. He contacted the boys . . . no, he contacted their parents. No, again. Maybe just one parent. The fewer people in on this affair the better. So he chose one—"

"Which one?"

Becker ran over the roster of names. "Richard Crompton Proctor, Nels's father."

"Why Proctor?"

"Because he's the most powerful man in town, the one with the widest contacts, the most influence, one of the richest if not *the* richest. It makes sense, Perry."

"I'm still listening."

"Okay, they cut a deal—Barney, old man Proctor and Nels.

The boys must be protected at all costs. But there's a witness, a witness who will not be bought off. Barney offers the solution: the witness must be eliminated.''

Maxwell shook his head in dissent. ''Nels. Wouldn't Mr. Proctor exclude his son, distance him even more from what was going down?''

Becker, on a roll, felt as if he had all the answers. ''Again, no. Barney insists Nels be in on the deal. It's a question of longevity. The father is getting on in years and his time is limited. Barney is looking for an annuity, a lifetime insurance policy.''

''Nels provides continuity.''

''It fits. Barney's future is guaranteed. When the old chief expires, Barney is leapfrogged over his senior fellow officer and named chief. Over the years, he is thrown an occasional economic bone. A few shares of stock for Christmas. A small part of a business the Horsemen enter into. Enough to keep him happy and on the string.''

''And in return, Barney kills David?''

Becker started to answer, stopped, and started again. ''Take care of David, might be the sort of suggestion that was made. Something nonspecific, leaving father and son free to say they never encouraged murder. But Barney knows that killing is the most efficient and conclusive way of closing the case. No chance of prosecution.''

''There's still Emily.''

''Not likely that she intends to bring charges. Two days have passed and she's said nothing. Besides, it would be her word against that of four clean-cut, upstanding youths, the pride of the community.''

''And Lauren?''

''Too frightened. Didn't want her parents to know she'd been up on the Point for even five minutes. I'll bet she had her eye on Jay Newell even then. Marrying him would be a profitable social and economic move for a girl from the Flats.''

''Now we come to Ortner?''

''Easy. A hospital for the county, why not? Everybody benefits and Ortner's the logical man to be put in charge. His lips are sealed forever.''

''It might have happened that way.''

''Sure it did, Perry.''

Maxwell wasn't convinced. ''According to your theory,

Barney had to keep the Luger. As smart as he is, why take the chance?''

"Nobody could trace it to him."

"All he had to do was toss it into the river or some mountain lake."

"As arrogant as he is, Barney never figured anybody would get on his case. He did the killing, kept his precious weapons, and was sure he would get away with it."

"That's a very creative story, Carl."

"It makes sense."

"If we could prove it. Nobody's going to testify. Not Lauren nor Ortner nor that secret witness of yours. And there's still your father's death to account for."

"More of the same. The Four Horsemen had to take possession of his property in order to complete their real estate holdings, in order to proceed with the mall."

"Pure conjecture."

"Not conjecture, fact. There was no way to erect the mall without Sam's land. I checked out the plans—Sam's farm, including his house, sliced into their parcel like an ax head, virtually cutting it in half. They had to have it. No other way to go. Millions of dollars were involved. Newell's bank made the initial loans that enabled them to buy most of the land they wanted. They cut off the source of water to the surrounding land of farmers who held out."

"The state wouldn't have permitted that."

"Don't be naive, Perry. The Environmental Protection Department makes those decisions. And who controls EPD? Hollis Whitehead, president of the General Assembly, the man who dealt out committee assignments, the man with a lot of political clout around the state. Hollis Whitehead, friend and follower of Nels Proctor, lead rider of the Horsemen."

"My head's beginning to spin."

"There's more. The rest of the money—one hundred and thirty-five million dollars in return for forty percent of the County Center, with options on future development—came from Fidelity Insurance Trust."

"All of it dependent on acquiring Sam's farm?"

"Damn right. That's why the bank had to call in Sam's loan when it did. That's why Jay Newell climbed all over Henry Streeter, forcing him to stop advancing any more money to my father. But Sam never gave up. He would have found another way, additional funds. My guess is he'd made a connection—maybe a friend, maybe a loan shark, who knows?—and the Horsemen found out about it. When it looked like he was about to pull it off, keep his land, they went after him. All they needed was a hit man.''

"You're saying they already had one?"

"Barney Grubb. That's the way it looks to me, Perry."

"Maybe here and now. But the Berkshire Diner and Pie Bakery is not a court of law. You tell me, Carl, would you want to prosecute this case on what we've got so far?"

"Maybe we can break it open."

"How?"

"Apply pressure. We go to the State Attorney with what we know."

"A great deal is conjecture, supposition, circumstantial."

"The Luger was used in two murders."

"One murder and one death currently labeled as a suicide."

"Let's not argue the point. That the Luger is Grubb's gun can be easily proven."

"That it *was* his gun."

"We have two violent deaths by gunshot, the same weapon each time. Coincidence will stretch only so far, Perry."

"You're a lawyer, Carl. Go ahead, put that weapon in Barney's hand either time. I don't believe you can do it. Can you place him at the scene of David's death? Again the answer is no. What we have been doing is casting the hook in the water without catching any fish."

Becker grew still. If Maxwell was right, he was locked in place with no place to go, defeated finally. But he was not yet ready to surrender. At least not until he talked it over with Molly.

Maybe she was right, and it was time for both of them to give it up, leave Old Brixton—its painful memories and mysteries—behind. He had come this far as much on her behalf as on his own and if a decision were to be made, it should be as much hers as his own.

Only a few days earlier he had spoken by phone to his superior in Washington. "When are you coming back, Carl? We're understaffed and I need you to take up your share of the work."

"In a few days," he had answered glibly, "maybe a week." But he hadn't meant it, thinking that to go back now would be a betrayal of his father and his father's struggles, to be beaten without giving it his best shot.

He spoke to Maxwell. "Let's talk to Molly, and right now."

When they arrived at Anna Slocum's house, they found her at the potter's wheel. She continued working while they explained why they had come.

"Molly left a few minutes ago," she answered. "On her way to Overlook Point. That girl is pretty upset by what's been happening. She's had a belly full of this town and its people, of all of us."

"I suppose it can wait until tomorrow," Becker said, masking his uneasiness.

"Hang around, if you like," Anna said as the phone started to ring. She rose, wiping her hands as she went. "Just don't expect me to entertain you boys." She picked up and said, "Hello . . ."

38

LAUREN REMAINED IN bed for three days. She ate nothing, drank only some fruit juice and an occasional cup of tea. Doctor Ortner was summoned but she refused to admit him to her room.

"What am I going to do?" Jay Newell asked the doctor, lamenting his wife's ill health.

"From what you've told me, what's needed here is a psychiatrist."

"Whenever I go near her, she cries. Three mornings ago she woke up crying and it's been going on ever since."

"Contact Harry Altman, in Boston. Use my name. Harry's the best there is."

"What could have brought this on?"

Ortner shrugged. "We may never know, unless she tells us. She may not know herself."

After Ortner departed, Newell went into the bedroom. Lauren, on her back, stared at the ceiling. He went to her side and in response she rolled away and curled up in the fetal position with her back to him.

"Please, Lauren, talk to me. I love you, I want to help."

Her sigh was fraught with despair. He touched her shoulder and she jerked away as if shocked.

"Don't you dare touch me." They were the first words she had spoken to him in days. "You are never to touch me again," she hissed.

"Please, Lauren, tell me what you're feeling. Ortner thinks you should see someone, a man named Altman in Boston."

"I don't want to look at you again," she said, her voice small and tight. "I don't want to look at myself."

"Can't you tell me what's wrong?" His pain was palpable and it moved her. But her own anguish was too great; she couldn't respond.

"Our lives are a fraud," she managed to get out. "A deceit. A terrible lie."

He felt like a child being punished without being told what he had done wrong. "I've never deceived you. In every way a man can be faithful to a woman, I've been true to you. There's never been anyone else. Never."

His inability to understand what really mattered was appalling to her. She turned sluggishly and forced herself to look at him. His eyes were swollen and his face looked bloated.

"I know," she said in a voice heavy with condemnation, "all about Emily. Everything there is to know."

He shrank back into himself, the horror and disbelief in his eyes confirming what she had denied for years. "I've known ever since that night. Emily came to me for help and I failed her. *Turned her away, my best friend*. All this time I lived with that—and with the knowledge that my husband raped my best friend."

He groaned and ground his teeth, collapsing alongside her on the bed, doubled over. "You don't understand."

"No more lies. I have existed side by side with lies and ugliness for too long. My own and yours, spoken and implicit. Emily told me everything. If I hadn't left when I did, it would've happened to me, too."

"Let me explain."

"Explain how that virtuous pillar of the community set it up, that stalwart pal of yours, Nels Proctor. Tell me about the bet you all made. How he led the way and how the rest of you finished that ugly job. What is it you men call it—oh, yes, sloppy seconds."

"You don't understand!" he groaned.

"I understand how incredibly evil all of it was, how evil it still is, including my role in all of it."

Hunched over, he began to sob. "I was there," he admitted, relieved to say it to another person at last. "Believe me, there were a hundred times I wanted to tell you, and I tried but lacked the courage. I was there but I didn't want any part of it."

Her scorn was withering. "They forced you to participate, is that what you're trying to tell me?"

"You don't know how Nels can be."

"My God, I loathe that man. But no one put a gun to your head. You were part of it because you wanted to be part of it. And now that bastard, Nels, with Molly Fairfax. He could be her father but that doesn't stop him. If I know our Nels, he enjoyed that possibility." Her gaze fixed on Jay. "Or maybe not, maybe you're Molly's father—"

"No, no." His head rocked steadily, his voice cracking. "You don't know how it was. They were all watching me. Nels and the others. It was done already, can't you see that? Each of them had done it."

"And you did nothing to stop them."

"They paid no attention to me. Everyone was drinking, they were drunk, don't you remember? After you left—my God!—we watched them together until he finished with her."

"And it was your turn."

"I didn't want to, but Nels insisted. They made fun of me, called me names."

She could no longer look at him.

He pleaded for understanding. "You don't know what it's like for a boy growing up. Trying to keep up. Nothing I did was right. Not to my father, not to my friends. Just to be accepted was a battle. I never wanted to get into fights or play football or do any of the things they did. People expect things of you—to look bad in front of your friends, it killed me. Nels challenged me."

"And you accepted the challenge."

"There was no way to back down."

"You raped Emily."

"No, I didn't. *Couldn't.* I was incapable of doing a thing like that. Impotent. I pretended, faked it. Acting out. In the dark, everybody half-drunk, no one could see what was going on. Nobody knew the difference. Not even Emily."

She sat up. "Why didn't you ever tell me?"

"It really didn't matter that I never penetrated her. Perhaps in a court of law it would have made a difference—oh, I don't know. I was so ashamed and so afraid. Afraid of my father. Afraid of Nels.''

"And what about me? You're supposed to love me. You're supposed to trust me.''

"Maybe I was afraid of you, too. Afraid of losing you.'' He raised his eyes to hers. "You never let on that you knew—you didn't trust me, either.''

"I guess I was afraid, too. Afraid of losing you, of losing the life we had, of hurting the children.''

"I have never been a man of strength and nobility, Lauren. I am not proud of the way I've lived. If it were possible, I'd make up for it.''

"You mean that?''

He drew back, suddenly wary and watchful. "What are you thinking?''

"We'll go to Molly, tell her everything. We'll go to the police.''

An icy finger of terror touched his spine. "I can't do that. Anyway, there's a statute of limitations.''

"Not for murder.''

"What are you saying? Nobody's been murdered.''

"David Colfax was.''

"A robber—''

"I never believed that. He was killed to keep him from testifying. He was up there, he saw it all—all of it, Jay. He was killed to silence him.

"I had no part in that.''

"You knew about it. You had to know, in your heart.''

"Maybe. Maybe I did guess.''

"We can put things right, Jay. Or at least as right as they can be after so long.''

"How? I'm not the problem. Even Nels has lost control—Barney, he's the one. Barney killed David. At least I think he did. I guess I always thought so. Nels as much as admitted that his father ordered Barney to stop David from bringing charges against us. Nels said it was done to protect us.''

"What was done made you all accessories to a murder. And no statute of limitations will protect you from that. Nels, it's always been Nels. None of you is cold enough or cruel enough to take a human life, only Nels.''

Jay hesitated. "There's another killing."

"Oh, no."

"Sam Becker."

"But he committed suicide."

"That had to be Barney, too."

"And Nels?"

Jay nodded. All the false fronts that had shielded him were being ripped away. His wife had always known him to be a weakling and soon his children would see him for what he truly was, a coward and a hypocrite. He cursed the memory of his father; if only he had followed his youthful yearnings, become an actor—more importantly, lived life his own way. Instead he had surrendered without ever trying.

"The mall," he said. "Without the section of Sam's land that jutted into the parcel, the mall couldn't be built. Sam refused to sell. We offered him money, a lot of money. He said the farm meant more to him than the money. We offered to buy just the piece of land we needed, leave him the rest. But his house was located there and he wouldn't give it up. The man was so damn stubborn."

"Because he wanted to stay on his own land, in his own house?"

"Nels insisted that I call in the loans. I figured that would make him give in. Instead he made other arrangements. Some friends said they'd come up with the cash, they could take out a second mortgage on a house, something like that. It looked as if he would be able to pay off the loans. Then all of a sudden he was dead and the loans went unpaid and the property reverted to the bank."

"How could you allow them to kill that poor man?"

"I didn't know they planned to kill him. No one ever told me. Besides, if I'd objected—Lauren, I was afraid."

"We've all been afraid, all of the time, and so we do nothing—while people like Nels and Grubb lie and cheat and kill with impunity. What's going to happen next?"

"What do you mean?"

"Tomorrow or next week or next year, what if Nels decides Hollis is in his way? Will he have him killed? Or Gary, or you? What if he decides that I've become a liability? Does Grubb come around one afternoon while I'm tending my orchids and put a bullet in my head? And what about Molly Fairfax? Surely she is a threat to every one of us."

The color drained from Jay's cheeks like a curtain being drawn.

"What is it?" Lauren said. "Is that it? Do they intend to kill Emily's girl as well?"

"She keeps nosing around."

"And?"

"And Barney believes she's trouble. Both of them, Molly and Carl Becker. He had one of his goons take a shot at them."

"We've got to do something," Lauren gasped.

"There's nothing anybody can do."

"You've got to stop it."

"Me! How can I stop it? Nels and Gary, they tried and failed. They tried to kill Barney. He was too smart for them, too tough."

She spoke in a monotone. "Everything's insane. Anything goes, is that the way we're going to live? No. No, no more. It has to stop somewhere."

"Stop Barney? You don't know how he is. Get in his way and he'll eliminate me, too."

But Lauren's eyes were shining. She had failed her friend—she would not fail her friend's daughter. "If you won't do something, Jay, I will."

"Stay out of this, please."

She reached for the phone and dialed hurriedly. "It's late, Jay, too late for us all."

Anna answered the call. "Hello."

"This is Lauren Newell."

Anna didn't show her surprise. "How have you been, Lauren?"

Lauren experienced a wave of apprehension. She had always liked Anna Slocum, yet had managed to keep her at arm's length. It was as if the independent nature of the older woman was an implicit criticism of her own insubstantial life. "May I talk to Molly, please?"

"She's gone out."

"Oh." Then with a rising sense of hysteria: "I've got to speak to her at once."

"Is something wrong, Lauren?"

In an emotional rush, she revealed what she knew, what she

thought she knew, what she feared might happen. "Somebody has to warn her."

"Carl Becker is here," Anna said. "Tell him what you've told me."

Becker listened intently. "I'll do what I can," he said when she finished. "Grubb may be after Molly," he told Maxwell. "I'm heading up to the Point to warn her."

"Why," Maxwell said in that matter-of-fact way of his, "don't I tag along?"

"That strikes me as a very good idea," Anna said, hurrying them out the door.

39

BARNEY GRUBB SLOUCHED down behind the wheel of his pickup, brooding over the way things were always left for him to take care of. The Four Horsemen; he repeated the name scathingly to himself. More like a quartet of geldings, not a real man in the group. Had it not been for their fathers; their grandfathers, that whole obscene succession of money-grubbing ancestors, not one of them would have amounted to a good piss in a rainstorm.

Take Proctor. He was the best of the lot, yet when push came to shove, when there was a man's job that needed doing, he always failed. That fouled-up deer hunt—thinking they could blow him away. Pathetic. Putting Overton on the gun was mistake number one. Gary was a plodder, hard working, stubborn—qualities people mistook for guts. Put his finger on the trigger of a delicate assignment and his nerves went back on him.

How easy it had been to spot him from nearly a hundred yards away, a squirming shadow in the stand. Kneeling, standing, scratching, shuffling, finally getting himself down into the prone position. And Nels, hanging back the way he did, making sure to keep himself out of the line of fire. Did they think he was a fool, that he wouldn't see, couldn't sense what was going on? Those kind of mistakes—amateur. Failure of nerve, failure of judgment. How easy it had been to leave Nels crouched behind a tree, to stalk Overton, to take him down.

Let them pay for their mistakes. Over and over again. The more they complained, the harder he was going to squeeze. His time had arrived at last and no one was going to block his path to the pot of gold. Least of all a nosy bitch intent on digging up buried skeletons.

He held steady behind the wheel when Molly Fairfax came out of the stone house. Parked in the shadows of a giant sugar maple, its leaves turning to golden flame, he drew no attention. He watched her walk, growing smaller in the distance.

As fine-looking a woman as he'd seen in a long time. The kind of looks and shape you saw in movies. The way she walked unloosed a warm flush in his groin and he watched the roll of her hips in counterpoint to the easy articulation of long legs, the rhythmic shift of her full round buttocks. Christ Almighty, a man could wallow a while in a body like that.

He straightened up and switched on the ignition, shifted into gear, and let the pickup inch ahead. He tried to imagine her with no clothes on, walking that way, coming toward him, thighs rubbing together, breasts jiggling. How come it was always the Nels Proctors of the world who got her kind? Always living high off the hog. First the mother, then the daughter.

Grubb would never have had the belly for that. Trying to screw your own flesh and blood, the act of a true deviate.

Keeping his distance, he followed her across New Bridge, past the Women's Club, hanging back until she turned up along the river's edge, until she reached the old path that led up to Overlook Point. Satisfied he knew her destination, he left the pickup behind the old cotton mill building where it was not likely to be spotted and went after her, keeping well to her rear. No need to alarm her any sooner than necessary.

At this time of year, dusk came early to Overlook Point. The autumn sun, low in the southwestern sky, cast long shadows broken only by patches of dappled light. A breeze rustled through the upper branches and an occasional leaf fluttered to the ground.

Molly hugged herself against the chill as she advanced into the clearing standing only yards from the big elm tree. She

looked around. Where had it happened? Perhaps on this very
ground. Emily had succumbed to the young Nels, sucked in by
his uncommon good looks, his charm, that flashing smile.
How easy it must have been to give in to him.

Both of them had been deceived.

Nels had never been concerned with love or affection or
even a case of healthy lust. For him it was always an exercise
of power, demonstrating his control over women, his ability to
manipulate them, to reduce them to objects of his will. Only
then was he satisfied, only then would he move on to the next
conquest.

On that Fourth of July night, an awful chain of cruelty and
crime had been set in motion. Rape and murder, pain and
despair. The destruction of families and an end to love. Her
eyes raked the clearing. Surrounded by walls of darkening
green shimmering in the evening breeze, she understood that
she was at last at the end of her search.

Everything she had come to Old Brixton to learn, she
had found. More, in fact, than she wanted to know. More
about Emily and the life she had led, more about her friends,
her family, her reasons for running away. Molly felt as if she
had discovered her mother all over again, a different Emily,
an Emily lost and fearful, out of control, on the run.

And in discovering this Emily, and learning to love her
anew, she had surrendered her father. Or had she? Emily had
given birth to Michael Fairfax even as she had given birth to
Molly. Breathed life into him and made him real to Molly, for
Molly. A loving father, brave and dedicated, a resourceful,
adventurous man to be proud of. A good father for a young
girl to have. Both father and mother would live in her memory
for the rest of her life.

It was time to leave Overlook Point, to put behind her what
had taken place so long ago. Time to put an end to her fanciful
notions of an idealized life in an idealized town, neither of
which were anything but images conjured up by her imagination. The breeze penetrated the wool sweater and she shivered.

The harsh reality of winter was on its way. Cold and
relentless, suffering no weakness or error. She didn't belong
here, had never belonged. Nothing remained of value for her.
She turned to go, to retrace her steps, and confronted Barney
Grubb, immense and menacing in the fading light, blocking
the path down to the river.

There was no comfort in that massive presence. No reassurance on that menacing face. His jaw was set, his eyes were hard and icy, giving nothing away. He wore wool pants and an aging leather jacket, boots on his big feet. His gnarled hands hung at his sides, flexing ominously.

She knew at once that this was no accidental meeting, and she looked for another way off the Point. But in the rapidly closing dusk, she could locate no opening in the surrounding walls of greenery.

"You've been following me."

He took a single step forward, branches snapping underfoot, emphasizing her vulnerability. He could snap her in two as easily as a dead branch.

"Why would I want to do that, miss? Unless you've broken the law. Have you done that, broken some law?"

She attempted to go around him. He shifted only slightly and managed to cut off access to the path. Summoning up a full measure of courage, she faced him.

"Is there something you wish to say to me, Chief Grubb? If not, I'd appreciate you allowing me to leave now."

He put his tongue in his cheek, moving it around in contemplation. "Mostly kids come up here. At night, to fool around a little. Is that what you're after, some action, miss?"

In the gloom he seemed taller and wider than usual, great and immovable. She shivered. "My friends are expecting me." He made no response. "Please, let me by, Chief."

"Sure, anything you say." He held his position, legs planted solidly apart. "We could've been friends, you and me, gotten along."

"Well, yes." She leaped at the chance. "Let's go somewhere warm, have a cup of coffee. We can talk."

"It's a nice idea, but I don't think so."

"You're keeping me here against my will."

"Thing is, this business with your mother, it's beginning to unsettle things."

"What did you have to do with my mother?"

"In the beginning, nothing. It's just that people around here—people like the Proctors and the Whiteheads, that kind—when they have a problem, they come looking for somebody to help. They come to me and I solve their problems for them."

Her legs began to tremble and she fought against the impulse to run. "I'm not interested in those people."

"Sure you are. You and Carl Becker, going around kicking over rocks, making a fuss, raising questions folks had just about forgot. You are getting on my nerves, like they say."

She retreated a step. "I'm leaving. Leaving Old Brixton, I mean. I won't be back."

"Ah," he said, a pained expression on his rugged face. "Too bad it ain't that easy anymore, but it ain't. There's your mother to think about. And David Colfax. And old Sam Becker. The longer you stayed, the more complicated things got. You should've stayed away. We'd all've been better off. You can see that, can't you?"

"My friends—"

"Your friends aren't about to interrupt us. Nobody is."

"What are you going to do?"

"If my man hadn't've missed that shot, had taken you and Becker out like he was supposed to, none of this would be necessary."

"You did try to kill us!" She backed away.

He stepped toward her. "I've got to make it look just right. Something that will stand up later on."

"What do you mean?"

"Killed by a stranger passing through. The way the Colfax boy was done. Neat and clean."

"No," she said, seeking an escape, this time locating the worn track that led down to the old fair grounds. "No," she said again and began to run.

The suddenness of her flight took him by surprise, cost him a second or two before he went after her. He angled through the brush, cutting off her way, making no effort to disguise his coming. No way she was going to get away from him.

He closed the gap between them. Hearing him, she realized she could not make it all the way down off the Point before he caught up. Swinging to the left, she plunged deeper into the woods. She cried out as branches whipped at her thighs, snapped at her face. She tripped and went down. Scrambling up, she set out again.

A quick backward glance put him no more than ten yards behind. She tried to make her legs move faster, straining, until her foot hooked a hidden vine and she fell heavily. Crawling, she made it up to her feet, lurched forward, changing direction, circling back toward the big elm tree. She was almost there when he caught up, yanking her backwards, flinging her to the ground. He planted one boot squarely across her middle.

"Understand," he said, unzipping his pants, "this is not the way I like to do things."

She struck at his heavy leg, struggling to free herself. She screamed and the sound was lost in the rustling leaves that formed a shifting canopy overhead.

"Understand," he said, reaching for her. "This is a means to an end. A diversion for the investigators later on." He pushed up her skirt, ripped her panties, then forced her legs apart, placing himself between her thighs. "They're logical men. The kind who put two and two together and come up with the answer that makes the most sense. Rape and murder, they'll decide, and that'll be the end of it." He lowered himself over her.

She fought him but her blows found no purchase. "You won't get away with this!" she screamed.

Sound broke out of him, a derisive snort that rolled into a rough cackle. "I put a bullet into Colfax and got away with that. I wasted old man Becker and got away with that. I'll get away with this." He grasped her arms and immobilized her. "Now hold still—"

"No!" She twisted away.

The laugh dissolved into a snarl. "Hold still, damnit. Don't make me hurt you unnecessarily. Nobody's coming along to help you. *Nobody*. First you, then Becker. And it'll all be over. You coming up here this way, you made it easier, that's all."

Pinned down, she continued to resist, strength waning, the immense power in his big body holding her in place. She set herself against his thrusts and jabs, determined not to give in.

He released one of her arms and guided himself, seeking entry, demanding that she lie still. In answer she ripped her nails along his cheeks, drawing blood. He pulled away and she rolled from under him, braced for another blow. Instead he stood up, head cocked, alert to some closing threat. He swore under his breath and adjusted his clothing. "Come on!" he said, pulling her to her feet, starting off again. "Make a sound and I'll bash you good."

She heard them now, crashing through the woods without caution, calling her name, gaining ground: Becker and Maxwell. Without hesitation, she screamed.

Grubb swung his big open hand against her cheek, driving her to her knees, numbed by the force of the blow. "One more time and I'll finish you off." Then he was on the move again, dragging her behind.

Stumbling, falling, she slowed his flight. Once, she managed to free herself, taking a few steps back in the direction from which they'd come before he took her down with a forearm shiver. Body racked with pain, she rolled as she hit the ground, coming up with a rock in her hand, flinging it wildly.

He threw another punch, his big fist landing on her breast. The pain left her breathless and silent, weak. He dragged her to her feet and went on. A dozen strides and he pulled up, breathing hard. Blocking the way, Perry Maxwell stood in a combat firing position, his .357 Magnum leveled and steady in the dusk.

"Don't make me shoot, Barney."

Grubb worked himself behind the girl, thoughts turning over rapidly, listening hard. To the rear, someone was closing in. Becker! This was the chance he'd been looking for, to take both of them out at the same time. What about Maxwell? A good cop, but unfortunately he'd have to go, too.

"You want her?" he snarled. "She's yours." Flinging her toward Maxwell, he ducked deeper into the woods, gone before the young cop could get a clean shot. He stopped only once, long enough to draw a snub-nosed .32 Smith & Wesson from his ankle holster. Now, he thought with grim satisfaction, let them try him on for size.

He heard them advancing noisily, calling to each other in the descending darkness, giving away their positions. He started off in a great circle to his left, stalking them the way he would a prize buck. It was the silence that stopped him this time, listening, hearing only the wind in the trees and a squirrel scampering for safety. He took one step and another when a shot rang out, the slug whining overhead.

He went to the ground, scanning the terrain in front of him. Maxwell appeared and disappeared, using the trees for cover, keeping to the shadows, moving swiftly. Nice movement, Grubb remarked to himself. Well trained, good reflexes. Grubb was pleased with the way the young cop handled himself under stress.

"Give it up, Perry!" he called.

"I've got to take you in, Barney."

"No chance."

Maxwell, bent low, went running for another position. Grubb snapped off a shot, the slug tearing through the leaves behind the sergeant. Well done, Grubb thought with professional objectivity. Maxwell had him spotted now and was counting shots.

"Perry!" Becker's voice floated toward Maxwell.

"Stay out of it, Carl!"

"I'm working my way behind him."

"Stay out of it, I told you. This is my job."

Grubb, listening, zeroed in on Becker. From the location of his voice, he had swung over toward the river, effectively cutting off Grubb's remaining escape route. But Becker and the girl would have to wait; Maxwell was the clear and present danger. Grubb felt around for a rock and heaved it in a high arc.

It did not surprise him when no shot followed; Maxwell was too smart to fall for an old trick like that.

"Give it up, Barney!"

Becker was closer, unable to keep from giving away his approach. It had been a long time since he'd tramped these or any other woods; he was a city boy now, out of his element.

Grubb willed his heartbeat to slow, controlled his breathing. He raised himself into a runner's crouch, the muscles in his thighs tense. When ready, he broke straight back to where he judged Becker to be. One shot and then another came winging after him. He veered and veered again, moving forward all the time.

"Carl, look out! He's coming at you!"

Becker pivoted at the exact moment Grubb crashed out of the bramble. Without thinking, he hurled a six-foot length of gnarled branch, thick and solid, at Grubb's churning legs. The big man crashed to the ground, the .32 flung loose. Both men dove for the weapon. Neither of them came up with it.

Becker delivered a karate chop to Grubb's thick neck. It had no appreciable effect. Grubb came up grunting, fists pumping. A looping right hand drove Becker to the soft carpet. It took only a fraction of a second for Grubb to locate the pistol and snatch it up just as Maxwell appeared.

Both men fired at once. Grubb, hit high on his left side, got off a second shot. Perry Maxwell took the slug between the fifth and sixth ribs, ripping up through his heart, lodging finally in the upper portion of the shoulder blade. He collapsed, the front of his uniform darkening rapidly, and lay without moving.

Becker ran back to Molly. "Perry's down and Grubb'll be after us next. Let's get out of here."

They had gone less than twenty yards when Grubb materialized out of the thicket. "Damn you both, causing all this trouble." He raised the .32.

Becker shoved Molly to one side and dove for safety as Grubb pulled the trigger. Becker came up charging. He launched a jarring heel kick that sent the policeman stumbling backwards. Becker followed with a straight left and a right cross that left Grubb shaking his head, but still standing. Another kick, aimed higher. This time Grubb grabbed, finding a hold, twisting and pulling at the same time. Becker went over on his back, Grubb pounding at his face.

Molly, a large rock held in both hands, looked for her chance, and brought it down on Grubb's head. He roared in rage and anguish, coming around to face this new attacker. She hit him again and he caved in.

Becker took the rock out of Molly's hands and raised it for a final blow.

"Don't!" Molly heard herself cry, the voice unrecognizable in her ears. "Don't kill him!"

Becker caught himself and allowed the rock to fall out of his hand, staring at the fallen policeman. He couldn't believe it was over.

Epilogue

THE FOLLOWING SPRING Barney Grubb was brought to trial. He was convicted of willful homicide in the death of police Sergeant Perry Maxwell and sentenced to life imprisonment. In a separate proceeding, he was charged with the attempted murders of Carl Becker and Molly Fairfax. Found guilty again, he was sentenced to twenty years on each charge. In the murders of David Colfax and Sam Becker, Grubb was again found guilty. The key to his conviction was the admission of guilt made to Molly Fairfax on Overlook Point. He was sentenced to life terms on each count.

In an attempt to plea bargain, Grubb incriminated Nelson Evan Proctor, insisting that Proctor was a conspirator to each of the killings. Jay Newell offered to testify for the prosecution but it was determined that he could supply only hearsay evidence. That left only Grubb's word against Proctor and, under state law, the testimony of a party to a crime was held insufficient to convict. The prosecution required hard evidence and none existed. No charges were brought against Proctor.

Not that Nels waited around to find out if they would be. On the morning after Barney Grubb was arrested, Nels visited

him in a holding cell in the basement of the station house. No
one ever learned what was said during the forty minutes they
were together. Conjecture was that Grubb threatened to in-
criminate Proctor unless some of the charges against him were
dropped and his subsequent sentence lightened, with early
parole guaranteed. Proctor, it was believed, pointed out that
he could promise nothing of the sort, but offered Barney a
substantial amount of money to keep his mouth shut, suggesting that he might be able to buy an easier time while in
prison. Infuriated by Proctor's response, Grubb attacked Nels
and the two men were found rolling on the floor of the cell,
throwing punches, when guards finally separated them. That
afternoon, Nels Proctor left Old Brixton, never to return.

Many rumors surfaced about Proctor over the next few
months. One had it that Nels had disappeared in the Amazon
River basin. Another put him in Algeria, living in a villa using
funds earlier deposited in a numbered Swiss bank account.
There, it was said, he lived in luxury, all his needs and pleasures served by beautiful young girls. Public opinion was
evenly divided about which rumor was the more likely to be
true until the following winter when definite news of his fate
became known.

Nels's lifeless body was found in an alley behind a homosex-
ual bar in Cap D'Antibes. His face had been disfigured by a
number of deep knife cuts and he had bled to death from
multiple stab wounds to the lower abdomen. His shirt and
jacket had been pulled up around his head and his trousers
had been cast aside. He had been robbed, beaten, and, according to police reports, sexually assaulted a number of times.

As word of the scandal surrounding the County Center Mall
spread around the state, construction ground to a halt. Potential renters canceled contracts and no replacements could be
found. The Fidelity Insurance Trust declined to put up any
more funds, nor would any other lenders take up the slack.

Soon after Grubb's first trial, Gary Overton moved out of
Old Brixton. He next surfaced along the Gulf Coast, in Ala-
bama, buying building lots and constructing one-family
homes, just as his father had done. At the same time, he tried
to form a syndicate to back a new shopping mall near the state
line. During a business meeting one afternoon, he suffered a
stroke which left him paralyzed and unable to speak. Despite

intensive therapy, he made no substantial progress toward
recovery and was placed in a nursing home where he could be
attended to full time.

Jay Newell remained in Old Brixton, still married to
Lauren. He resigned as president of the bank and lived quietly
on the wealth he'd accumulated. The Newells seldom went
anywhere. They accepted no invitations and never entertained.
None of their children were ever seen in town again. Some
people claimed Lauren had begun using Valium to excess, but
that was never confirmed.

Soon after Grubb's arrest, Hollis Whitehead issued a written statement through his press secretary denying any involvement in . . ."the supposed assault of one Emily Fowler." He
claimed no knowledge of the "alleged homicides" and only an
incidental acquaintance with the accused. He resigned as a
member of the General Assembly and he and Bunny moved to
Palm Beach where Hollis spent a great deal of his time drinking and staring from his terrace at the Atlantic Ocean.

Henry Streeter died the week Grubb's trial began, of natural
causes.

Ralph Ortner sold his interest in the medical complex and
moved to Arizona.

B.J. Miller continued to live in the trailer park, unnoticed
for the most part, tied to a distant past that evoked sad,
nostalgic memories, and she was unwilling still to confront the
truth.

As for Anna Slocum, she stayed on in her stone house,
spending more and more time at the potter's wheel. Shops in
Newport, in Provincetown, in Bar Harbor, offered to sell
whatever items she would make for them, but she refused.
After much persuasion, she agreed to allow Molly to in-
corporate some of her work into a gallery show entitled
"Native Crafts." Everything on display was sold in the first
two days of the show, with orders enough to keep Anna occupied for nearly a year. A buyer for Bloomingdale's wanted
the store to deal exclusively with her ceramics, guaranteeing
her a yearly income that far exceeded anything she'd ever
made before; Anna declined the offer.

"It would mean employing people," she told Molly over
dinner at a Mexican restaurant in Greenwich Village. "Finding larger work space, storage, a large inventory. That's not

what I want, to become a machine."

The conversation turned, as it inevitably did, to what had occurred during Molly's stay in Old Brixton. "Mixed feelings," Molly said, with forced cheerfulness. "That's what I'm left with."

"About Nels?"

"About all of it. As for Nels—well, there are those dark moments when I'm alone at night when I still begin to believe that even once I truly knew he was my father, I wanted him to make love to me anyway."

"You can't be sure that he was your father."

Molly's bright, green eyes clouded over. "But what if I did know, what if I sensed it, and still wanted him? The feelings —those unexplained longings, the obsessive cravings that I thought only he could satisfy. Will I ever come to terms with it? What sort of woman does that make me?"

Anna held her hand, sharing her strength, reassuring the younger woman. "You're like my pots. Soft and pliable at the start, vulnerable to outside forces, tempered under intense heat. But unlike my pots, you won't become hard and rigid. I know you, Molly. You'll never break. You're a good woman, better than most. Still changing, still growing, still in the making."

An extended silence followed before Anna spoke again. "If I'm out of line, say so. Have you been in touch with Carl?"

Molly, sliding into that soft drawl, answered, "He came by a few weeks ago. On his way back from Old Brixton. He had his father moved to the family grave site."

"And will you see him again?"

"I wonder about that," Molly said with an incomplete gesture, thinking back to the day they'd been shot at, the day Becker had kissed her. How odd that he'd never kissed her again, or even tried. She'd wondered a lot about that. Even now she could almost taste him, experience again the penetrating warmth and wetness of his tongue, the soft pliancy of his lips. She shivered. "He doesn't appear to be very interested . . ."

"Don't be a fool."

"What if he doesn't come back to see me?"

Anna raised her brows and made a strenuous effort to keep from laughing out loud. What a burden to bear, being young.

What an incredible adventure, being young. She addressed Molly with mock seriousness. "Oh, I'm sure he will."

"Soon?" Molly asked, flashing a small, plaintive smile.

"Soon enough."

The *Choice* for Bestsellers
also offers a handsome and
sturdy book rack for your
prized novels at $9.95 each.
Write to:

The <u>Choice</u> for Bestsellers
120 Brighton Road
P.O. Box 5092
Clifton, NJ 07015-5092
Attn: Customer Service Group